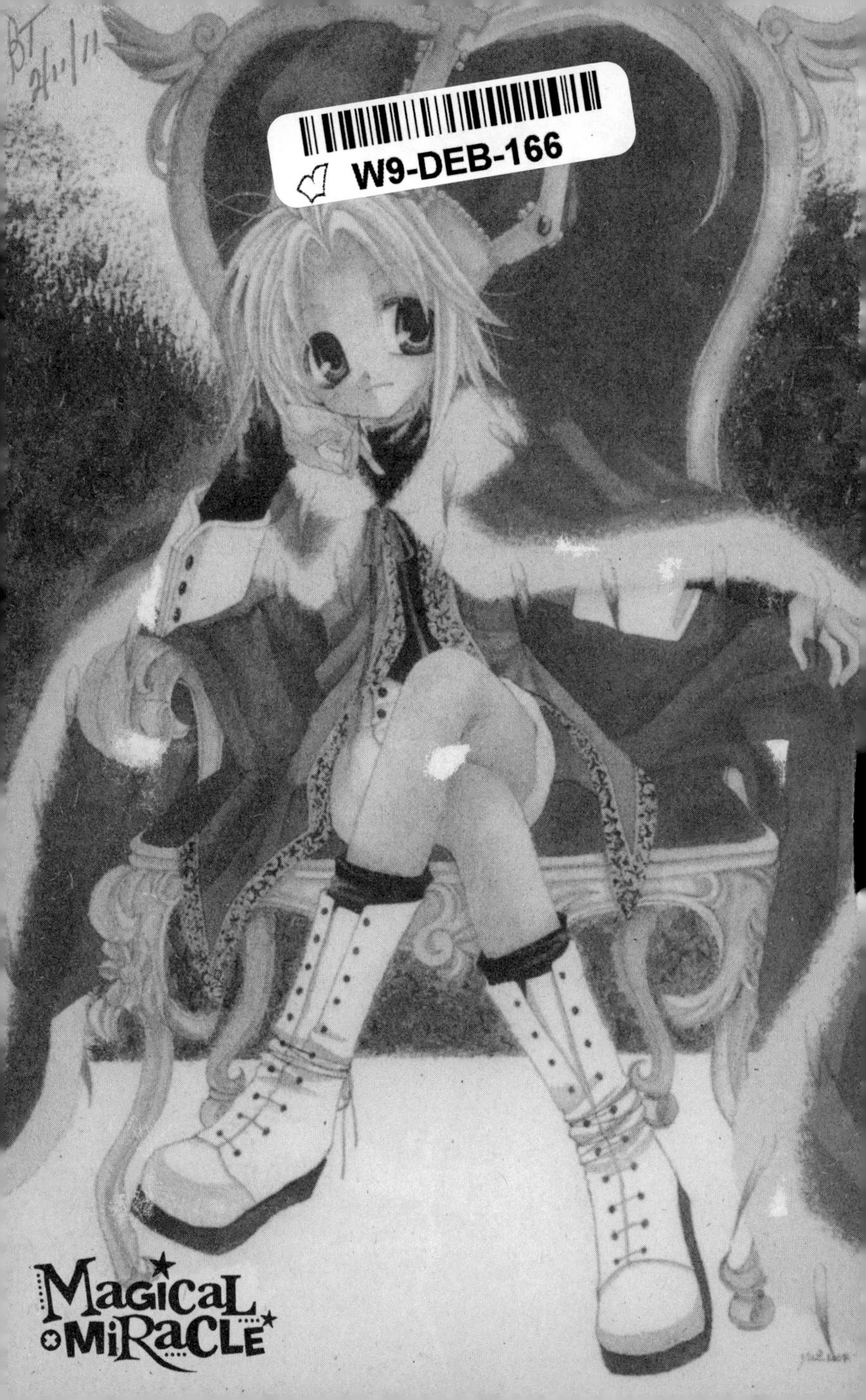
Magical
Miracle

CONTENTS

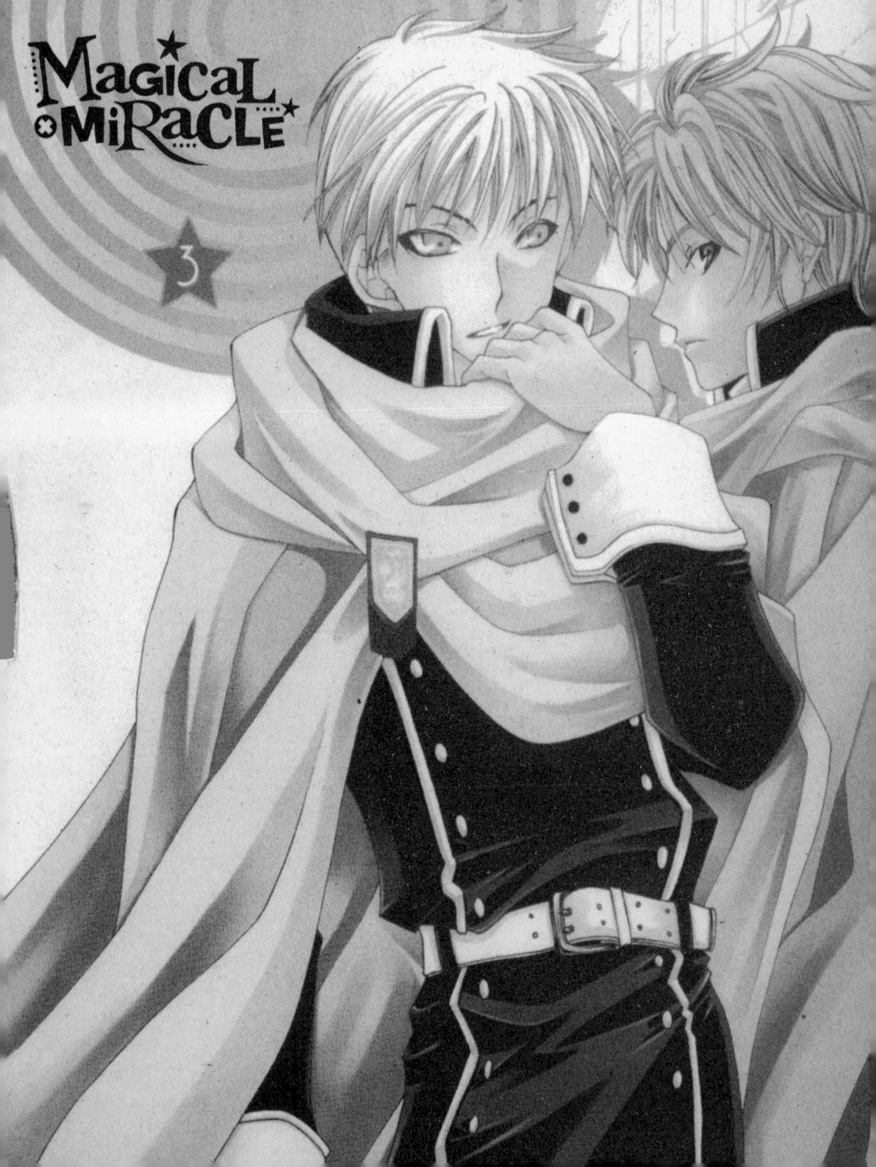
MAGICAL MIRACLE
3

Magical Miracle

Volume 3

By
Yuzu Mizutani

TOKYOPOP®

HAMBURG // LONDON // LOS ANGELES // TOKYO

Magical x Miracle Vol.3
Created by Yuzu Mizutani

Translation - Yoohae Yang
English Adaptation - Mark Ilvedson
Retouch and Lettering - Amit Gogia
Production Artist - Courtney Geter
Graphic Designer - James Lee

Editor - Hope Donovan
Digital Imaging Manager - Chris Buford
Pre-Production Supervisor - Erika Terriquez
Art Director - Anne Marie Horne
Production Manager - Elisabeth Brizzi
Managing Editor - Vy Nguyen
VP of Production - Ron Klamert
Editor-in-Chief - Rob Tokar
Publisher - Mike Kiley
President and C.O.O. - John Parker
C.E.O. and Chief Creative Officer - Stuart Levy

A  Manga

TOKYOPOP Inc.
5900 Wilshire Blvd. Suite 2000
Los Angeles, CA 90036

E-mail: info@TOKYOPOP.com
Come visit us online at www.TOKYOPOP.com

ISBN: 1-59816-330-2

First TOKYOPOP printing: December 2006
10 9 8 7 6 5 4 3 2 1
Printed in the USA

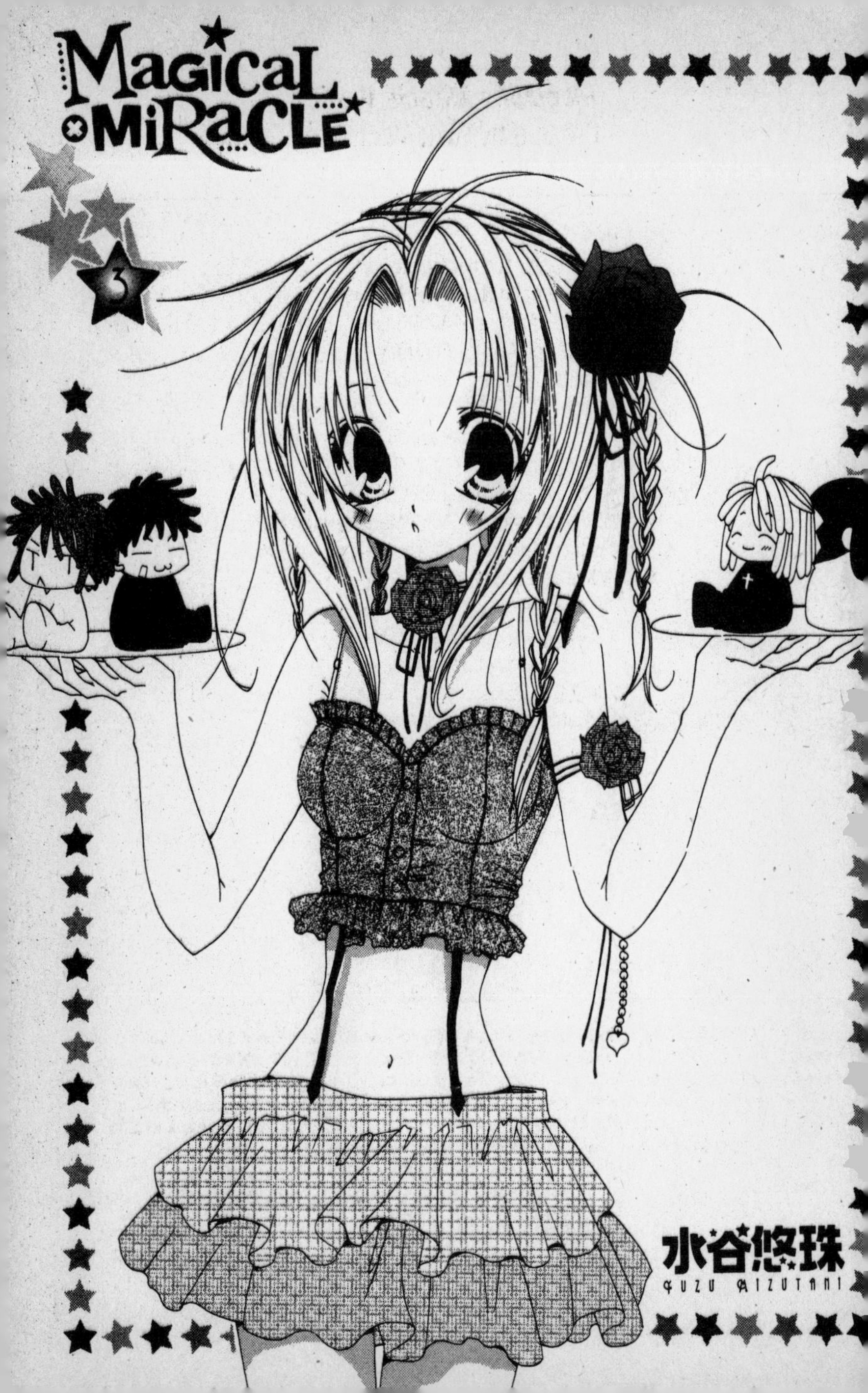
Magical
Miracle
3
水谷悠珠
YUZU MIZUTANI

MAGICAL ★ MIRACLE ★

Character Introductions

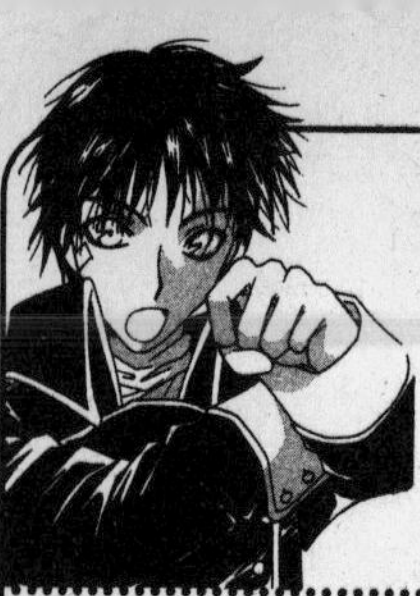

VAITH
A LOYAL FOLLOWER OF THE MASTER WIZARD AS WELL AS CAPTAIN OF THE BLACK KNIGHTS. HANDSOME AND DECEPTIVELY SMOOTH.

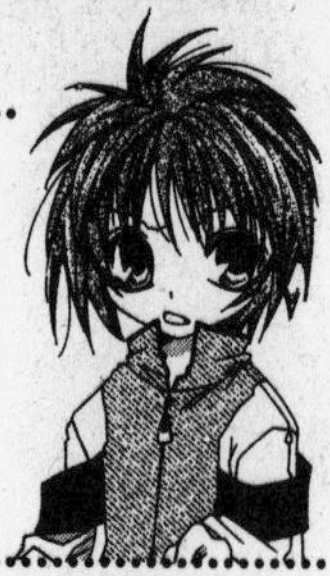

FERN
THE MOST FEISTY AND RUDE OF ALL THE MASTER WIZARD'S FOLLOWERS.

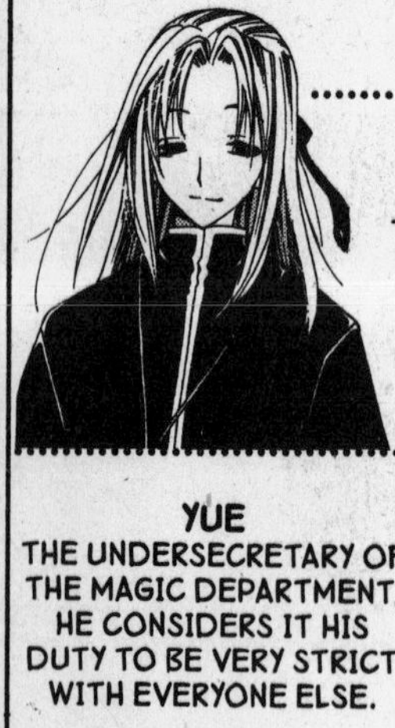

GLENN
IN ADDITION TO SERVING THE MASTER WIZARD, THIS SWEET PRIEST PROVIDES EDUCATION TO MANY OF THE TOWN'S CHILDREN.

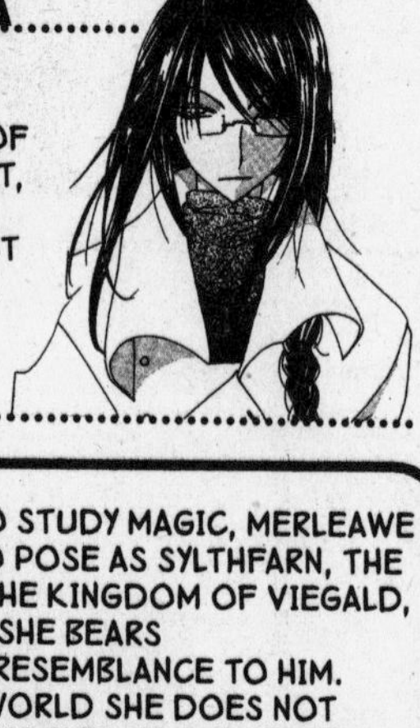

YUE
THE UNDERSECRETARY OF THE MAGIC DEPARTMENT, HE CONSIDERS IT HIS DUTY TO BE VERY STRICT WITH EVERYONE ELSE.

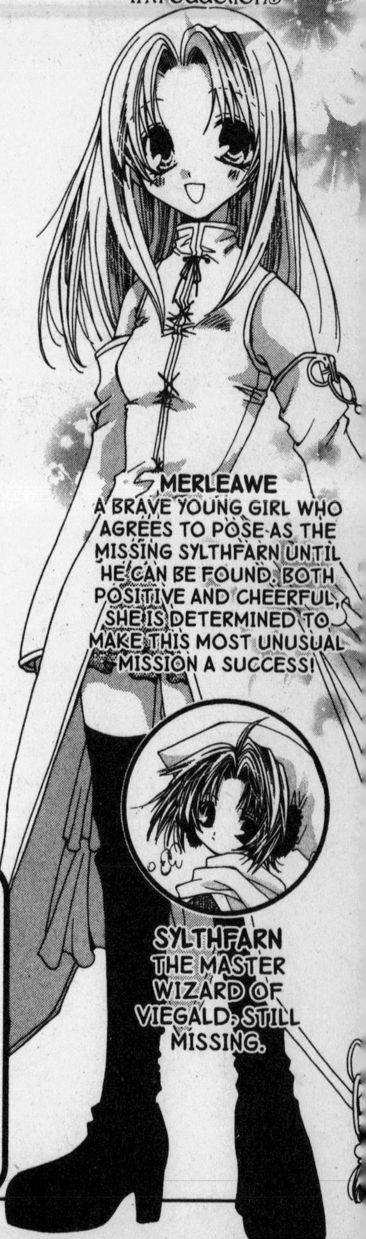

MERLEAWE
A BRAVE YOUNG GIRL WHO AGREES TO POSE AS THE MISSING SYLTHFARN UNTIL HE CAN BE FOUND. BOTH POSITIVE AND CHEERFUL, SHE IS DETERMINED TO MAKE THIS MOST UNUSUAL MISSION A SUCCESS!

SYLTHFARN
THE MASTER WIZARD OF VIEGALD, STILL MISSING.

STORY

JUST AS SHE BEGAN TO STUDY MAGIC, MERLEAWE WAS CALLED UPON TO POSE AS SYLTHFARN, THE MASTER WIZARD OF THE KINGDOM OF VIEGALD, SINCE SHE BEARS SUCH A STRIKING RESEMBLANCE TO HIM. CAUGHT UP IN A WORLD SHE DOES NOT KNOW, SHE NOW STRUGGLES TO DO HER BEST IMPERSONATION, WITH THE FULL SUPPORT OF SYLTHFARN'S FOLLOWERS. HOPING AND PRAYING THAT SHE IS DOING THE RIGHT THING, SHE BATTLES INTENSE FEELINGS OF GUILT FOR HAVING TO LIE TO SO MANY, EVEN IF FOR A GOOD CAUSE...

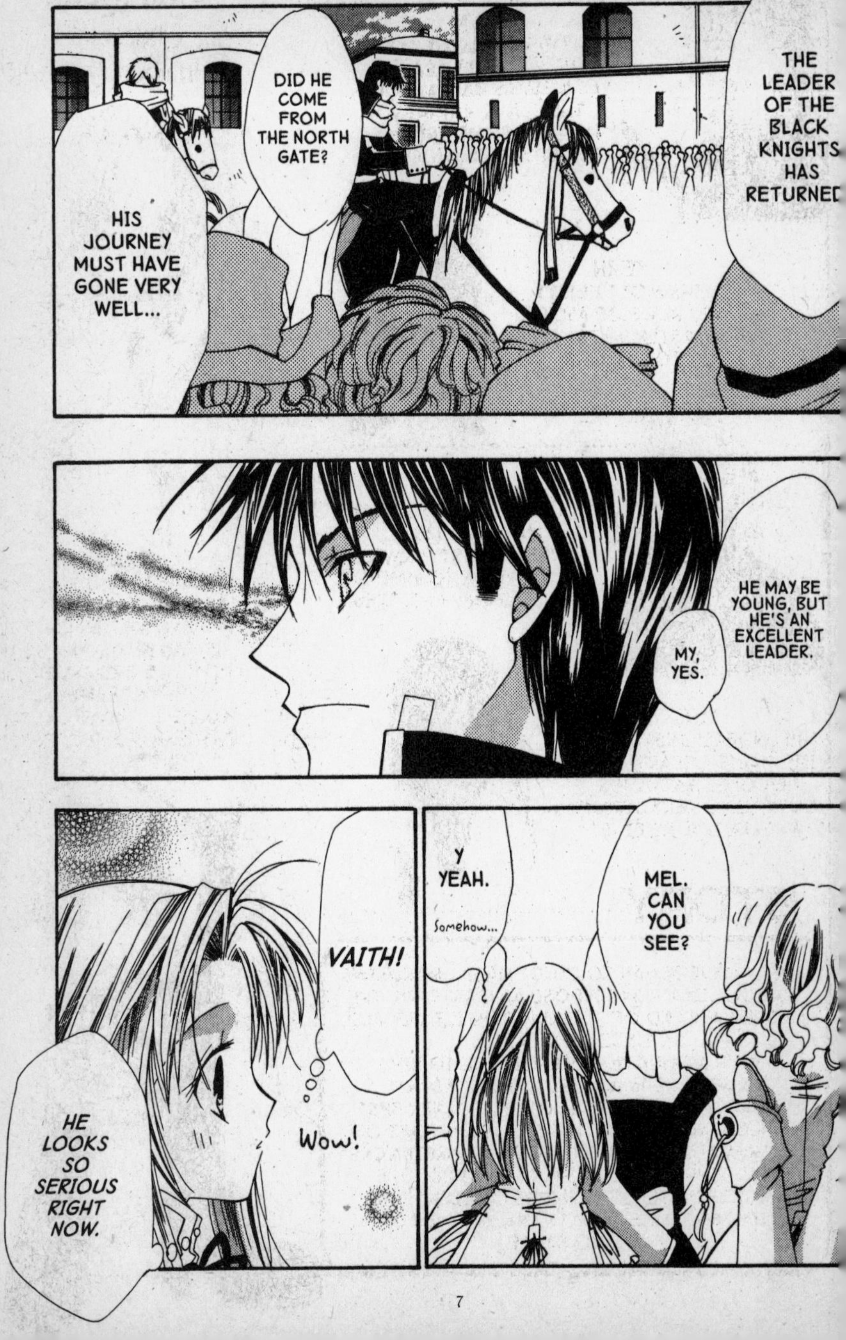
THE LEADER OF THE BLACK KNIGHTS HAS RETURNED
DID HE COME FROM THE NORTH GATE?
HIS JOURNEY MUST HAVE GONE VERY WELL...
HE MAY BE YOUNG, BUT HE'S AN EXCELLENT LEADER.
MY, YES.
MEL. CAN YOU SEE?
Y YEAH.
Somehow...
VAITH!
Wow!
HE LOOKS SO SERIOUS RIGHT NOW.

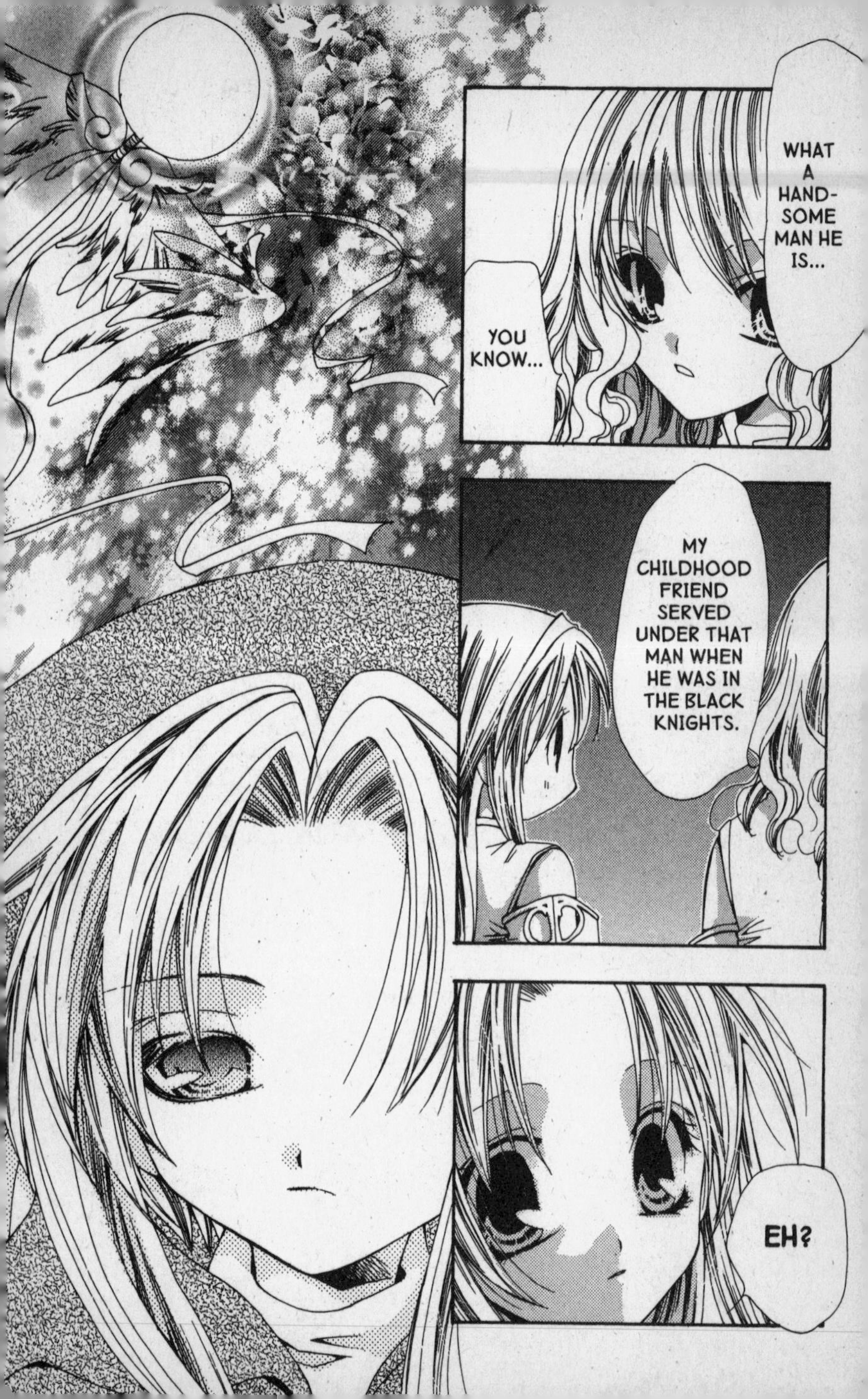
WHAT A HAND-SOME MAN HE IS...
YOU KNOW...
MY CHILDHOOD FRIEND SERVED UNDER THAT MAN WHEN HE WAS IN THE BLACK KNIGHTS.
EH?

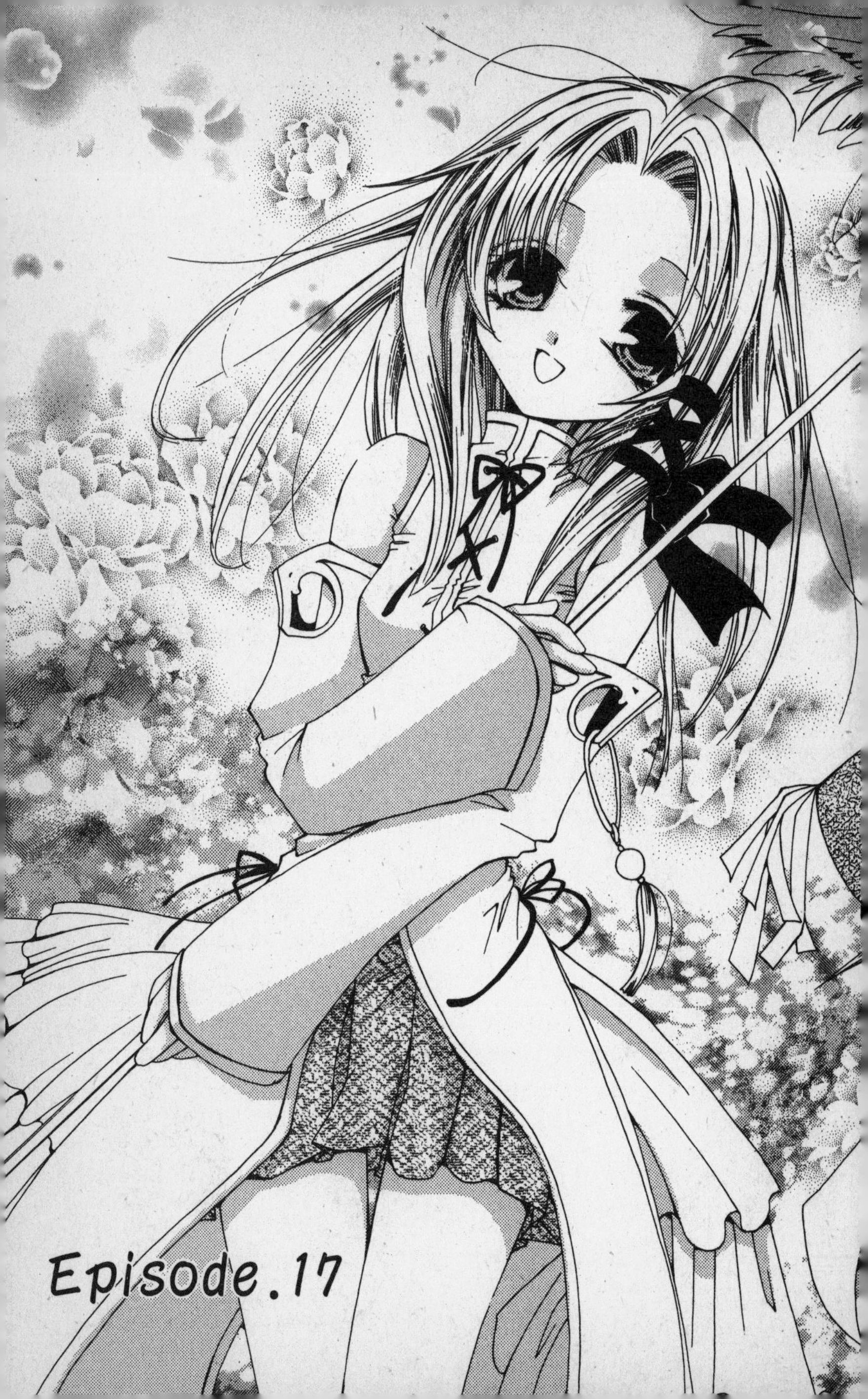
Episode.17

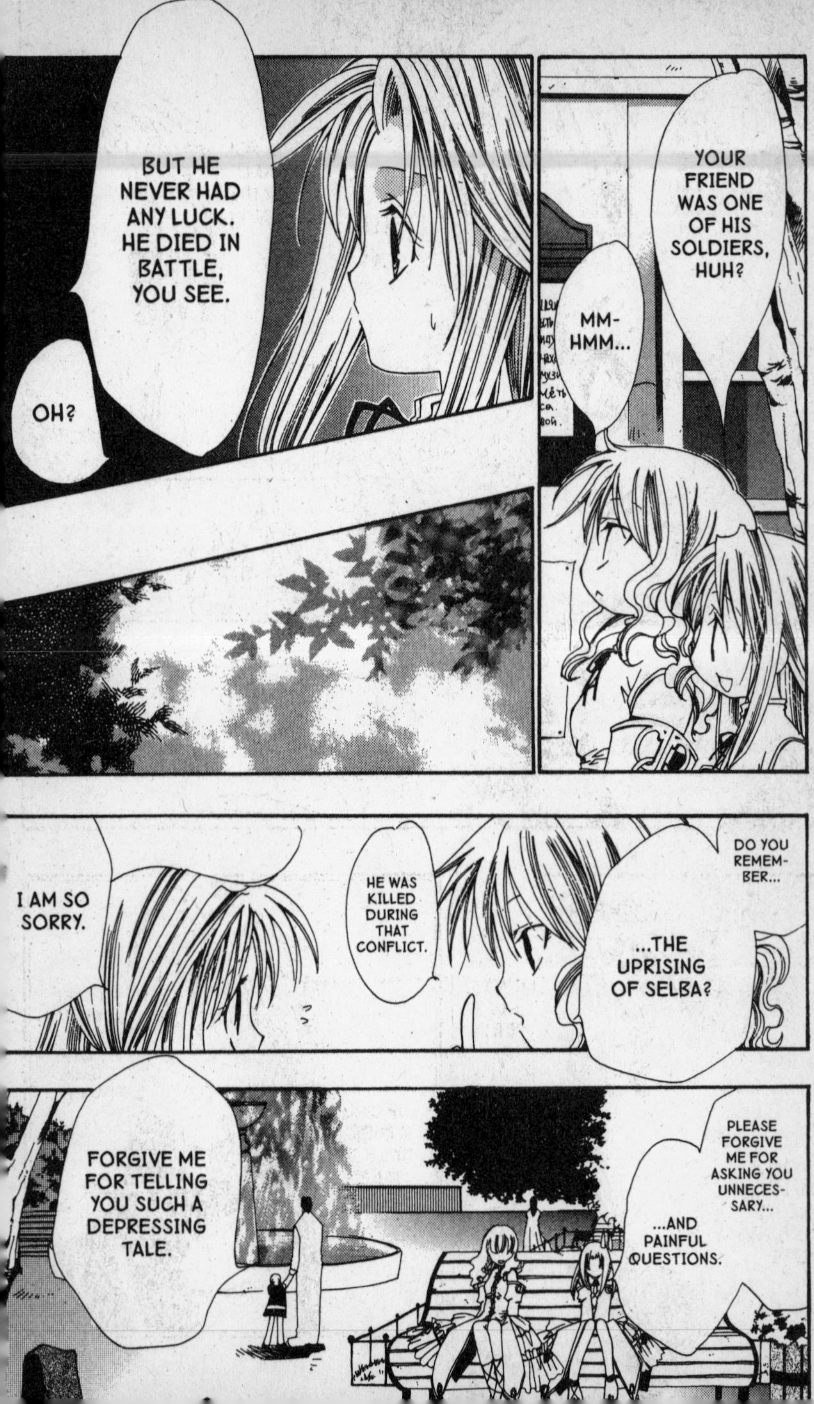
YOUR FRIEND WAS ONE OF HIS SOLDIERS, HUH?
MM-HMM...
BUT HE NEVER HAD ANY LUCK. HE DIED IN BATTLE, YOU SEE.
OH?
DO YOU REMEMBER...
...THE UPRISING OF SELBA?
HE WAS KILLED DURING THAT CONFLICT.
I AM SO SORRY.
PLEASE FORGIVE ME FOR ASKING YOU UNNECESSARY...
...AND PAINFUL QUESTIONS.
FORGIVE ME FOR TELLING YOU SUCH A DEPRESSING TALE.

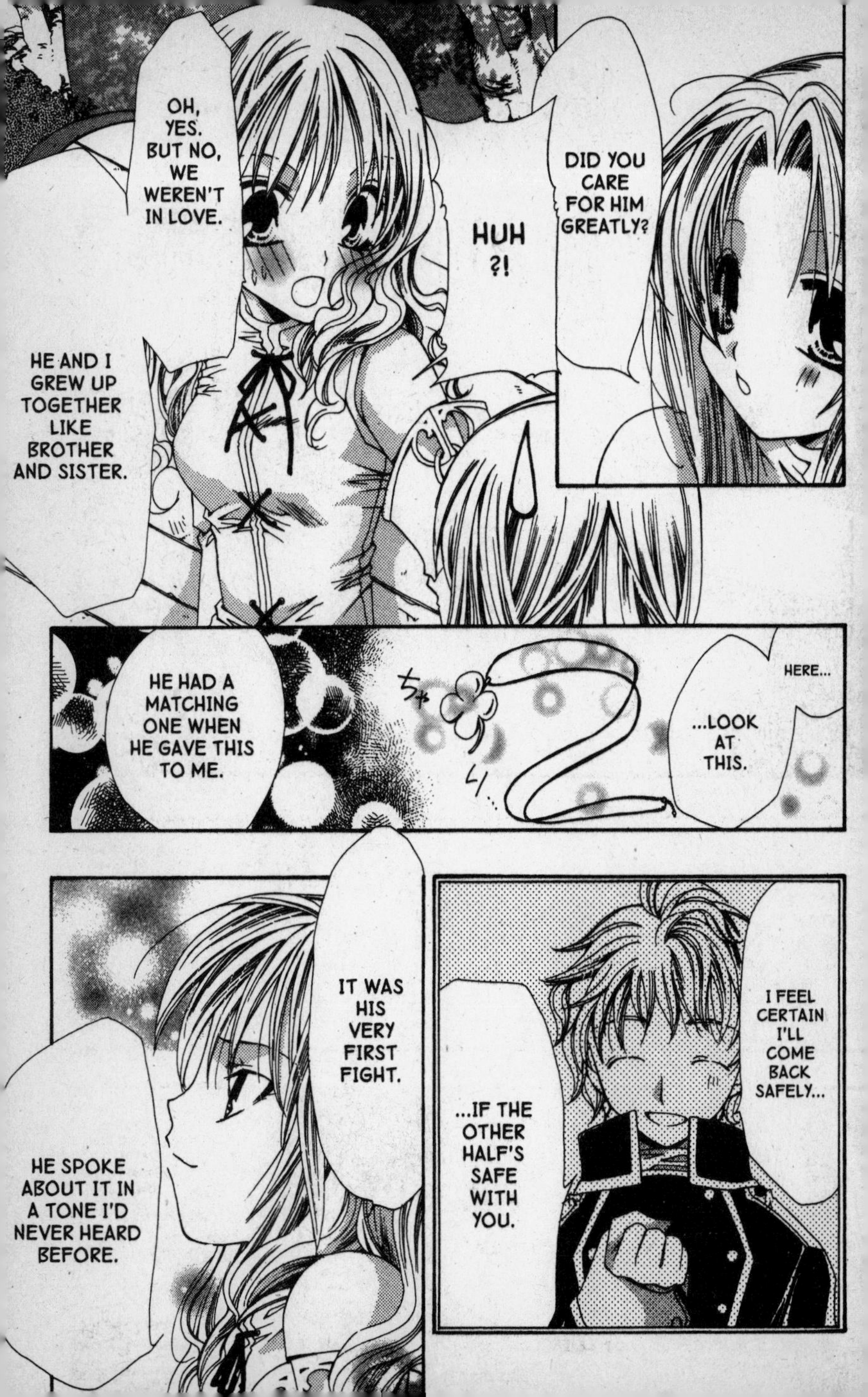
DID YOU CARE FOR HIM GREATLY?
HUH ?!
OH, YES. BUT NO, WE WEREN'T IN LOVE.
HE AND I GREW UP TOGETHER LIKE BROTHER AND SISTER.
HERE...
...LOOK AT THIS.
HE HAD A MATCHING ONE WHEN HE GAVE THIS TO ME.
I FEEL CERTAIN I'LL COME BACK SAFELY...
...IF THE OTHER HALF'S SAFE WITH YOU.
IT WAS HIS VERY FIRST FIGHT.
HE SPOKE ABOUT IT IN A TONE I'D NEVER HEARD BEFORE.

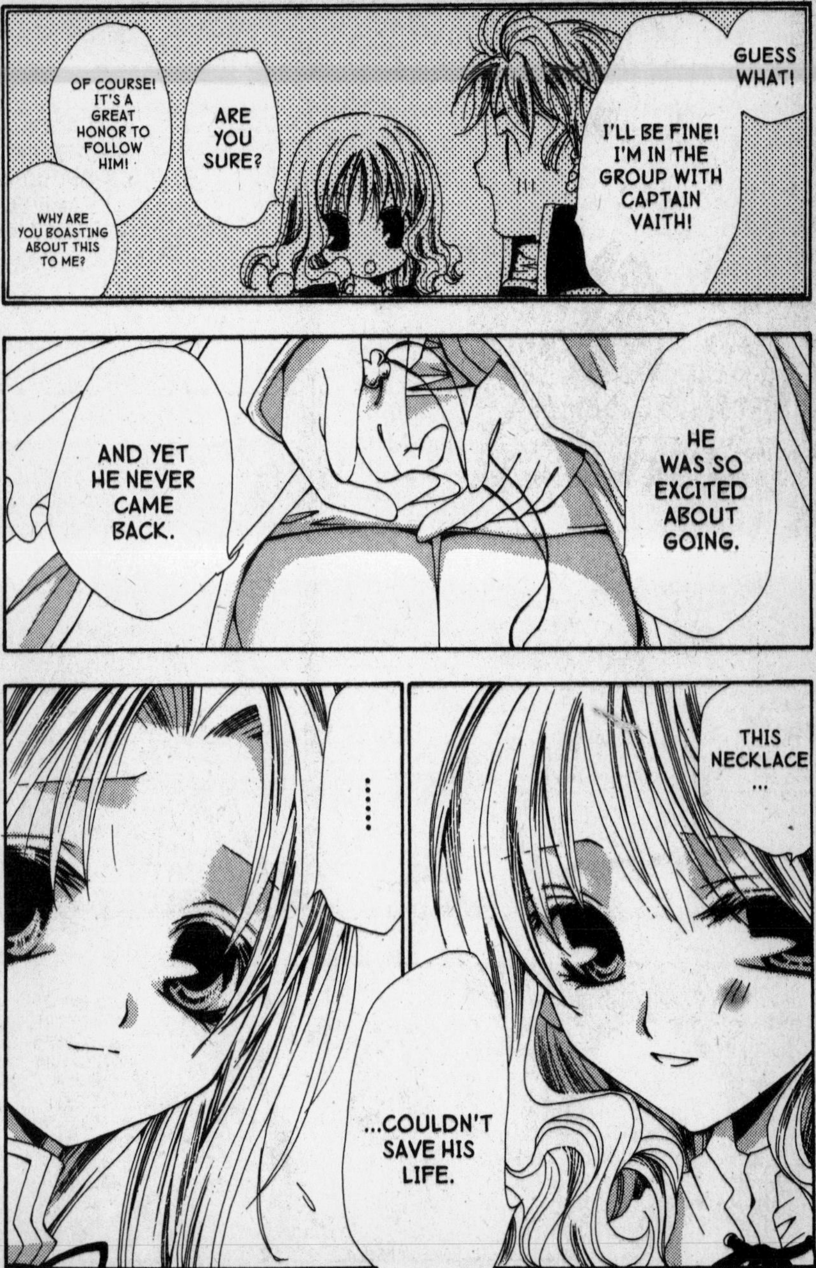
GUESS WHAT!
I'LL BE FINE! I'M IN THE GROUP WITH CAPTAIN VAITH!
ARE YOU SURE?
OF COURSE! IT'S A GREAT HONOR TO FOLLOW HIM!
WHY ARE YOU BOASTING ABOUT THIS TO ME?
HE WAS SO EXCITED ABOUT GOING.
AND YET HE NEVER CAME BACK.
THIS NECKLACE ...
...COULDN'T SAVE HIS LIFE.
......

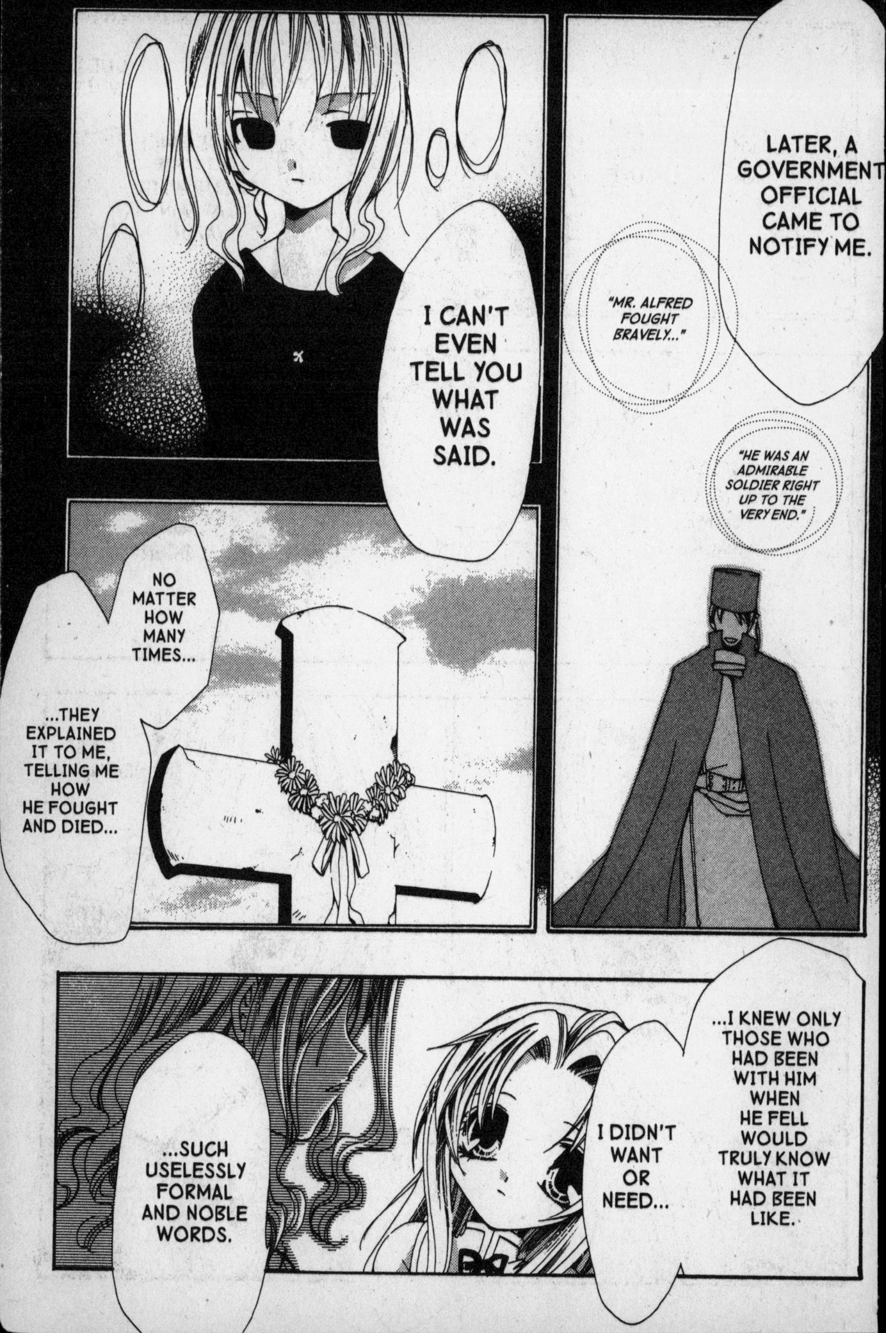
LATER, A GOVERNMENT OFFICIAL CAME TO NOTIFY ME.
"MR. ALFRED FOUGHT BRAVELY..."
"HE WAS AN ADMIRABLE SOLDIER RIGHT UP TO THE VERY END."
I CAN'T EVEN TELL YOU WHAT WAS SAID.
NO MATTER HOW MANY TIMES...
...THEY EXPLAINED IT TO ME, TELLING ME HOW HE FOUGHT AND DIED...
...I KNEW ONLY THOSE WHO HAD BEEN WITH HIM WHEN HE FELL WOULD TRULY KNOW WHAT IT HAD BEEN LIKE.
I DIDN'T WANT OR NEED...
...SUCH USELESSLY FORMAL AND NOBLE WORDS.

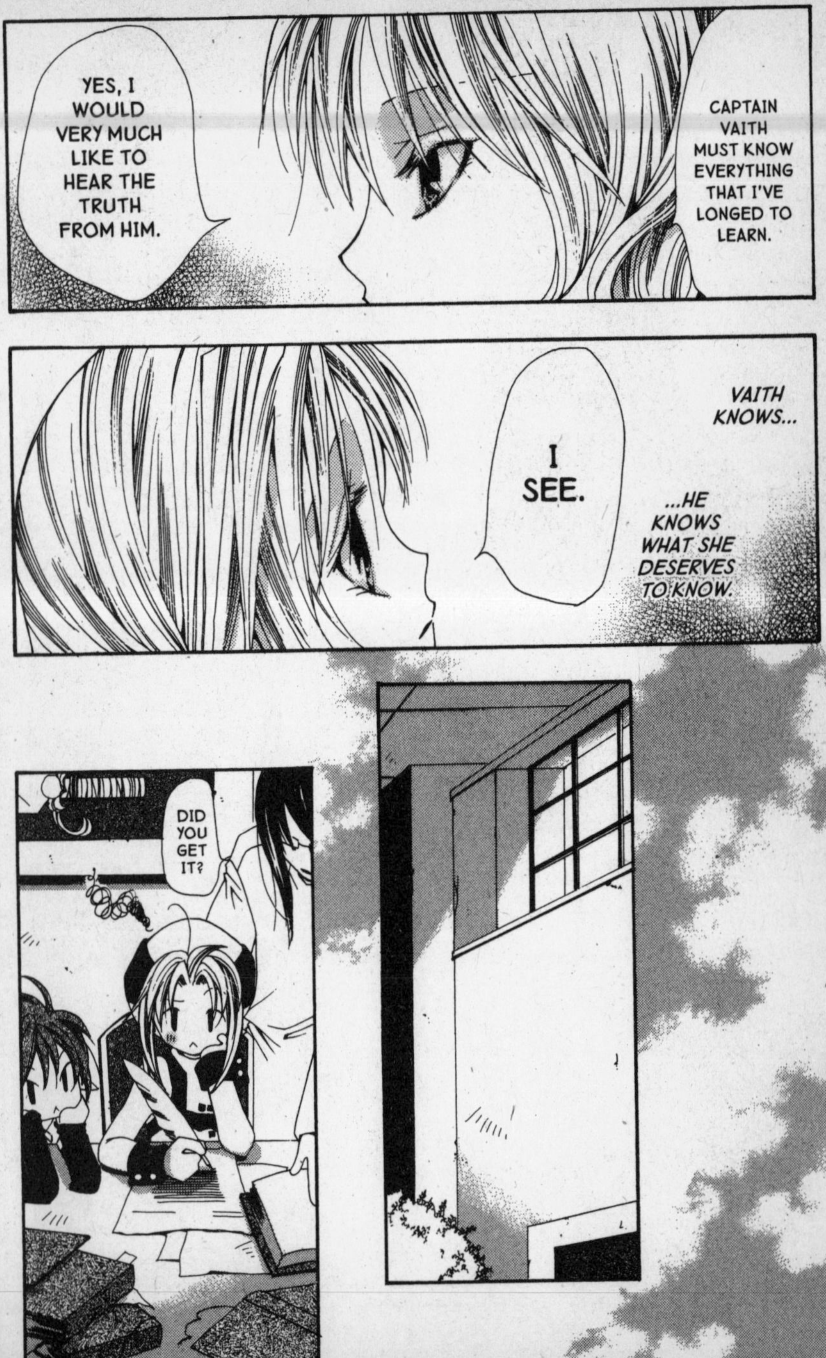
CAPTAIN VAITH MUST KNOW EVERYTHING THAT I'VE LONGED TO LEARN.
YES, I WOULD VERY MUCH LIKE TO HEAR THE TRUTH FROM HIM.
VAITH KNOWS...
I SEE.
...HE KNOWS WHAT SHE DESERVES TO KNOW.
DID YOU GET IT?

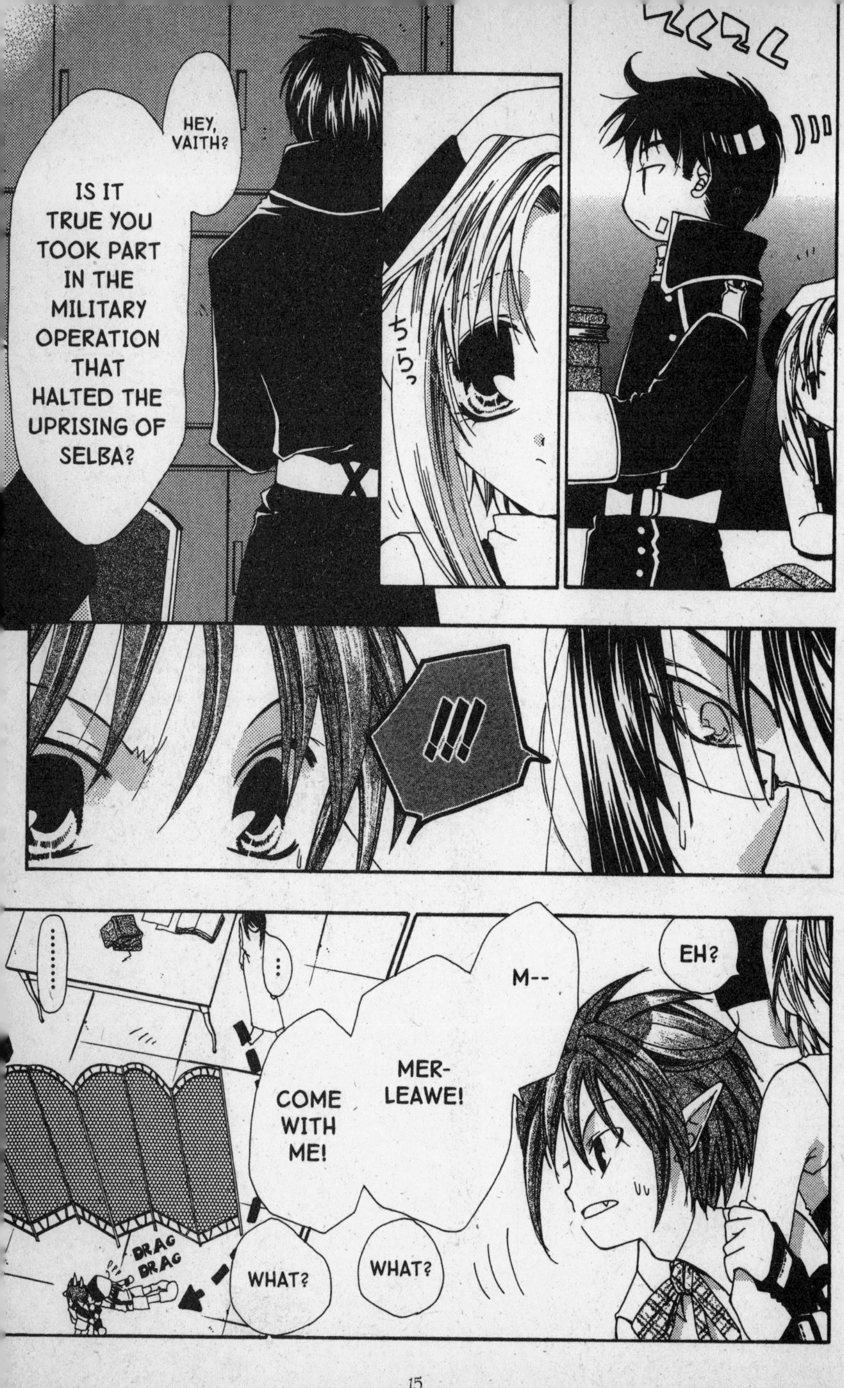
HEY, VAITH?
IS IT TRUE YOU TOOK PART IN THE MILITARY OPERATION THAT HALTED THE UPRISING OF SELBA?
!!!
EH?
M--
MER-LEAWE!
COME WITH ME!
WHAT?
WHAT?
......
...
DRAG DRAG

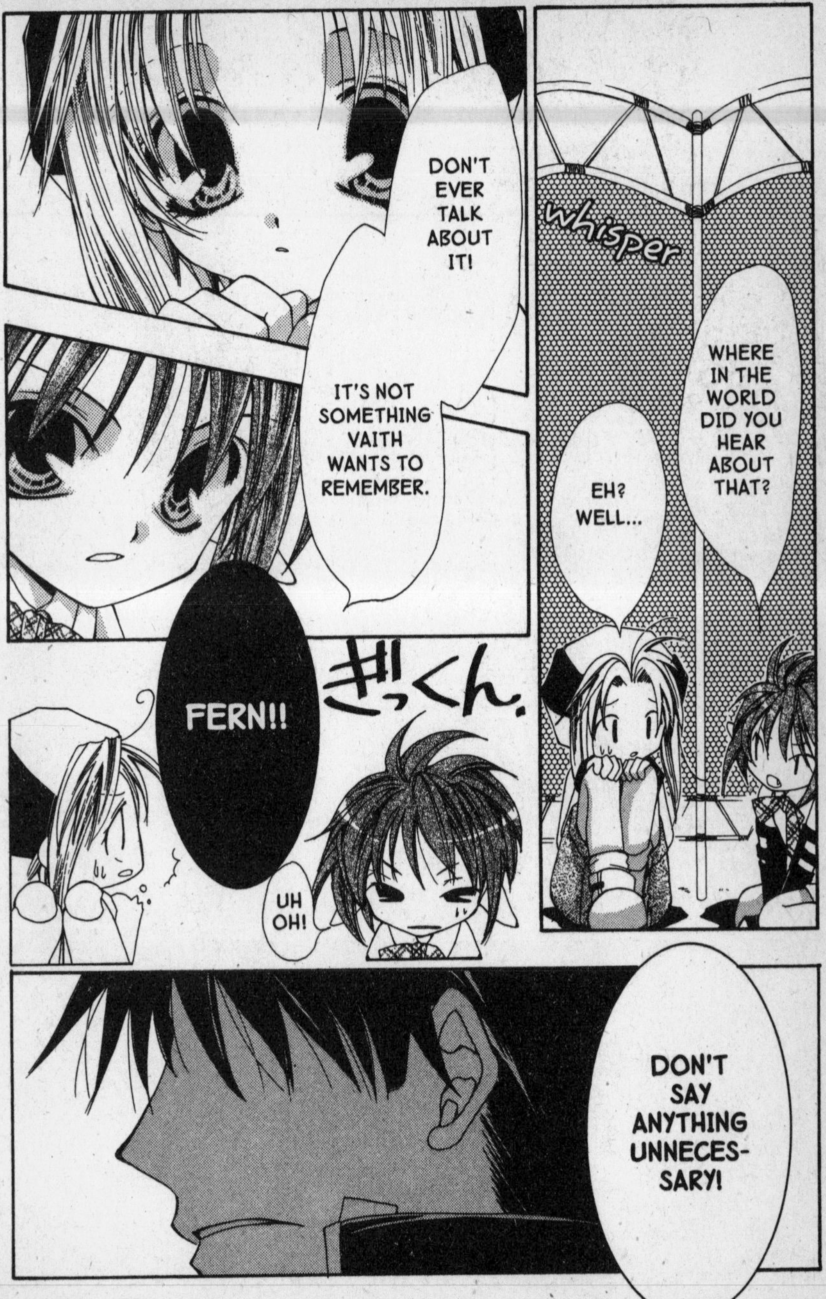
whisper
WHERE IN THE WORLD DID YOU HEAR ABOUT THAT?
EH? WELL...
DON'T EVER TALK ABOUT IT!
IT'S NOT SOMETHING VAITH WANTS TO REMEMBER.
FERN!!
ぎっくん
UH OH!
DON'T SAY ANYTHING UNNECES-SARY!

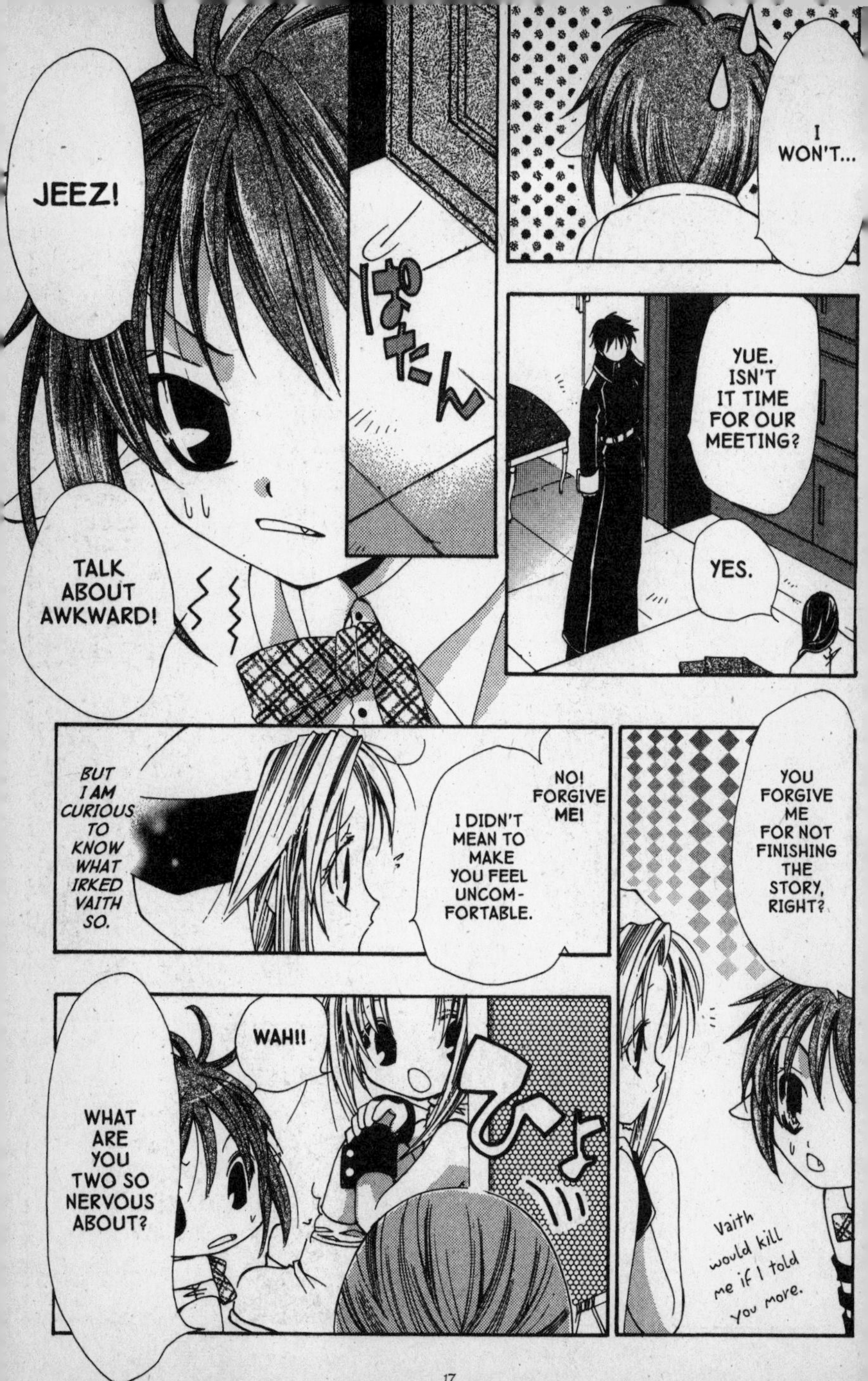
I WON'T...
YUE. ISN'T IT TIME FOR OUR MEETING?
YES.
ぱたん
JEEZ!
TALK ABOUT AWKWARD!
YOU FORGIVE ME FOR NOT FINISHING THE STORY, RIGHT?
Vaith would kill me if I told you more.
NO! FORGIVE ME!
I DIDN'T MEAN TO MAKE YOU FEEL UNCOM-FORTABLE.
BUT I AM CURIOUS TO KNOW WHAT IRKED VAITH SO.
WAH!!
ひょ
WHAT ARE YOU TWO SO NERVOUS ABOUT?

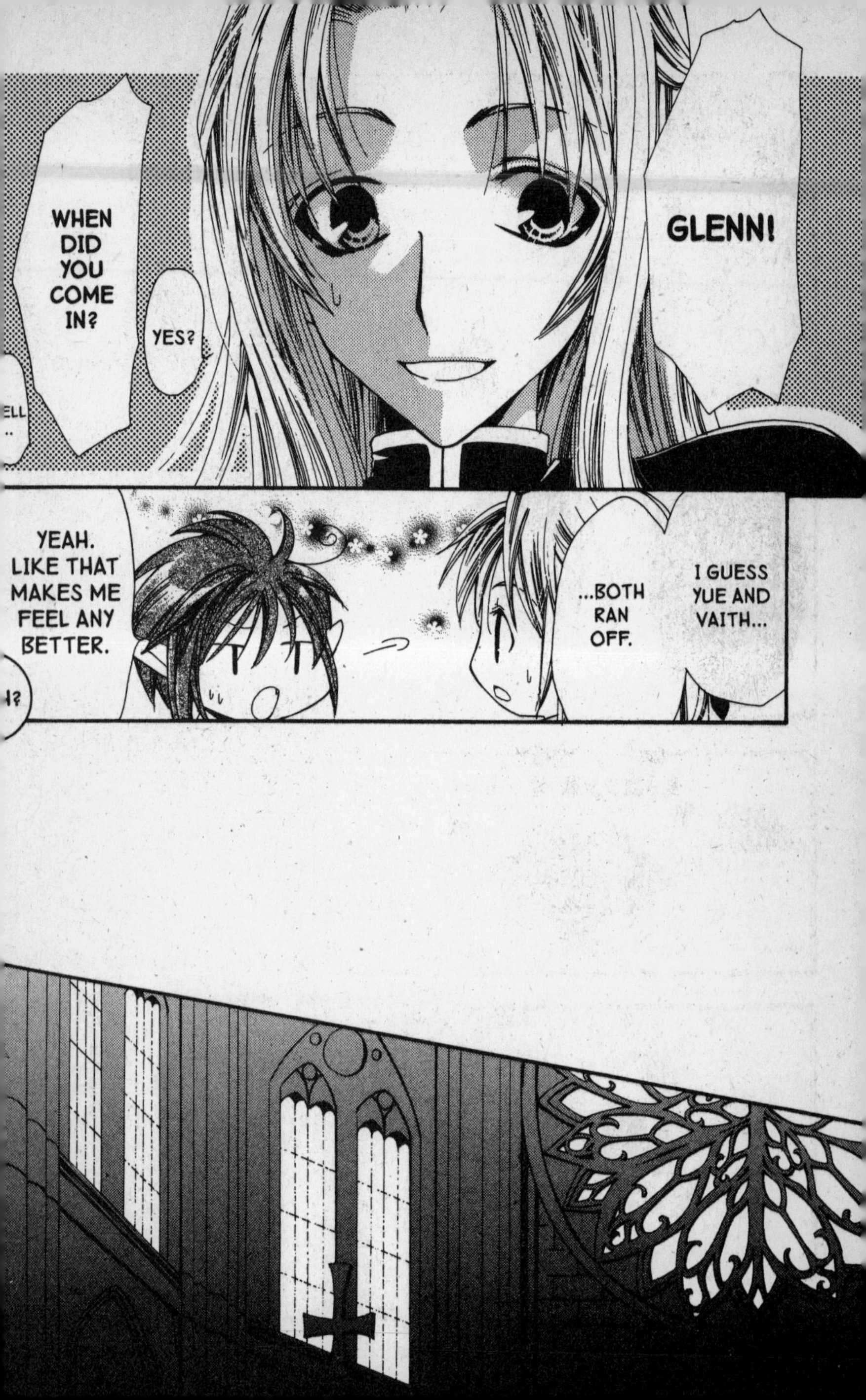
GLENN!
YES?
WHEN DID YOU COME IN?
I GUESS YUE AND VAITH...
...BOTH RAN OFF.
YEAH. LIKE THAT MAKES ME FEEL ANY BETTER.

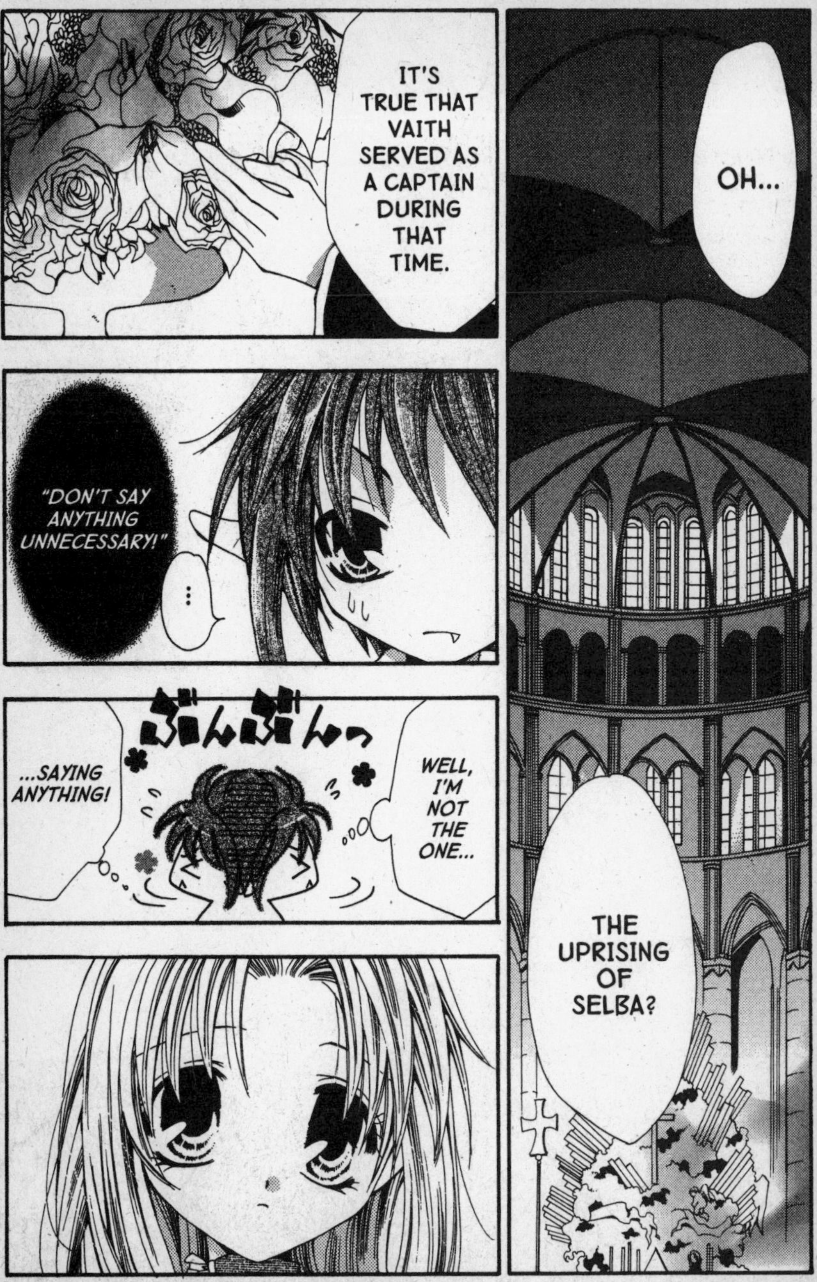
OH...
THE UPRISING OF SELBA?
IT'S TRUE THAT VAITH SERVED AS A CAPTAIN DURING THAT TIME.
...
"DON'T SAY ANYTHING UNNECESSARY!"
WELL, I'M NOT THE ONE...
ぶんぶんっ
...SAYING ANYTHING!

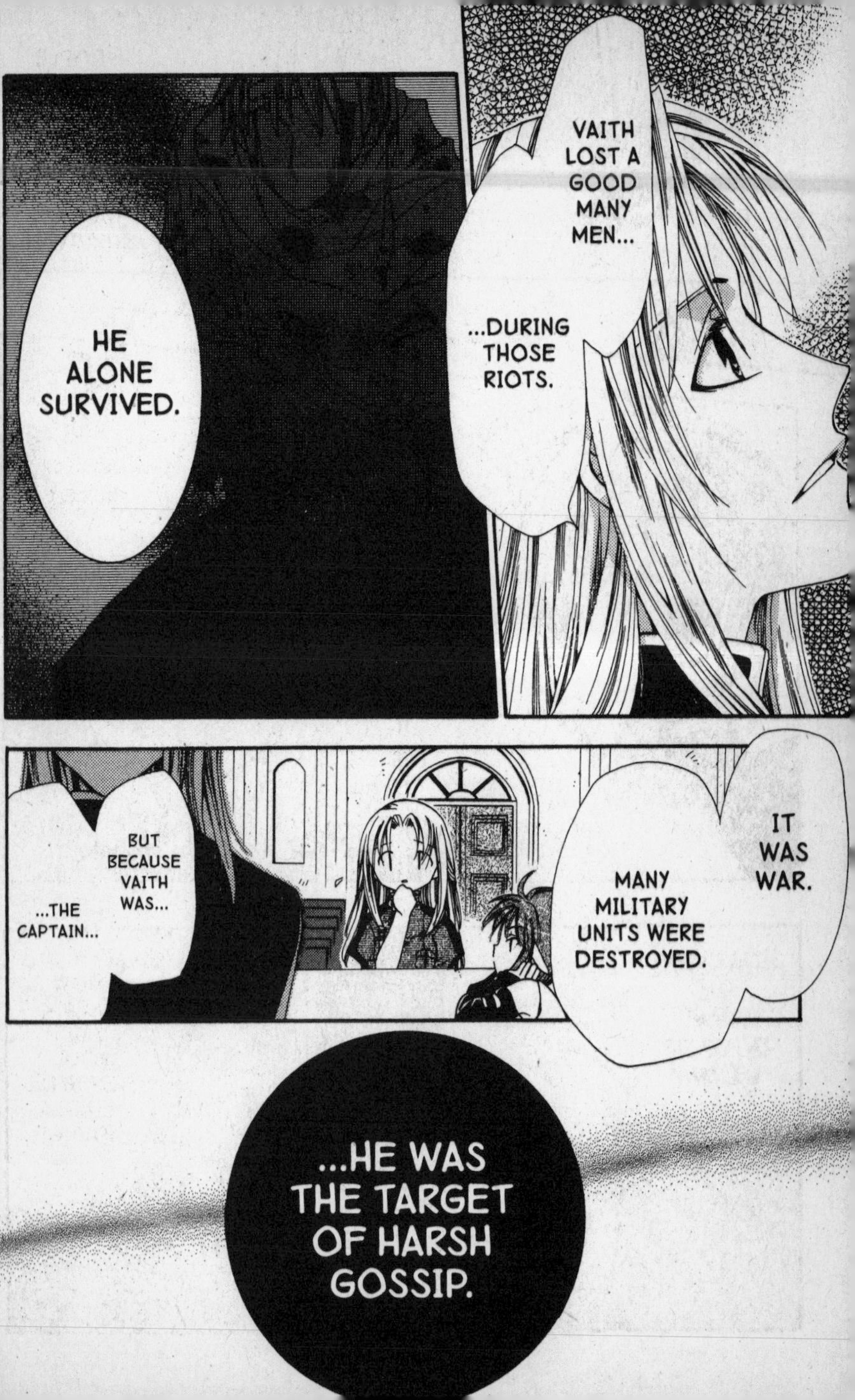
VAITH LOST A GOOD MANY MEN...
...DURING THOSE RIOTS.
HE ALONE SURVIVED.
IT WAS WAR.
MANY MILITARY UNITS WERE DESTROYED.
BUT BECAUSE VAITH WAS...
...THE CAPTAIN...
...HE WAS THE TARGET OF HARSH GOSSIP.

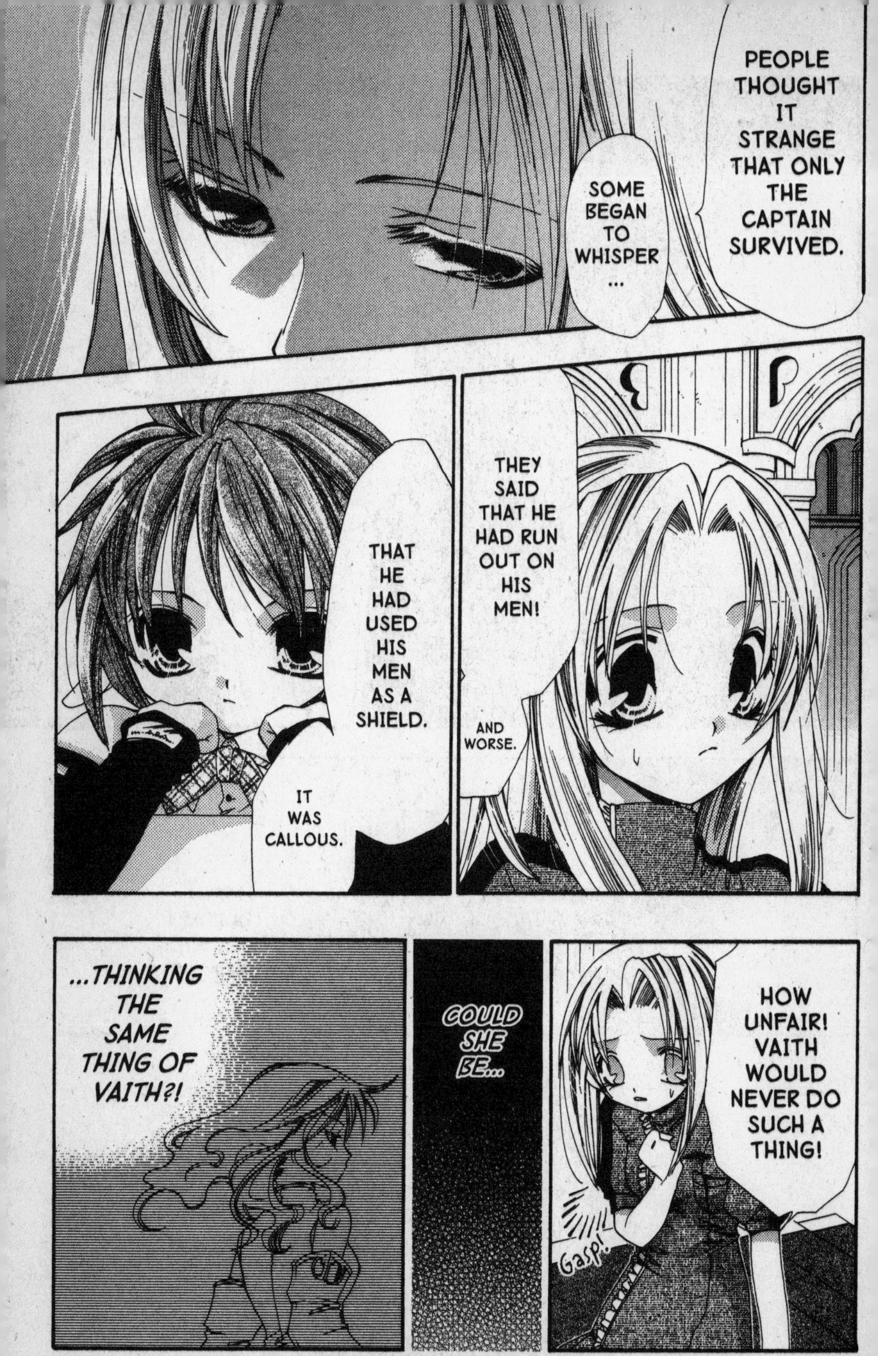
PEOPLE THOUGHT IT STRANGE THAT ONLY THE CAPTAIN SURVIVED.
SOME BEGAN TO WHISPER ...
THEY SAID THAT HE HAD RUN OUT ON HIS MEN!
AND WORSE.
THAT HE HAD USED HIS MEN AS A SHIELD.
IT WAS CALLOUS.
HOW UNFAIR! VAITH WOULD NEVER DO SUCH A THING!
Gasp!
COULD SHE BE...
...THINKING THE SAME THING OF VAITH?!

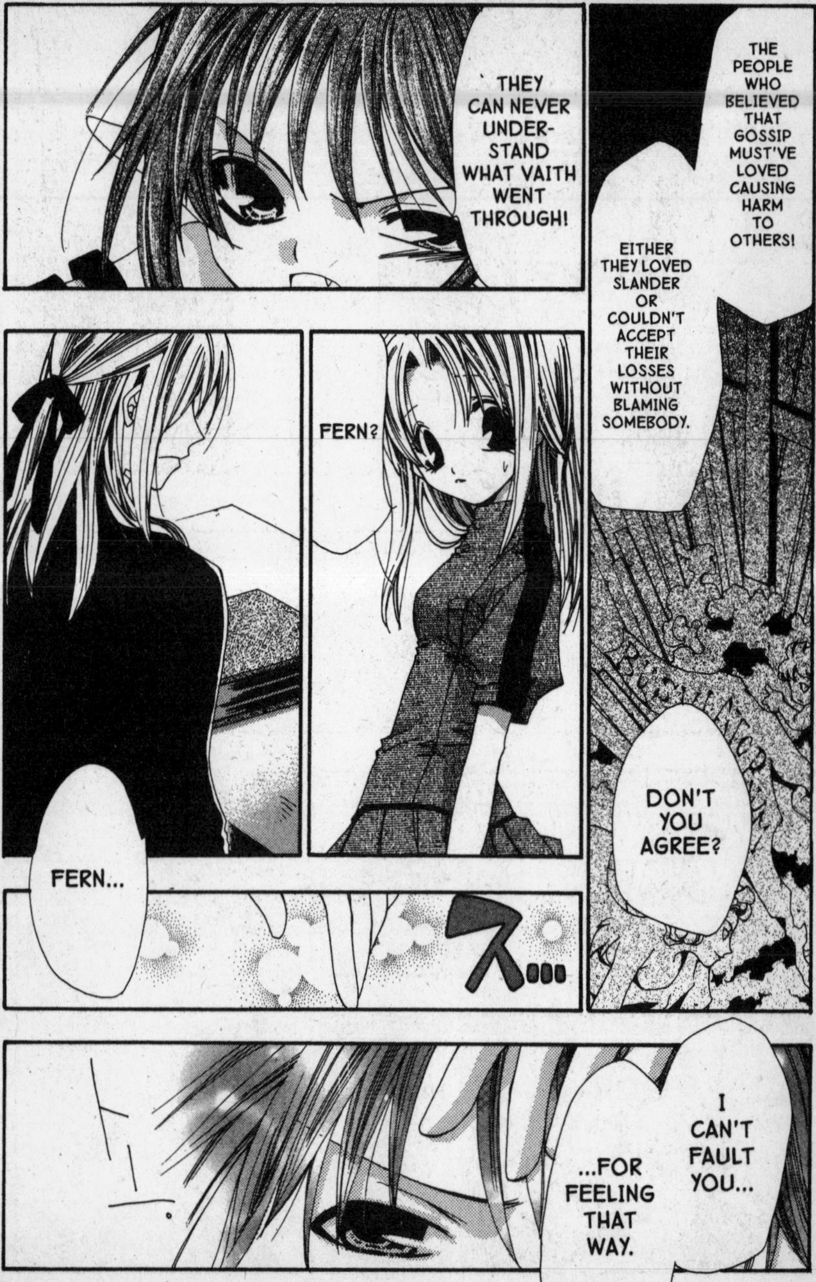
THE PEOPLE WHO BELIEVED THAT GOSSIP MUST'VE LOVED CAUSING HARM TO OTHERS!
EITHER THEY LOVED SLANDER OR COULDN'T ACCEPT THEIR LOSSES WITHOUT BLAMING SOMEBODY.
DON'T YOU AGREE?
THEY CAN NEVER UNDER-STAND WHAT VAITH WENT THROUGH!
FERN?
FERN...
ス...
I CAN'T FAULT YOU...
...FOR FEELING THAT WAY.

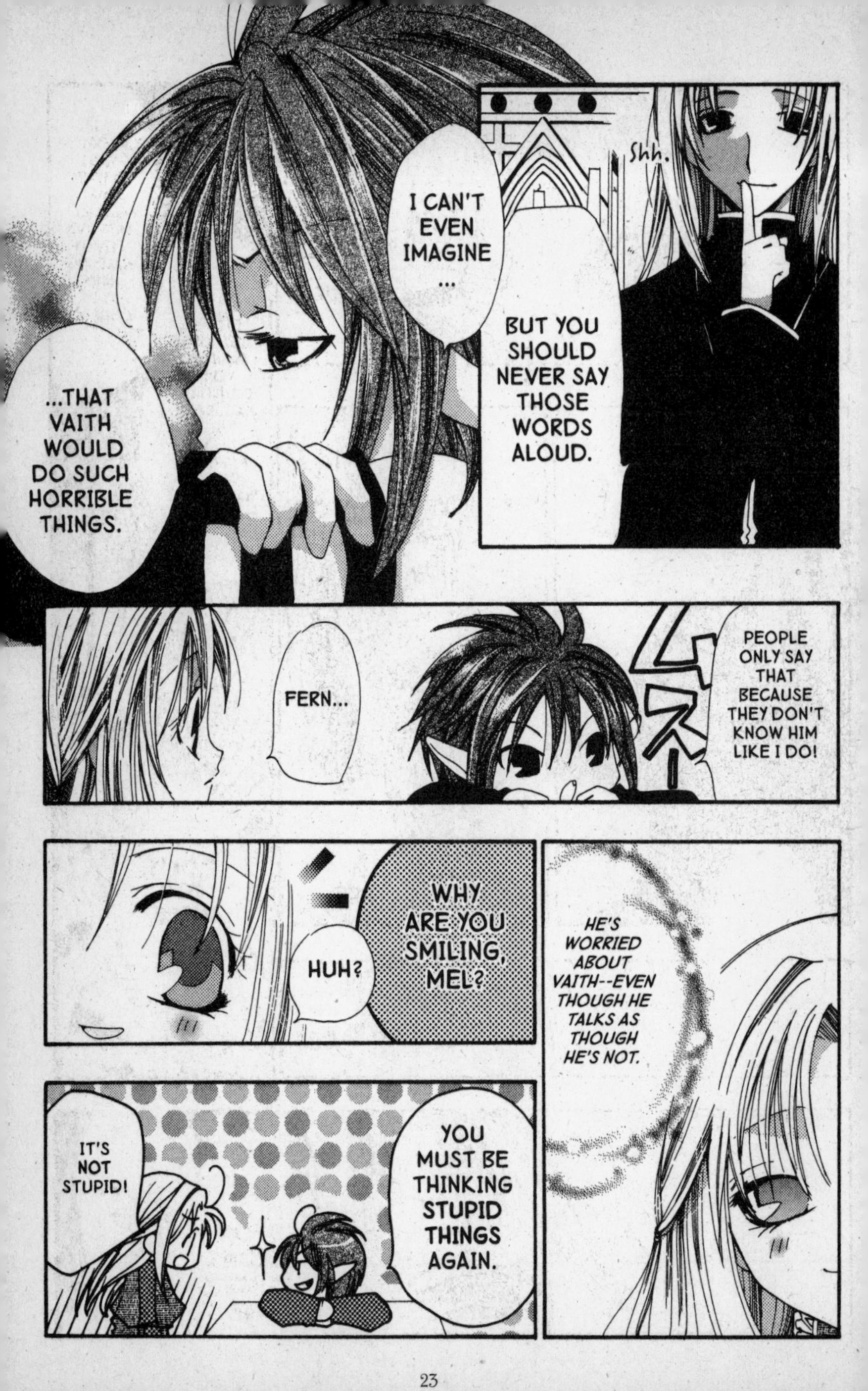
Shh.
BUT YOU SHOULD NEVER SAY THOSE WORDS ALOUD.
I CAN'T EVEN IMAGINE ...
...THAT VAITH WOULD DO SUCH HORRIBLE THINGS.
PEOPLE ONLY SAY THAT BECAUSE THEY DON'T KNOW HIM LIKE I DO!
ムスー
FERN...
HE'S WORRIED ABOUT VAITH--EVEN THOUGH HE TALKS AS THOUGH HE'S NOT.
WHY ARE YOU SMILING, MEL?
HUH?
YOU MUST BE THINKING STUPID THINGS AGAIN.
IT'S NOT STUPID!

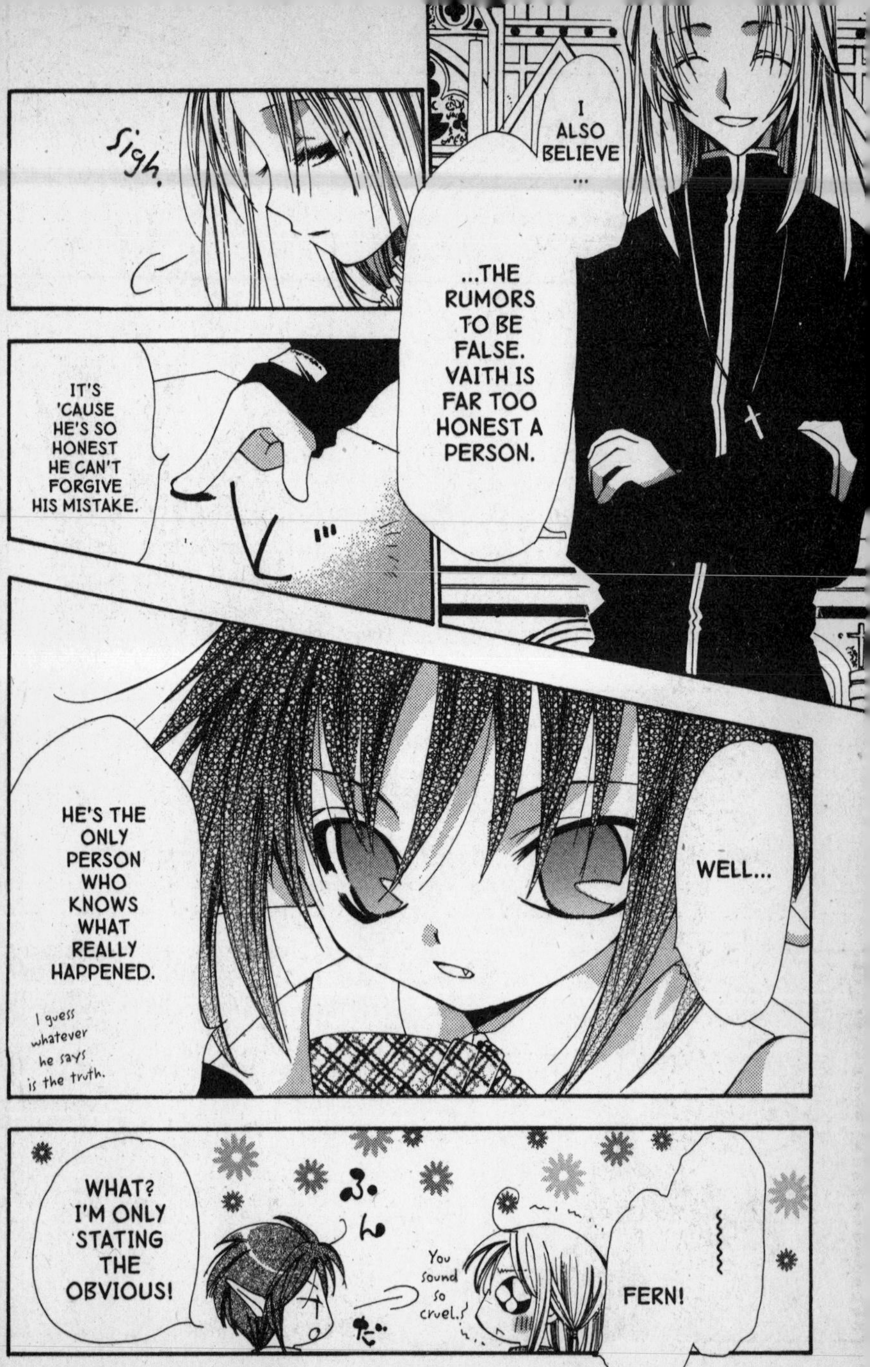

I ALSO BELIEVE ...
...THE RUMORS TO BE FALSE. VAITH IS FAR TOO HONEST A PERSON.
Sigh.
IT'S 'CAUSE HE'S SO HONEST HE CAN'T FORGIVE HIS MISTAKE.
WELL...
HE'S THE ONLY PERSON WHO KNOWS WHAT REALLY HAPPENED.
I guess whatever he says is the truth.
FERN!
~n...
You sound so cruel.
ふん
WHAT? I'M ONLY STATING THE OBVIOUS!

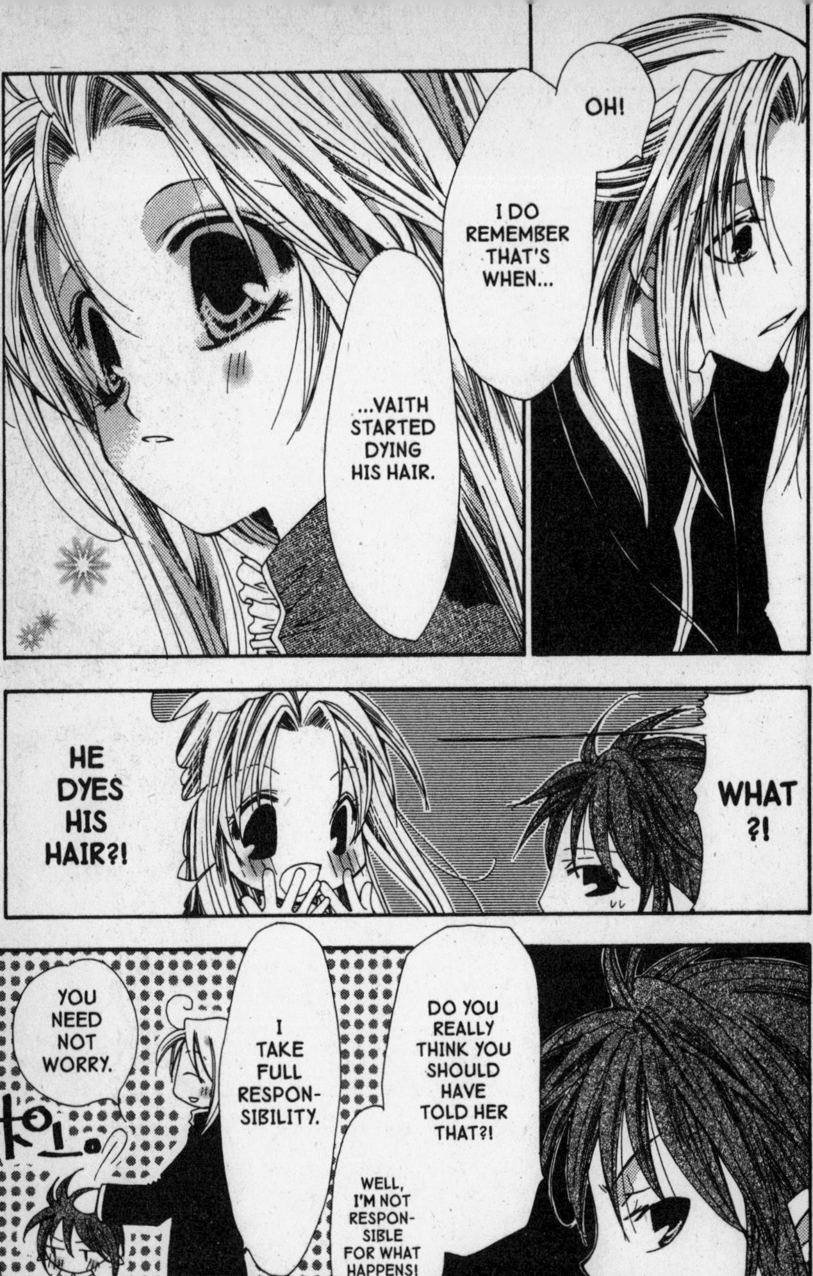
OH!
I DO REMEMBER THAT'S WHEN...
...VAITH STARTED DYING HIS HAIR.
WHAT ?!
HE DYES HIS HAIR?!
DO YOU REALLY THINK YOU SHOULD HAVE TOLD HER THAT?!
WELL, I'M NOT RESPON-SIBLE FOR WHAT HAPPENS!
I TAKE FULL RESPON-SIBILITY.
YOU NEED NOT WORRY.
...

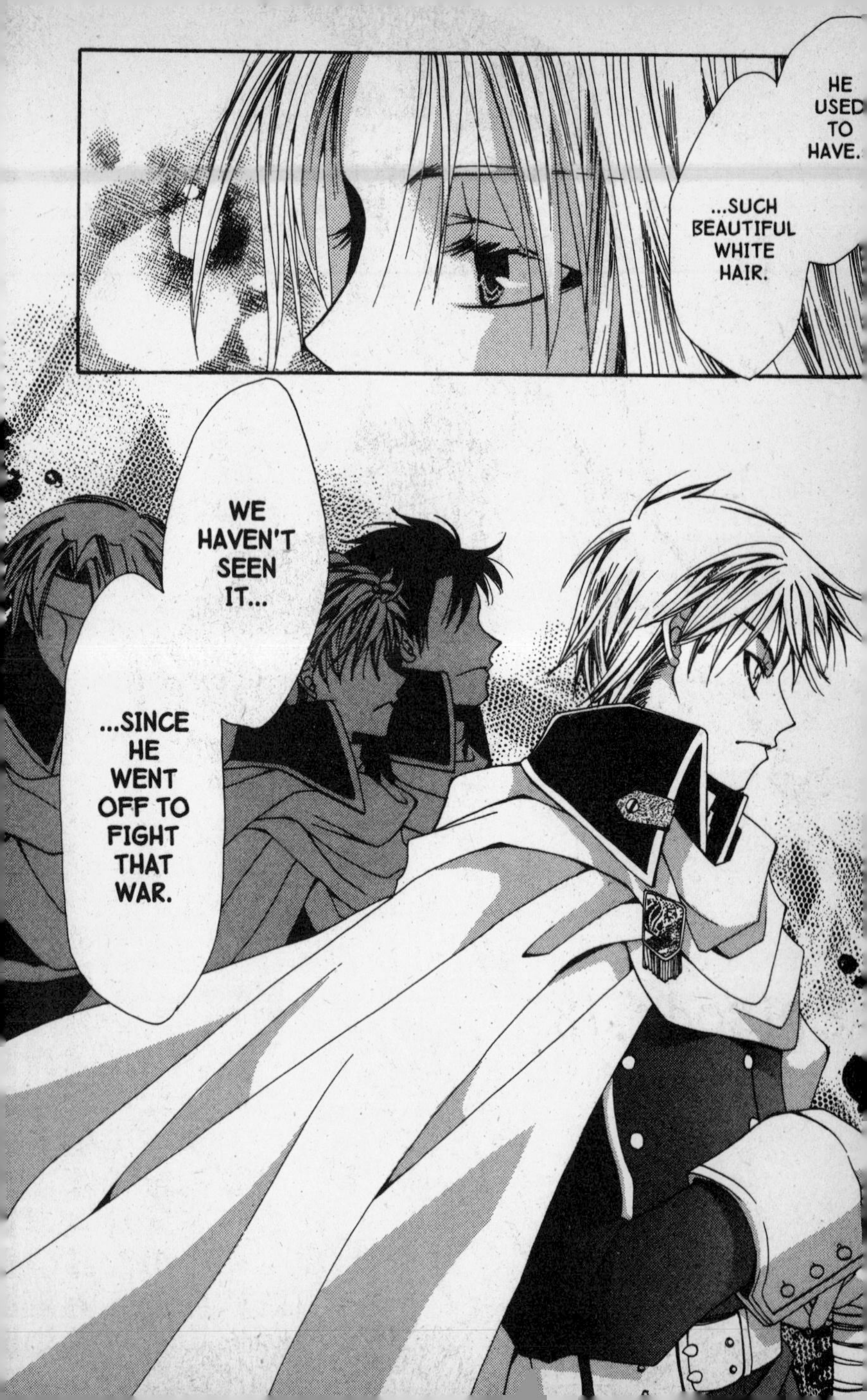
HE USED TO HAVE.
...SUCH BEAUTIFUL WHITE HAIR.
WE HAVEN'T SEEN IT...
...SINCE HE WENT OFF TO FIGHT THAT WAR.

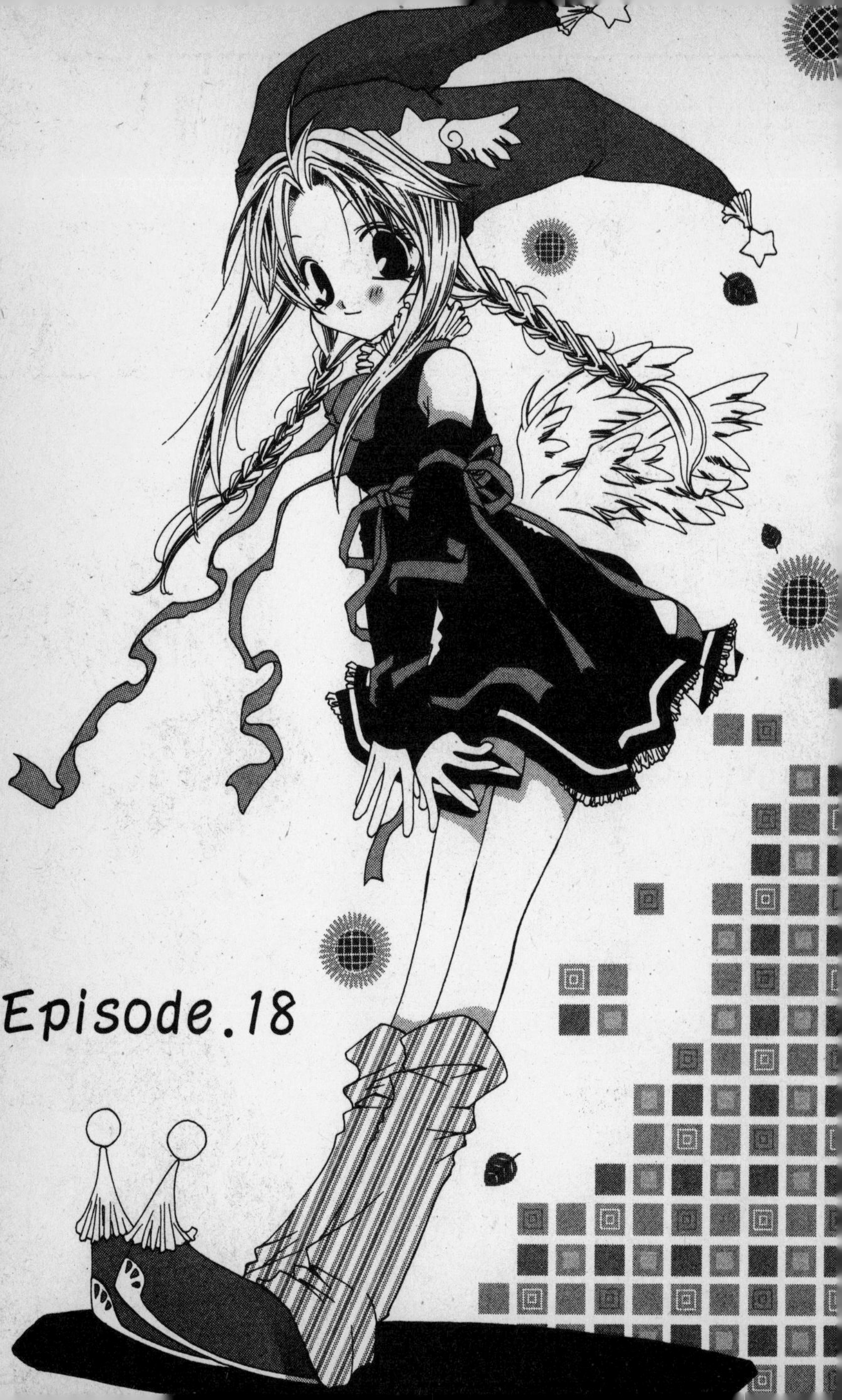
Episode.18

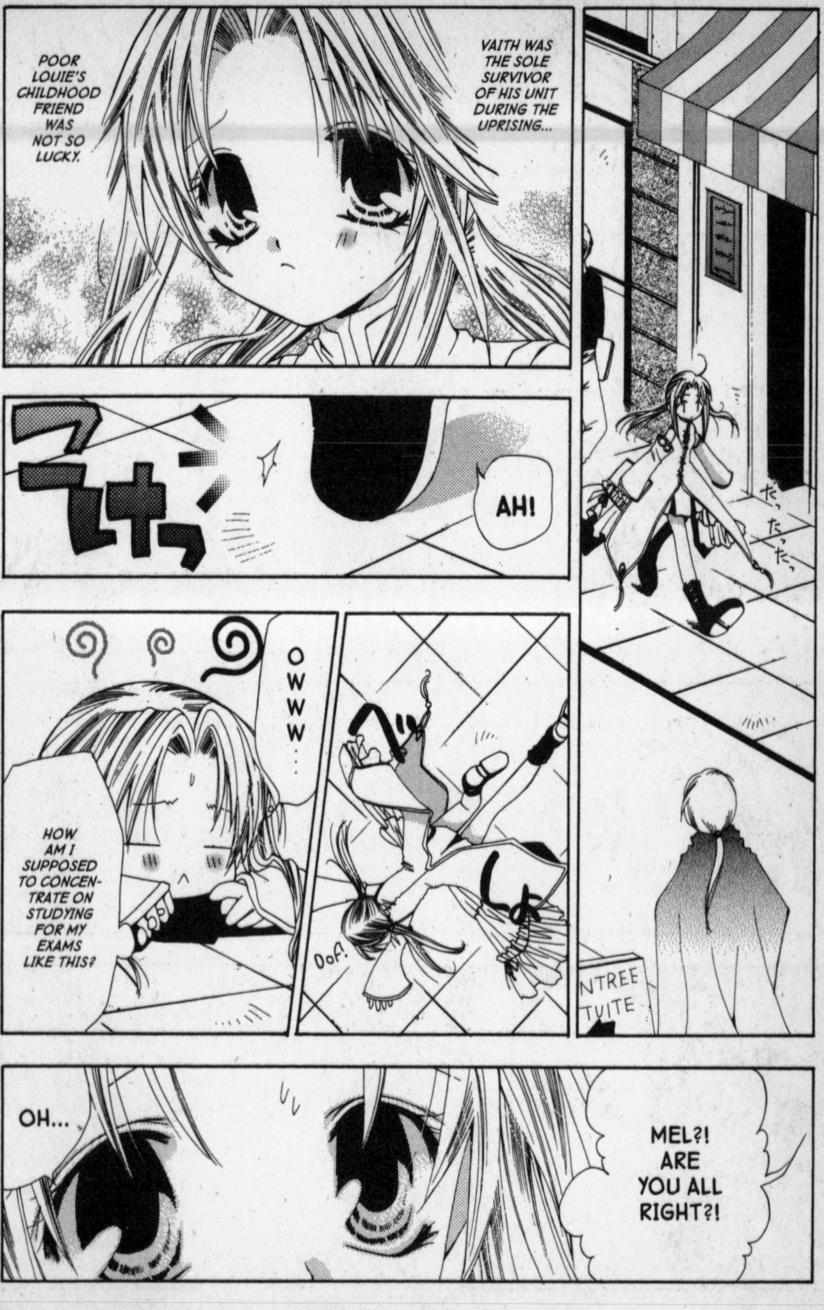
だっ、だっ、だっ
NTREE
TUITE
VAITH WAS THE SOLE SURVIVOR OF HIS UNIT DURING THE UPRISING...
POOR LOUIE'S CHILDHOOD FRIEND WAS NOT SO LUCKY.
AH!
べしょ
Dof!
OWWW...
HOW AM I SUPPOSED TO CONCENTRATE ON STUDYING FOR MY EXAMS LIKE THIS?
MEL?! ARE YOU ALL RIGHT?!
OH...

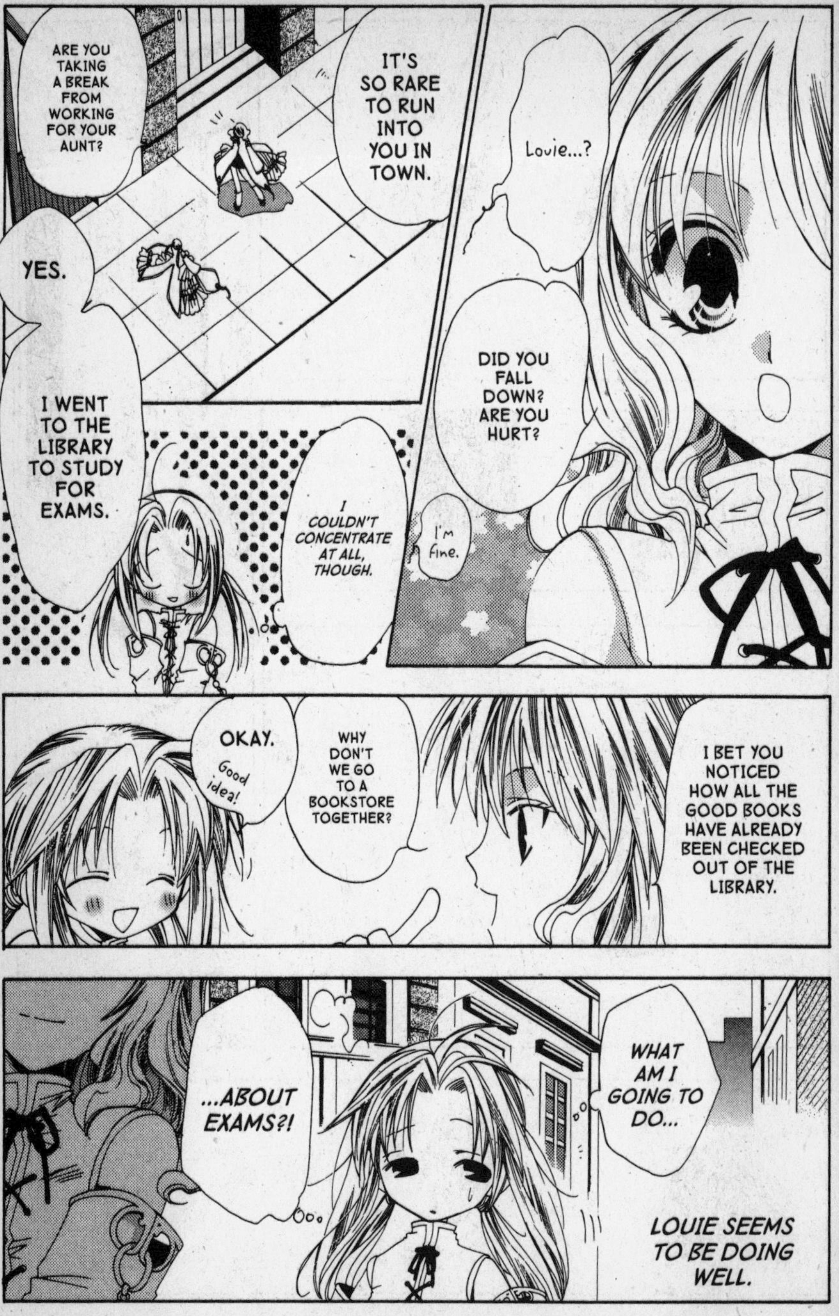
Louie...?
DID YOU FALL DOWN? ARE YOU HURT?
I'm fine.
IT'S SO RARE TO RUN INTO YOU IN TOWN.
ARE YOU TAKING A BREAK FROM WORKING FOR YOUR AUNT?
YES.
I WENT TO THE LIBRARY TO STUDY FOR EXAMS.
I COULDN'T CONCENTRATE AT ALL, THOUGH.
I BET YOU NOTICED HOW ALL THE GOOD BOOKS HAVE ALREADY BEEN CHECKED OUT OF THE LIBRARY.
WHY DON'T WE GO TO A BOOKSTORE TOGETHER?
OKAY.
Good idea!
WHAT AM I GOING TO DO...
...ABOUT EXAMS?!
LOUIE SEEMS TO BE DOING WELL.

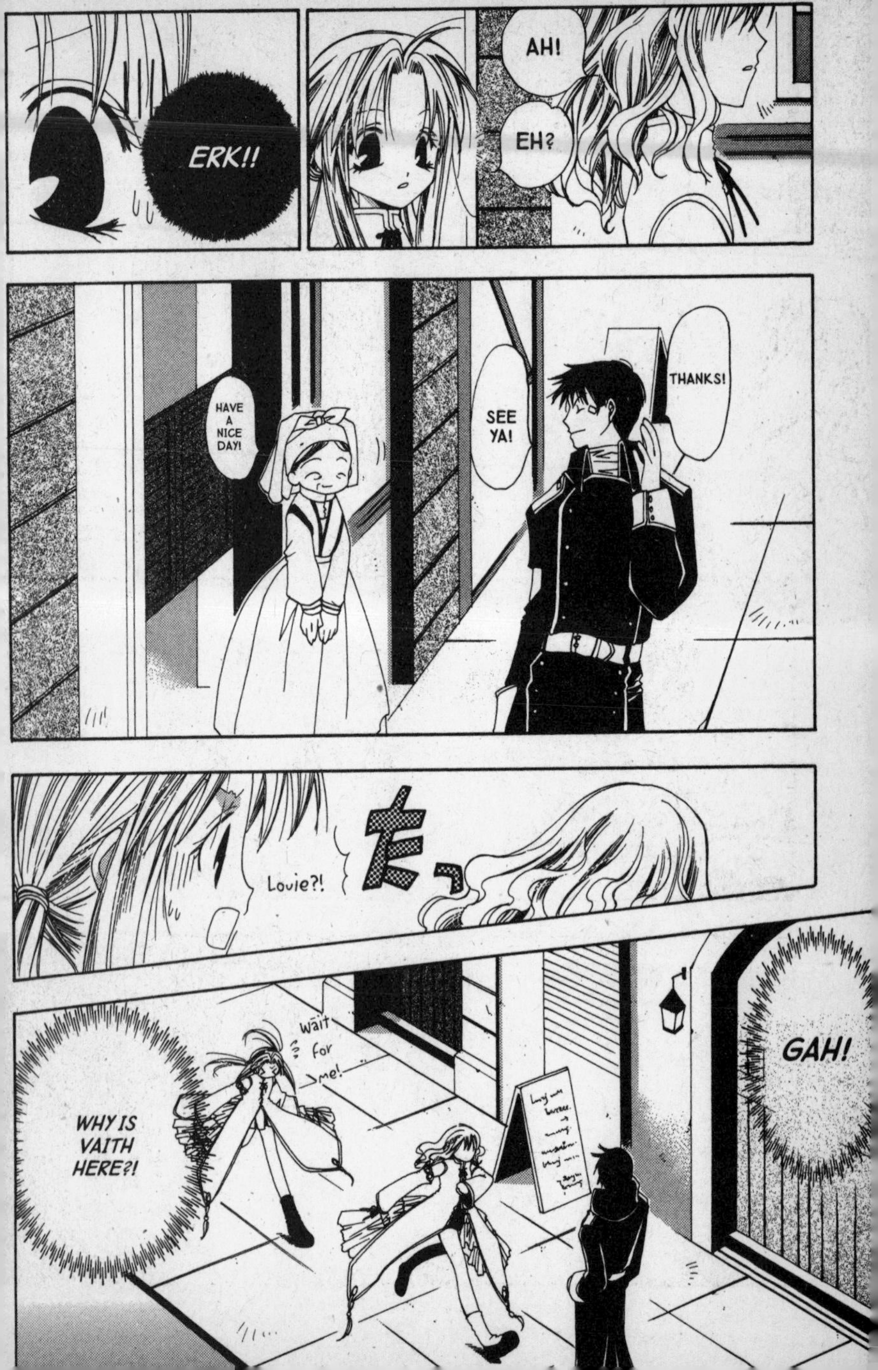
AH!
EH?
ERK!!
THANKS!
SEE YA!
HAVE A NICE DAY!
たっ
Louie?!
GAH!
Wait for me!
WHY IS VAITH HERE?!

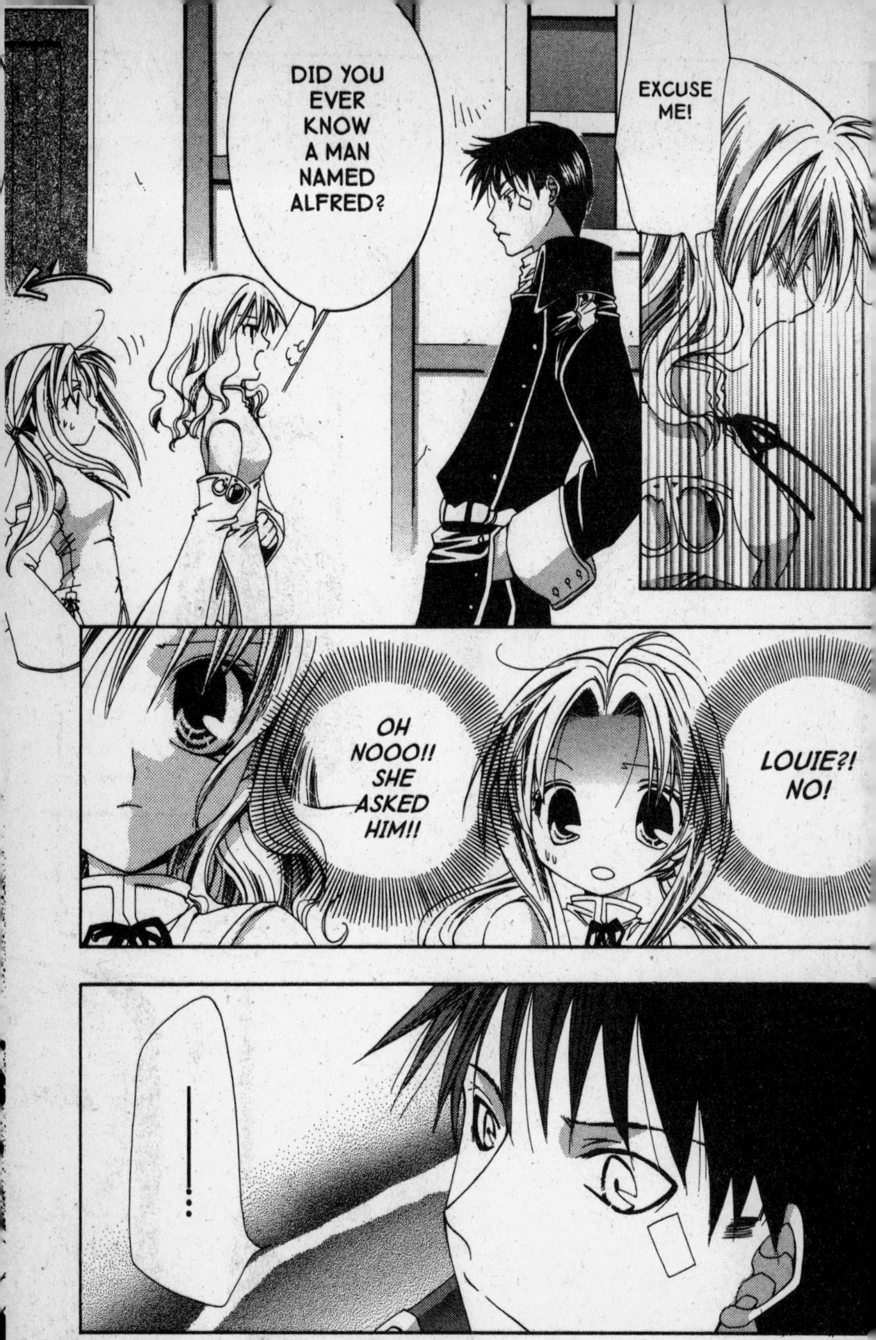
EXCUSE ME!
DID YOU EVER KNOW A MAN NAMED ALFRED?
LOUIE?! NO!
OH NOOO!! SHE ASKED HIM!!

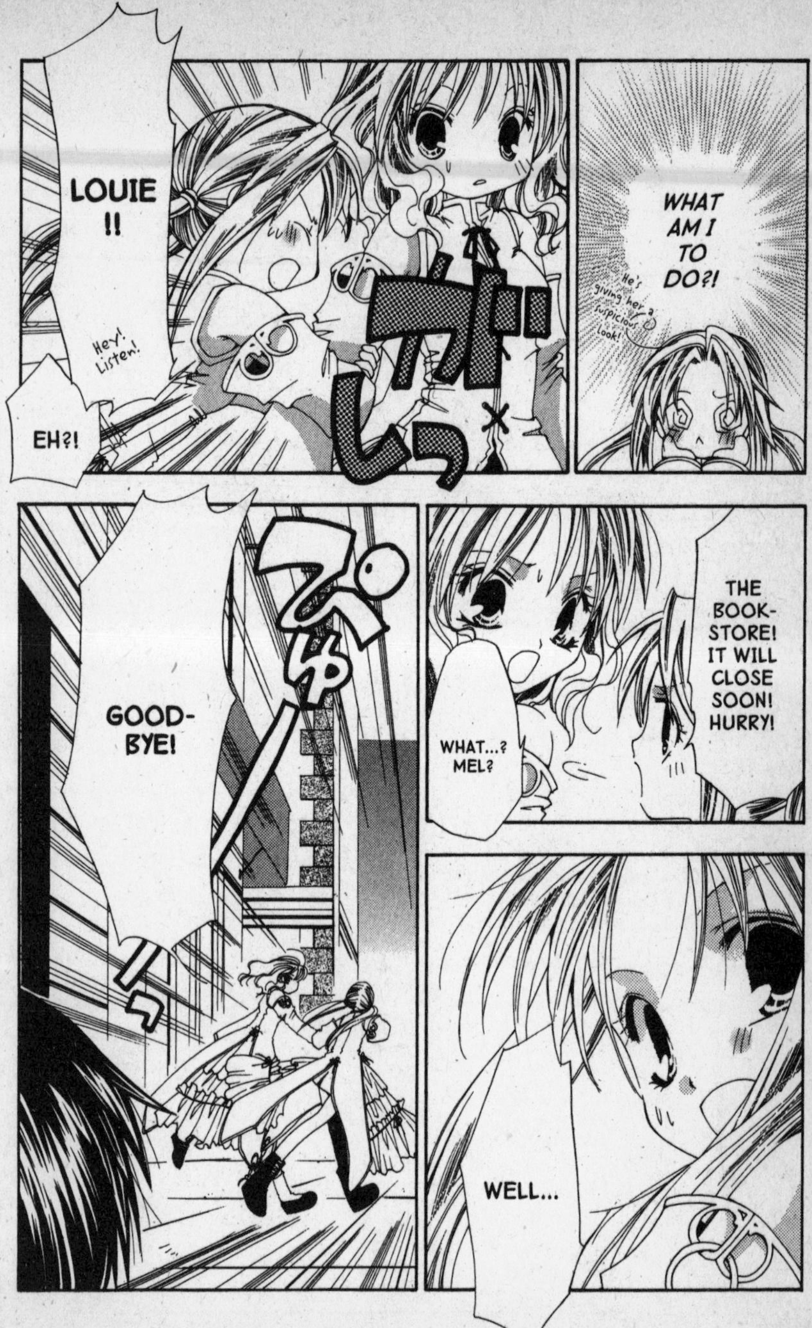
WHAT AM I TO DO?!
He's giving her a suspicious look!
LOUIE !!
Hey! Listen!
ガバしっ
EH?!
THE BOOK-STORE! IT WILL CLOSE SOON! HURRY!
WHAT...? MEL?
WELL...
GOOD-BYE!
ぴゅ〜ん

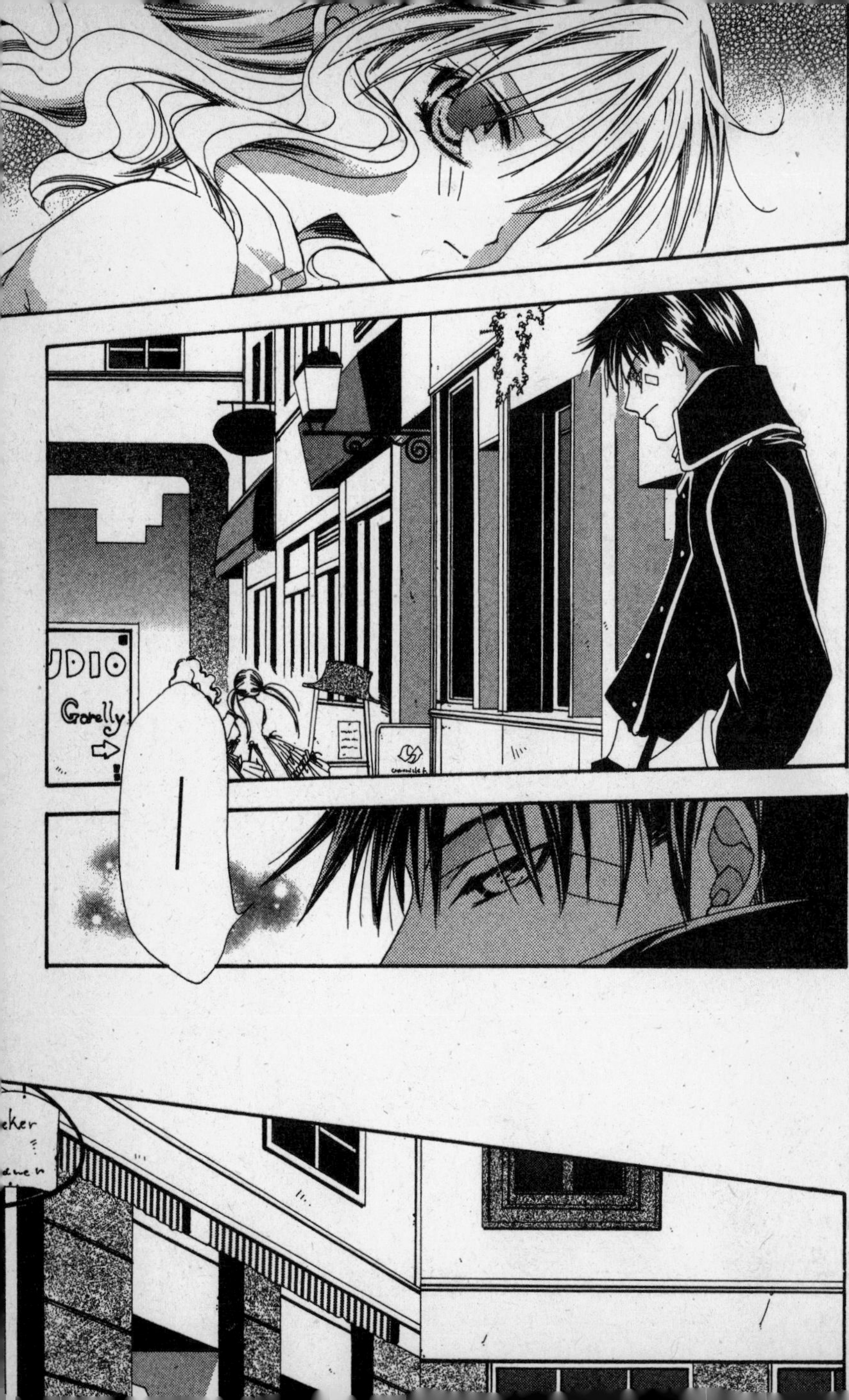
UDIO
Garelly

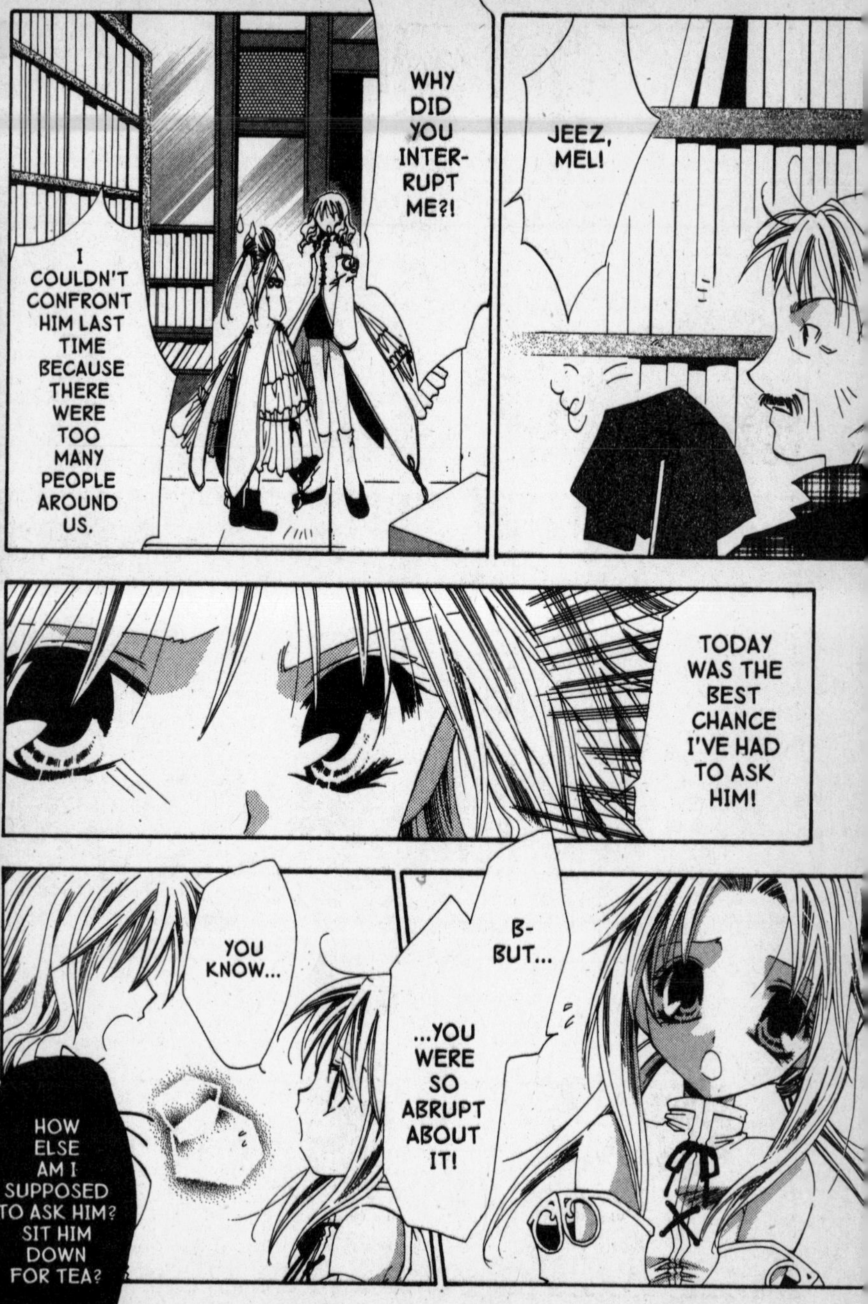
JEEZ, MEL!
WHY DID YOU INTERRUPT ME?!
I COULDN'T CONFRONT HIM LAST TIME BECAUSE THERE WERE TOO MANY PEOPLE AROUND US.
TODAY WAS THE BEST CHANCE I'VE HAD TO ASK HIM!
B-BUT...
...YOU WERE SO ABRUPT ABOUT IT!
YOU KNOW...
HOW ELSE AM I SUPPOSED TO ASK HIM? SIT HIM DOWN FOR TEA?

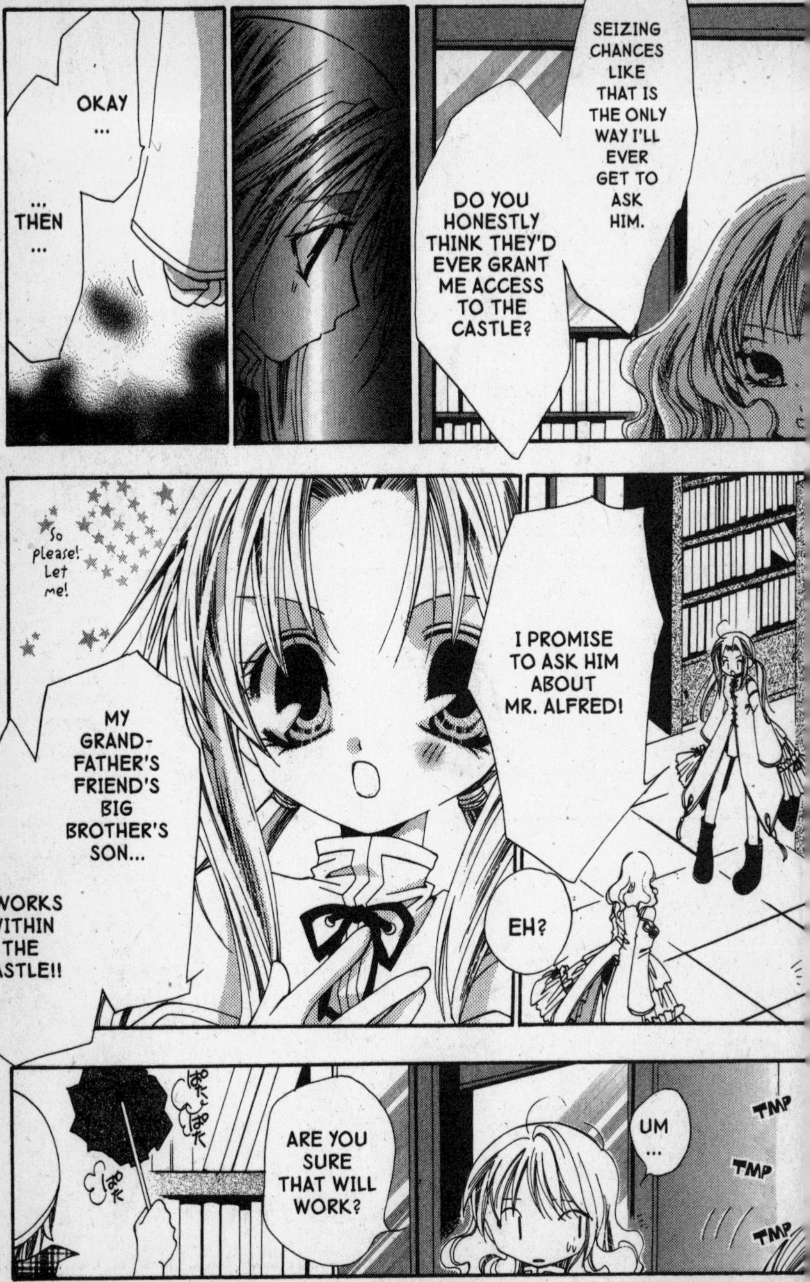
SEIZING CHANCES LIKE THAT IS THE ONLY WAY I'LL EVER GET TO ASK HIM.
DO YOU HONESTLY THINK THEY'D EVER GRANT ME ACCESS TO THE CASTLE?
OKAY ...
... THEN ...
I PROMISE TO ASK HIM ABOUT MR. ALFRED!
EH?
So please! Let me!
MY GRAND-FATHER'S FRIEND'S BIG BROTHER'S SON...
...WORKS WITHIN THE CASTLE!!
TMP
TMP
TMP
UM ...
ぱたぱた
ぱた
ARE YOU SURE THAT WILL WORK?

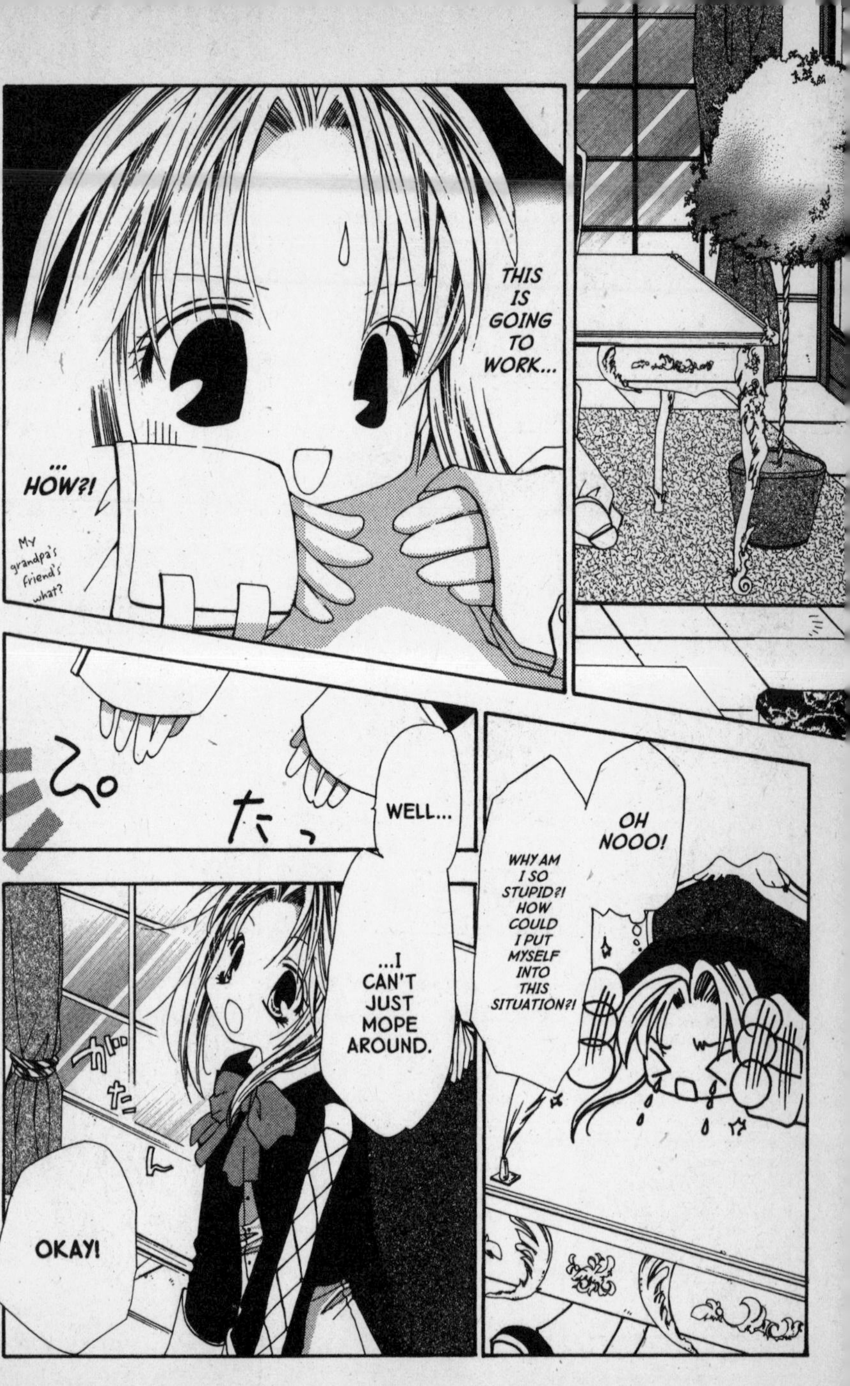
THIS IS GOING TO WORK...
...HOW?!
My grandpa's friend's what?
OH NOOO!
WHY AM I SO STUPID?! HOW COULD I PUT MYSELF INTO THIS SITUATION?!
たっ
WELL...
...I CAN'T JUST MOPE AROUND.
OKAY!

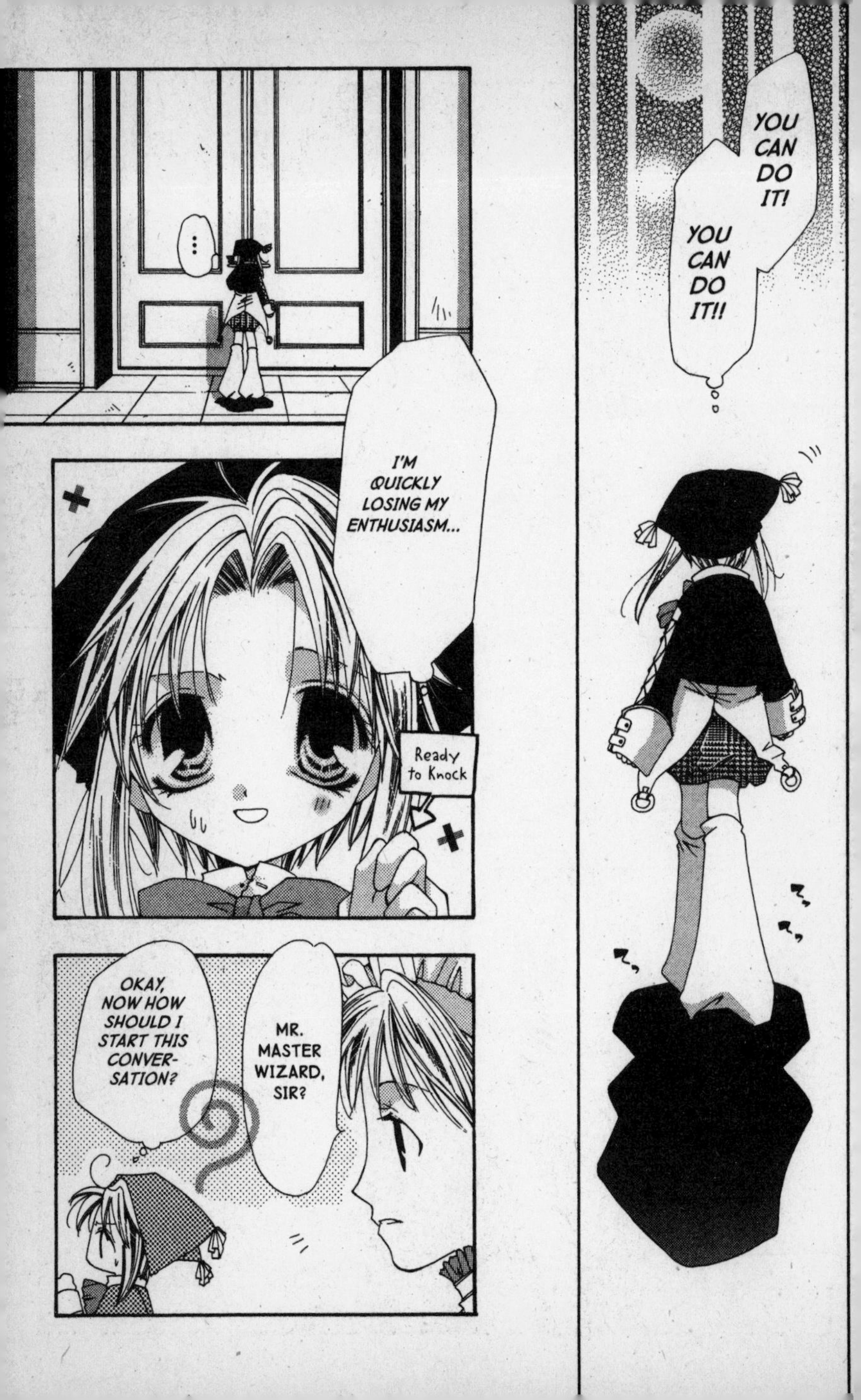
YOU CAN DO IT!
YOU CAN DO IT!!
...
I'M QUICKLY LOSING MY ENTHUSIASM...
Ready to Knock
MR. MASTER WIZARD, SIR?
OKAY, NOW HOW SHOULD I START THIS CONVER-SATION?

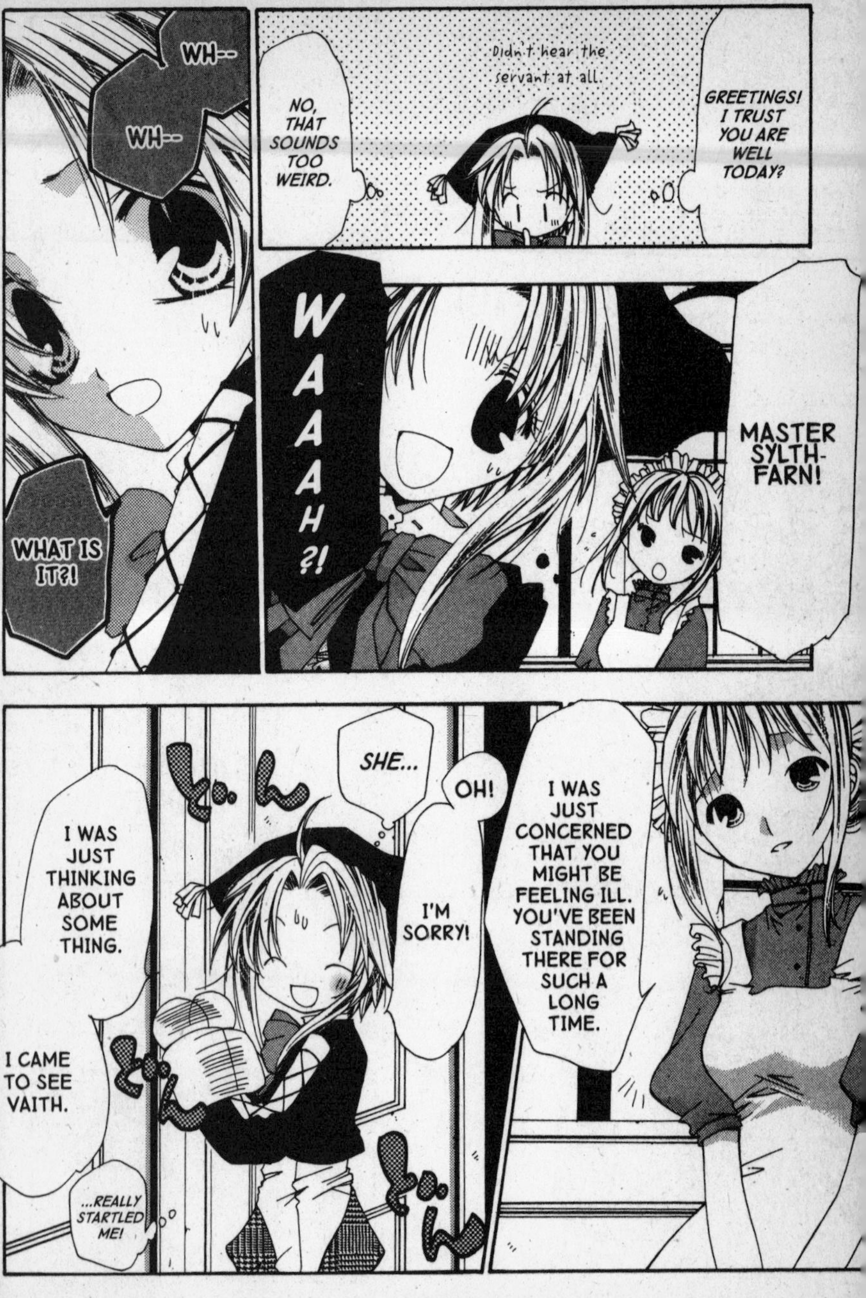
GREETINGS! I TRUST YOU ARE WELL TODAY?
Didn't hear the servant at all.
NO, THAT SOUNDS TOO WEIRD.
MASTER SYLTH-FARN!
WAAAAH?!
WH--
WH--
WHAT IS IT?!
I WAS JUST CONCERNED THAT YOU MIGHT BE FEELING ILL. YOU'VE BEEN STANDING THERE FOR SUCH A LONG TIME.
OH!
SHE...
I'M SORRY!
I WAS JUST THINKING ABOUT SOME THING.
I CAME TO SEE VAITH.
...REALLY STARTLED ME!

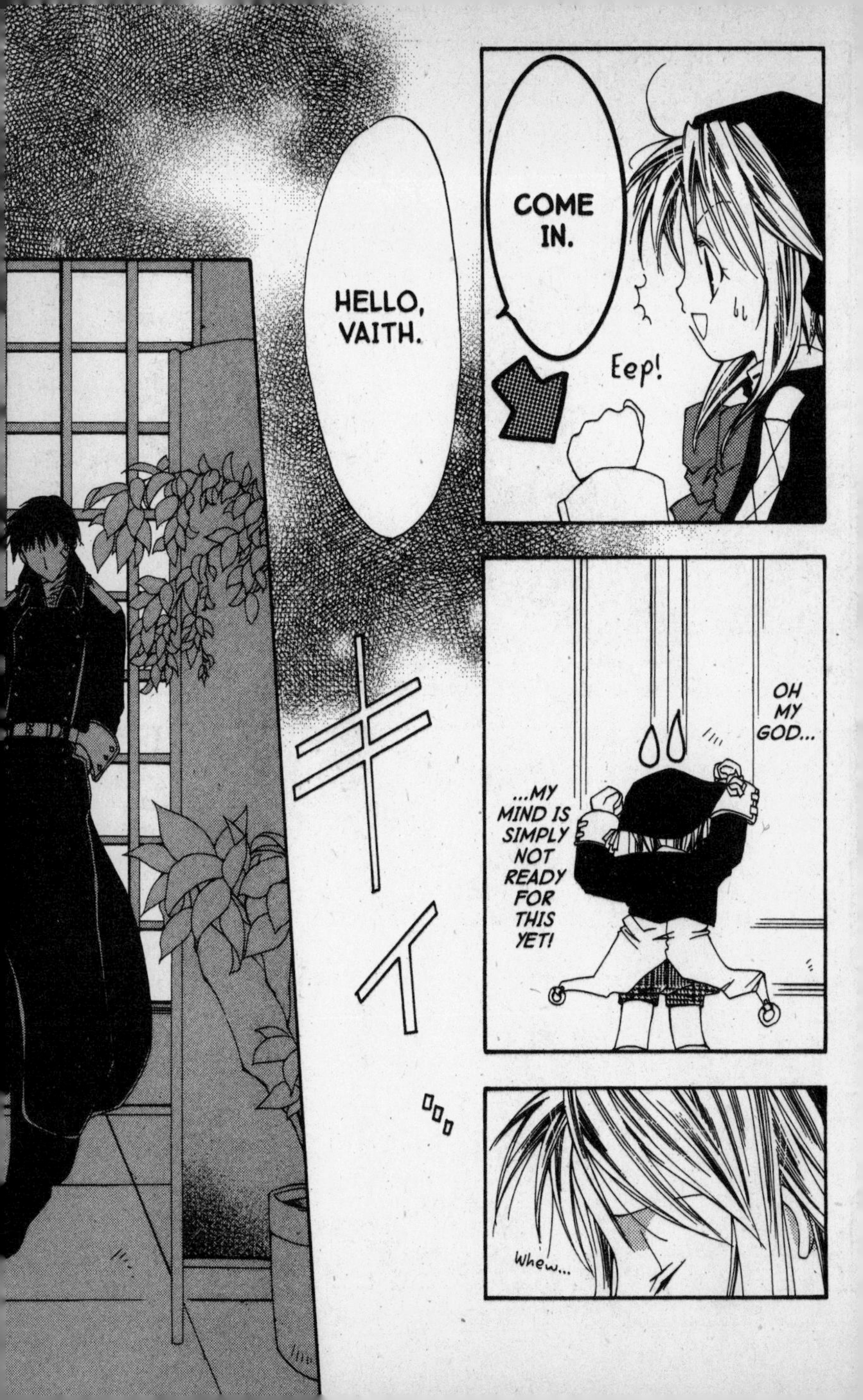
COME IN.
Eep!
OH MY GOD...
...MY MIND IS SIMPLY NOT READY FOR THIS YET!
Whew...
HELLO, VAITH.

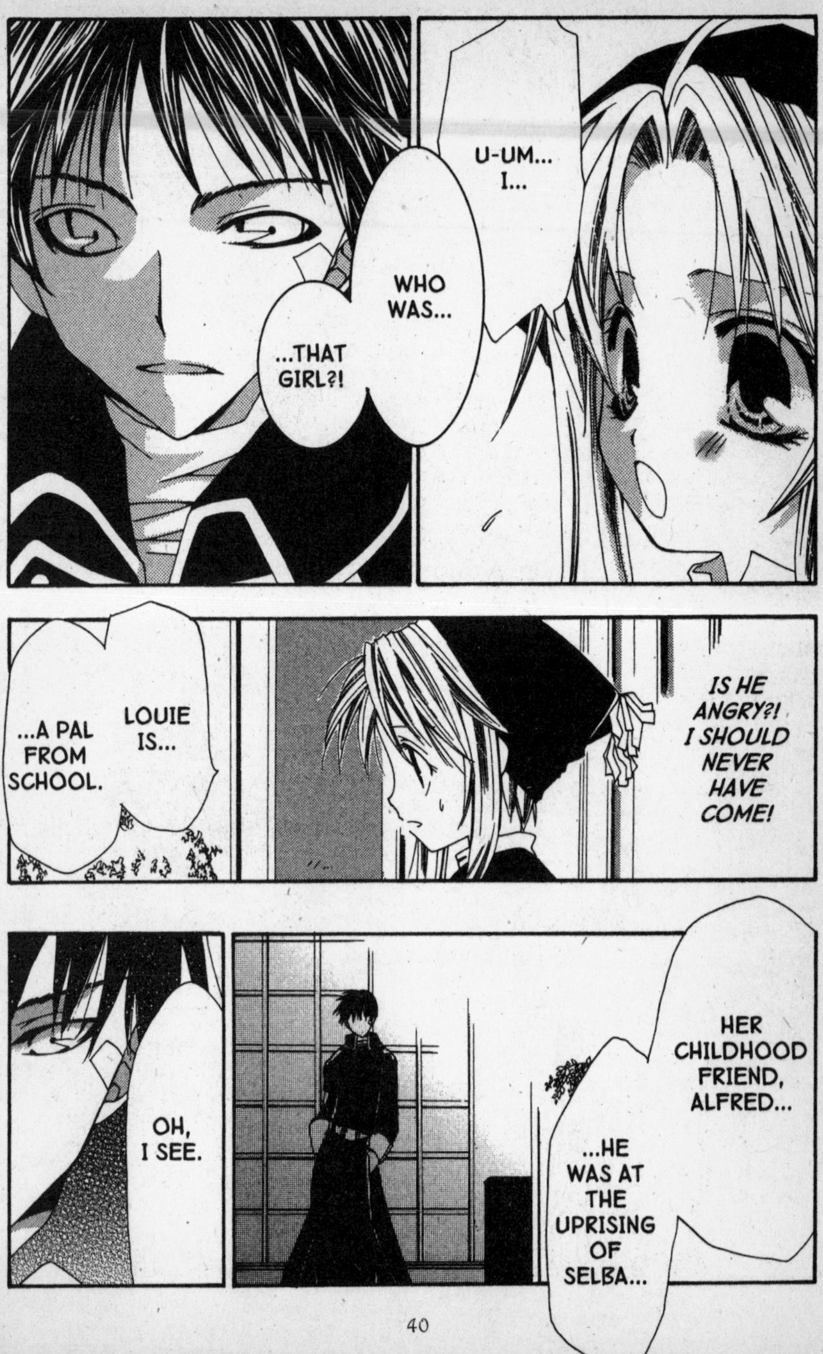
U-UM... I...
WHO WAS...
...THAT GIRL?!
IS HE ANGRY?! I SHOULD NEVER HAVE COME!
LOUIE IS...
...A PAL FROM SCHOOL.
HER CHILDHOOD FRIEND, ALFRED...
...HE WAS AT THE UPRISING OF SELBA...
OH, I SEE.

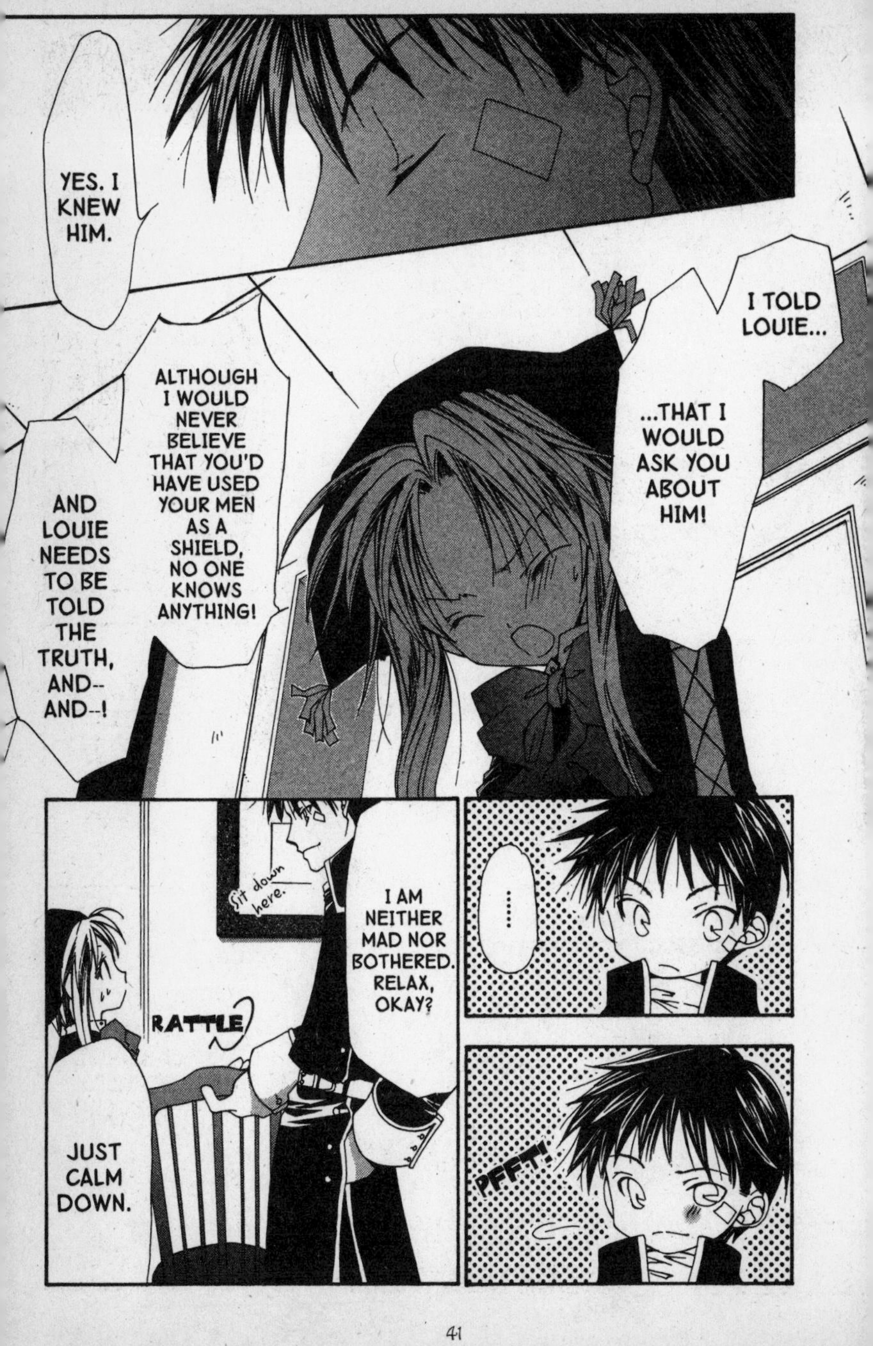
YES. I KNEW HIM.
I TOLD LOUIE...
...THAT I WOULD ASK YOU ABOUT HIM!
ALTHOUGH I WOULD NEVER BELIEVE THAT YOU'D HAVE USED YOUR MEN AS A SHIELD, NO ONE KNOWS ANYTHING!
AND LOUIE NEEDS TO BE TOLD THE TRUTH, AND-- AND--!
......
PFFT!
Sit down here.
I AM NEITHER MAD NOR BOTHERED. RELAX, OKAY?
RATTLE
JUST CALM DOWN.

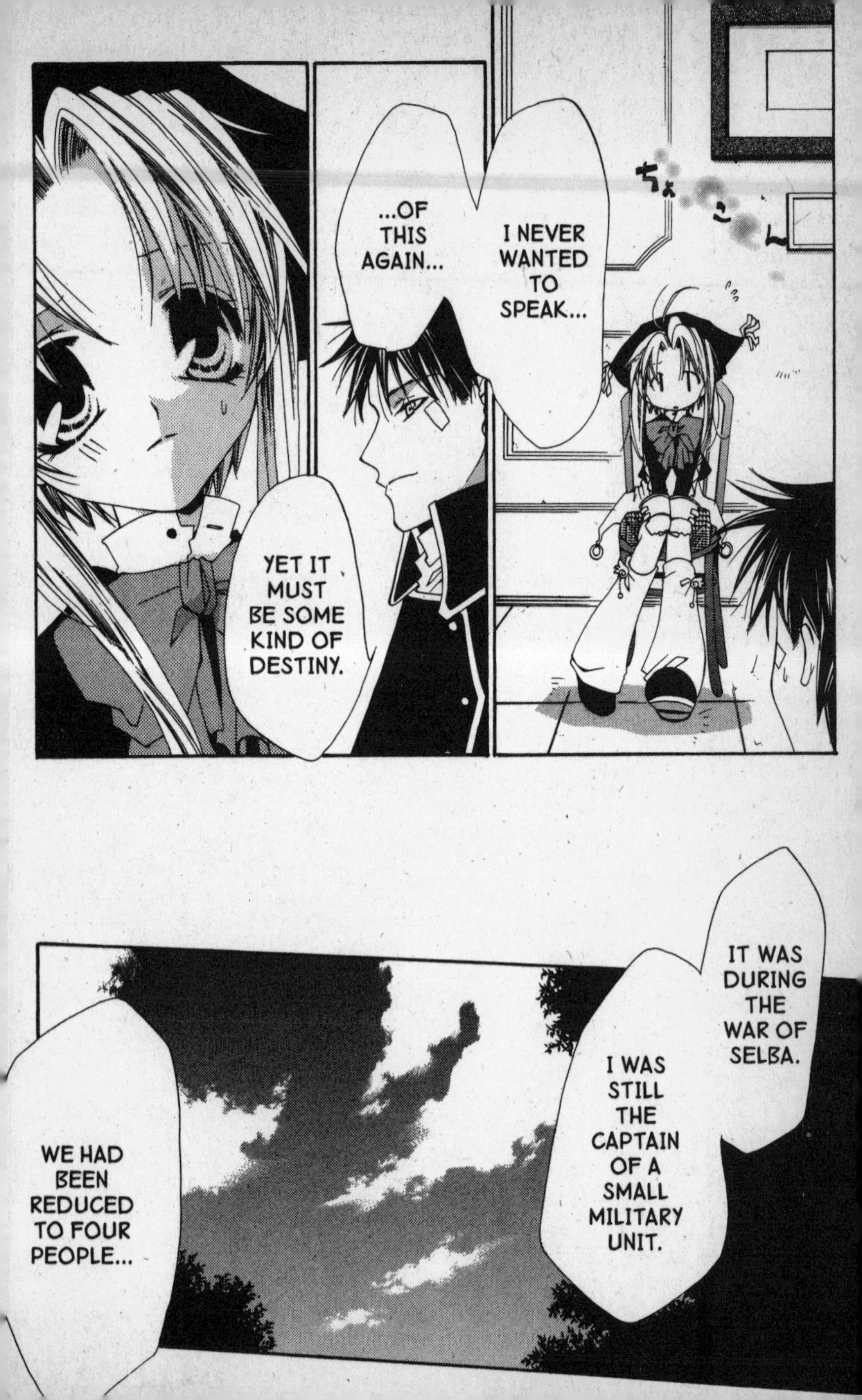

ちょこん
I NEVER WANTED TO SPEAK...
...OF THIS AGAIN...
YET IT MUST BE SOME KIND OF DESTINY.
IT WAS DURING THE WAR OF SELBA.
I WAS STILL THE CAPTAIN OF A SMALL MILITARY UNIT.
WE HAD BEEN REDUCED TO FOUR PEOPLE...

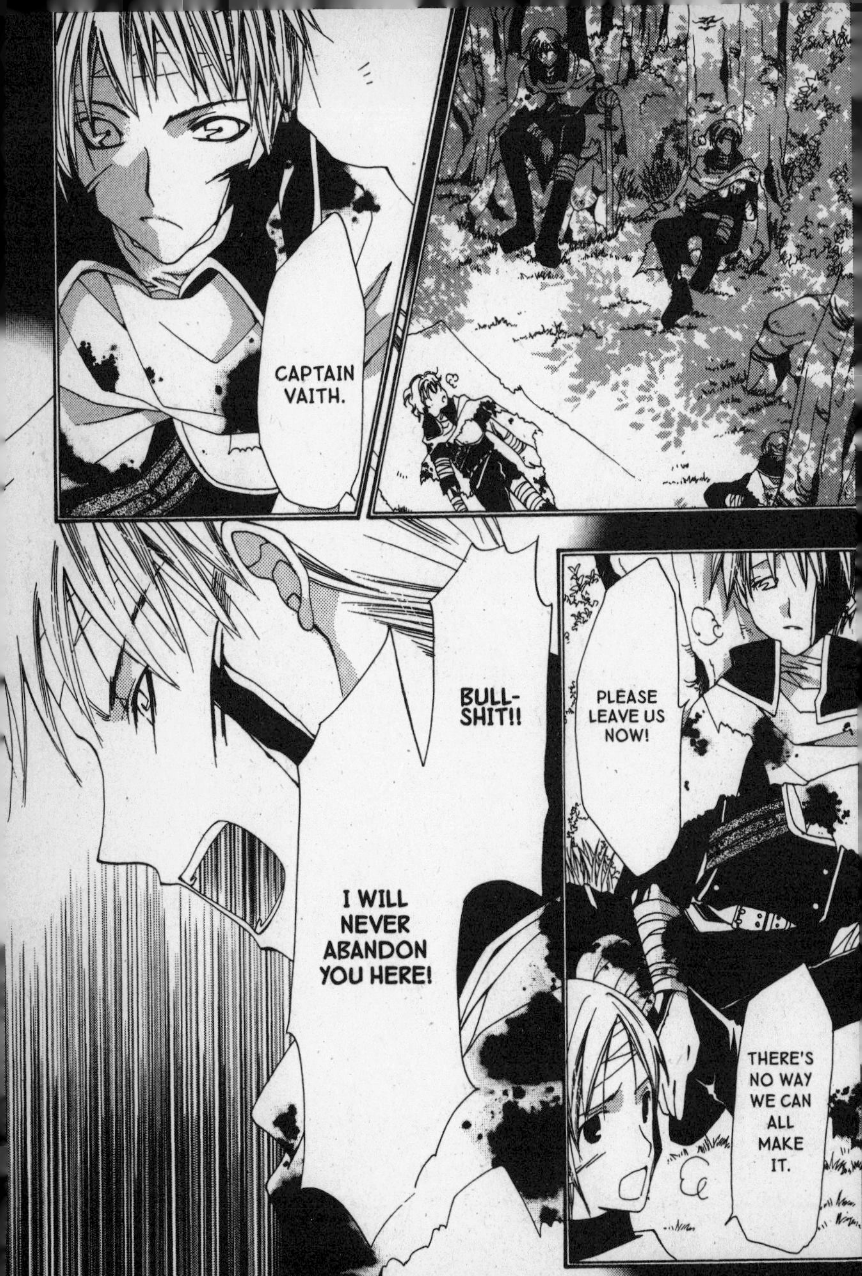
CAPTAIN VAITH.
PLEASE LEAVE US NOW!
THERE'S NO WAY WE CAN ALL MAKE IT.
BULL-SHIT!!
I WILL NEVER ABANDON YOU HERE!

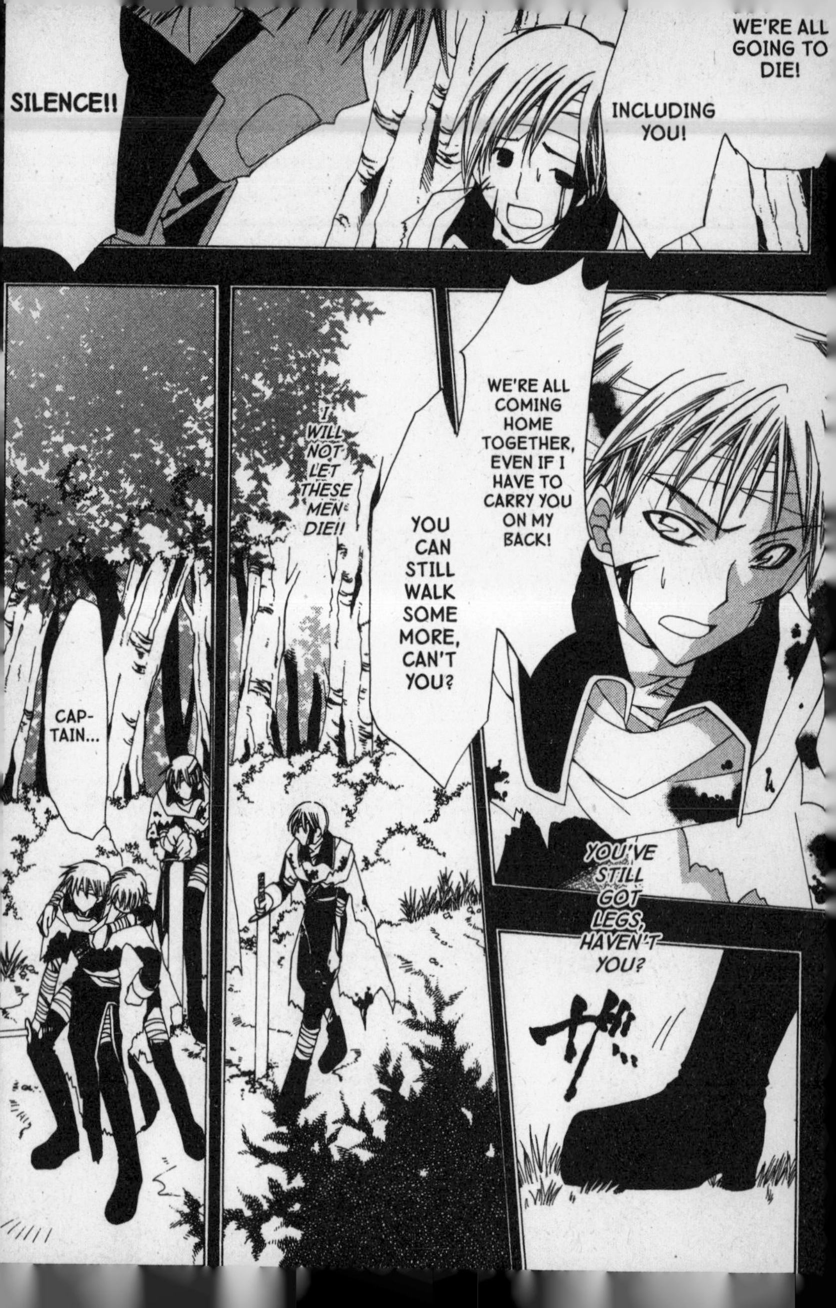
WE'RE ALL GOING TO DIE!
INCLUDING YOU!
SILENCE!!
WE'RE ALL COMING HOME TOGETHER, EVEN IF I HAVE TO CARRY YOU ON MY BACK!
YOU CAN STILL WALK SOME MORE, CAN'T YOU?
YOU'VE STILL GOT LEGS, HAVEN'T YOU?
I WILL NOT LET THESE MEN DIE!!
CAP-TAIN...

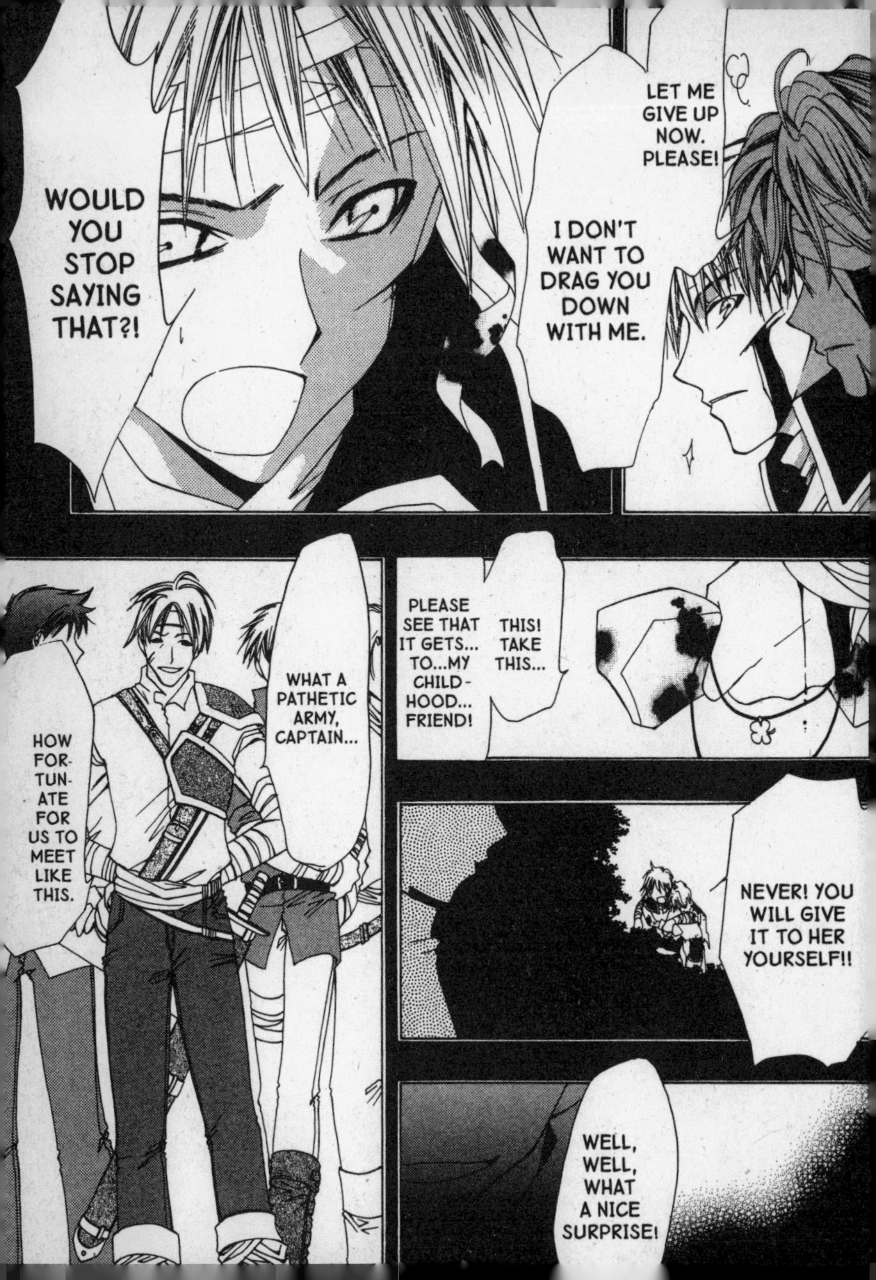
LET ME GIVE UP NOW. PLEASE!
I DON'T WANT TO DRAG YOU DOWN WITH ME.
WOULD YOU STOP SAYING THAT?!
THIS! TAKE THIS...
PLEASE SEE THAT IT GETS... TO...MY CHILD-HOOD... FRIEND!
NEVER! YOU WILL GIVE IT TO HER YOURSELF!!
WELL, WELL, WHAT A NICE SURPRISE!
WHAT A PATHETIC ARMY, CAPTAIN...
HOW FOR-TUN-ATE FOR US TO MEET LIKE THIS.

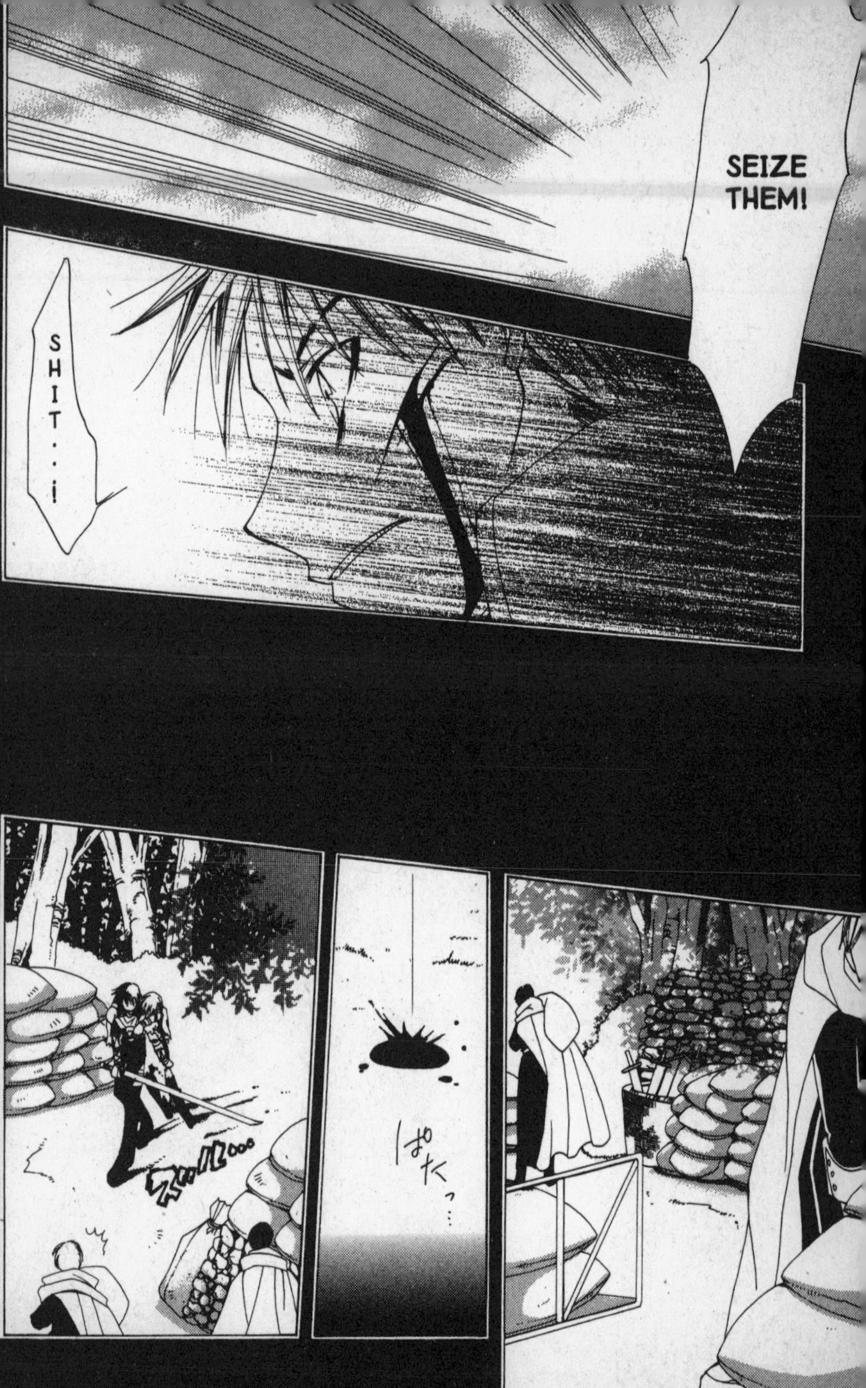
SEIZE THEM!
SHIT...!
ぱたっ…

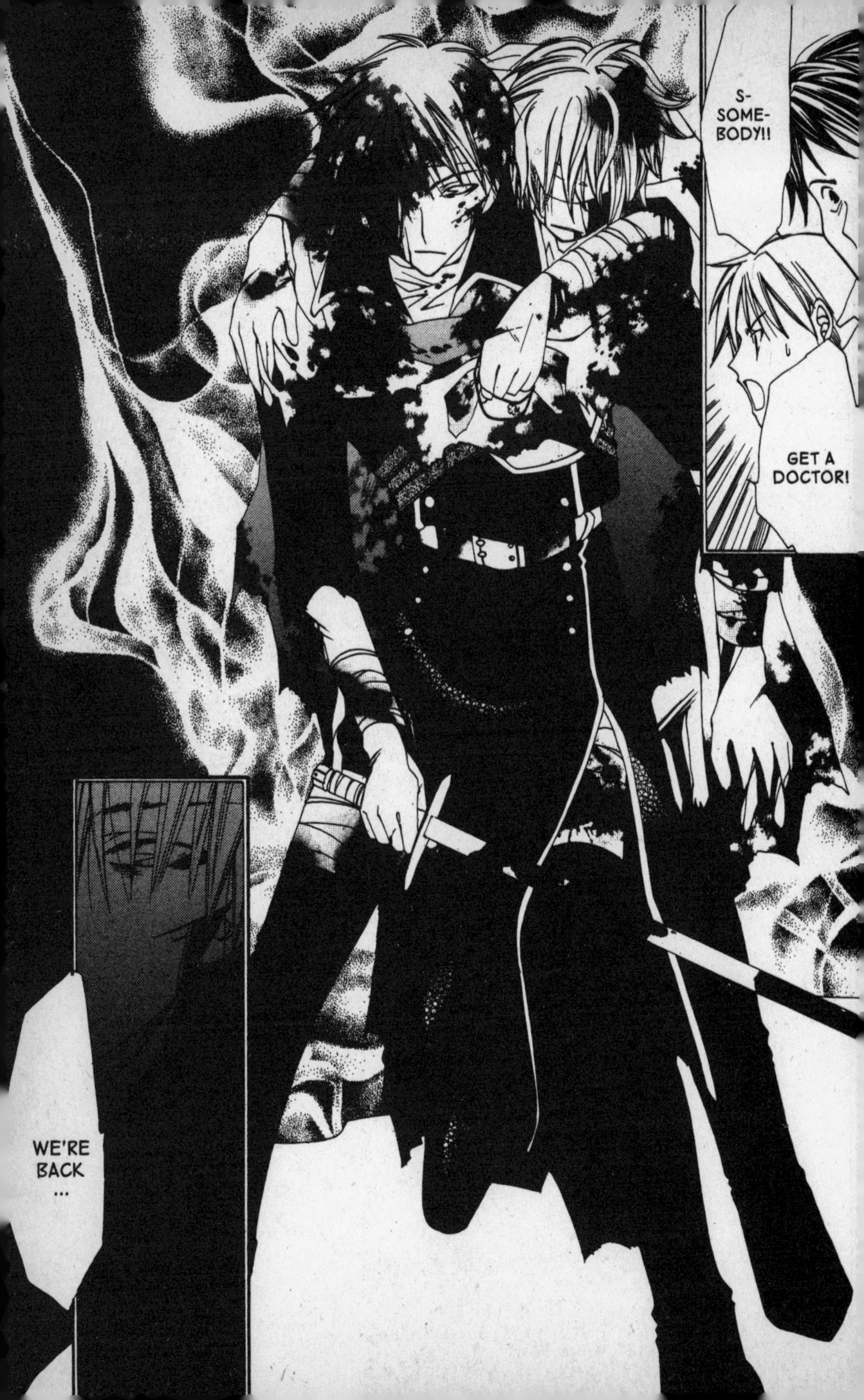
S-SOME-BODY!!
GET A DOCTOR!
WE'RE BACK ...

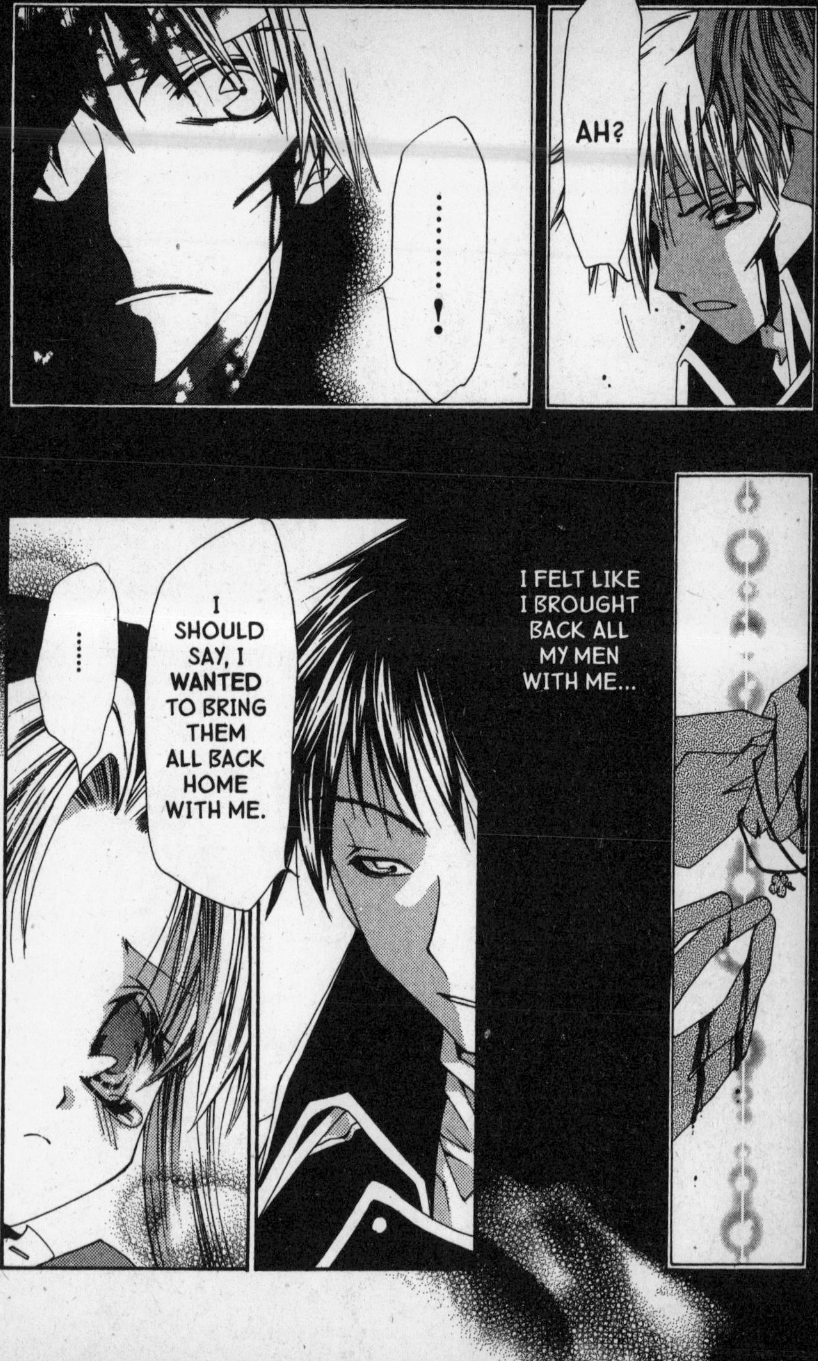
AH?
.........!
I FELT LIKE I BROUGHT BACK ALL MY MEN WITH ME...
I SHOULD SAY, I WANTED TO BRING THEM ALL BACK HOME WITH ME.
......

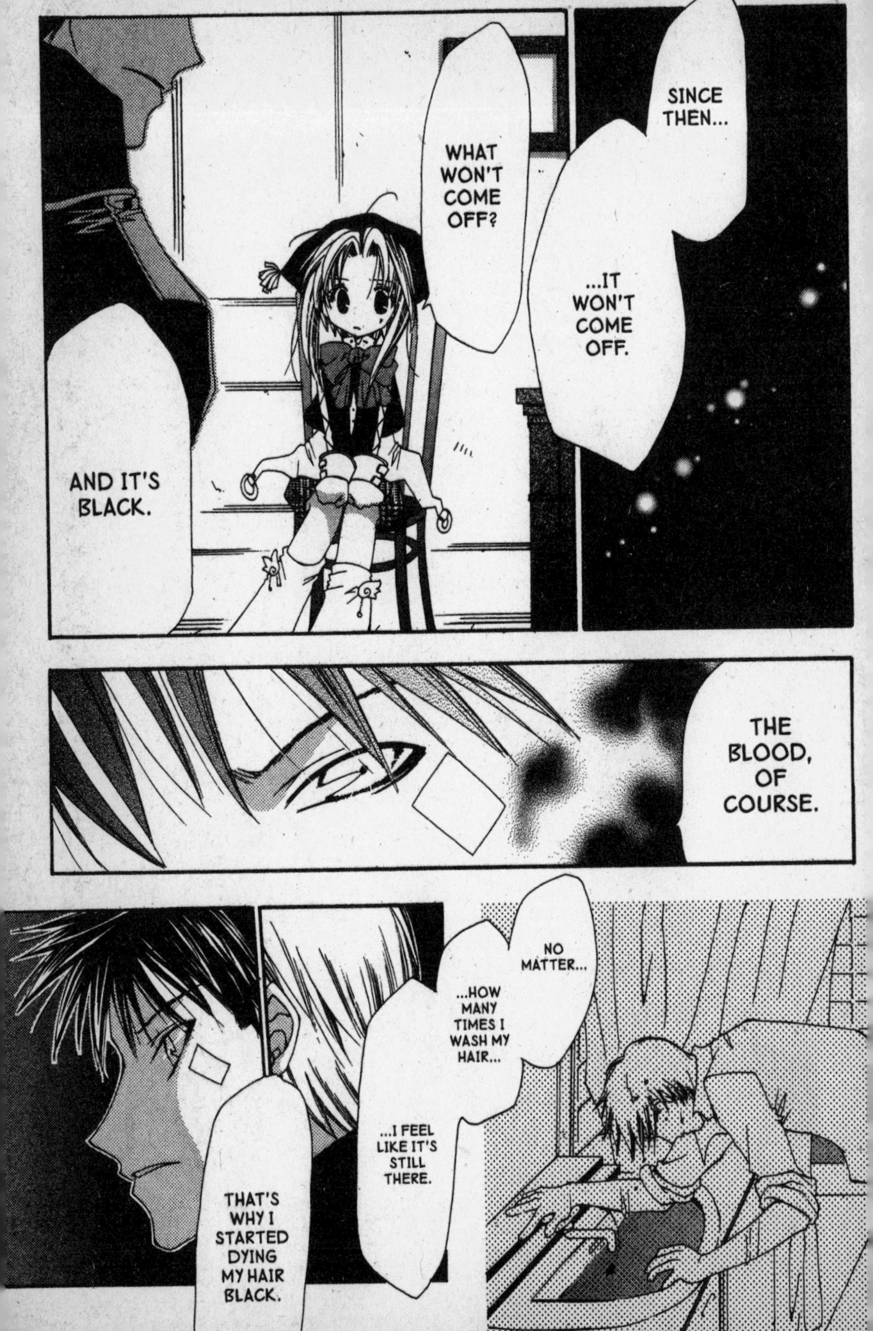
SINCE THEN...
...IT WON'T COME OFF.
WHAT WON'T COME OFF?
AND IT'S BLACK.
THE BLOOD, OF COURSE.
NO MATTER...
...HOW MANY TIMES I WASH MY HAIR...
...I FEEL LIKE IT'S STILL THERE.
THAT'S WHY I STARTED DYING MY HAIR BLACK.

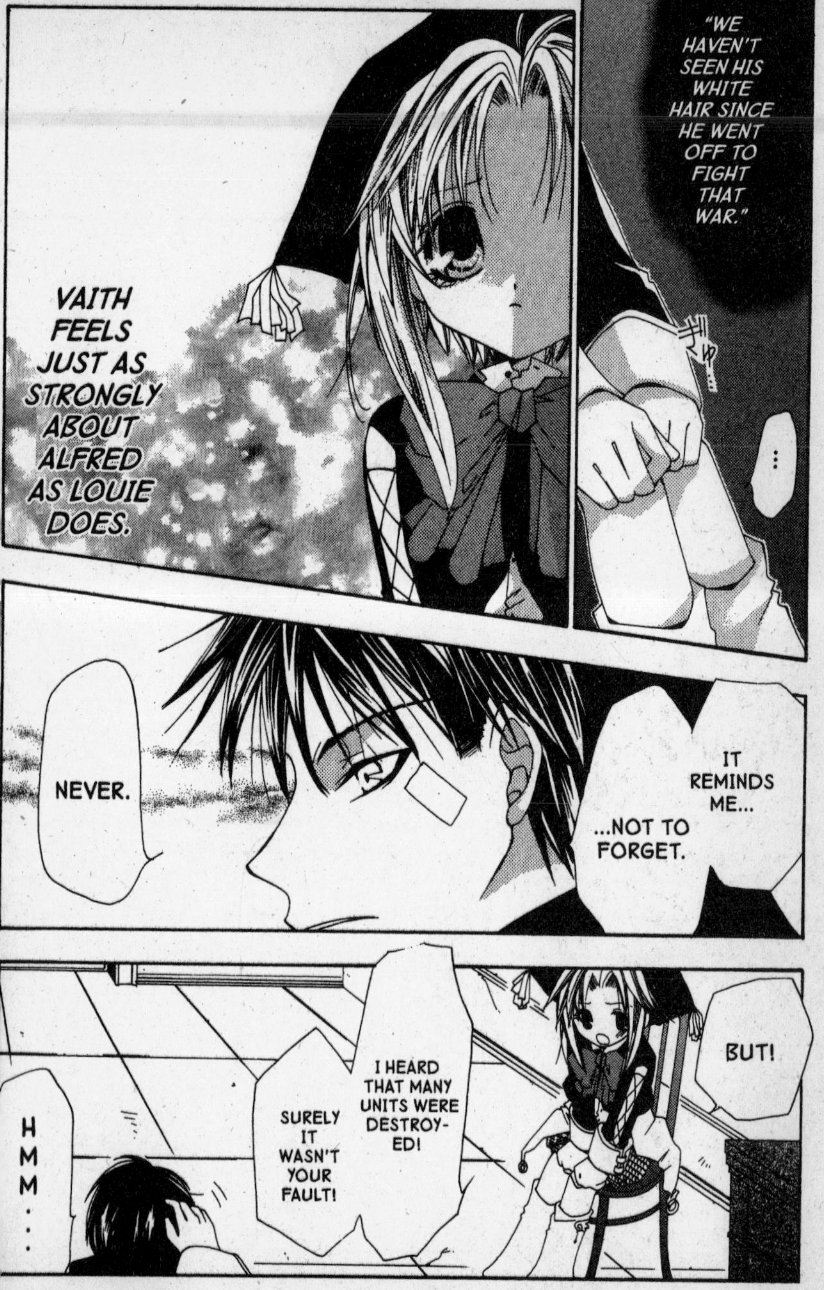
"WE HAVEN'T SEEN HIS WHITE HAIR SINCE HE WENT OFF TO FIGHT THAT WAR."
...
VAITH FEELS JUST AS STRONGLY ABOUT ALFRED AS LOUIE DOES.
IT REMINDS ME...
...NOT TO FORGET.
NEVER.
BUT!
I HEARD THAT MANY UNITS WERE DESTROY-ED!
SURELY IT WASN'T YOUR FAULT!
HMM...

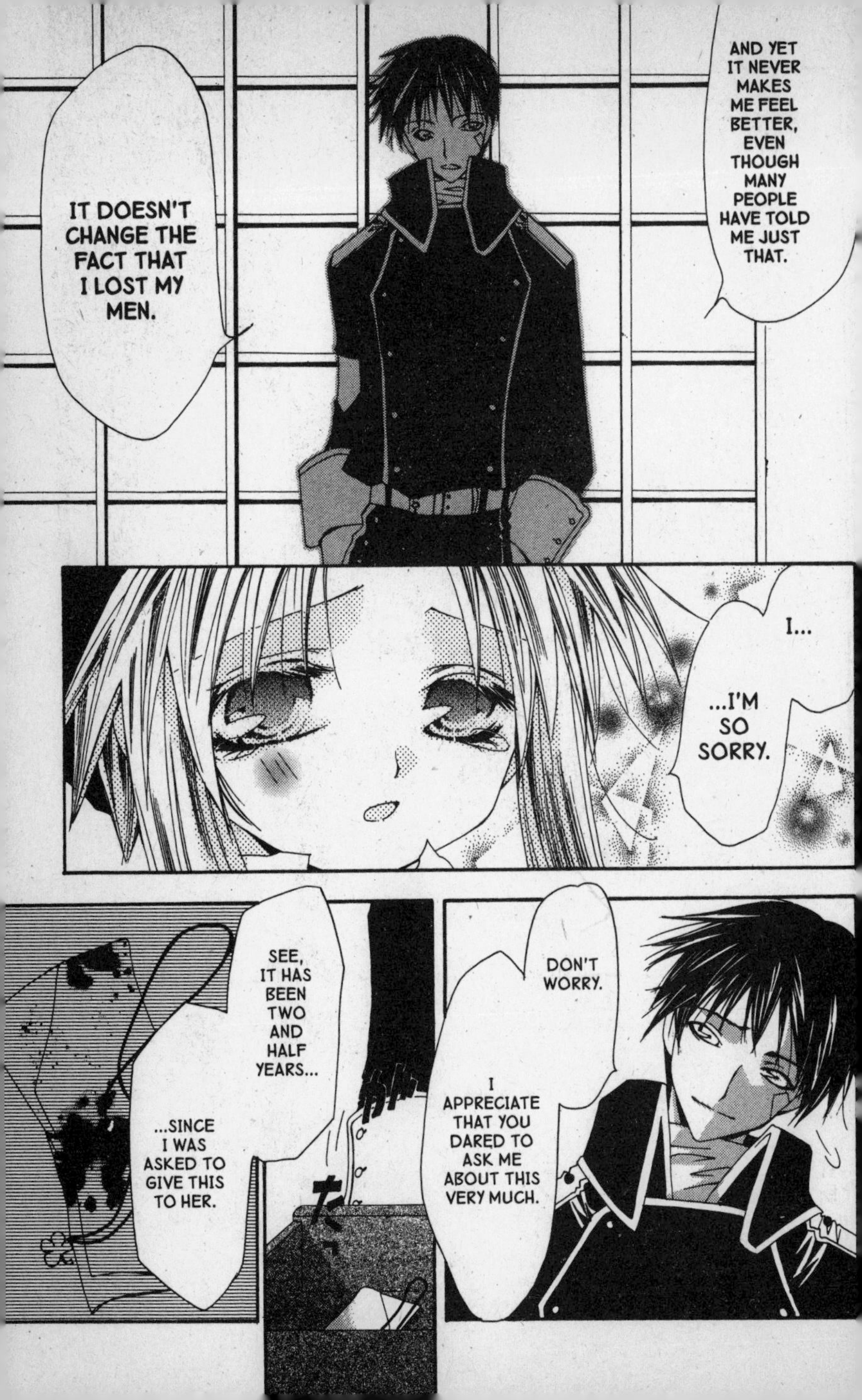
AND YET IT NEVER MAKES ME FEEL BETTER, EVEN THOUGH MANY PEOPLE HAVE TOLD ME JUST THAT.
IT DOESN'T CHANGE THE FACT THAT I LOST MY MEN.
I...
...I'M SO SORRY.
DON'T WORRY.
I APPRECIATE THAT YOU DARED TO ASK ME ABOUT THIS VERY MUCH.
SEE, IT HAS BEEN TWO AND HALF YEARS...
...SINCE I WAS ASKED TO GIVE THIS TO HER.

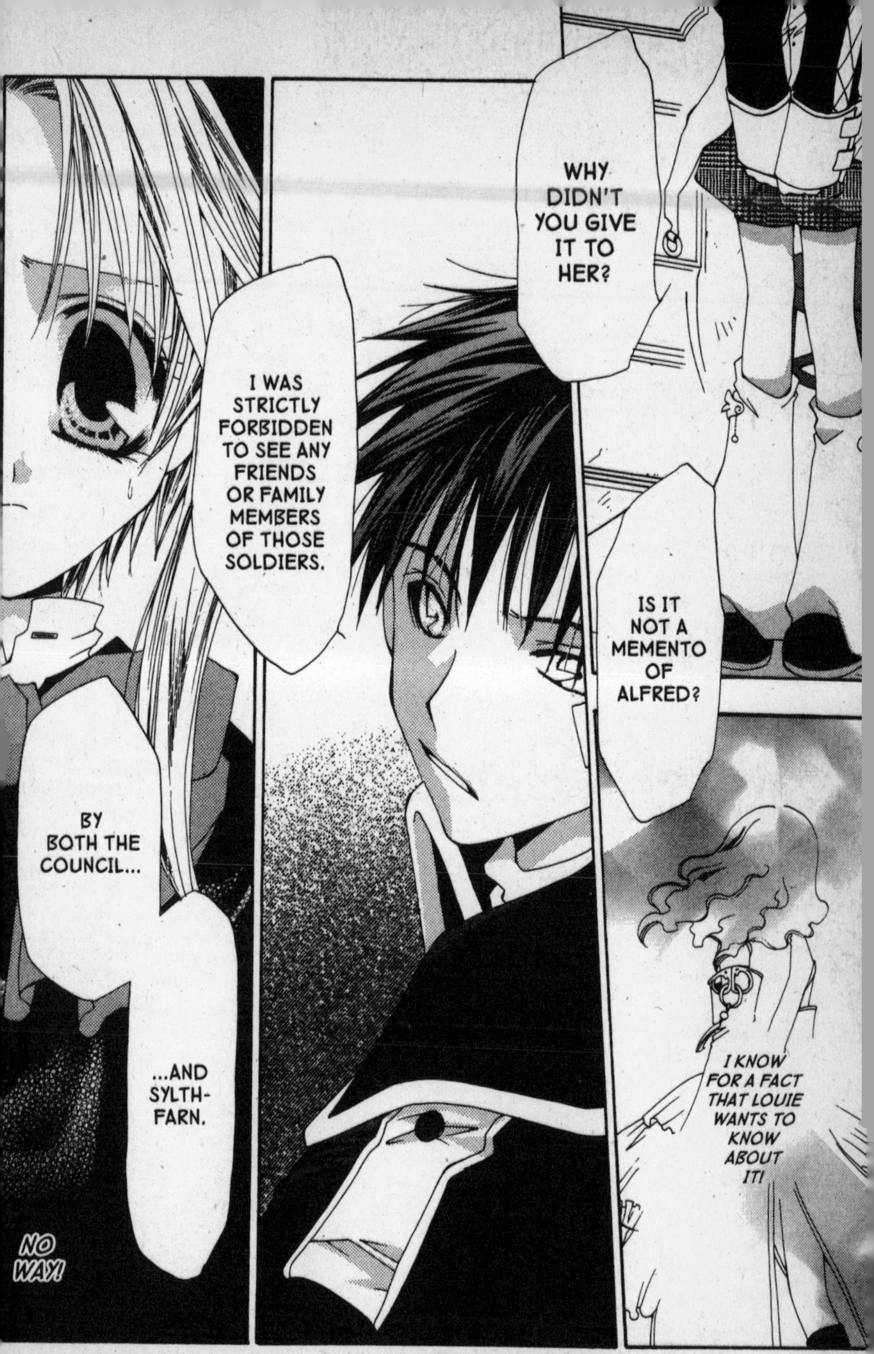
WHY DIDN'T YOU GIVE IT TO HER?
IS IT NOT A MEMENTO OF ALFRED?
I KNOW FOR A FACT THAT LOUIE WANTS TO KNOW ABOUT IT!
I WAS STRICTLY FORBIDDEN TO SEE ANY FRIENDS OR FAMILY MEMBERS OF THOSE SOLDIERS.
BY BOTH THE COUNCIL...
...AND SYLTH-FARN.
NO WAY!

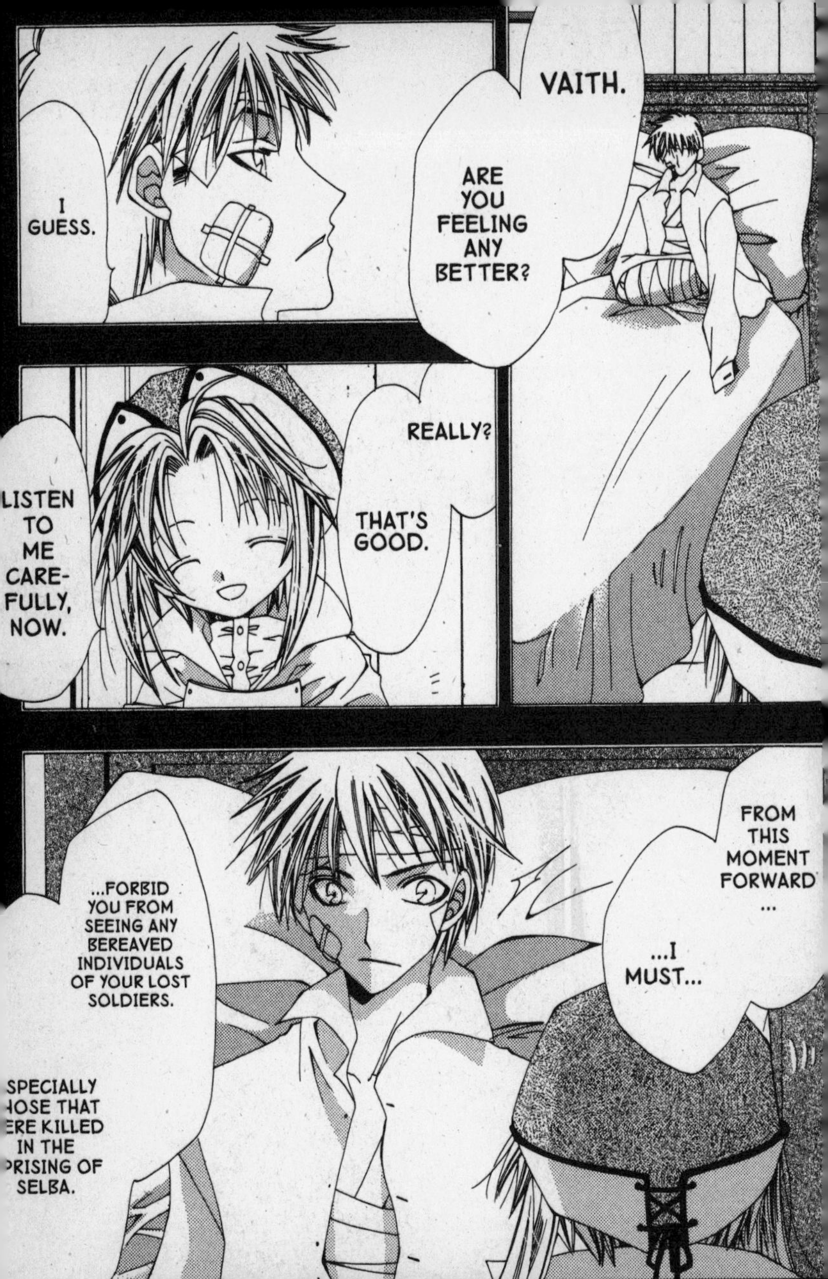
VAITH.
ARE YOU FEELING ANY BETTER?
I GUESS.
REALLY? THAT'S GOOD.
LISTEN TO ME CARE-FULLY, NOW.
FROM THIS MOMENT FORWARD...
...I MUST...
...FORBID YOU FROM SEEING ANY BEREAVED INDIVIDUALS OF YOUR LOST SOLDIERS.
SPECIALLY HOSE THAT ERE KILLED IN THE PRISING OF SELBA.

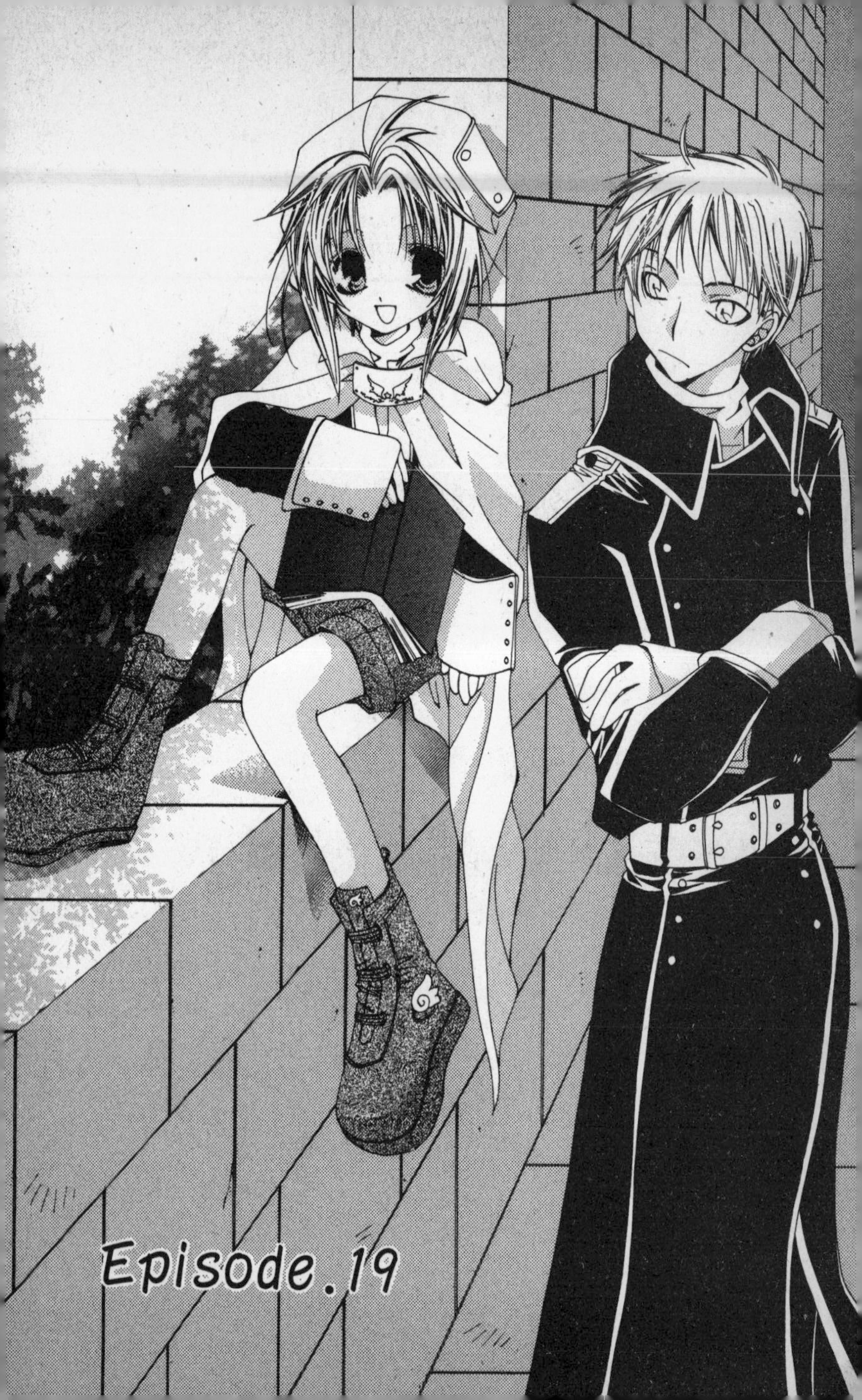
Episode.19

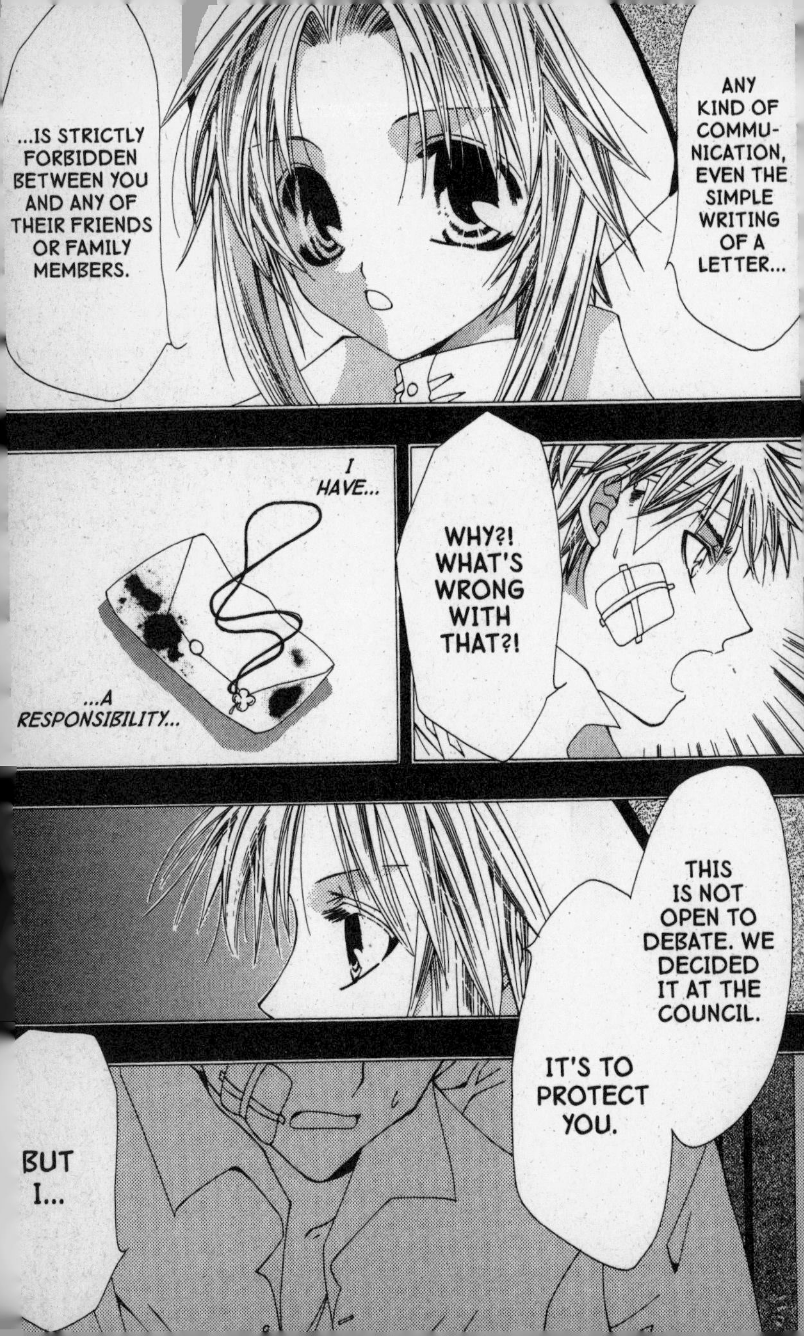
ANY KIND OF COMMUNICATION, EVEN THE SIMPLE WRITING OF A LETTER...
...IS STRICTLY FORBIDDEN BETWEEN YOU AND ANY OF THEIR FRIENDS OR FAMILY MEMBERS.
WHY?! WHAT'S WRONG WITH THAT?!
I HAVE...
...A RESPONSIBILITY...
THIS IS NOT OPEN TO DEBATE. WE DECIDED IT AT THE COUNCIL.
IT'S TO PROTECT YOU.
BUT I...

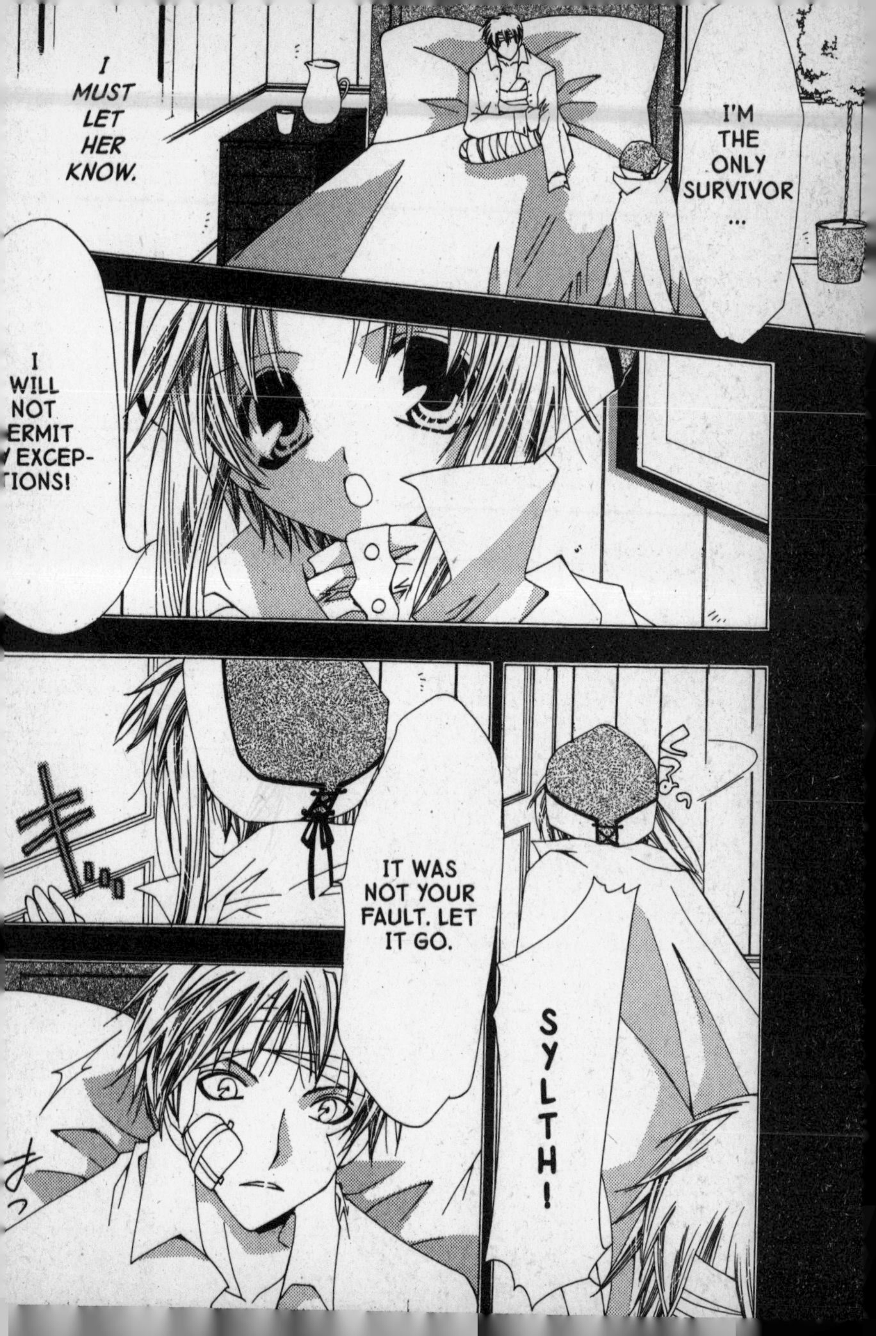
I'M THE ONLY SURVIVOR ...
I MUST LET HER KNOW.
I WILL NOT ERMIT EXCEP- TIONS!
SYLTH!
IT WAS NOT YOUR FAULT. LET IT GO.

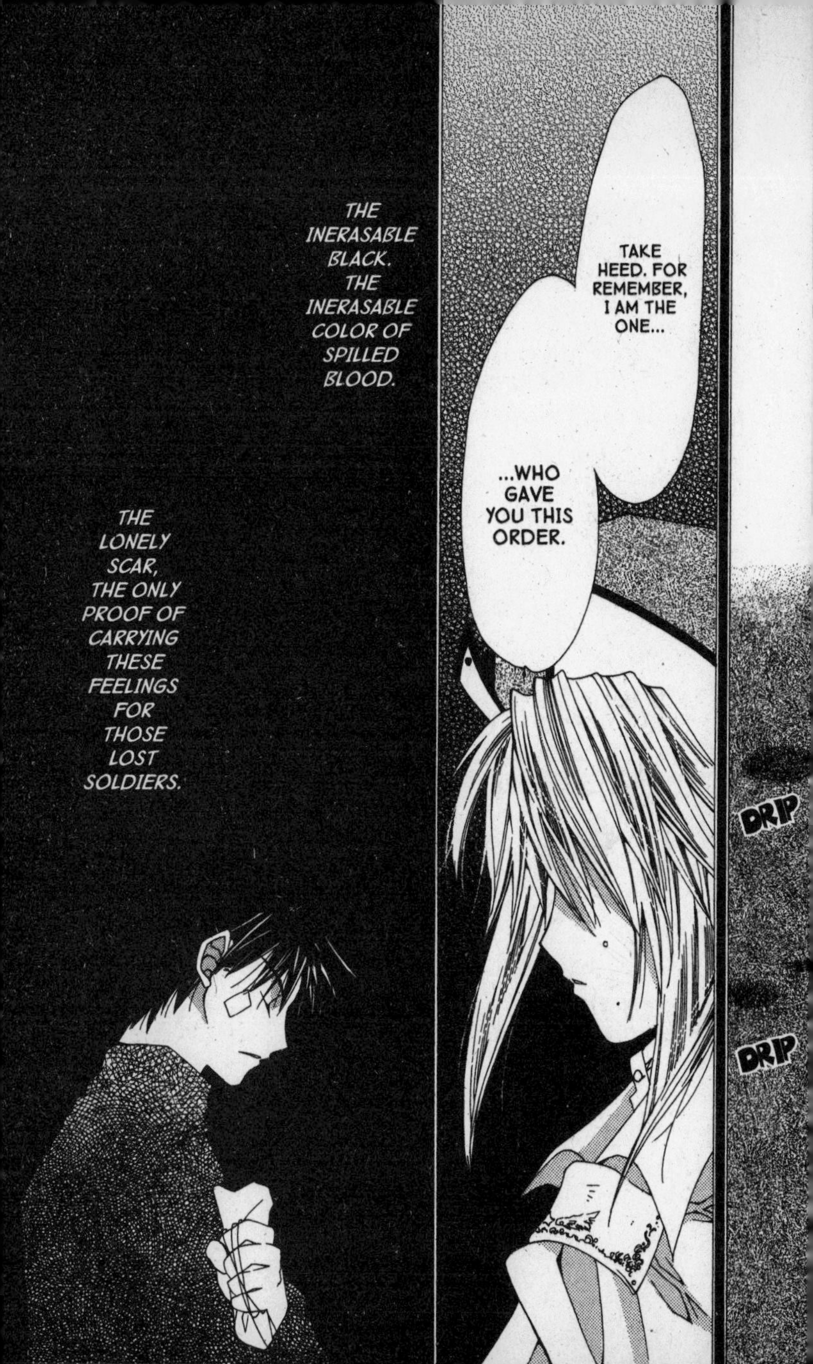
DRIP
DRIP
TAKE HEED. FOR REMEMBER, I AM THE ONE...
...WHO GAVE YOU THIS ORDER.
THE INERASABLE BLACK. THE INERASABLE COLOR OF SPILLED BLOOD.
THE LONELY SCAR, THE ONLY PROOF OF CARRYING THESE FEELINGS FOR THOSE LOST SOLDIERS.

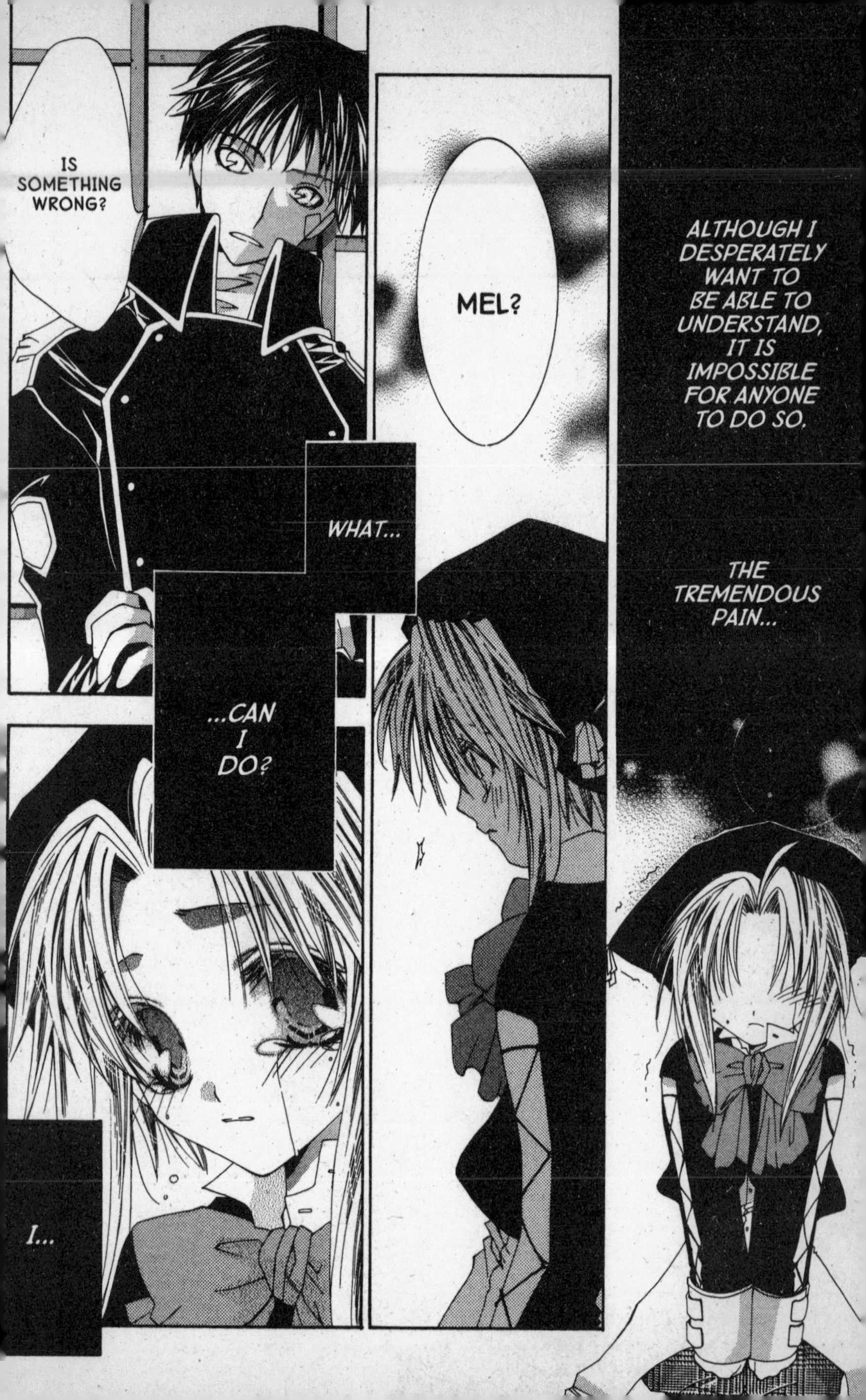

ALTHOUGH I DESPERATELY WANT TO BE ABLE TO UNDERSTAND, IT IS IMPOSSIBLE FOR ANYONE TO DO SO.
THE TREMENDOUS PAIN...
MEL?
IS SOMETHING WRONG?
WHAT...
...CAN I DO?
I...

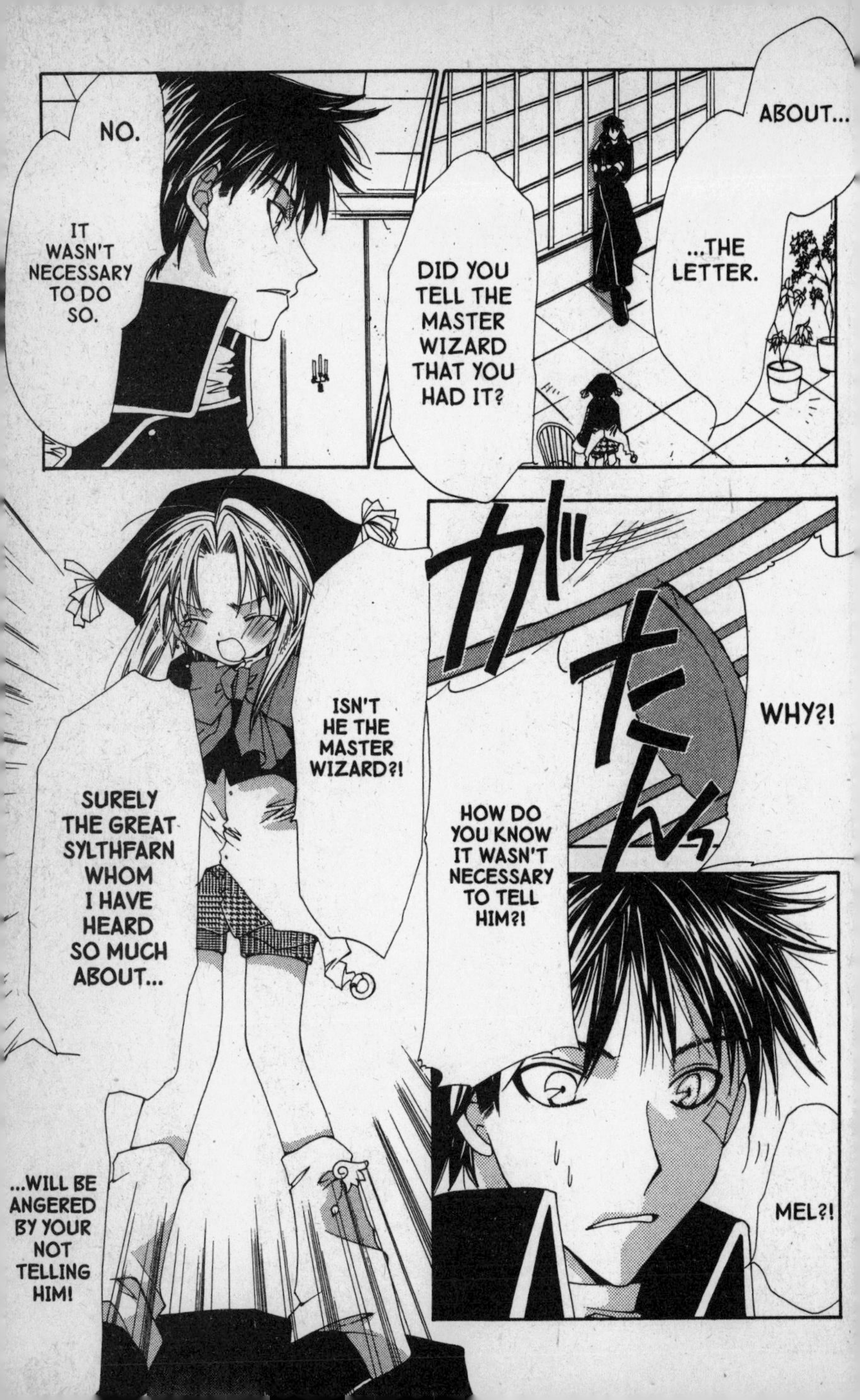
ABOUT...
...THE LETTER.
DID YOU TELL THE MASTER WIZARD THAT YOU HAD IT?
NO.
IT WASN'T NECESSARY TO DO SO.
ガたん
WHY?!
HOW DO YOU KNOW IT WASN'T NECESSARY TO TELL HIM?!
MEL?!
ISN'T HE THE MASTER WIZARD?!
SURELY THE GREAT SYLTHFARN WHOM I HAVE HEARD SO MUCH ABOUT...
...WILL BE ANGERED BY YOUR NOT TELLING HIM!

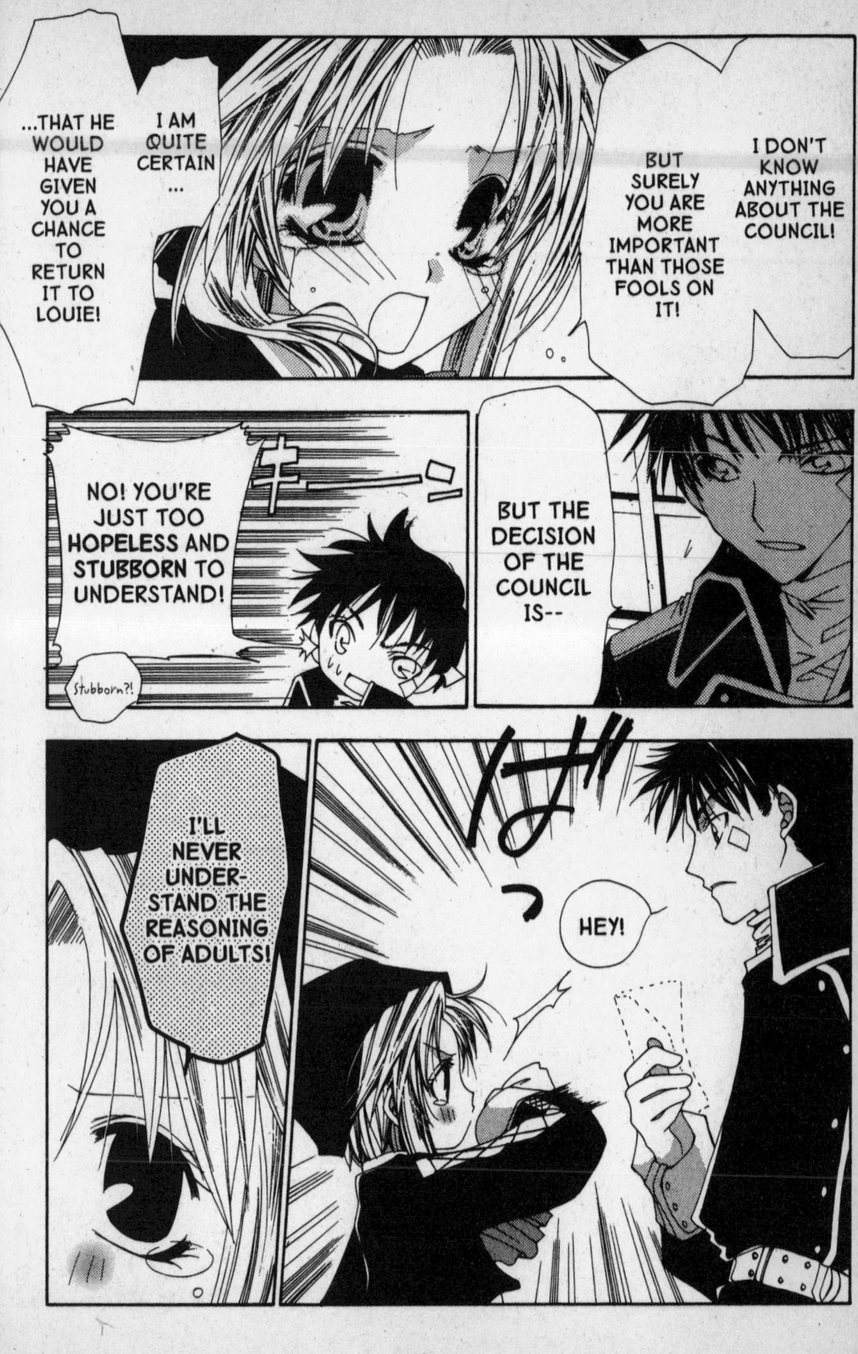
I DON'T KNOW ANYTHING ABOUT THE COUNCIL!
BUT SURELY YOU ARE MORE IMPORTANT THAN THOSE FOOLS ON IT!
I AM QUITE CERTAIN ...
...THAT HE WOULD HAVE GIVEN YOU A CHANCE TO RETURN IT TO LOUIE!
BUT THE DECISION OF THE COUNCIL IS--
NO! YOU'RE JUST TOO HOPELESS AND STUBBORN TO UNDERSTAND!
Stubborn?!
HEY!
I'LL NEVER UNDER-STAND THE REASONING OF ADULTS!

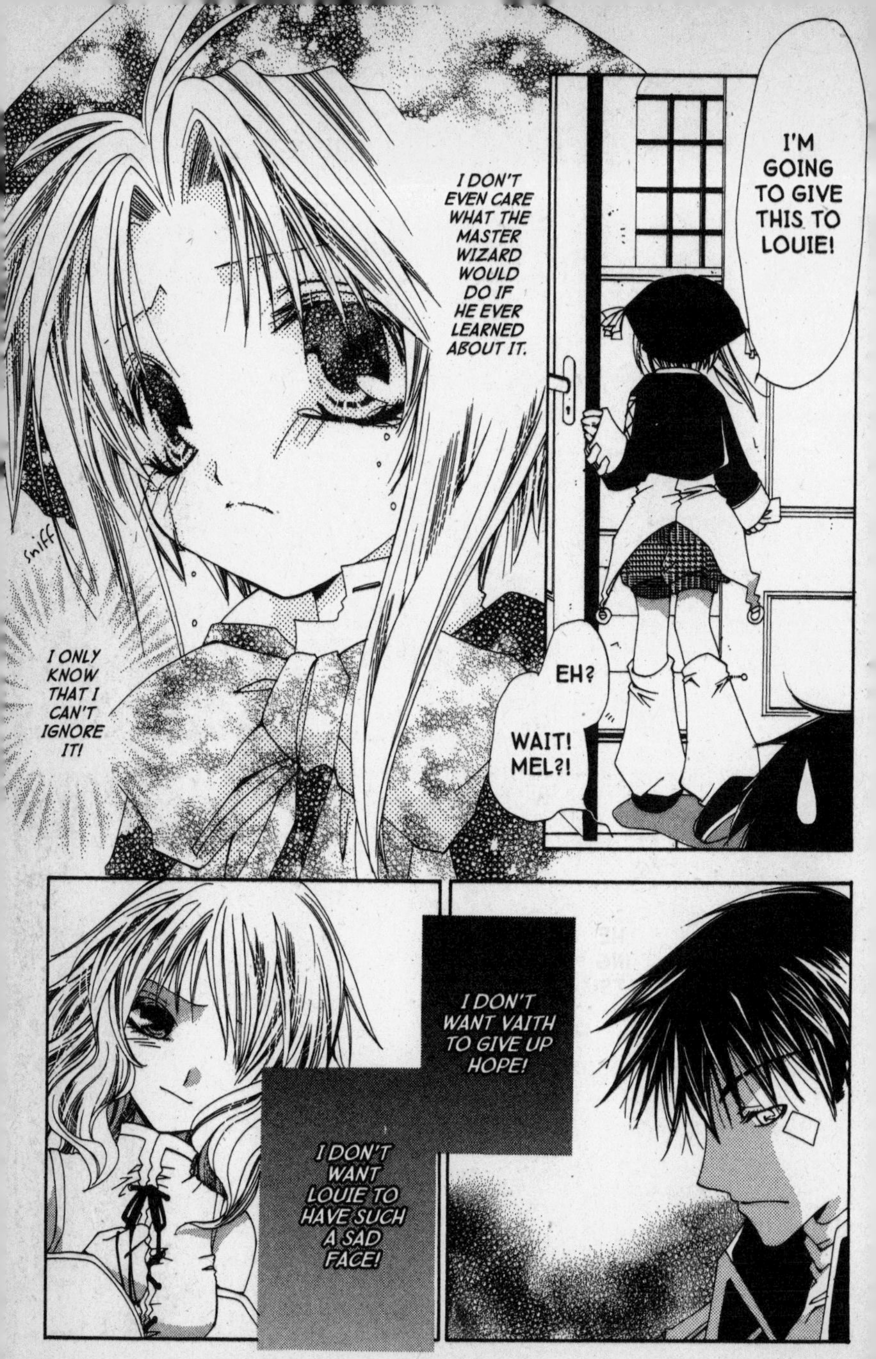
I'M GOING TO GIVE THIS TO LOUIE!
EH?
WAIT! MEL?!
I DON'T EVEN CARE WHAT THE MASTER WIZARD WOULD DO IF HE EVER LEARNED ABOUT IT.
sniff
I ONLY KNOW THAT I CAN'T IGNORE IT!
I DON'T WANT VAITH TO GIVE UP HOPE!
I DON'T WANT LOUIE TO HAVE SUCH A SAD FACE!

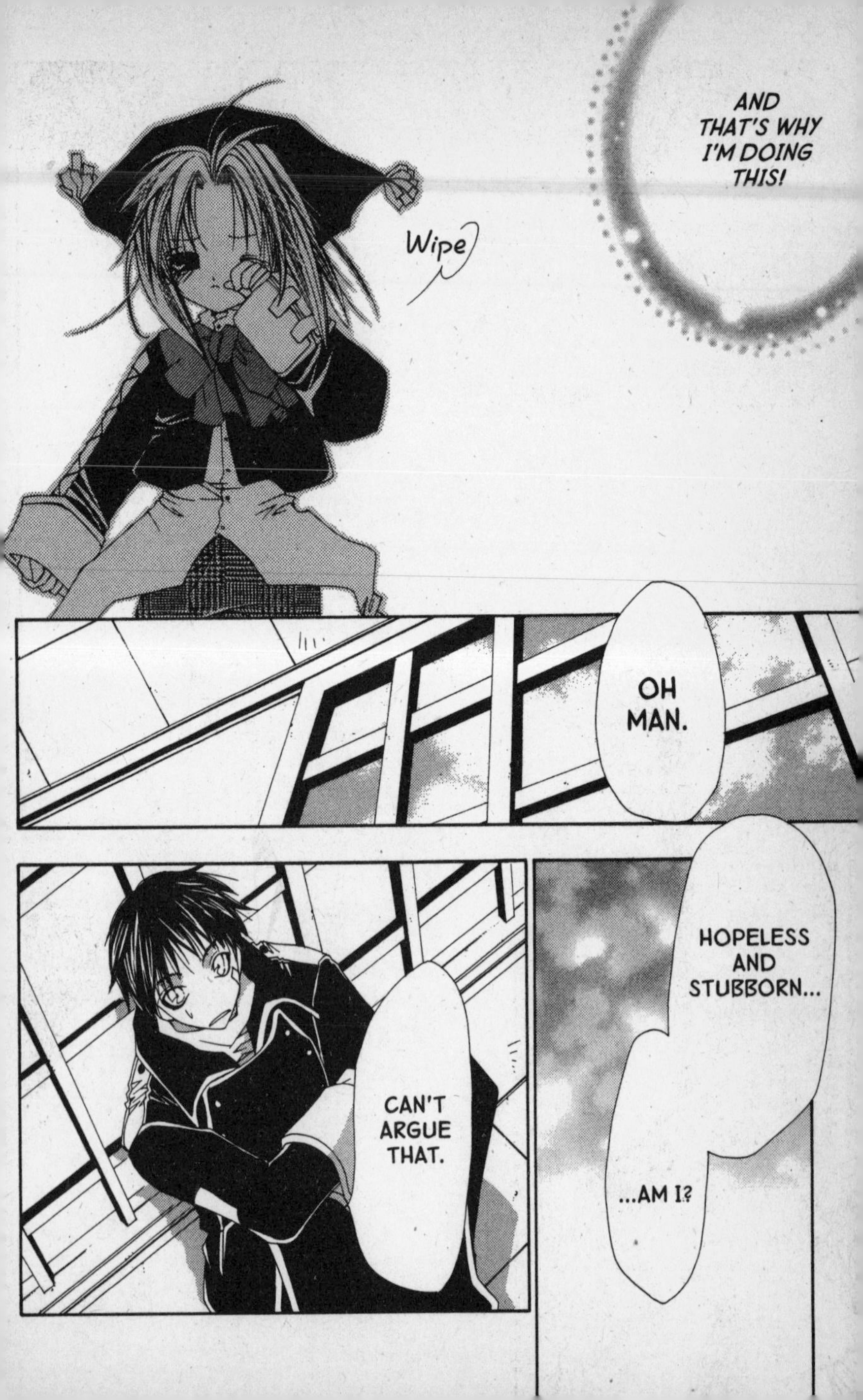
AND THAT'S WHY I'M DOING THIS!
Wipe
OH MAN.
HOPELESS AND STUBBORN...
...AM I?
CAN'T ARGUE THAT.

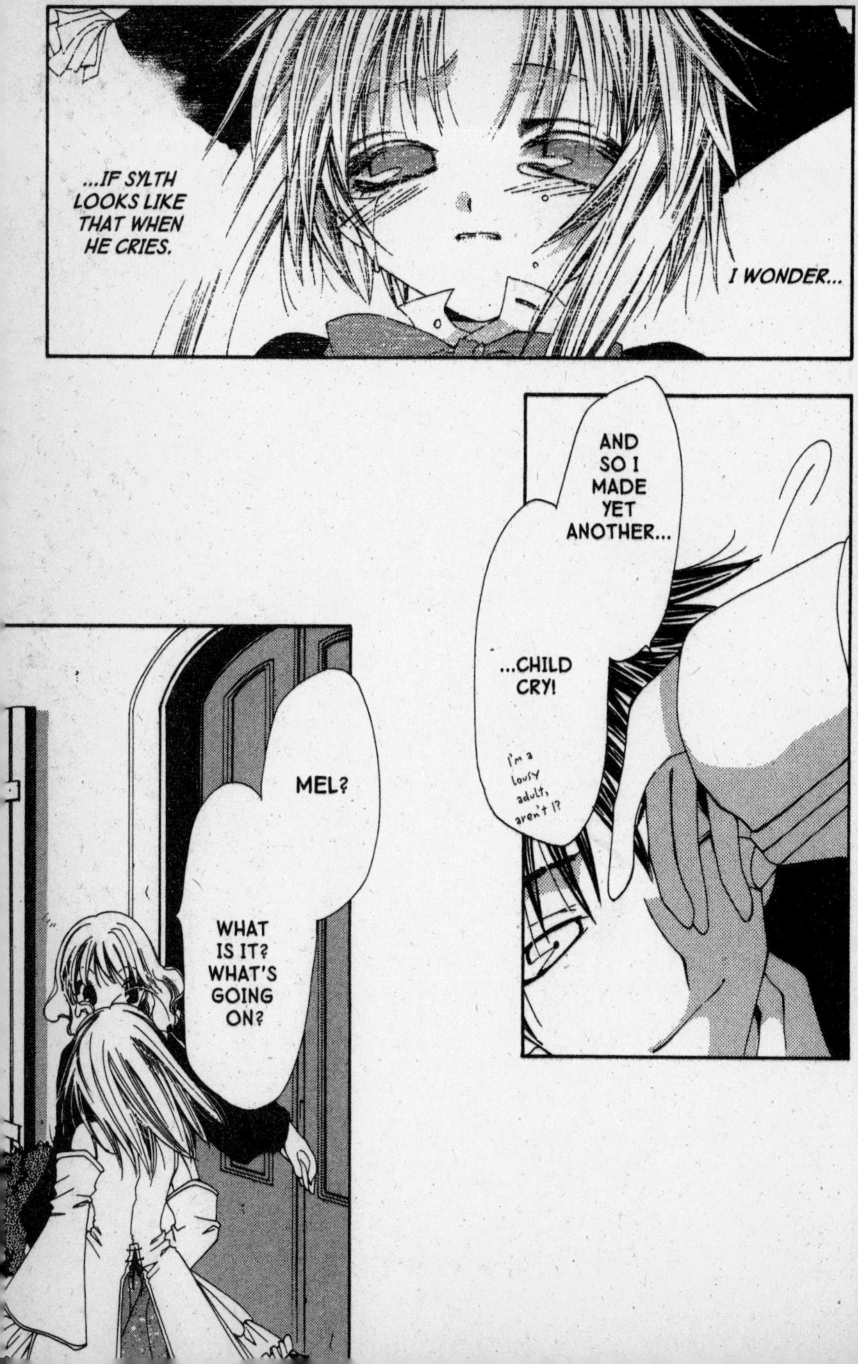
I WONDER...
...IF SYLTH LOOKS LIKE THAT WHEN HE CRIES.
AND SO I MADE YET ANOTHER...
...CHILD CRY!
I'm a lousy adult, aren't I?
MEL?
WHAT IS IT? WHAT'S GOING ON?

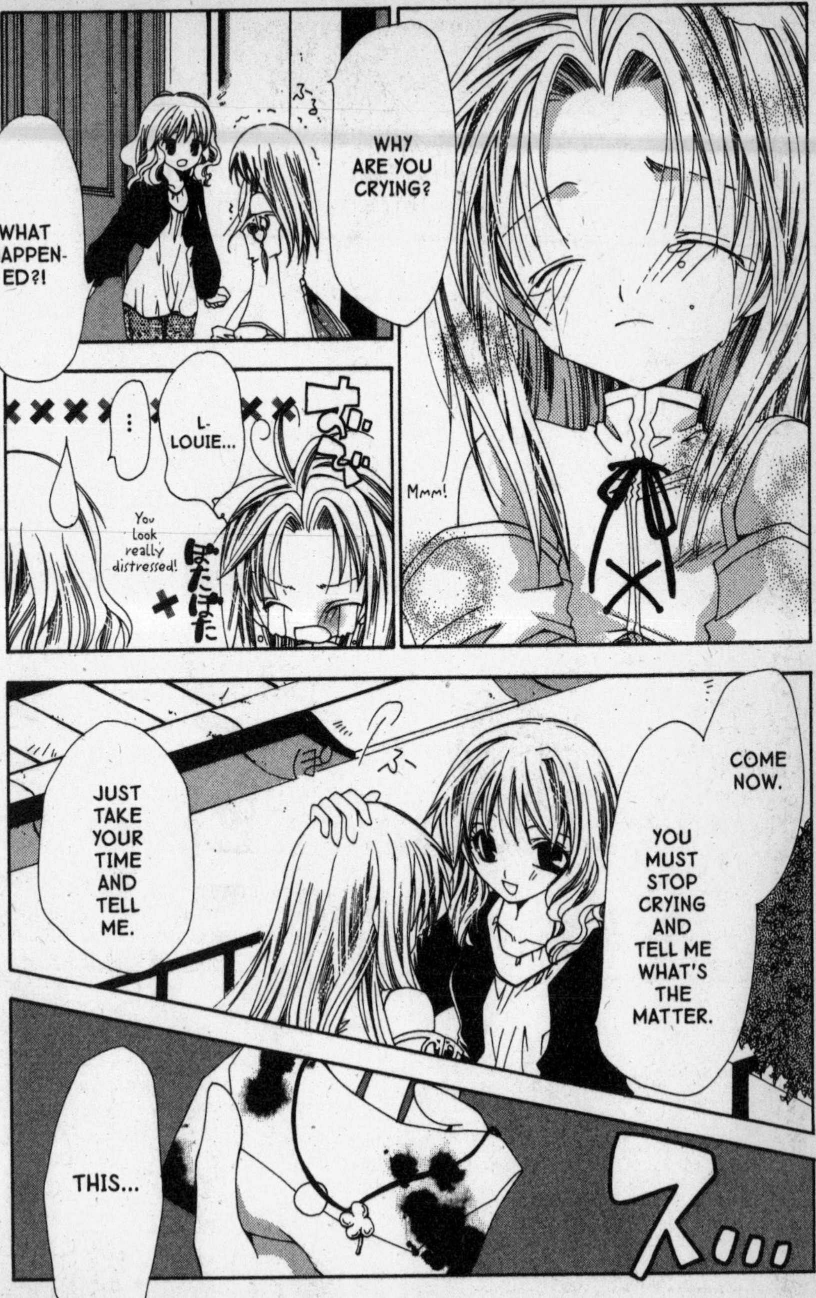
WHY ARE YOU CRYING?
Mmm!
WHAT HAPPEN-ED?!
L-LOUIE...
...
You look really distressed!
COME NOW.
YOU MUST STOP CRYING AND TELL ME WHAT'S THE MATTER.
JUST TAKE YOUR TIME AND TELL ME.
THIS...

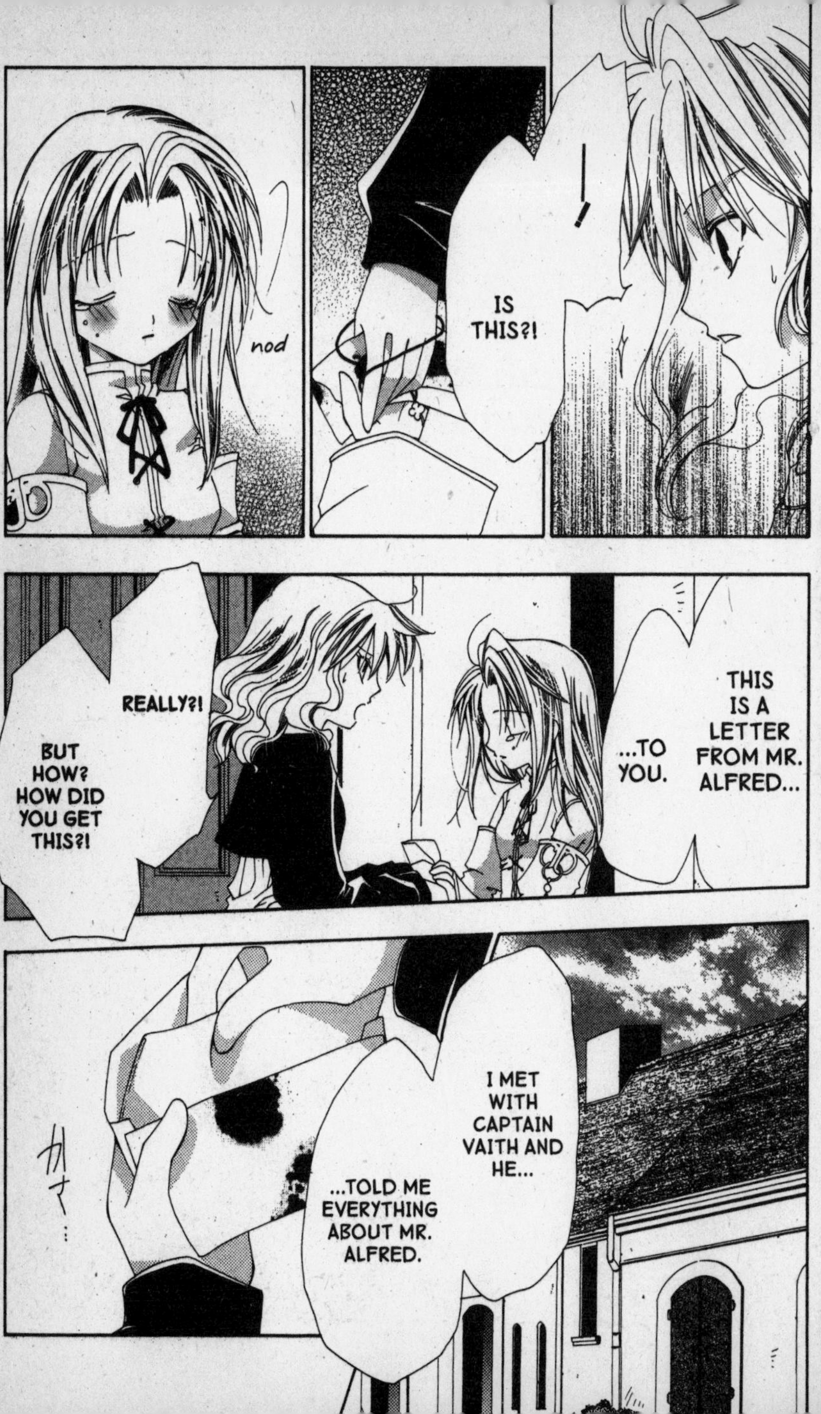
!
IS THIS?!
nod
THIS IS A LETTER FROM MR. ALFRED...
...TO YOU.
REALLY?!
BUT HOW? HOW DID YOU GET THIS?!
I MET WITH CAPTAIN VAITH AND HE...
...TOLD ME EVERYTHING ABOUT MR. ALFRED.
カサ…

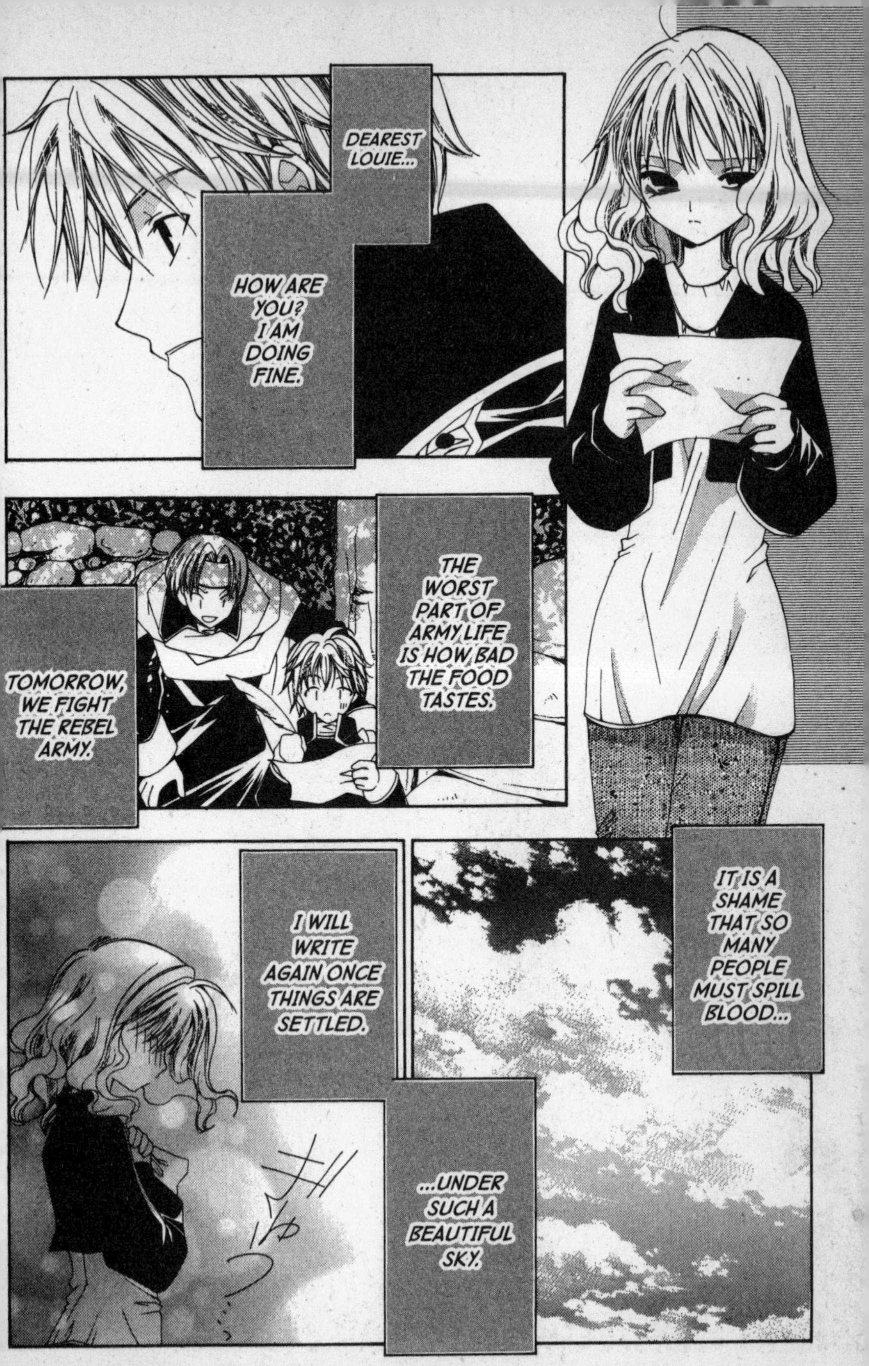
DEAREST LOUIE...
HOW ARE YOU? I AM DOING FINE.
THE WORST PART OF ARMY LIFE IS HOW BAD THE FOOD TASTES.
TOMORROW, WE FIGHT THE REBEL ARMY.
IT IS A SHAME THAT SO MANY PEOPLE MUST SPILL BLOOD...
...UNDER SUCH A BEAUTIFUL SKY.
I WILL WRITE AGAIN ONCE THINGS ARE SETTLED.

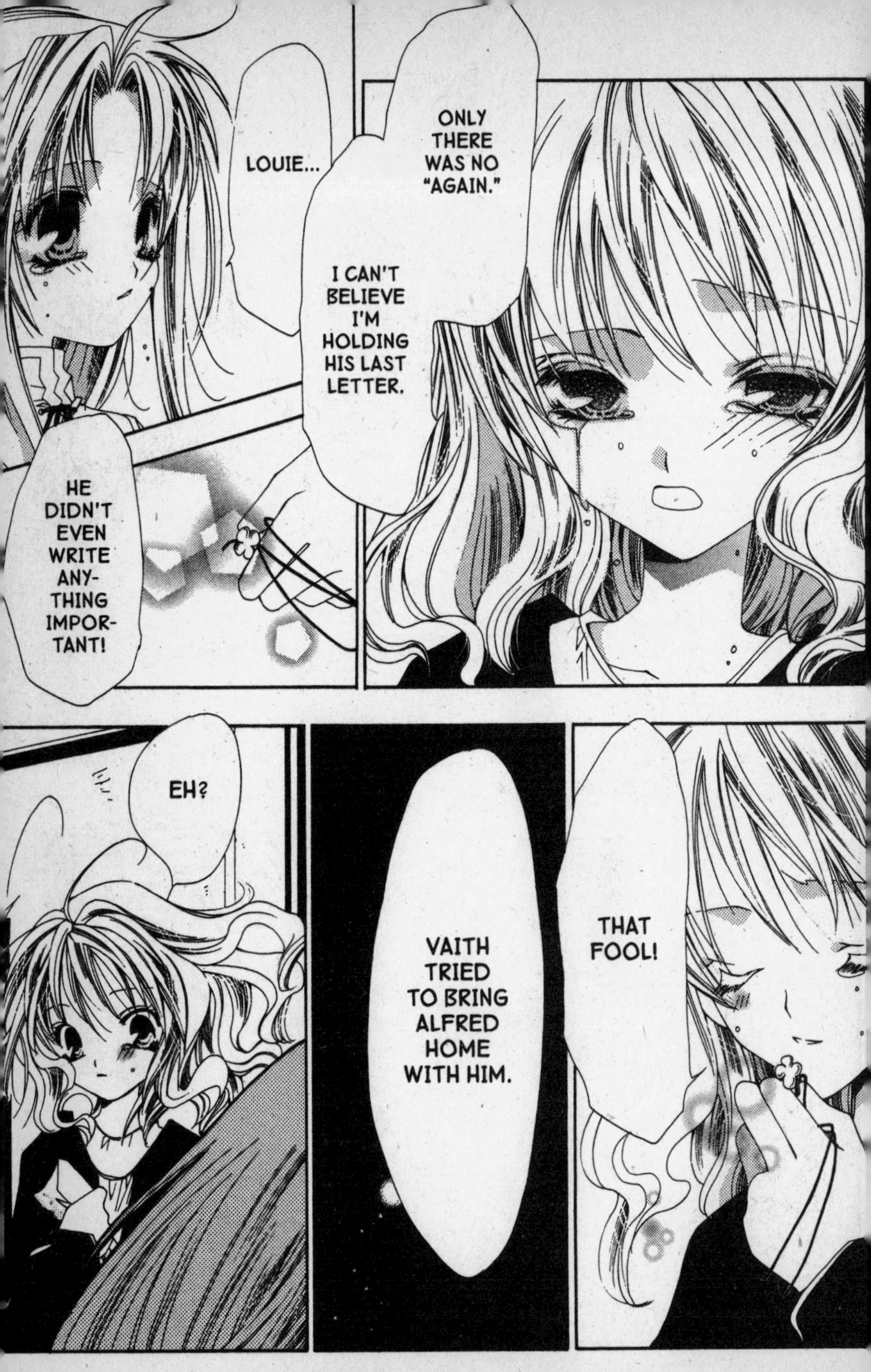
ONLY THERE WAS NO "AGAIN."
I CAN'T BELIEVE I'M HOLDING HIS LAST LETTER.
LOUIE...
HE DIDN'T EVEN WRITE ANY-THING IMPOR-TANT!
THAT FOOL!
VAITH TRIED TO BRING ALFRED HOME WITH HIM.
EH?

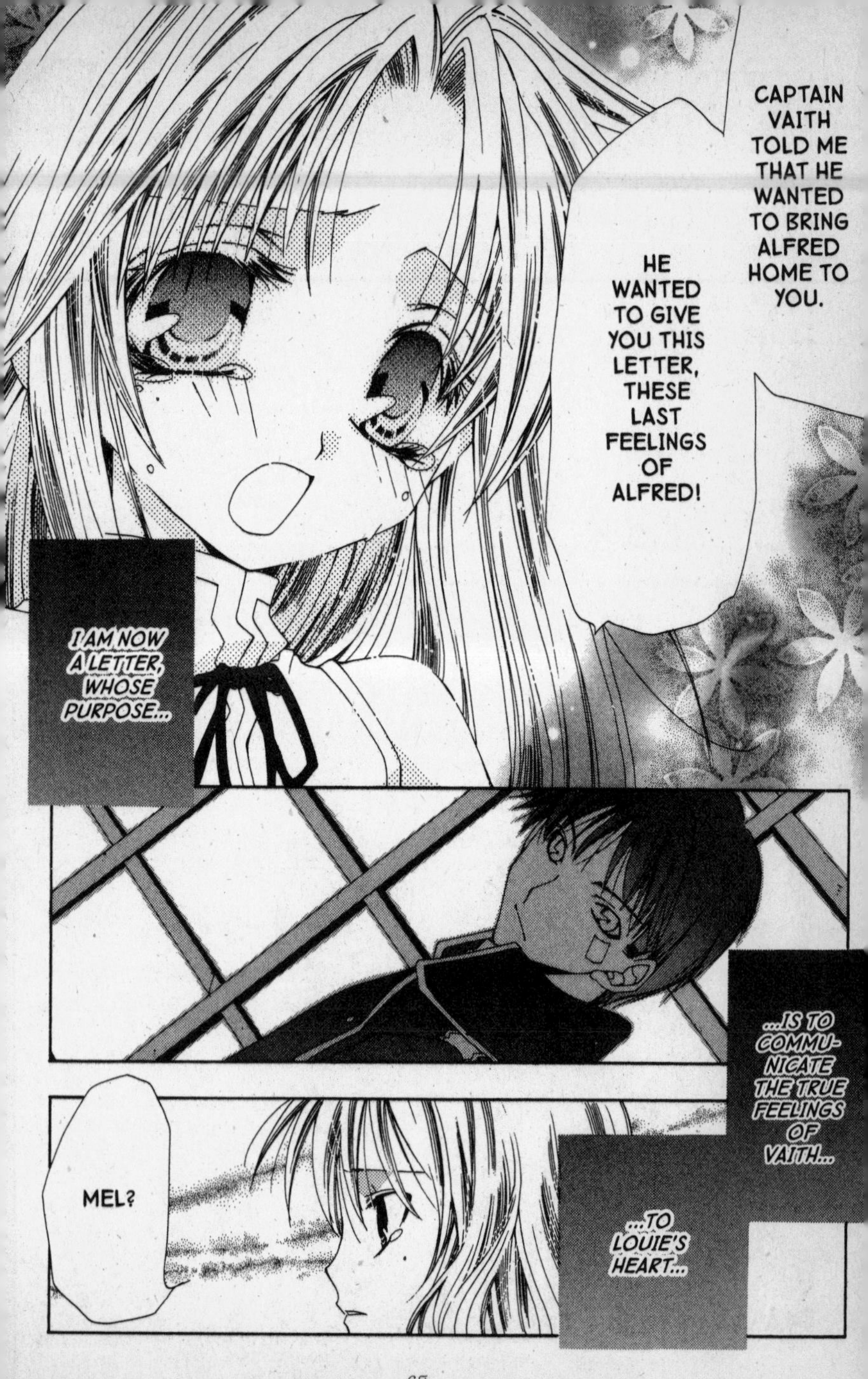
CAPTAIN VAITH TOLD ME THAT HE WANTED TO BRING ALFRED HOME TO YOU.
HE WANTED TO GIVE YOU THIS LETTER, THESE LAST FEELINGS OF ALFRED!
I AM NOW A LETTER, WHOSE PURPOSE...
...IS TO COMMUNICATE THE TRUE FEELINGS OF VAITH...
...TO LOUIE'S HEART...
MEL?

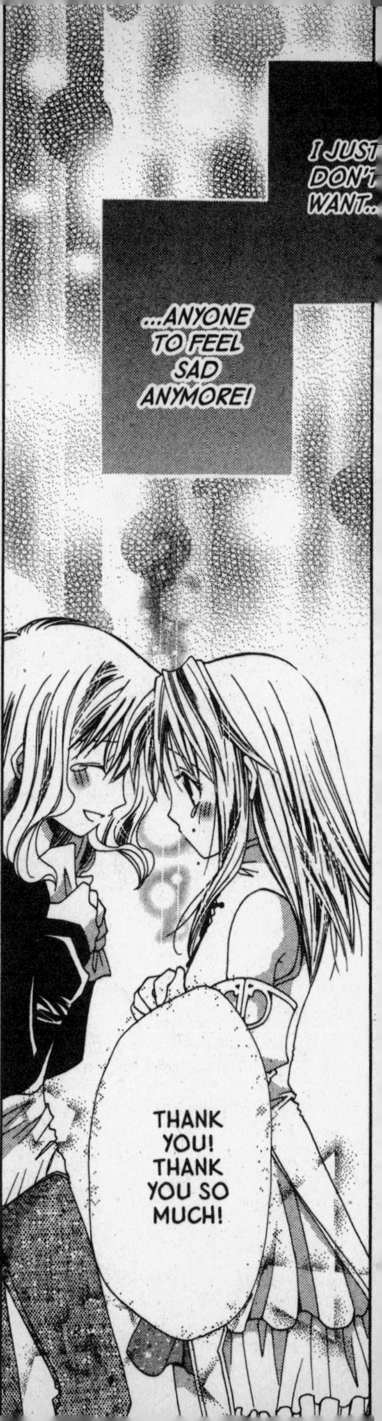
I JUST DON'T WANT...
...ANYONE TO FEEL SAD ANYMORE!
THANK YOU! THANK YOU SO MUCH!
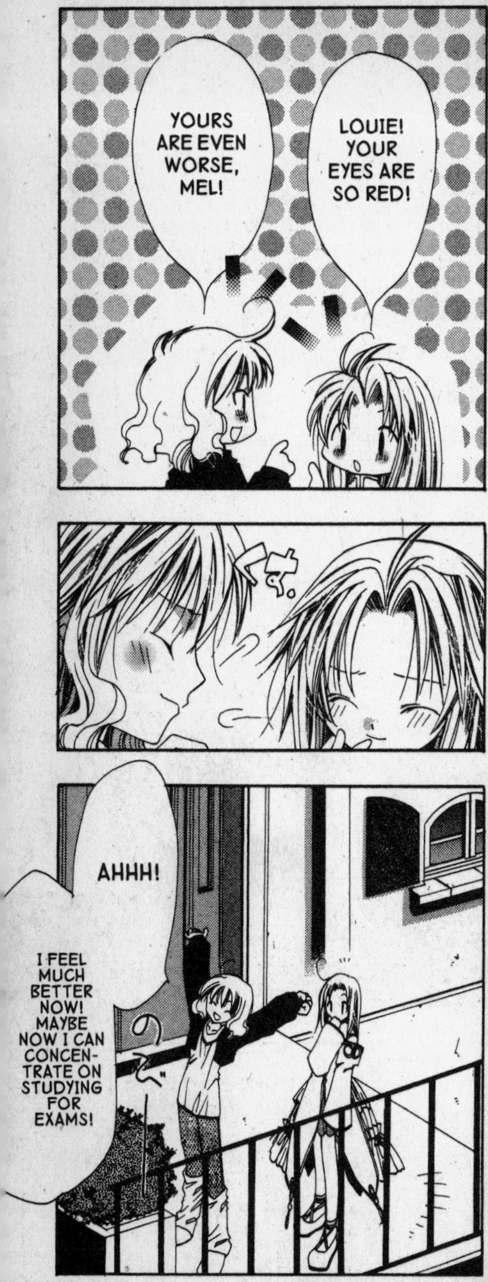
LOUIE! YOUR EYES ARE SO RED!
YOURS ARE EVEN WORSE, MEL!
AHHH!
I FEEL MUCH BETTER NOW! MAYBE NOW I CAN CONCEN-TRATE ON STUDYING FOR EXAMS!

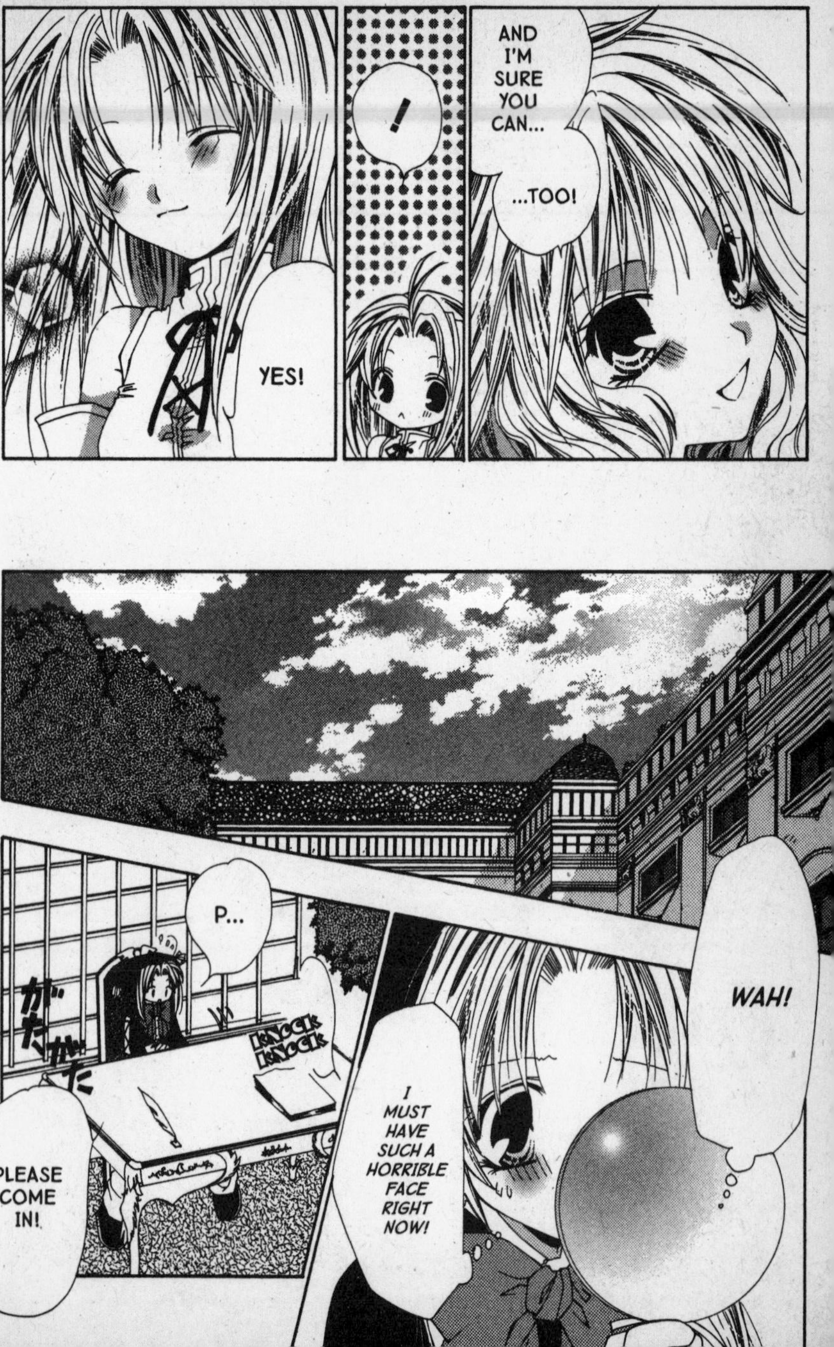
AND I'M SURE YOU CAN...
...TOO!
!
YES!
WAH!
I MUST HAVE SUCH A HORRIBLE FACE RIGHT NOW!
KNOCK KNOCK
P...
PLEASE COME IN!

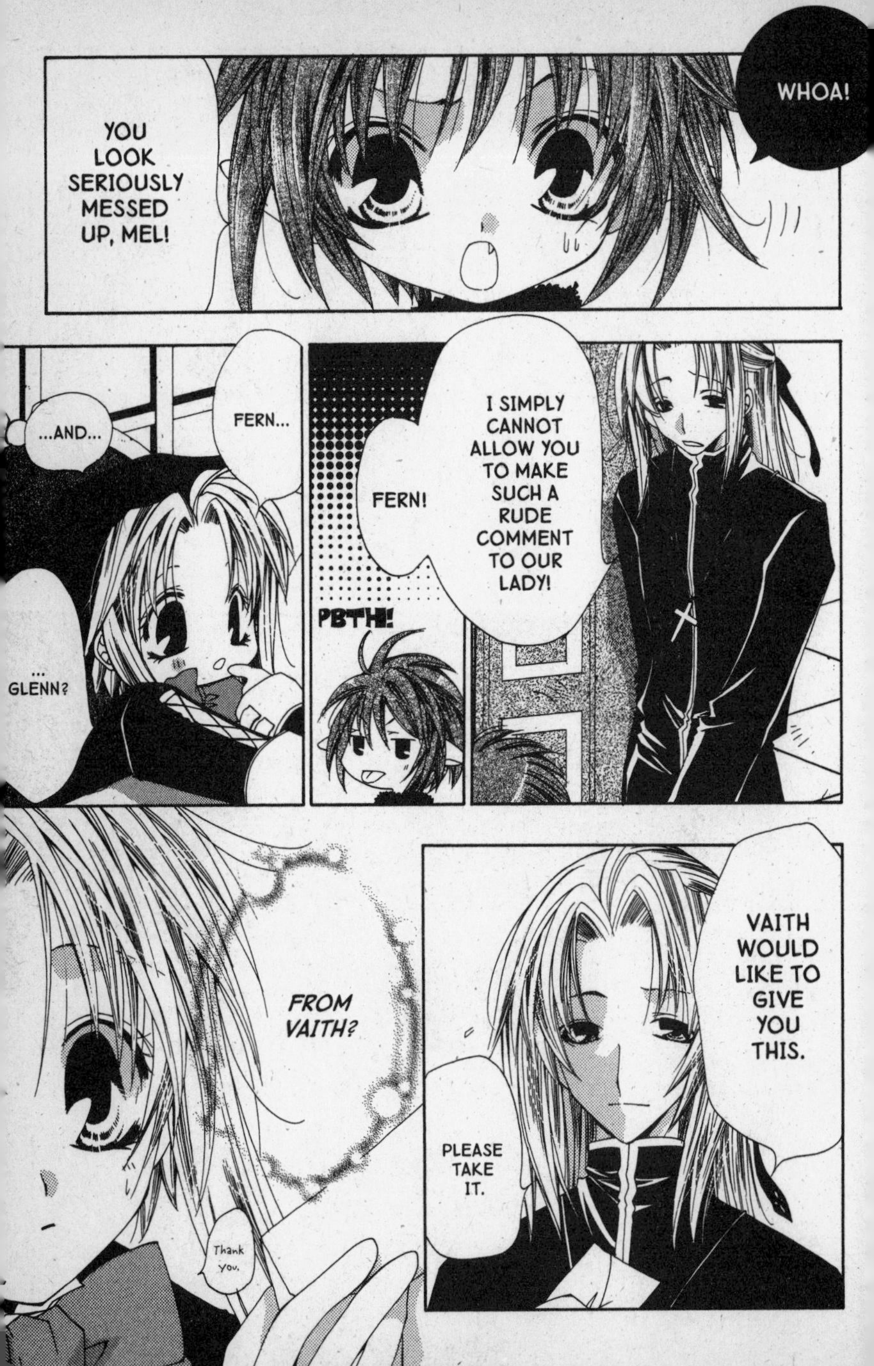
WHOA!
YOU LOOK SERIOUSLY MESSED UP, MEL!
I SIMPLY CANNOT ALLOW YOU TO MAKE SUCH A RUDE COMMENT TO OUR LADY!
FERN!
PBTH!
FERN...
...AND...
... GLENN?
VAITH WOULD LIKE TO GIVE YOU THIS.
PLEASE TAKE IT.
FROM VAITH?
Thank you.

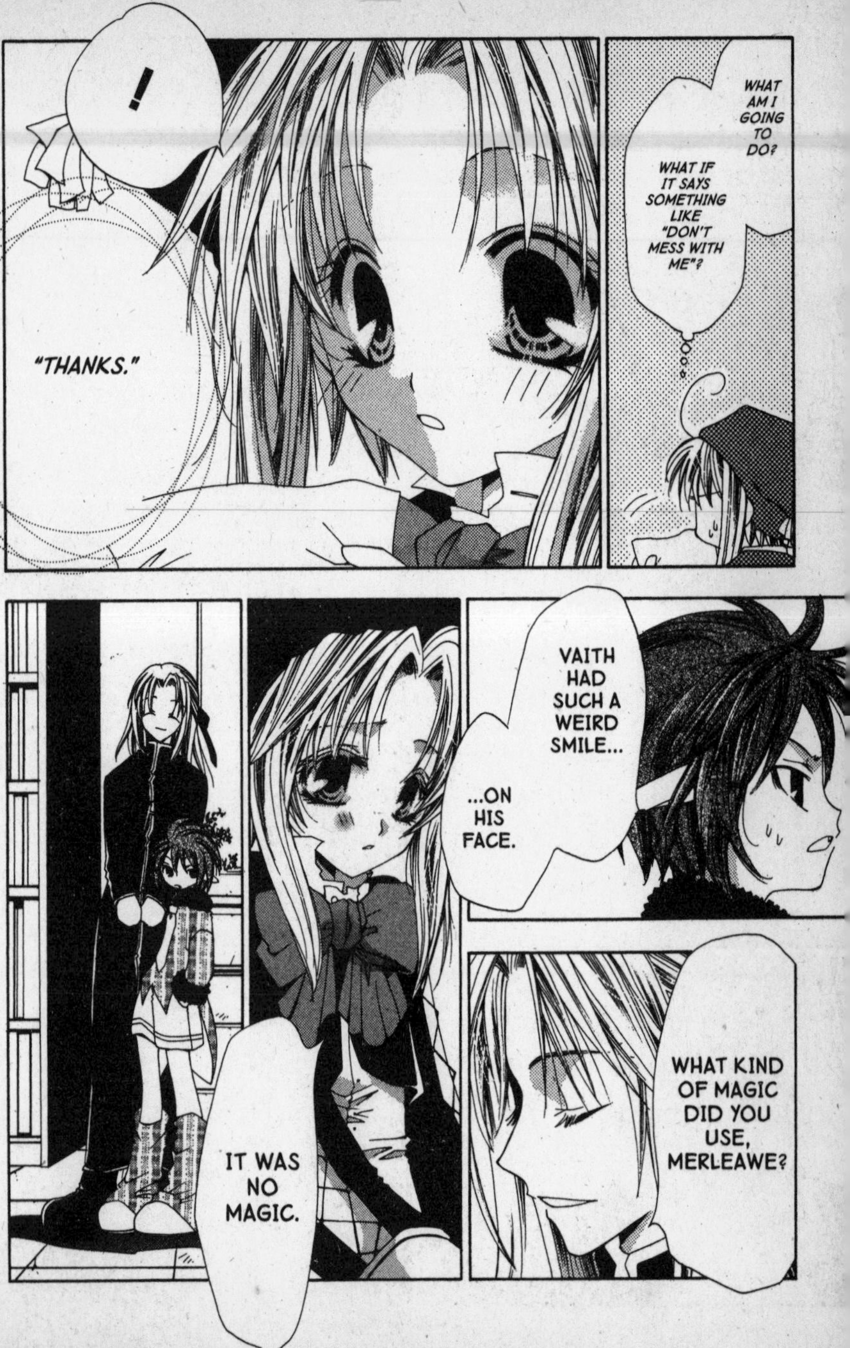
WHAT AM I GOING TO DO?
WHAT IF IT SAYS SOMETHING LIKE "DON'T MESS WITH ME"?
!
"THANKS."
VAITH HAD SUCH A WEIRD SMILE...
...ON HIS FACE.
WHAT KIND OF MAGIC DID YOU USE, MERLEAWE?
IT WAS NO MAGIC.

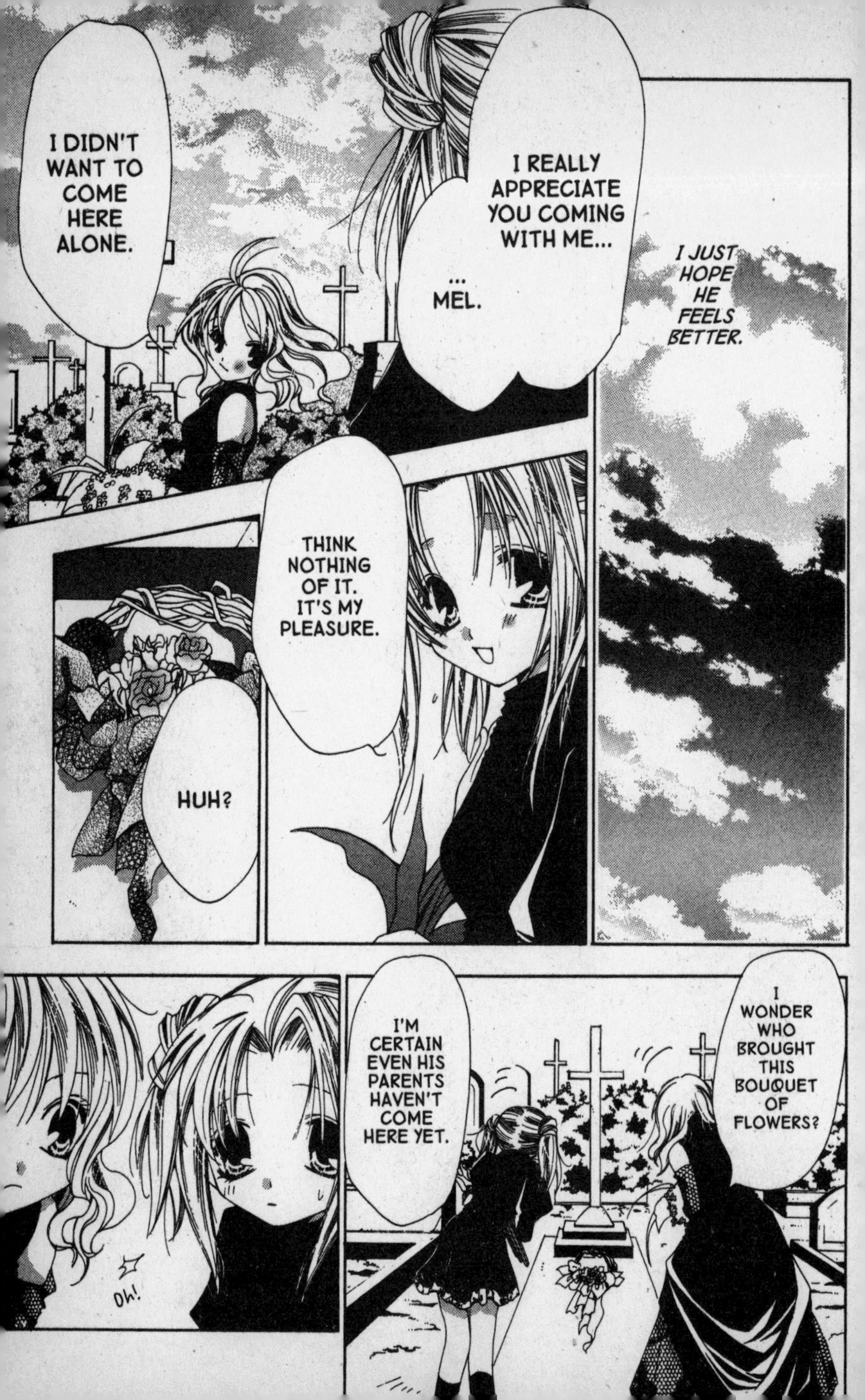
I JUST HOPE HE FEELS BETTER.
I REALLY APPRECIATE YOU COMING WITH ME...
... MEL.
I DIDN'T WANT TO COME HERE ALONE.
THINK NOTHING OF IT. IT'S MY PLEASURE.
HUH?
I WONDER WHO BROUGHT THIS BOUQUET OF FLOWERS?
I'M CERTAIN EVEN HIS PARENTS HAVEN'T COME HERE YET.
Oh!

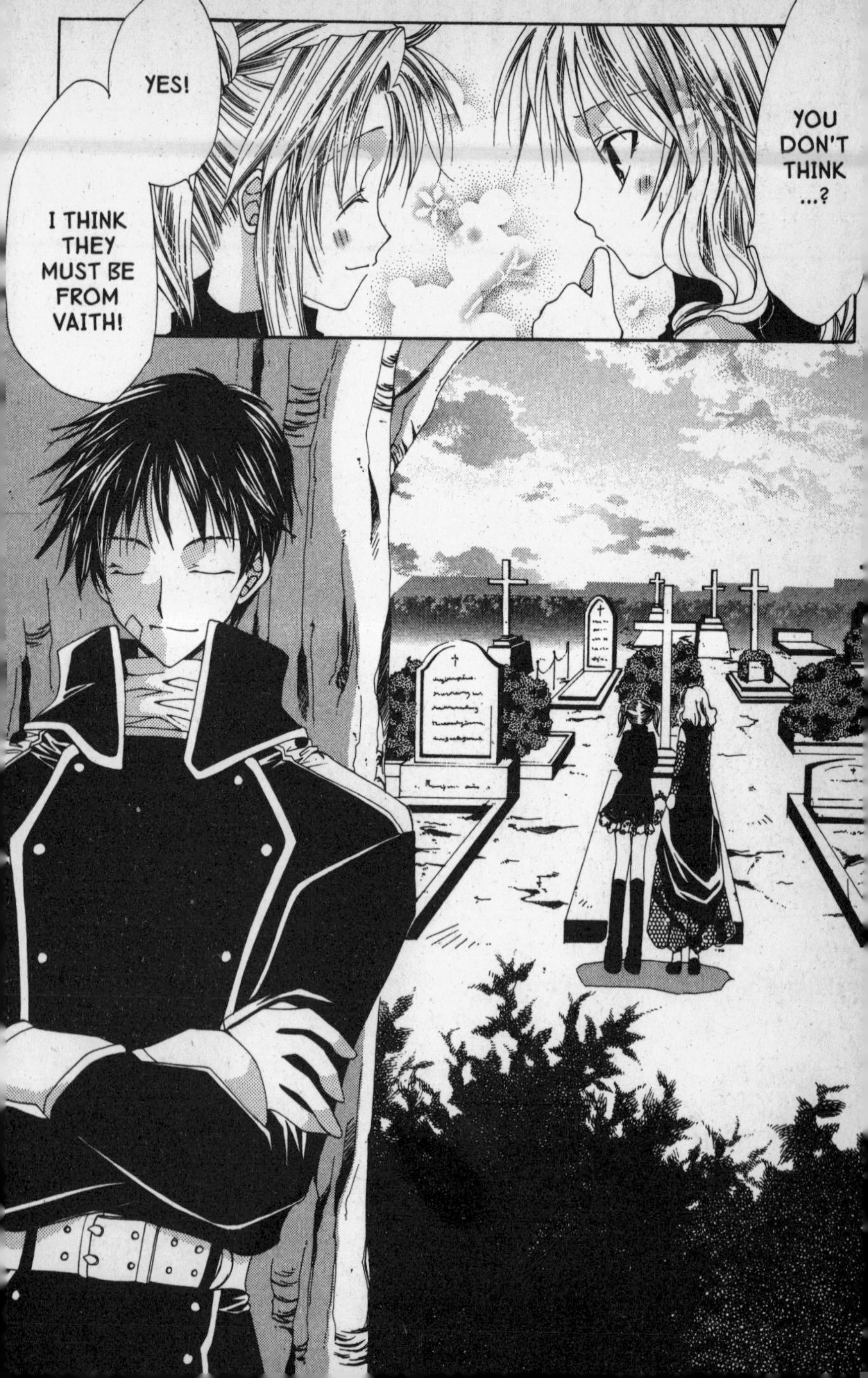
YOU DON'T THINK ...?
YES!
I THINK THEY MUST BE FROM VAITH!

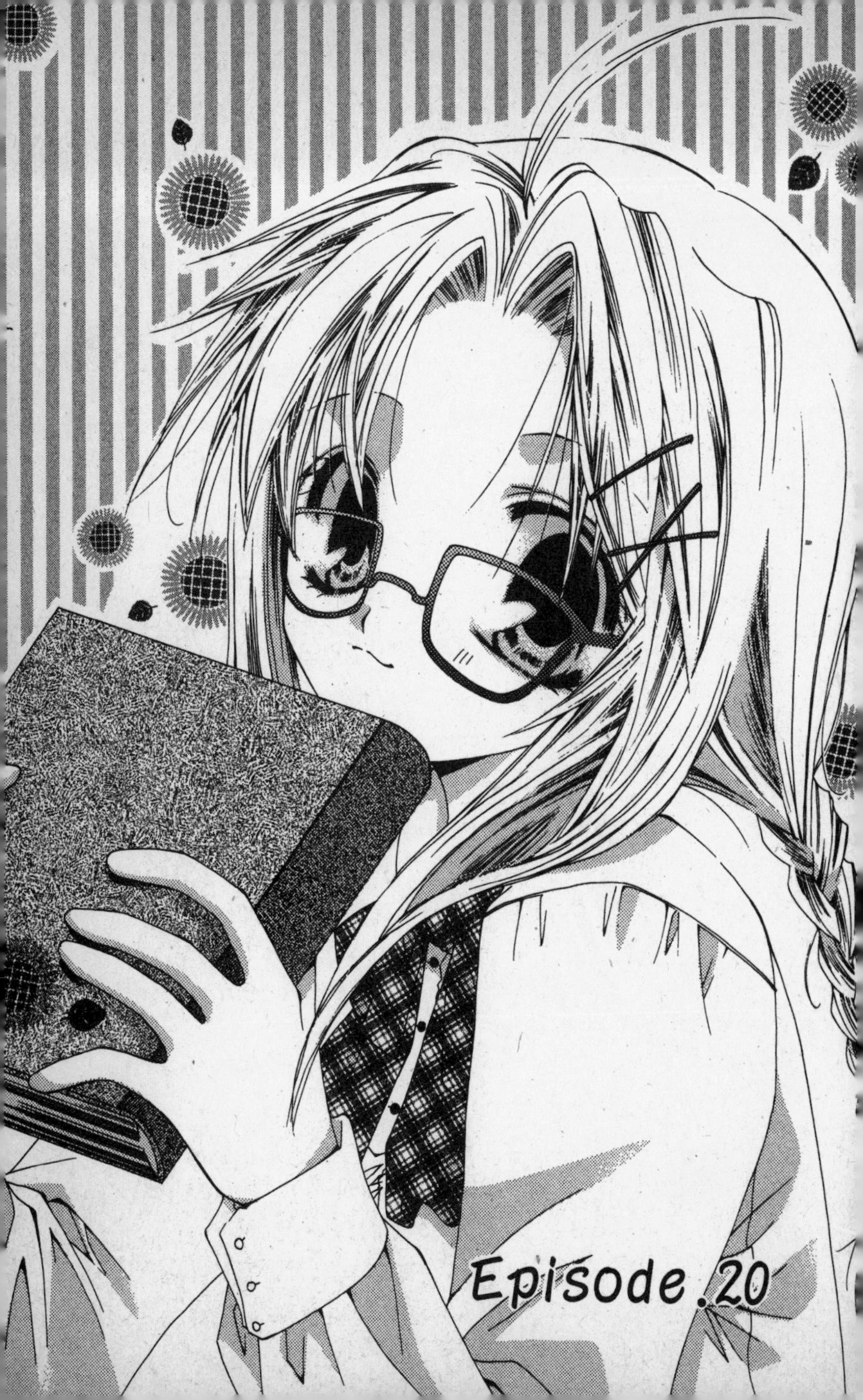
Episode .20

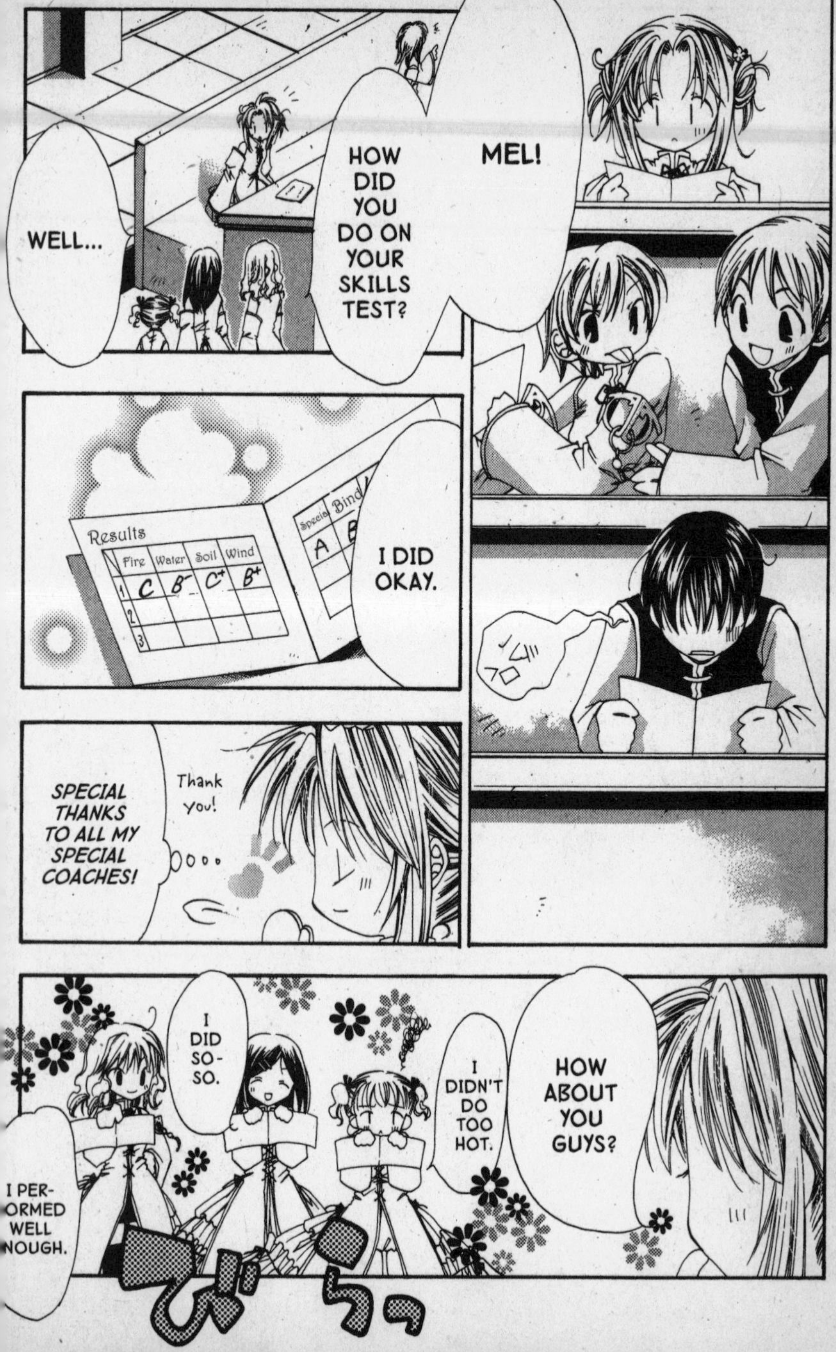
MEL!
HOW DID YOU DO ON YOUR SKILLS TEST?
WELL...
Results
Fire Water Soil Wind
1 C B- C+ B+
2
3
Special Bind
A B
I DID OKAY.
Thank you!
SPECIAL THANKS TO ALL MY SPECIAL COACHES!
HOW ABOUT YOU GUYS?
I DIDN'T DO TOO HOT.
I DID SO-SO.
I PER-ORMED WELL NOUGH.

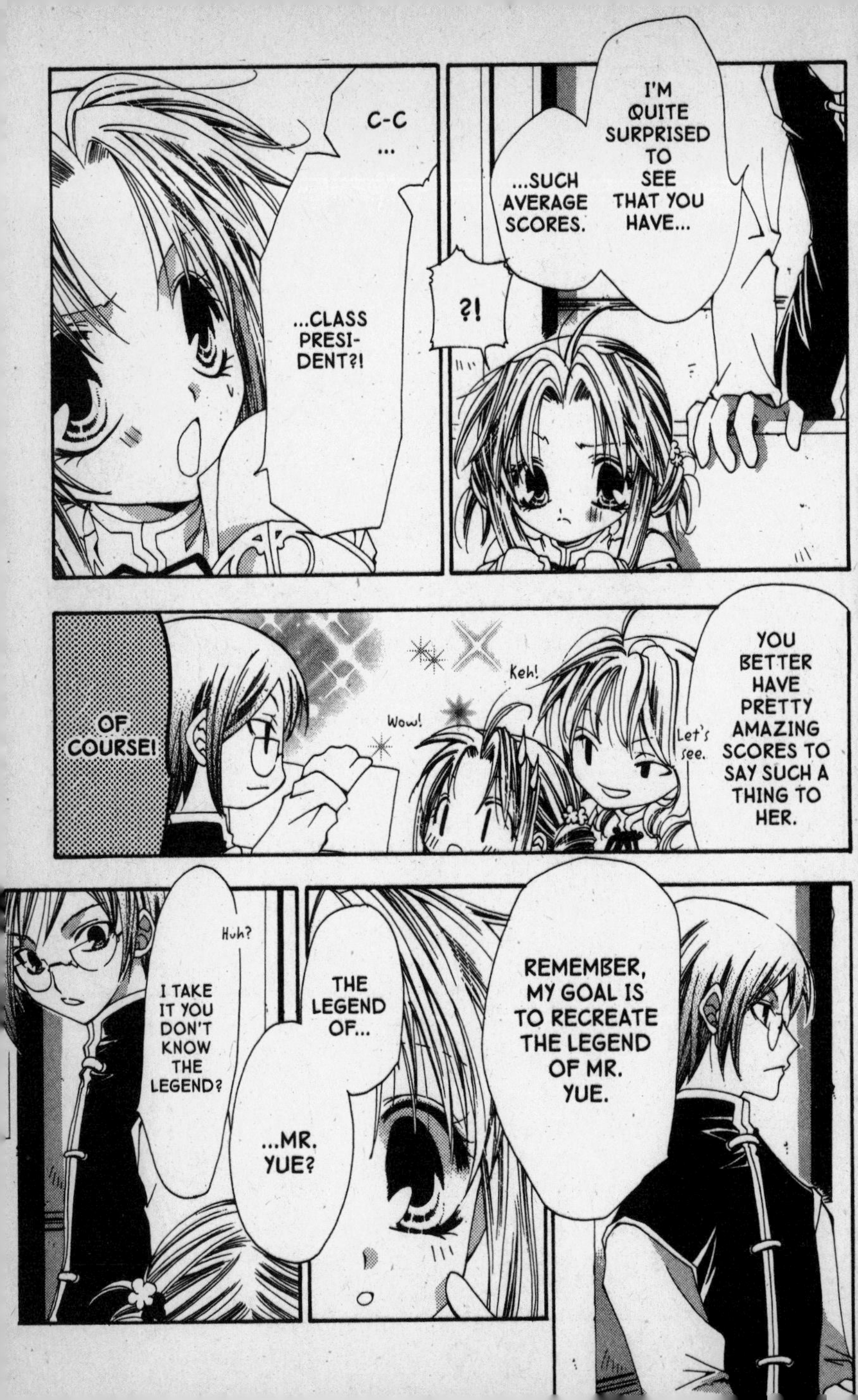
I'M QUITE SURPRISED TO SEE THAT YOU HAVE...
...SUCH AVERAGE SCORES.
?!
C-C...
...CLASS PRESIDENT?!
YOU BETTER HAVE PRETTY AMAZING SCORES TO SAY SUCH A THING TO HER.
Let's see.
Keh!
Wow!
OF COURSE!
REMEMBER, MY GOAL IS TO RECREATE THE LEGEND OF MR. YUE.
THE LEGEND OF...
...MR. YUE?
Huh?
I TAKE IT YOU DON'T KNOW THE LEGEND?

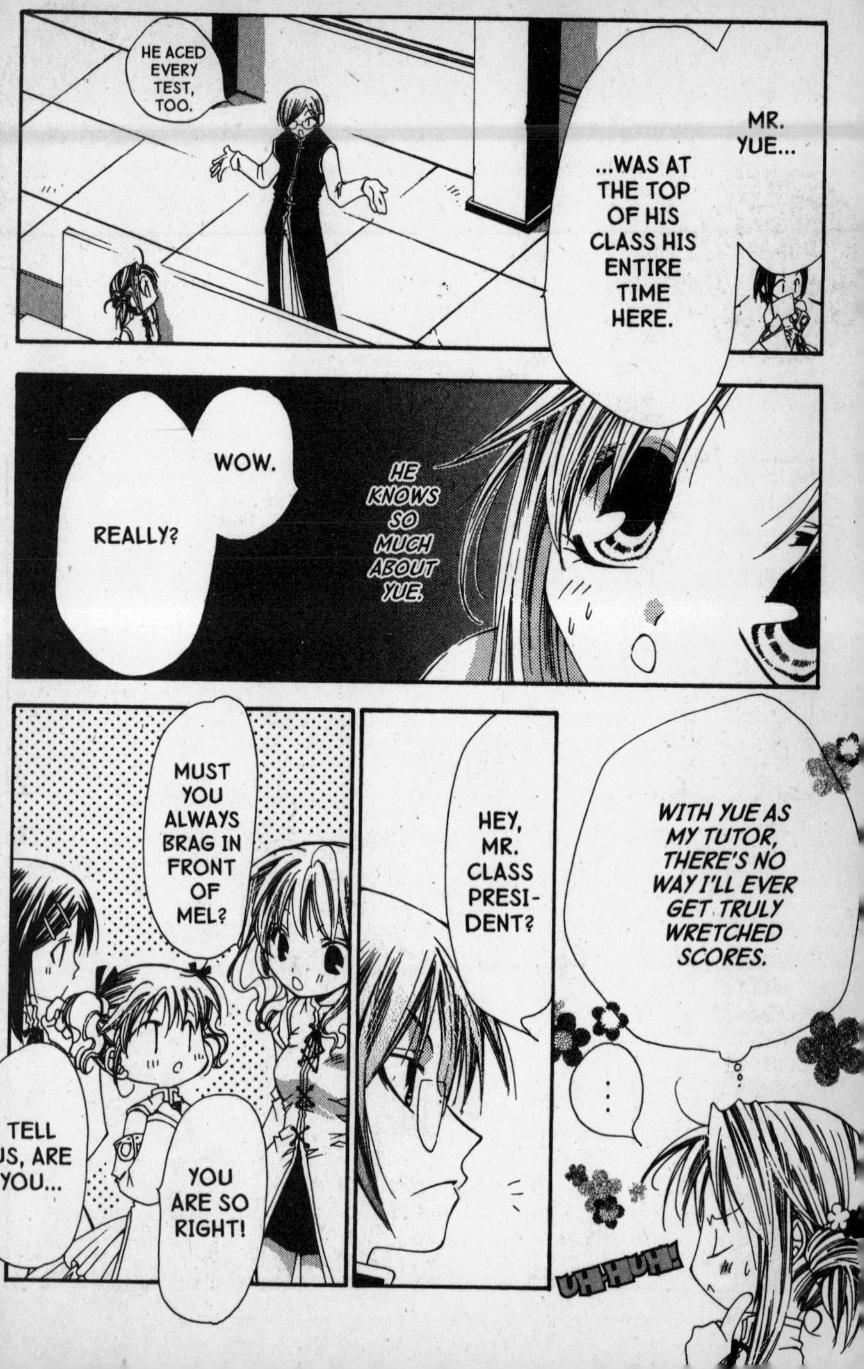

MR. YUE...
...WAS AT THE TOP OF HIS CLASS HIS ENTIRE TIME HERE.
HE ACED EVERY TEST, TOO.
HE KNOWS SO MUCH ABOUT YUE.
WOW.
REALLY?
WITH YUE AS MY TUTOR, THERE'S NO WAY I'LL EVER GET TRULY WRETCHED SCORES.
...
UH-HUH!
HEY, MR. CLASS PRESI-DENT?
MUST YOU ALWAYS BRAG IN FRONT OF MEL?
YOU ARE SO RIGHT!
TELL US, ARE YOU...

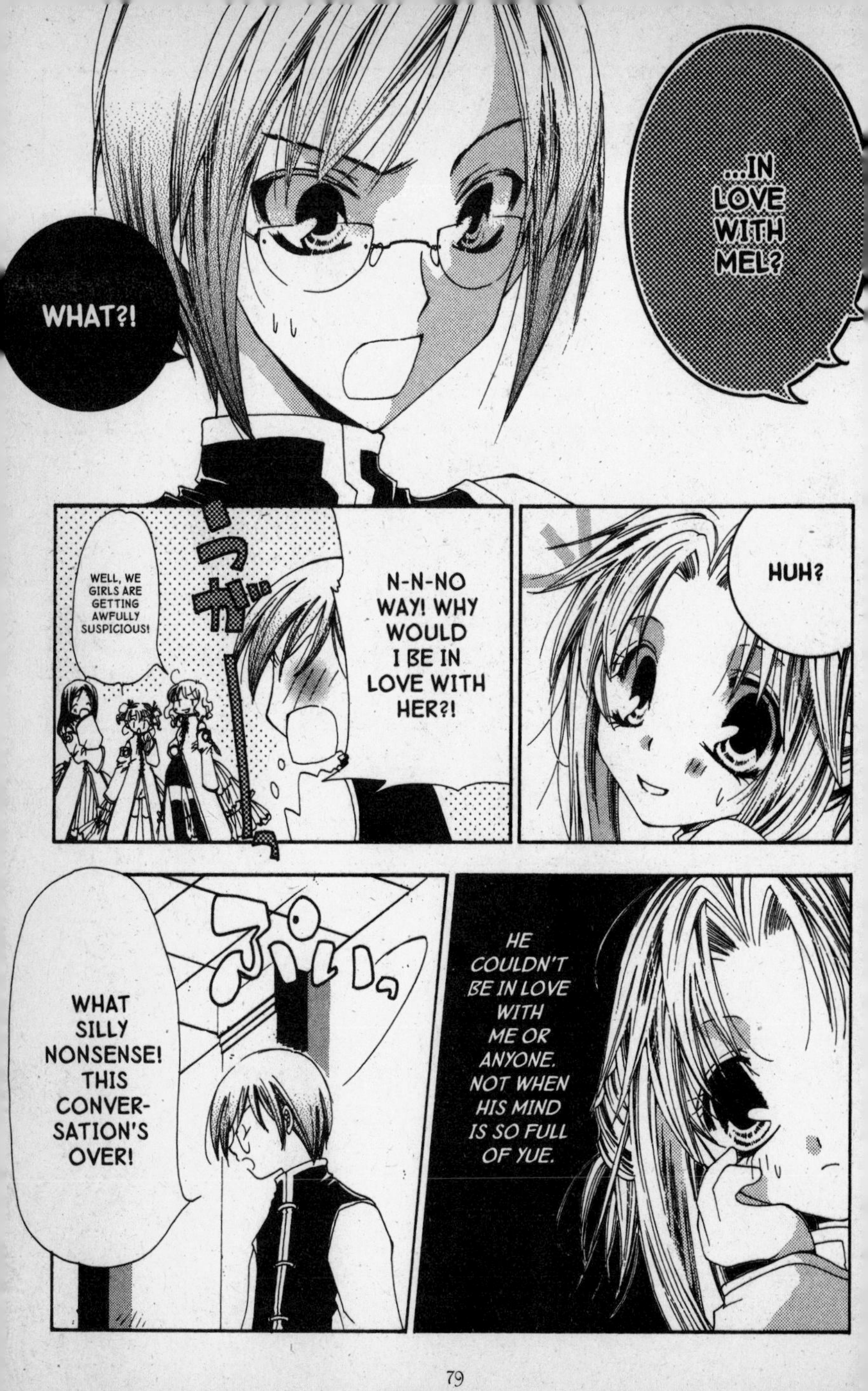
...IN LOVE WITH MEL?
WHAT?!
HUH?
N-N-NO WAY! WHY WOULD I BE IN LOVE WITH HER?!
WELL, WE GIRLS ARE GETTING AWFULLY SUSPICIOUS!
HE COULDN'T BE IN LOVE WITH ME OR ANYONE. NOT WHEN HIS MIND IS SO FULL OF YUE.
WHAT SILLY NONSENSE! THIS CONVER-SATION'S OVER!

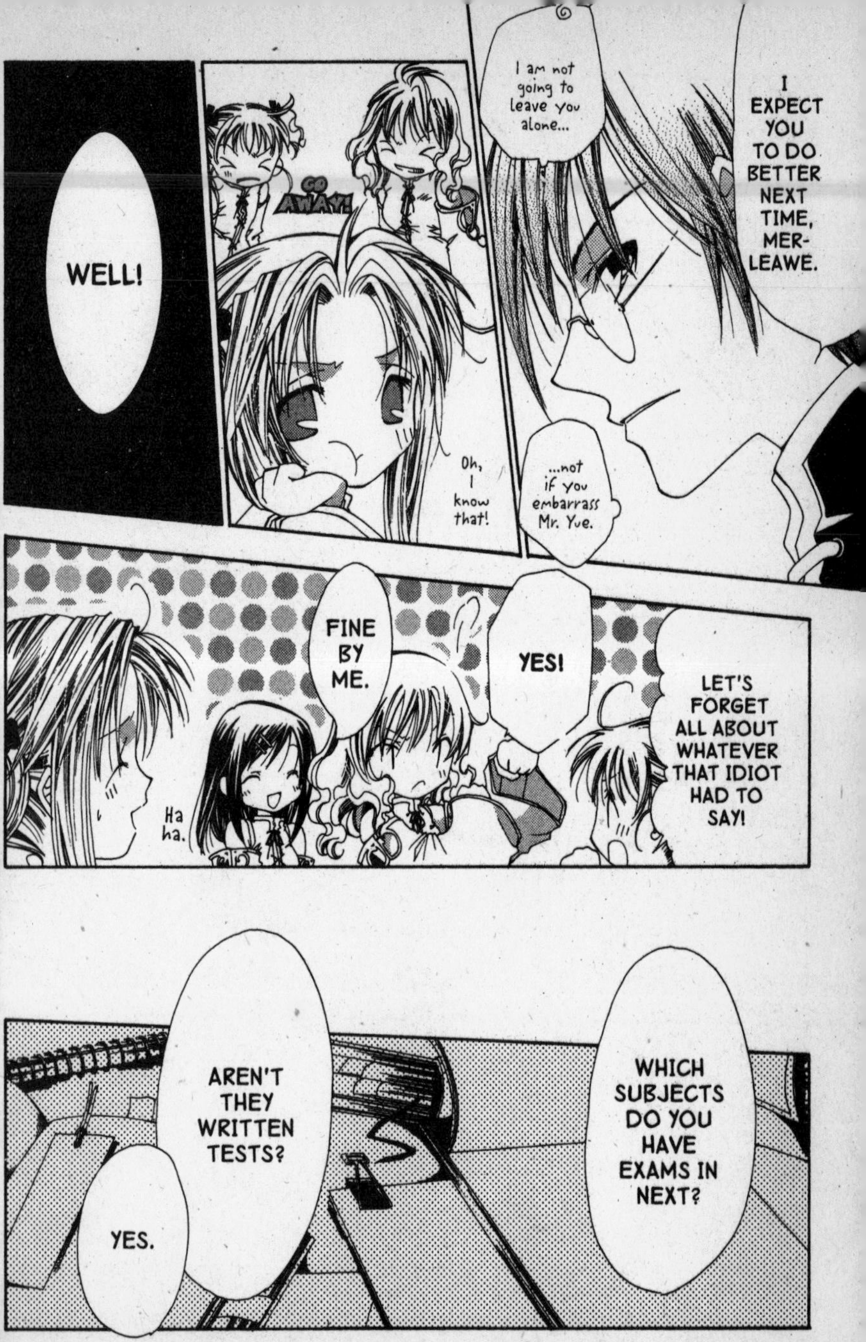
I EXPECT YOU TO DO BETTER NEXT TIME, MER-LEAWE.
I am not going to leave you alone...
...not if you embarrass Mr. Yue.
GO AWAY!
Oh, I know that!
WELL!
LET'S FORGET ALL ABOUT WHATEVER THAT IDIOT HAD TO SAY!
YES!
FINE BY ME.
Ha ha.
WHICH SUBJECTS DO YOU HAVE EXAMS IN NEXT?
AREN'T THEY WRITTEN TESTS?
YES.

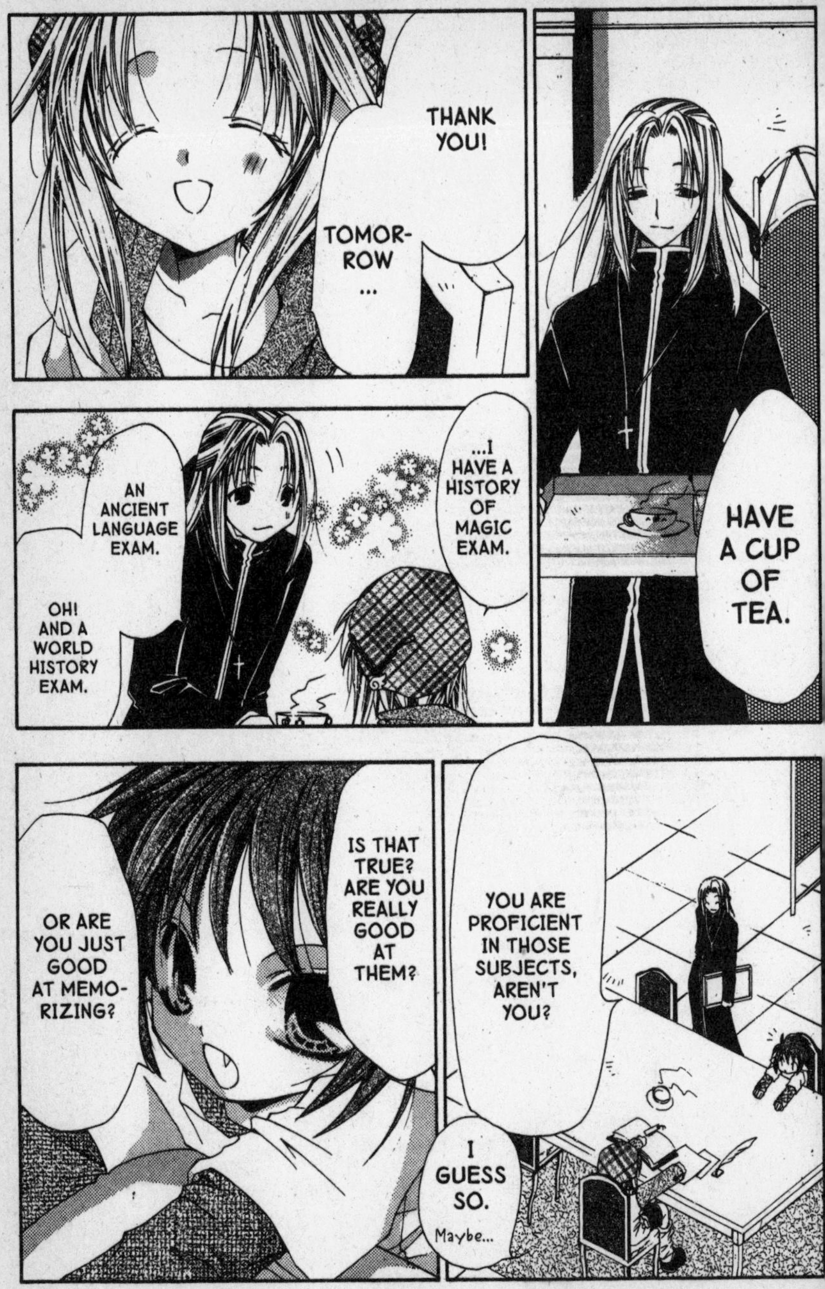
HAVE A CUP OF TEA.
THANK YOU!
TOMORROW...
...I HAVE A HISTORY OF MAGIC EXAM.
AN ANCIENT LANGUAGE EXAM.
OH! AND A WORLD HISTORY EXAM.
YOU ARE PROFICIENT IN THOSE SUBJECTS, AREN'T YOU?
I GUESS SO.
Maybe...
IS THAT TRUE? ARE YOU REALLY GOOD AT THEM?
OR ARE YOU JUST GOOD AT MEMORIZING?

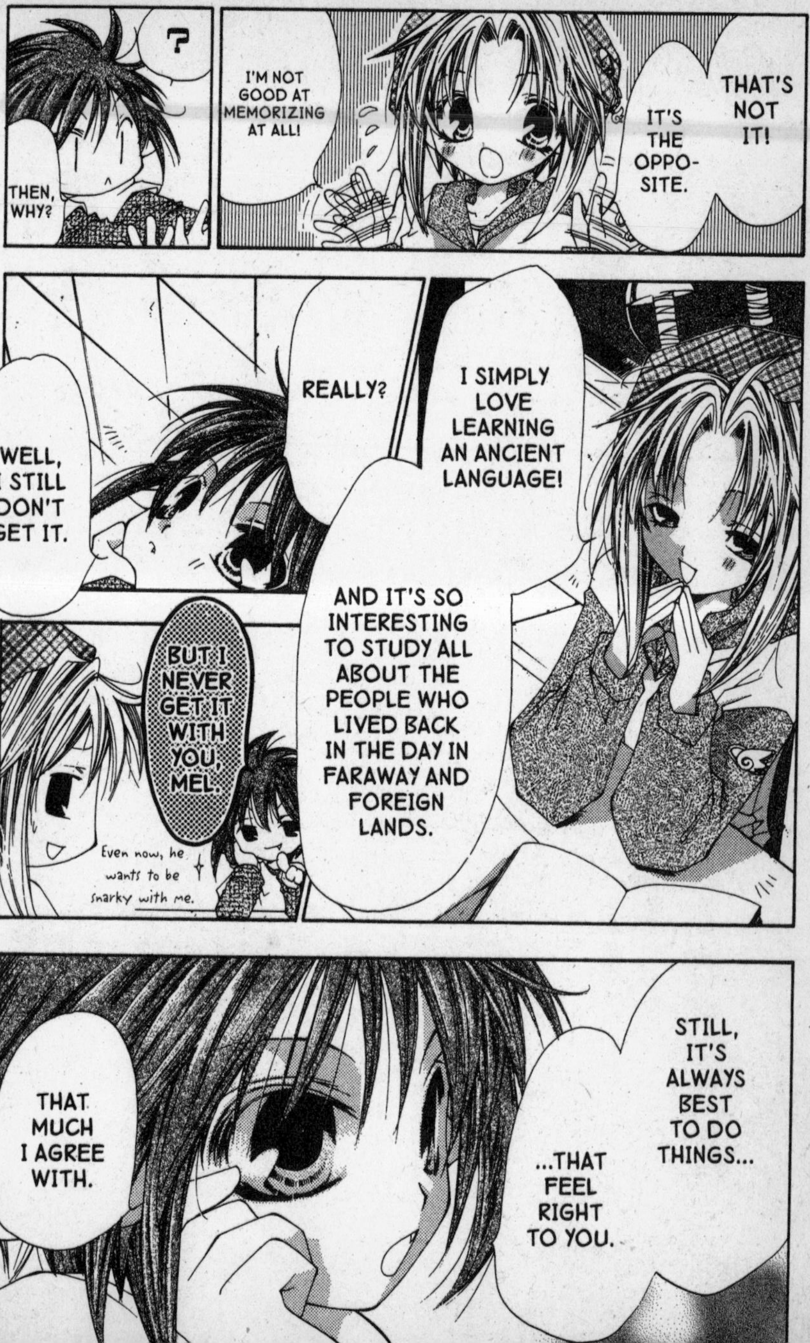
THAT'S NOT IT!
IT'S THE OPPO-SITE.
I'M NOT GOOD AT MEMORIZING AT ALL!
?
THEN, WHY?
I SIMPLY LOVE LEARNING AN ANCIENT LANGUAGE!
AND IT'S SO INTERESTING TO STUDY ALL ABOUT THE PEOPLE WHO LIVED BACK IN THE DAY IN FARAWAY AND FOREIGN LANDS.
REALLY?
WELL, I STILL DON'T GET IT.
BUT I NEVER GET IT WITH YOU, MEL.
Even now, he wants to be snarky with me.
STILL, IT'S ALWAYS BEST TO DO THINGS...
...THAT FEEL RIGHT TO YOU.
THAT MUCH I AGREE WITH.

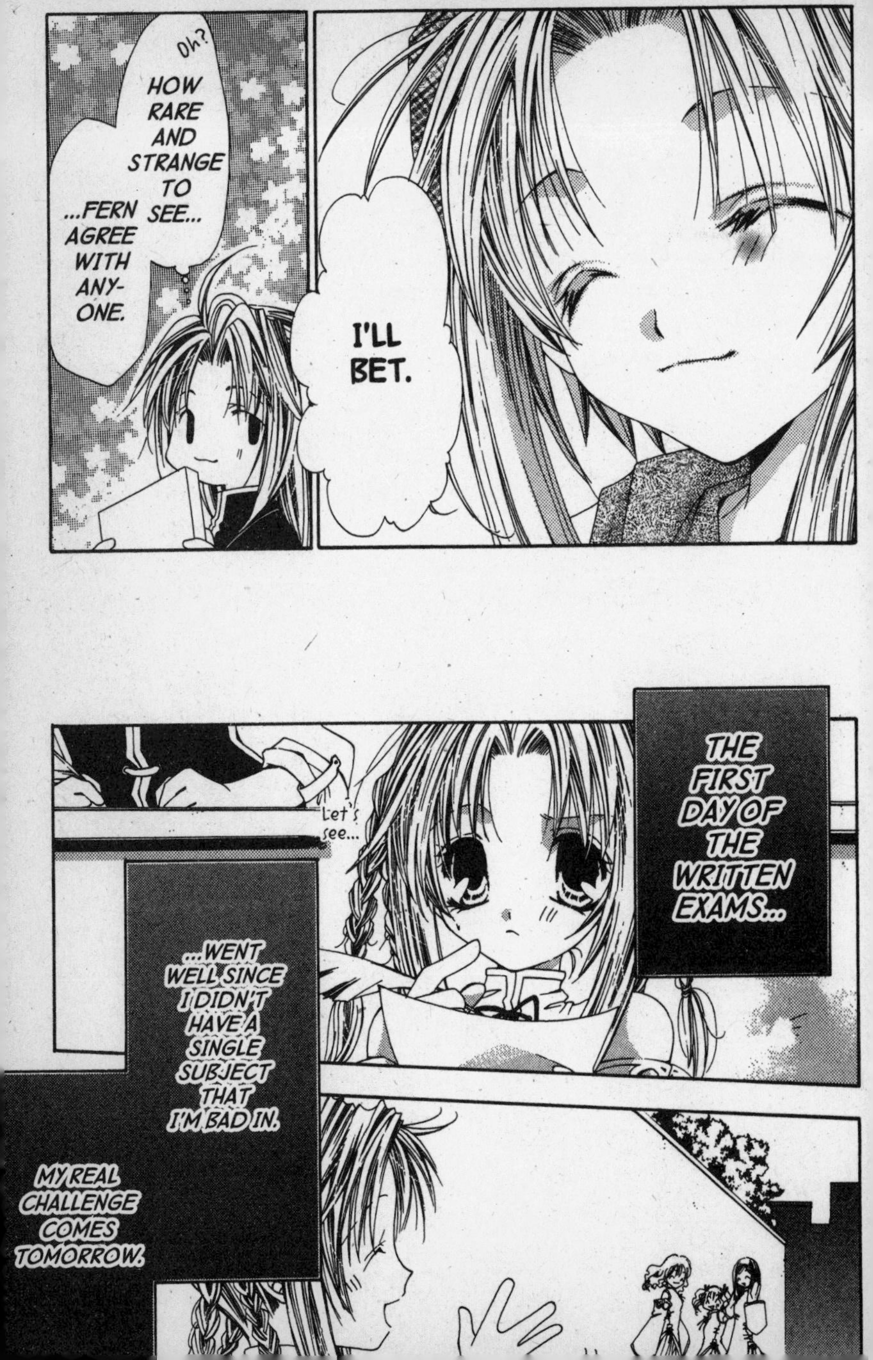
I'LL BET.
Oh?
HOW RARE AND STRANGE TO SEE... ...FERN AGREE WITH ANYONE.
THE FIRST DAY OF THE WRITTEN EXAMS...
Let's see...
...WENT WELL SINCE I DIDN'T HAVE A SINGLE SUBJECT THAT I'M BAD IN.
MY REAL CHALLENGE COMES TOMORROW.

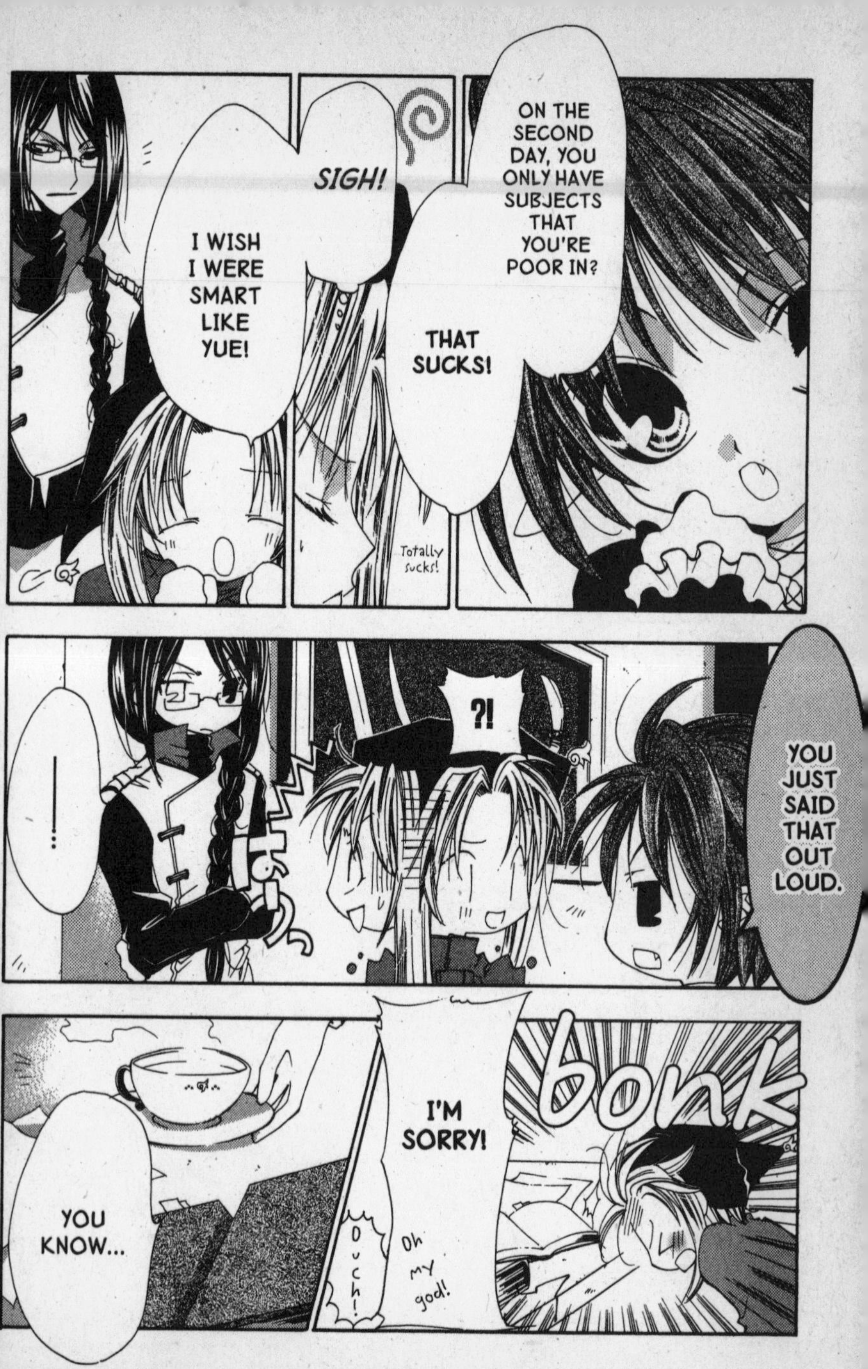
ON THE SECOND DAY, YOU ONLY HAVE SUBJECTS THAT YOU'RE POOR IN?
THAT SUCKS!
Totally sucks!
SIGH!
I WISH I WERE SMART LIKE YUE!
YOU JUST SAID THAT OUT LOUD.
?!
...!
bonk
I'M SORRY!
Oh my god!
Ouch!
YOU KNOW...

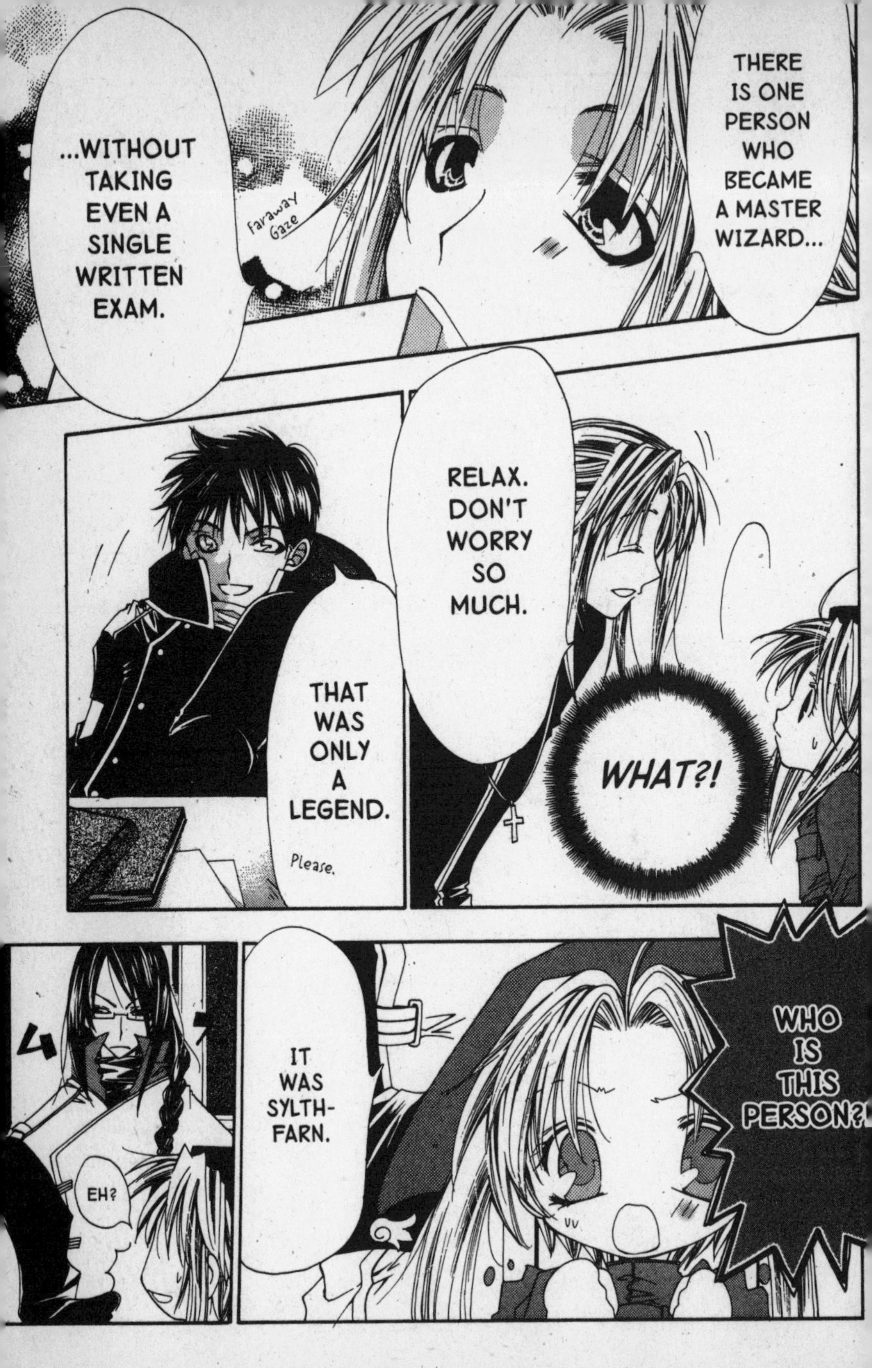
THERE IS ONE PERSON WHO BECAME A MASTER WIZARD...
Faraway Gaze
...WITHOUT TAKING EVEN A SINGLE WRITTEN EXAM.
RELAX. DON'T WORRY SO MUCH.
WHAT?!
THAT WAS ONLY A LEGEND.
Please.
WHO IS THIS PERSON?!
IT WAS SYLTH-FARN.
EH?

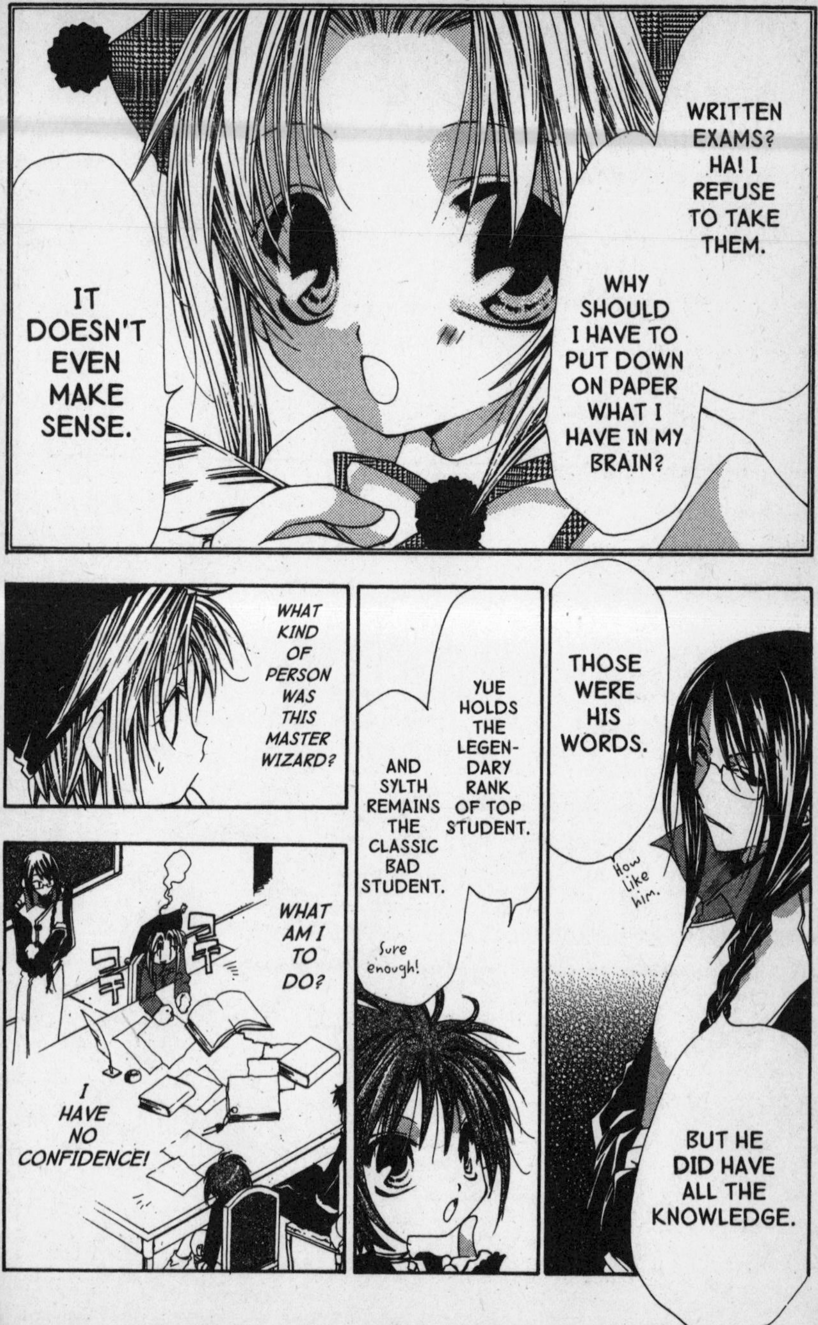
WRITTEN EXAMS? HA! I REFUSE TO TAKE THEM.
WHY SHOULD I HAVE TO PUT DOWN ON PAPER WHAT I HAVE IN MY BRAIN?
IT DOESN'T EVEN MAKE SENSE.
THOSE WERE HIS WORDS.
How like him.
BUT HE DID HAVE ALL THE KNOWLEDGE.
YUE HOLDS THE LEGEN-DARY RANK OF TOP STUDENT.
AND SYLTH REMAINS THE CLASSIC BAD STUDENT.
Sure enough!
WHAT KIND OF PERSON WAS THIS MASTER WIZARD?
WHAT AM I TO DO?
I HAVE NO CONFIDENCE!

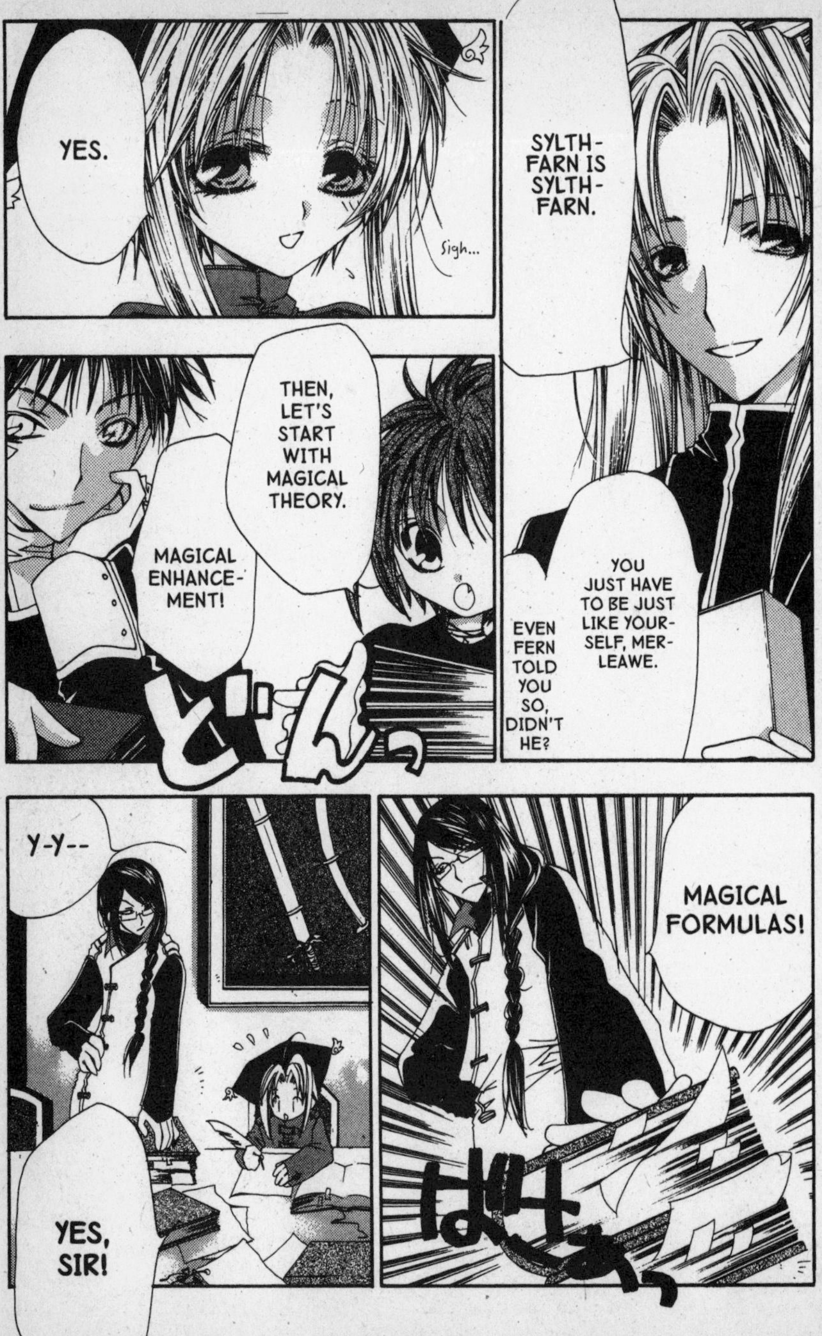

SYLTH-FARN IS SYLTH-FARN.
YOU JUST HAVE TO BE JUST LIKE YOURSELF, MERLEAWE.
EVEN FERN TOLD YOU SO, DIDN'T HE?
YES.
Sigh...
THEN, LET'S START WITH MAGICAL THEORY.
MAGICAL ENHANCEMENT!
どんっ
MAGICAL FORMULAS!
Y-Y--
YES, SIR!

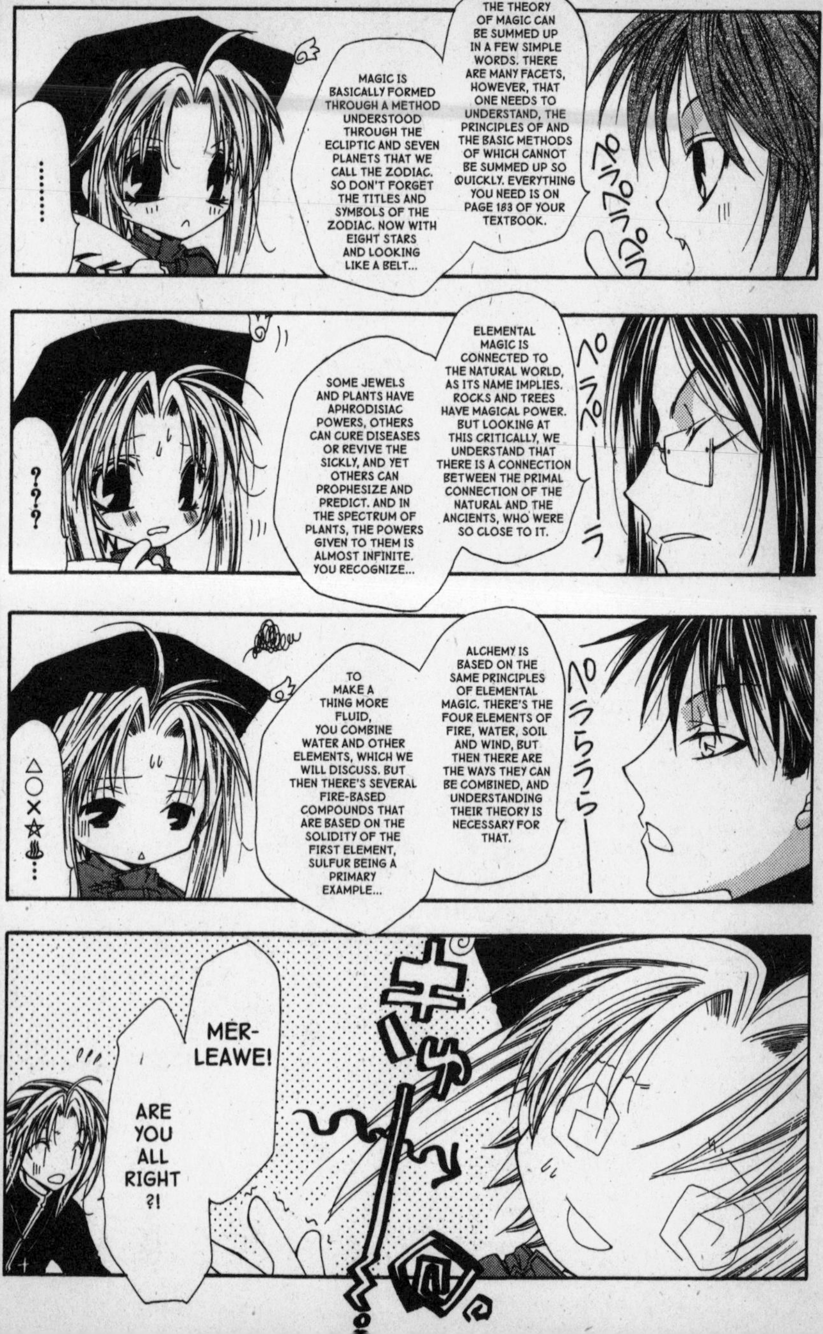
THE THEORY OF MAGIC CAN BE SUMMED UP IN A FEW SIMPLE WORDS. THERE ARE MANY FACETS, HOWEVER, THAT ONE NEEDS TO UNDERSTAND, THE PRINCIPLES OF AND THE BASIC METHODS OF WHICH CANNOT BE SUMMED UP SO QUICKLY. EVERYTHING YOU NEED IS ON PAGE 183 OF YOUR TEXTBOOK.
MAGIC IS BASICALLY FORMED THROUGH A METHOD UNDERSTOOD THROUGH THE ECLIPTIC AND SEVEN PLANETS THAT WE CALL THE ZODIAC. SO DON'T FORGET THE TITLES AND SYMBOLS OF THE ZODIAC. NOW WITH EIGHT STARS AND LOOKING LIKE A BELT...
....
ELEMENTAL MAGIC IS CONNECTED TO THE NATURAL WORLD, AS ITS NAME IMPLIES. ROCKS AND TREES HAVE MAGICAL POWER. BUT LOOKING AT THIS CRITICALLY, WE UNDERSTAND THAT THERE IS A CONNECTION BETWEEN THE PRIMAL CONNECTION OF THE NATURAL AND THE ANCIENTS, WHO WERE SO CLOSE TO IT.
SOME JEWELS AND PLANTS HAVE APHRODISIAC POWERS, OTHERS CAN CURE DISEASES OR REVIVE THE SICKLY, AND YET OTHERS CAN PROPHESIZE AND PREDICT. AND IN THE SPECTRUM OF PLANTS, THE POWERS GIVEN TO THEM IS ALMOST INFINITE. YOU RECOGNIZE...
???
ALCHEMY IS BASED ON THE SAME PRINCIPLES OF ELEMENTAL MAGIC. THERE'S THE FOUR ELEMENTS OF FIRE, WATER, SOIL AND WIND, BUT THEN THERE ARE THE WAYS THEY CAN BE COMBINED, AND UNDERSTANDING THEIR THEORY IS NECESSARY FOR THAT.
TO MAKE A THING MORE FLUID, YOU COMBINE WATER AND OTHER ELEMENTS, WHICH WE WILL DISCUSS. BUT THEN THERE'S SEVERAL FIRE-BASED COMPOUNDS THAT ARE BASED ON THE SOLIDITY OF THE FIRST ELEMENT, SULFUR BEING A PRIMARY EXAMPLE...
△○×☆...
MER-LEAWE!
ARE YOU ALL RIGHT ?!

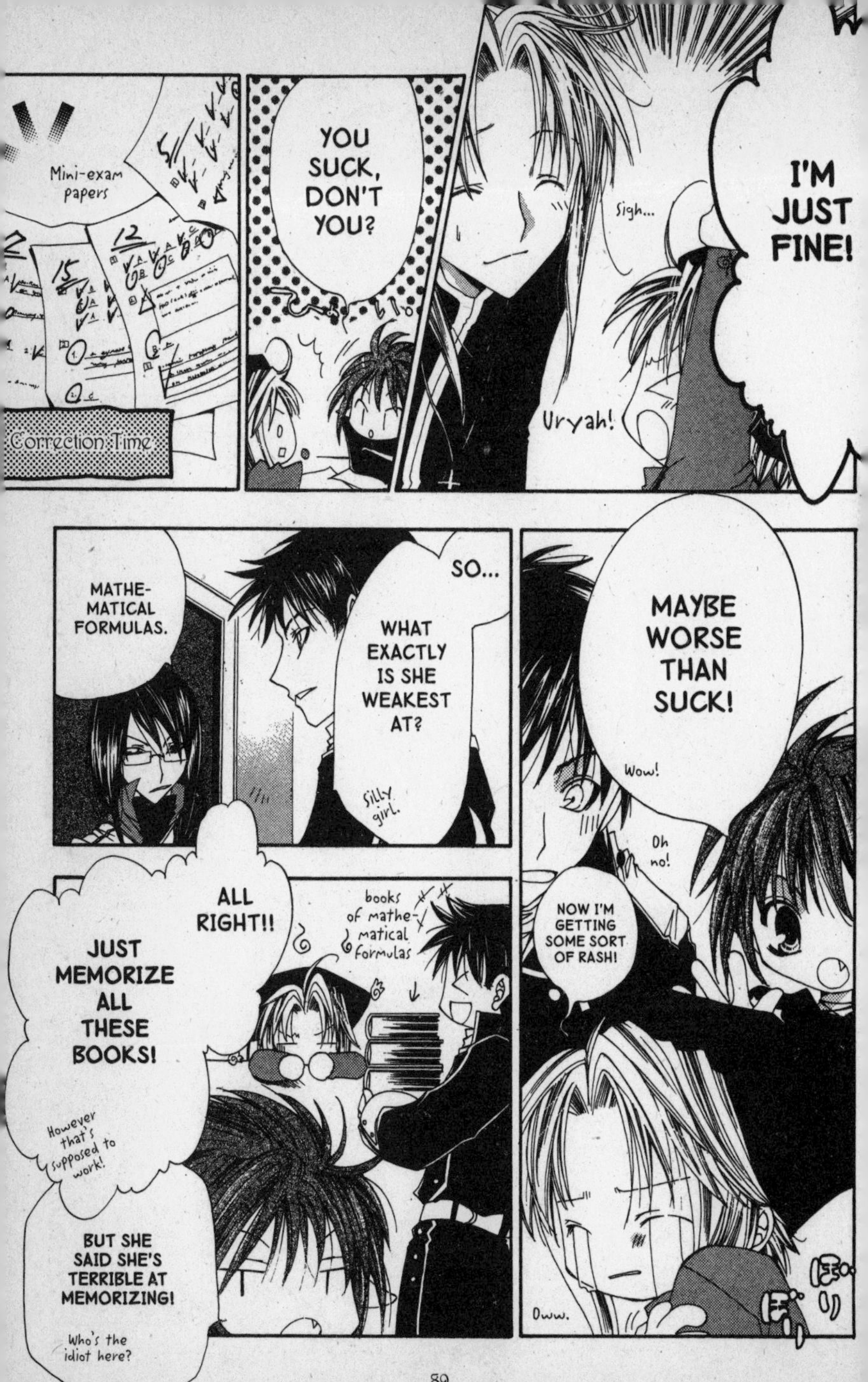
I'M JUST FINE!
Sigh...
Uryah!
YOU SUCK, DON'T YOU?
Mini-exam papers
Correction Time
MAYBE WORSE THAN SUCK!
Wow!
Oh no!
NOW I'M GETTING SOME SORT OF RASH!
Oww.
SO...
WHAT EXACTLY IS SHE WEAKEST AT?
silly girl.
MATHE-MATICAL FORMULAS.
ALL RIGHT!!
books of mathe-matical formulas
JUST MEMORIZE ALL THESE BOOKS!
However that's supposed to work!
BUT SHE SAID SHE'S TERRIBLE AT MEMORIZING!
Who's the idiot here?

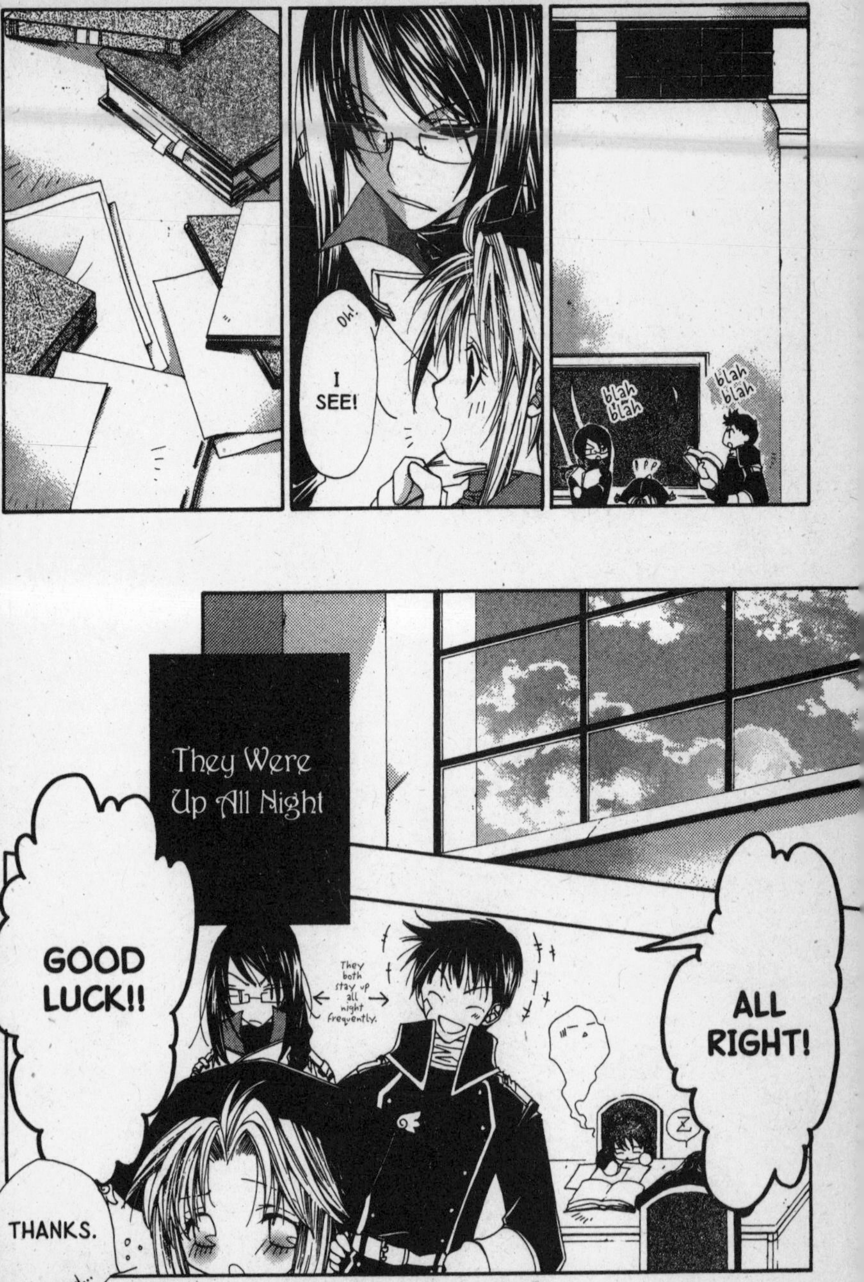

blah blah
blah blah
Oh! I SEE!
They Were Up All Night
ALL RIGHT!
They both stay up all night frequently.
GOOD LUCK!!
THANKS.
Bed...

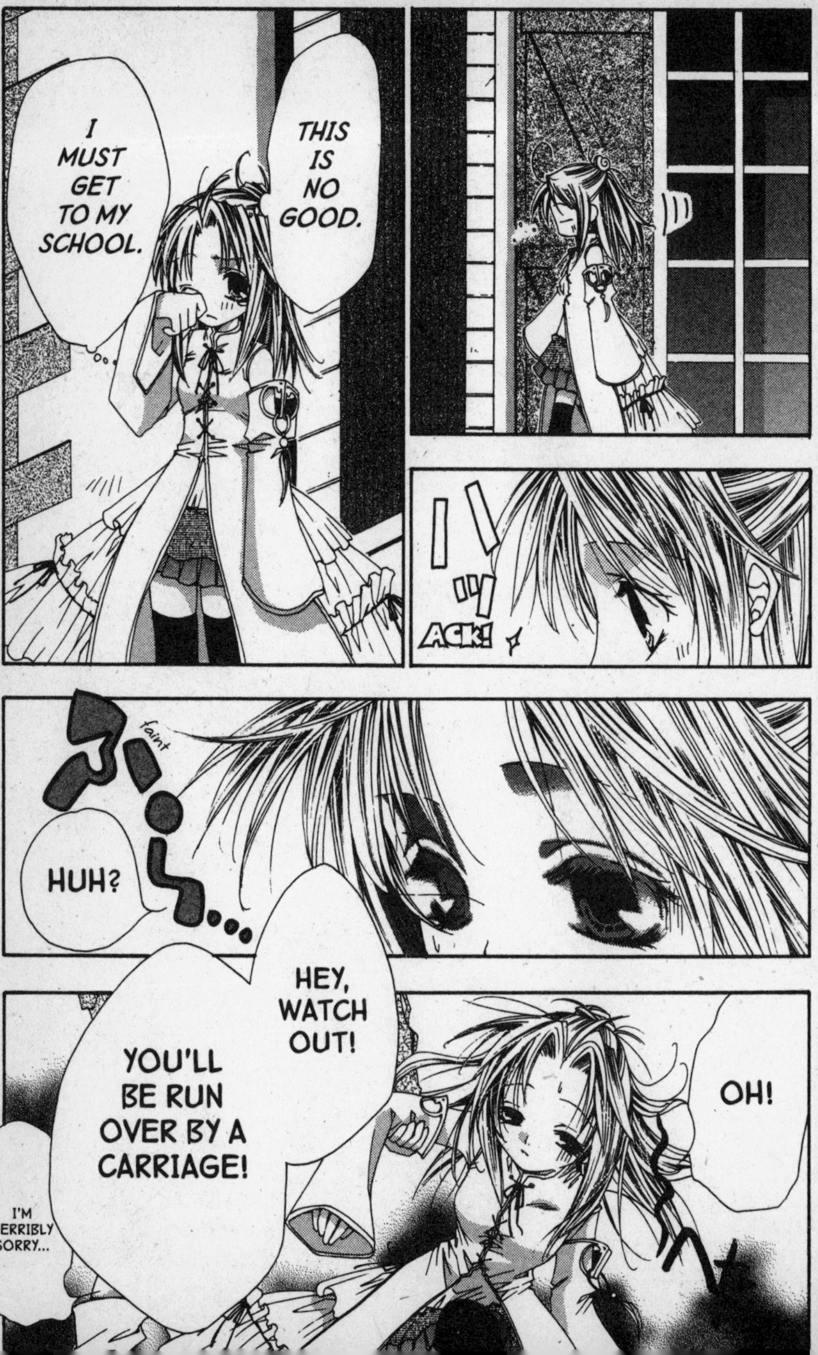
ACK!
THIS IS NO GOOD.
I MUST GET TO MY SCHOOL.
faint
HUH?
OH!
HEY, WATCH OUT!
YOU'LL BE RUN OVER BY A CARRIAGE!
I'M TERRIBLY SORRY...

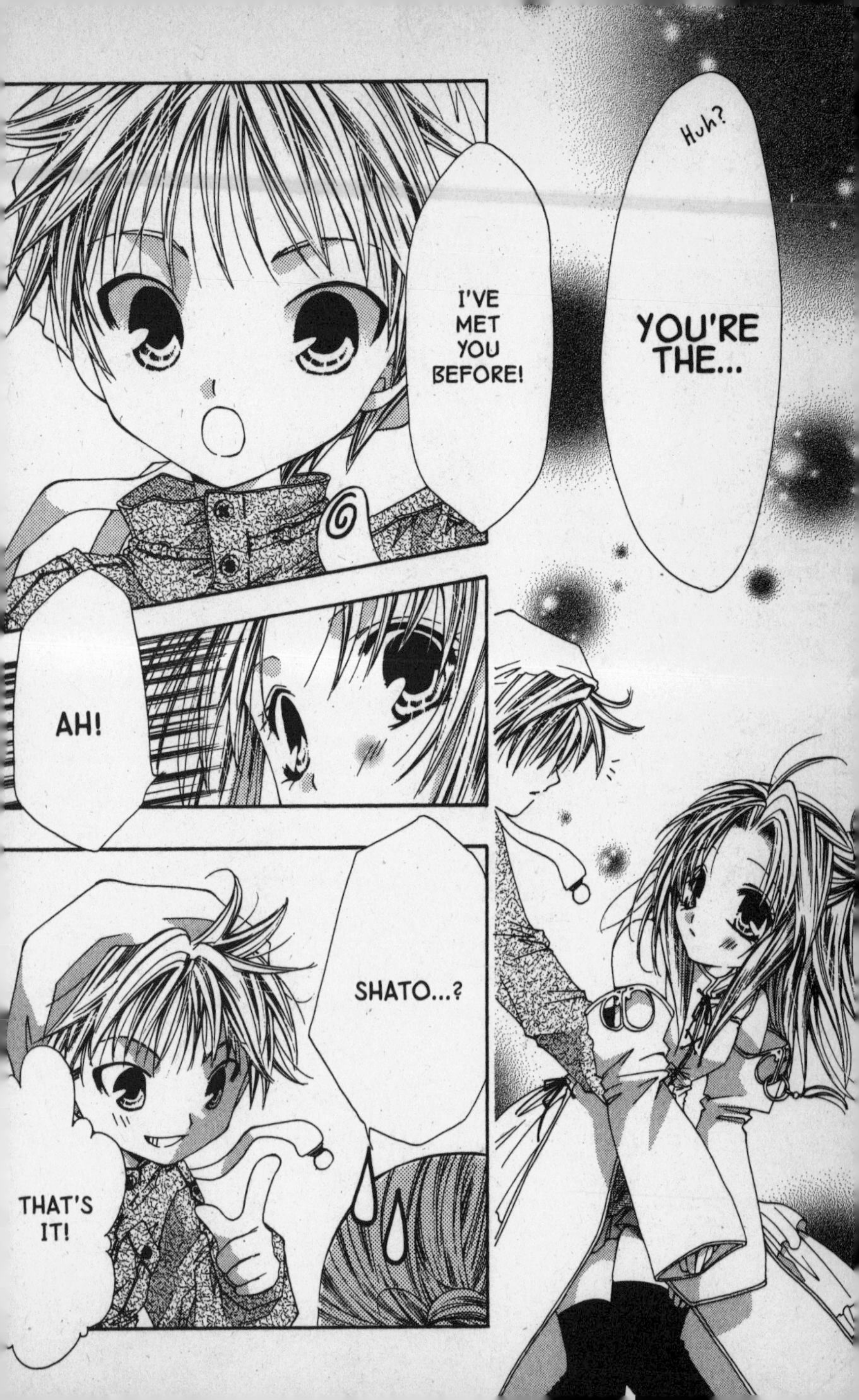
Huh?
YOU'RE THE...
I'VE MET YOU BEFORE!
AH!
SHATO...?
THAT'S IT!

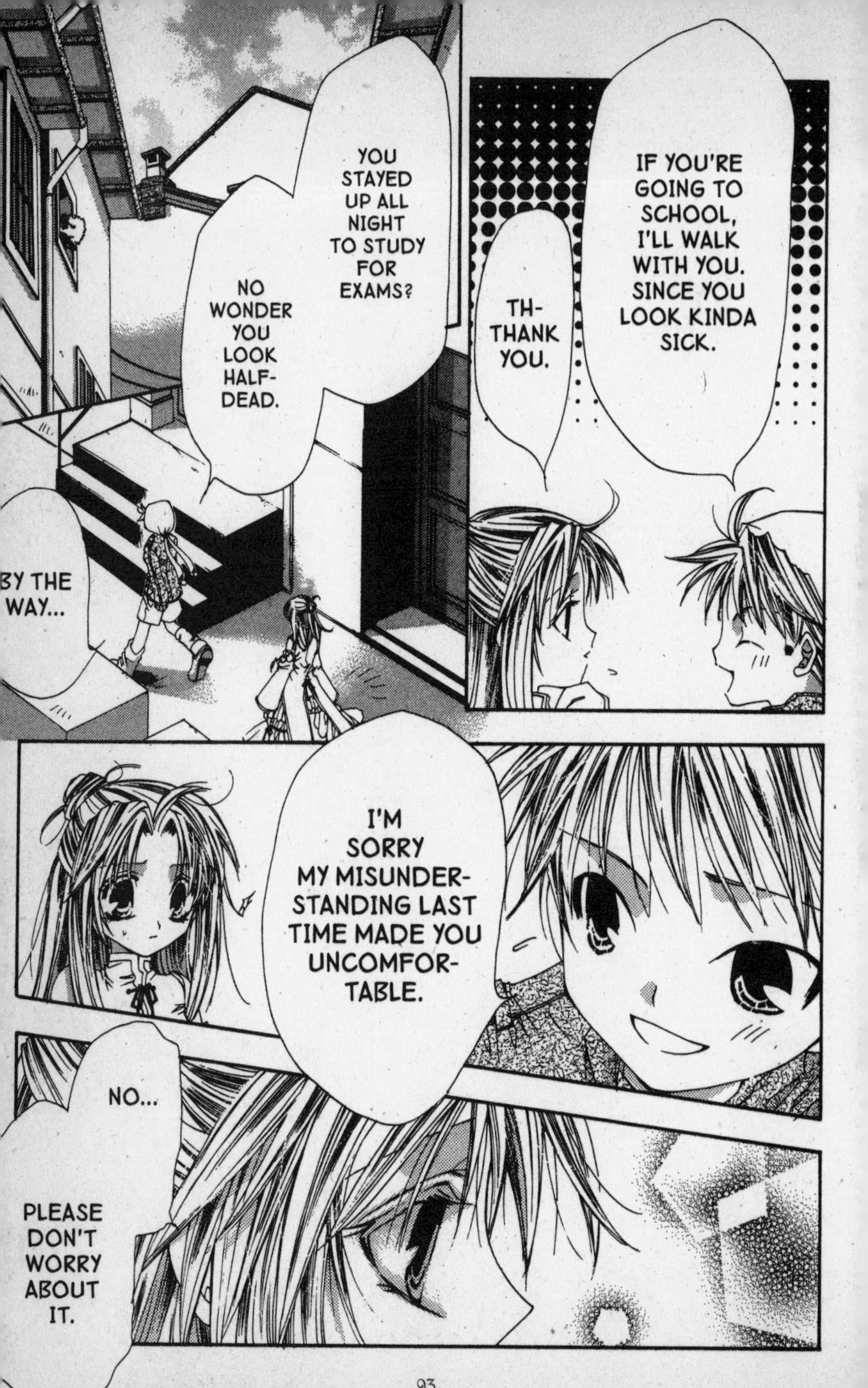
IF YOU'RE GOING TO SCHOOL, I'LL WALK WITH YOU. SINCE YOU LOOK KINDA SICK.
TH- THANK YOU.
YOU STAYED UP ALL NIGHT TO STUDY FOR EXAMS?
NO WONDER YOU LOOK HALF-DEAD.
BY THE WAY...
I'M SORRY MY MISUNDER-STANDING LAST TIME MADE YOU UNCOMFOR-TABLE.
NO...
PLEASE DON'T WORRY ABOUT IT.

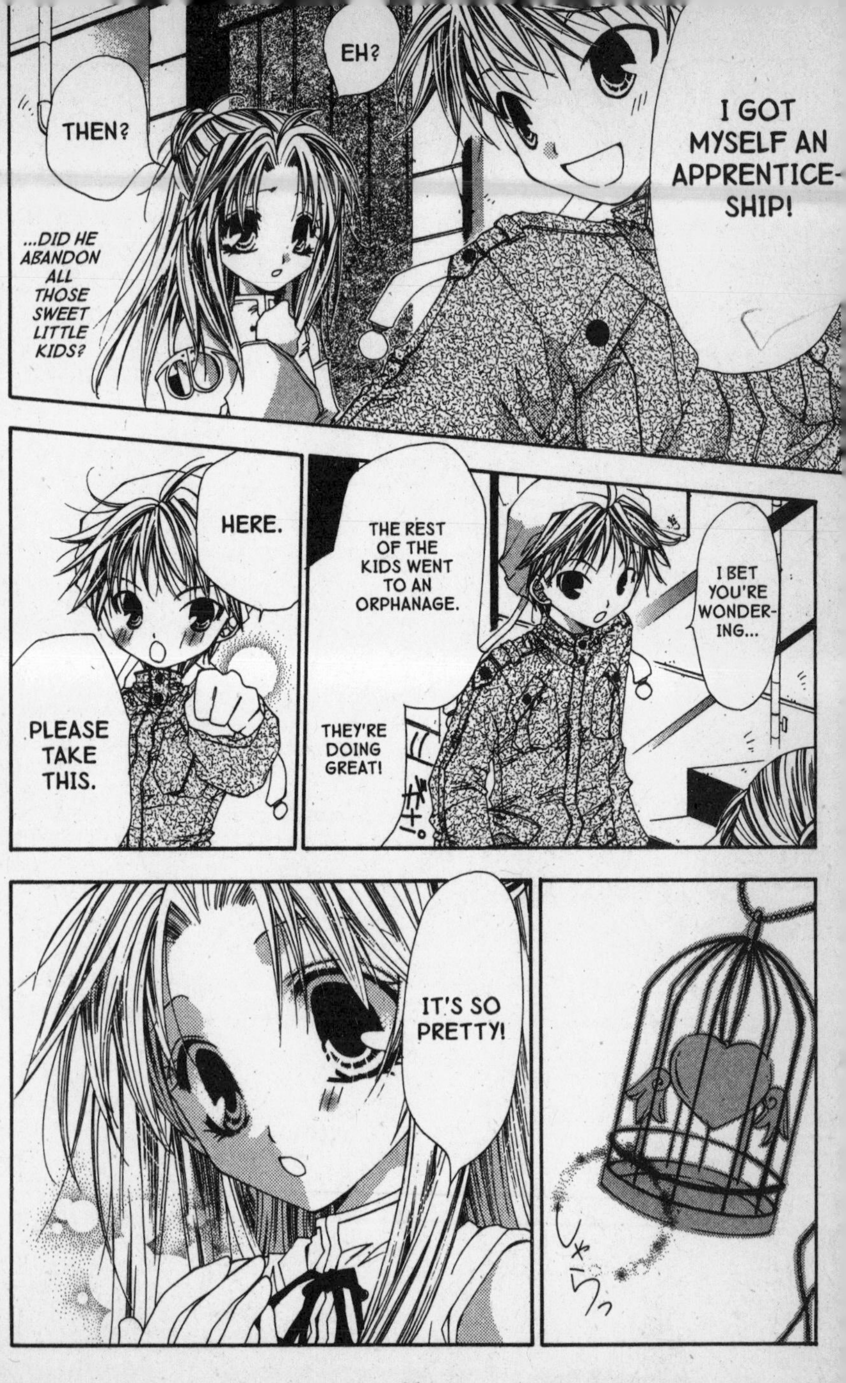

I GOT MYSELF AN APPRENTICE-SHIP!
EH?
THEN?
...DID HE ABANDON ALL THOSE SWEET LITTLE KIDS?
I BET YOU'RE WONDER-ING...
THE REST OF THE KIDS WENT TO AN ORPHANAGE.
THEY'RE DOING GREAT!
HERE.
PLEASE TAKE THIS.
しゃらっ
IT'S SO PRETTY!

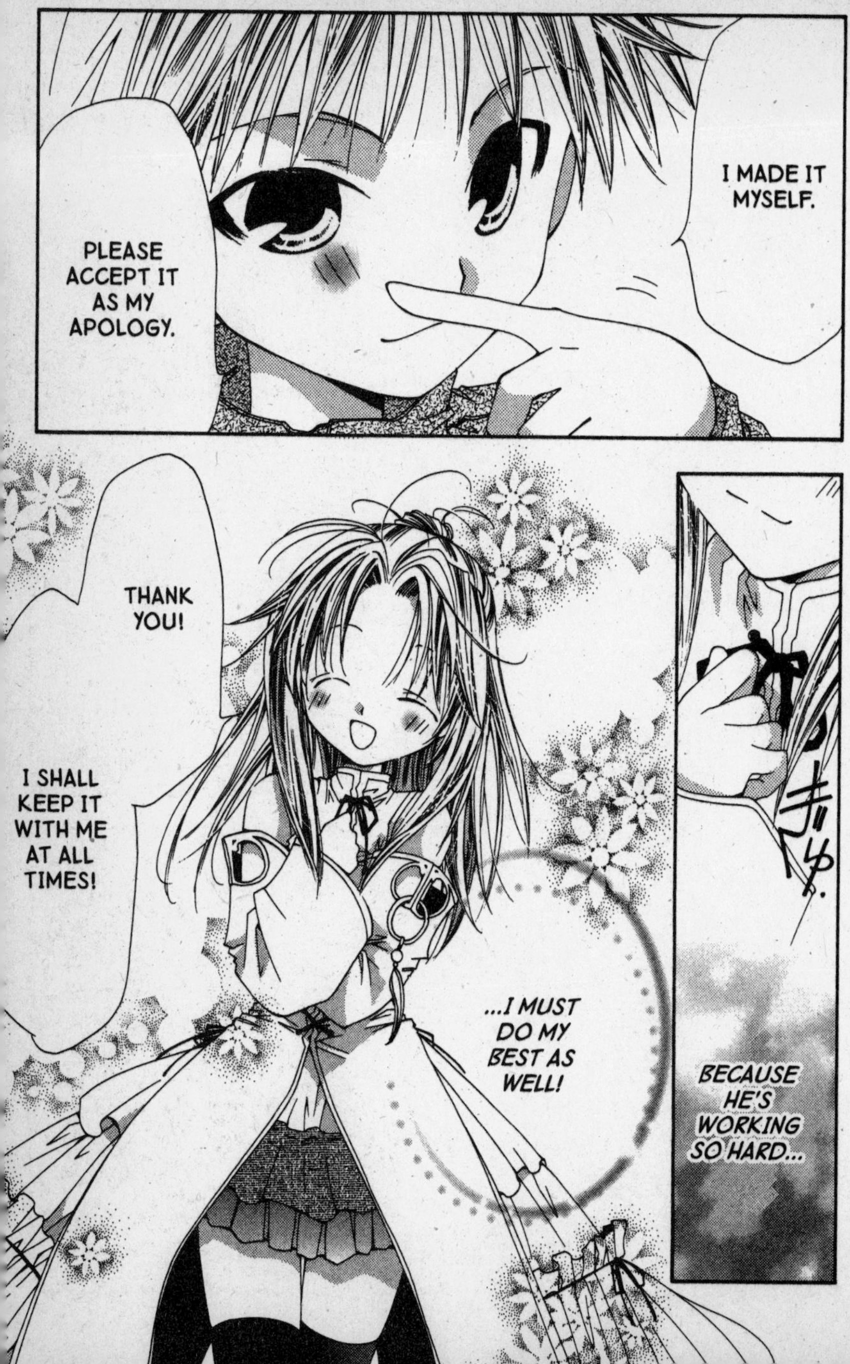
I MADE IT MYSELF.
PLEASE ACCEPT IT AS MY APOLOGY.
BECAUSE HE'S WORKING SO HARD...
...I MUST DO MY BEST AS WELL!
THANK YOU!
I SHALL KEEP IT WITH ME AT ALL TIMES!

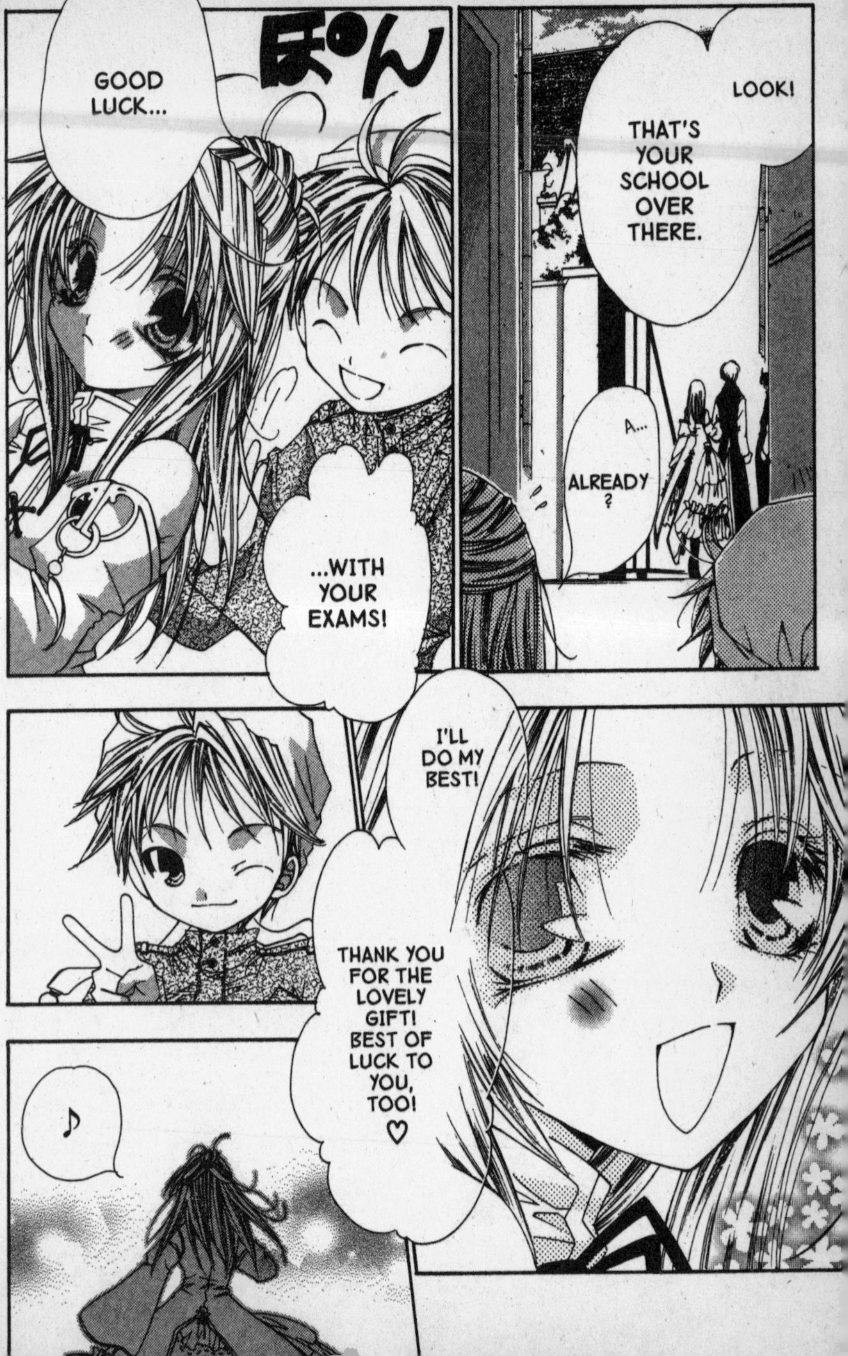
LOOK!
THAT'S YOUR SCHOOL OVER THERE.
A... ALREADY?
ぽん
GOOD LUCK...
...WITH YOUR EXAMS!
I'LL DO MY BEST!
THANK YOU FOR THE LOVELY GIFT! BEST OF LUCK TO YOU, TOO! ♡
♪

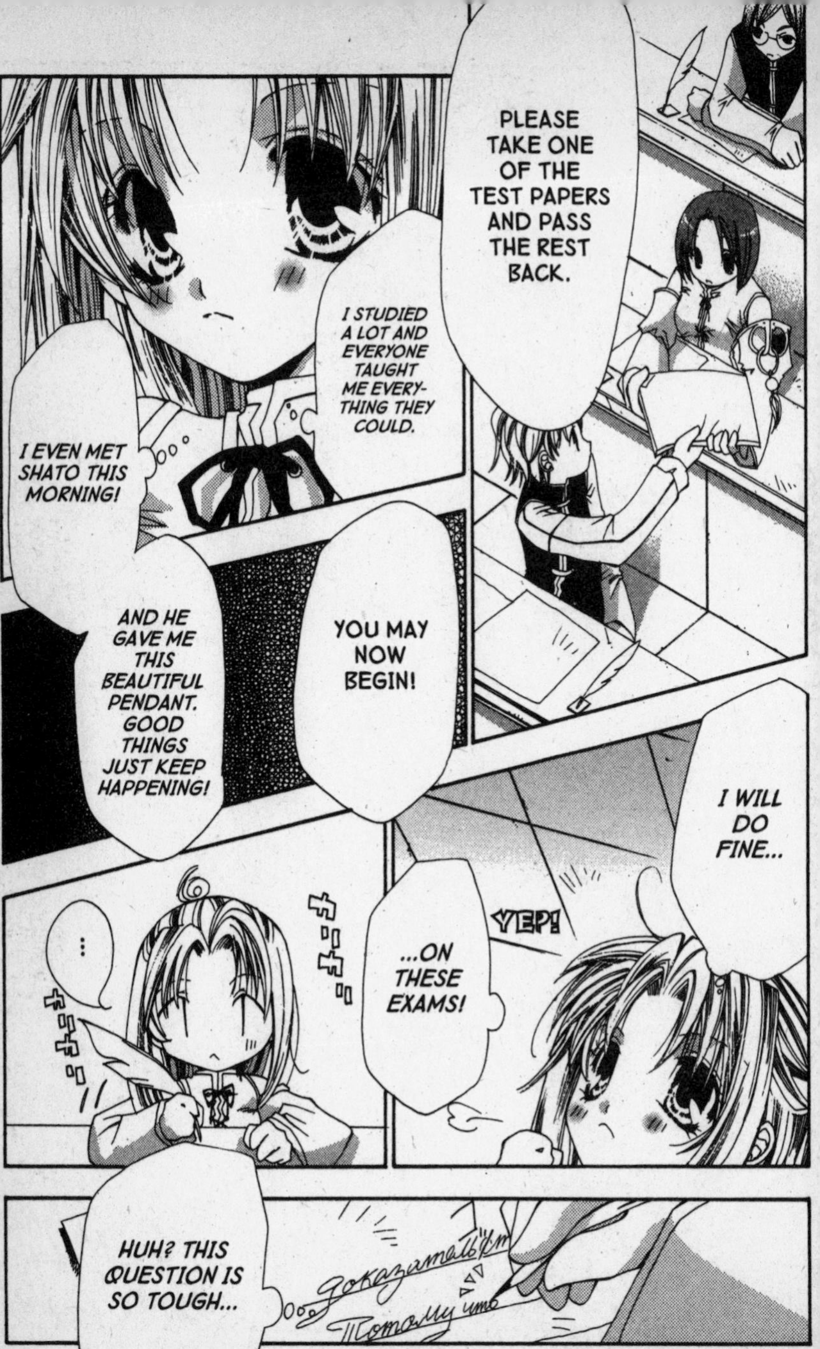
PLEASE TAKE ONE OF THE TEST PAPERS AND PASS THE REST BACK.
I STUDIED A LOT AND EVERYONE TAUGHT ME EVERY-THING THEY COULD.
I EVEN MET SHATO THIS MORNING!
AND HE GAVE ME THIS BEAUTIFUL PENDANT. GOOD THINGS JUST KEEP HAPPENING!
YOU MAY NOW BEGIN!
I WILL DO FINE...
YEP!
...ON THESE EXAMS!
...
HUH? THIS QUESTION IS SO TOUGH...

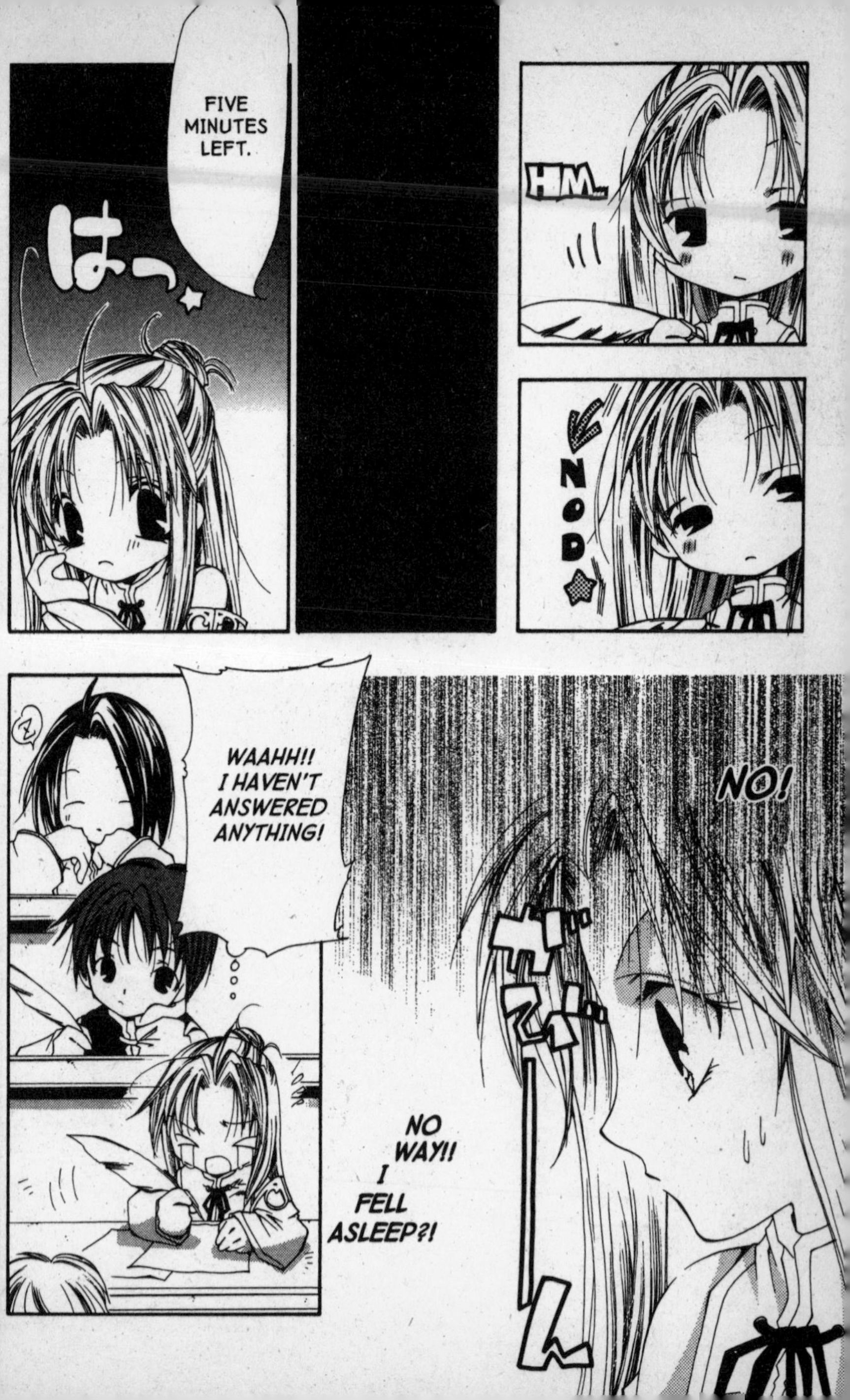
HM...
NOD
FIVE MINUTES LEFT.
はっ
NO!
NO WAY!! I FELL ASLEEP?!
WAAHH!! I HAVEN'T ANSWERED ANYTHING!

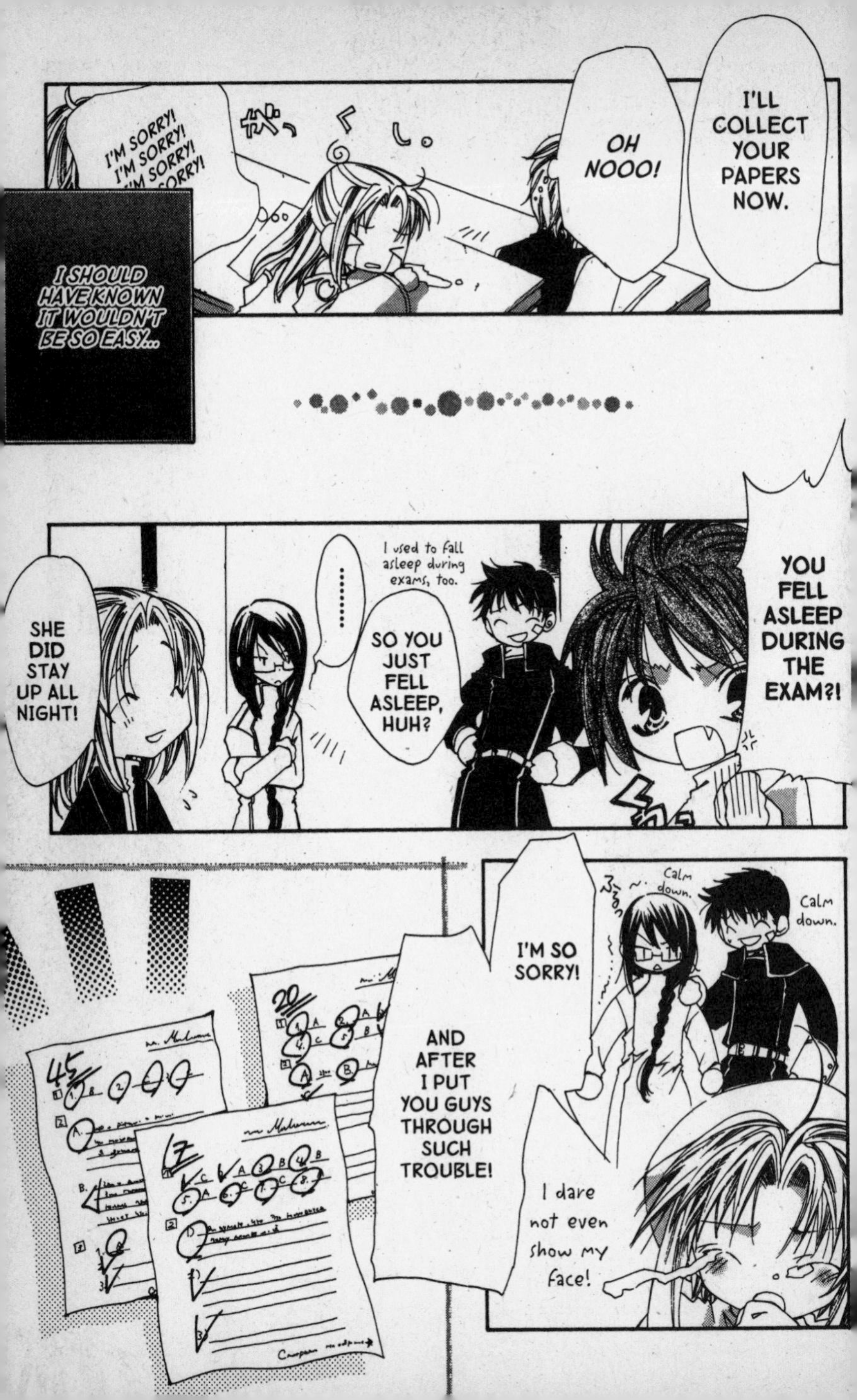
I'LL COLLECT YOUR PAPERS NOW.
OH NOOO!
I'M SORRY! I'M SORRY! I'M SORRY!
I SHOULD HAVE KNOWN IT WOULDN'T BE SO EASY...
YOU FELL ASLEEP DURING THE EXAM?!
I used to fall asleep during exams, too.
SO YOU JUST FELL ASLEEP, HUH?
......
SHE DID STAY UP ALL NIGHT!
Calm down.
Calm down.
I'M SO SORRY!
AND AFTER I PUT YOU GUYS THROUGH SUCH TROUBLE!
I dare not even show my face!

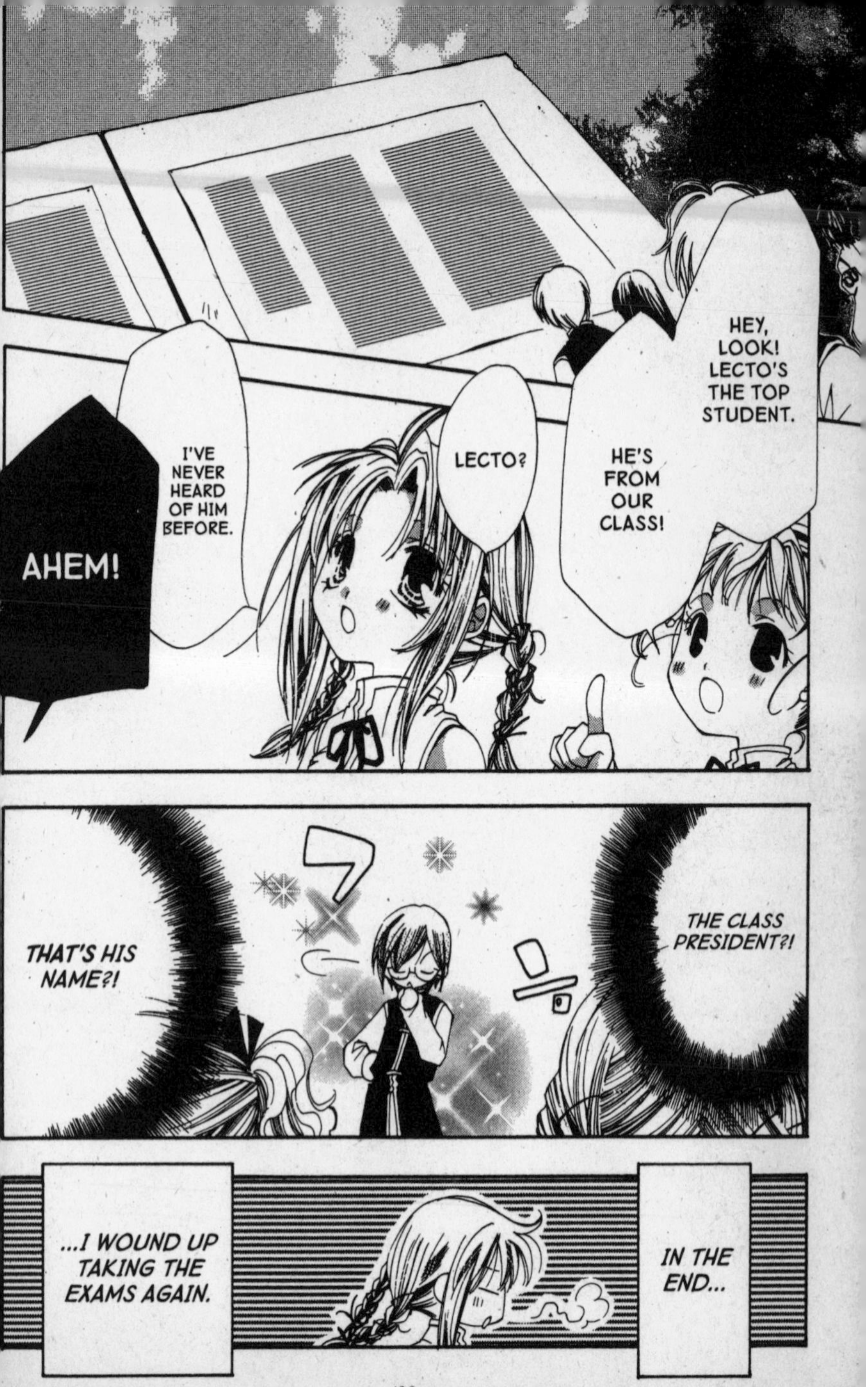
HEY, LOOK! LECTO'S THE TOP STUDENT.
HE'S FROM OUR CLASS!
LECTO?
I'VE NEVER HEARD OF HIM BEFORE.
AHEM!
THE CLASS PRESIDENT?!
THAT'S HIS NAME?!
IN THE END...
...I WOUND UP TAKING THE EXAMS AGAIN.

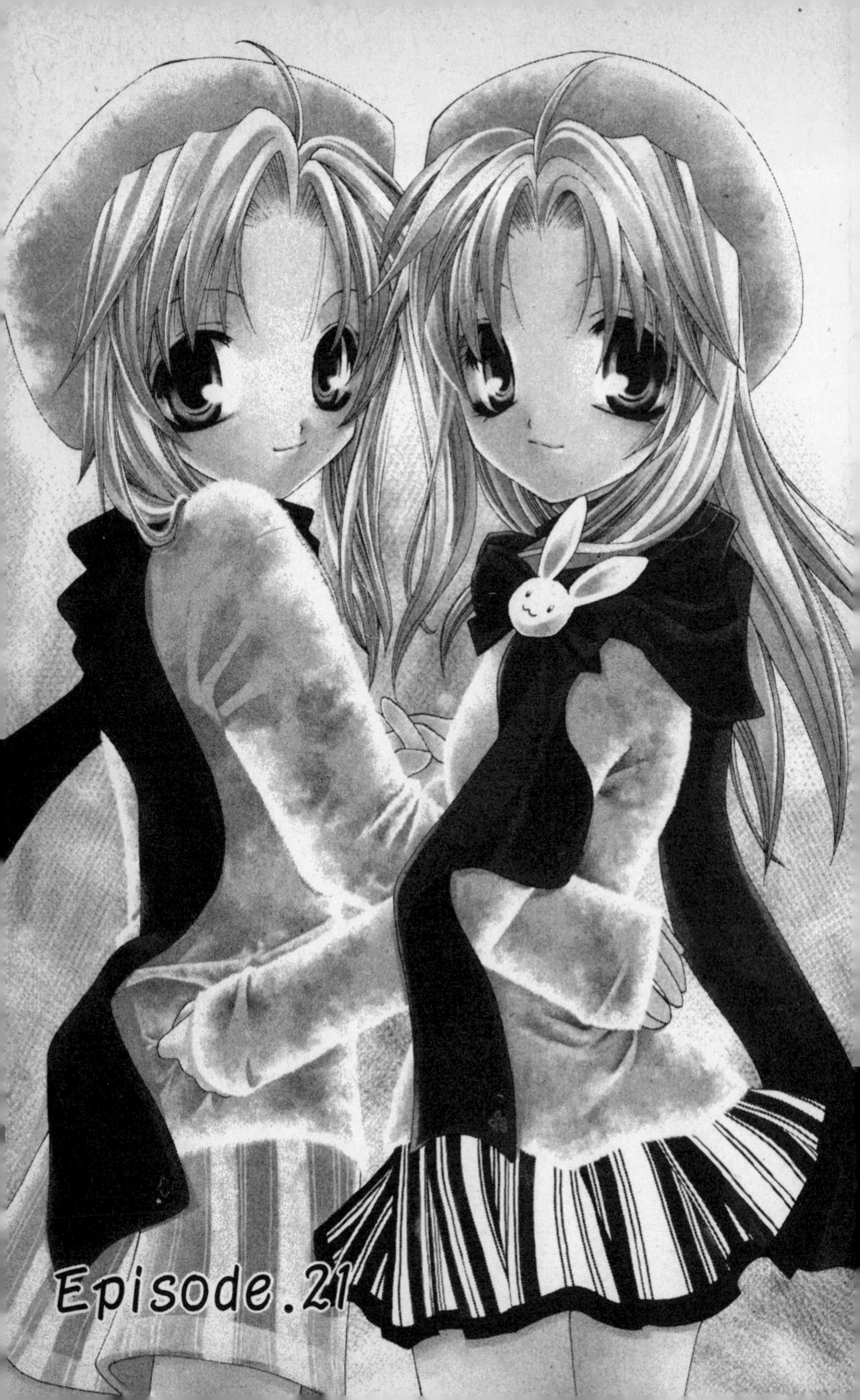
Episode.21

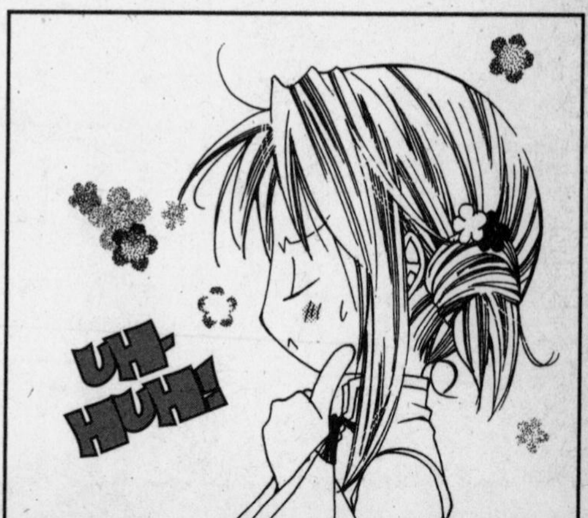
UH-HUH!

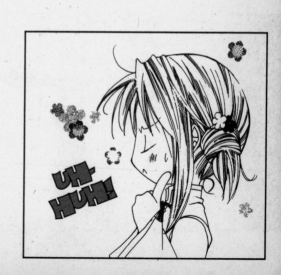

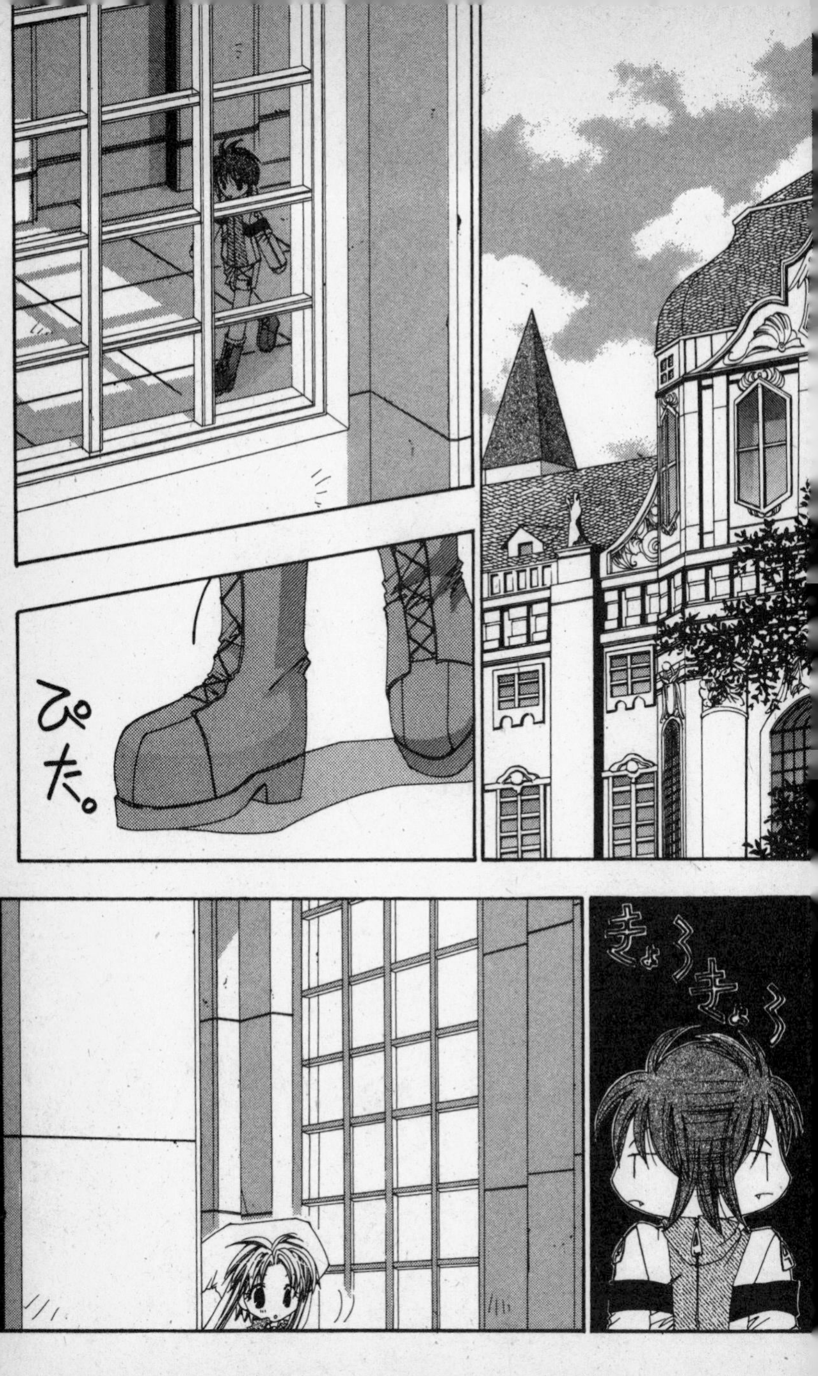
ぴた。
きょろきょろ

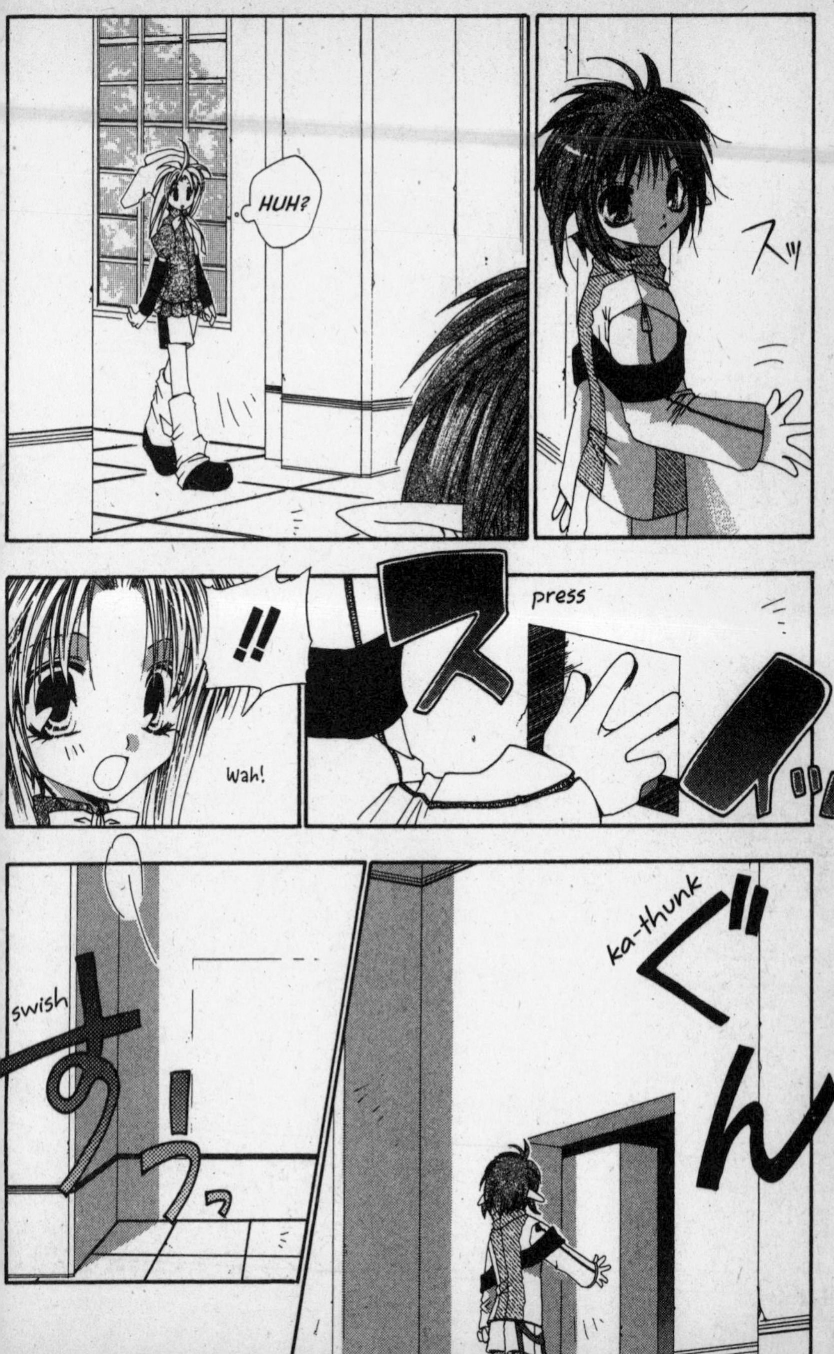

スッ
HUH?
press
!!
Wah!
ka-thunk
ぐん
swish
すっ
!

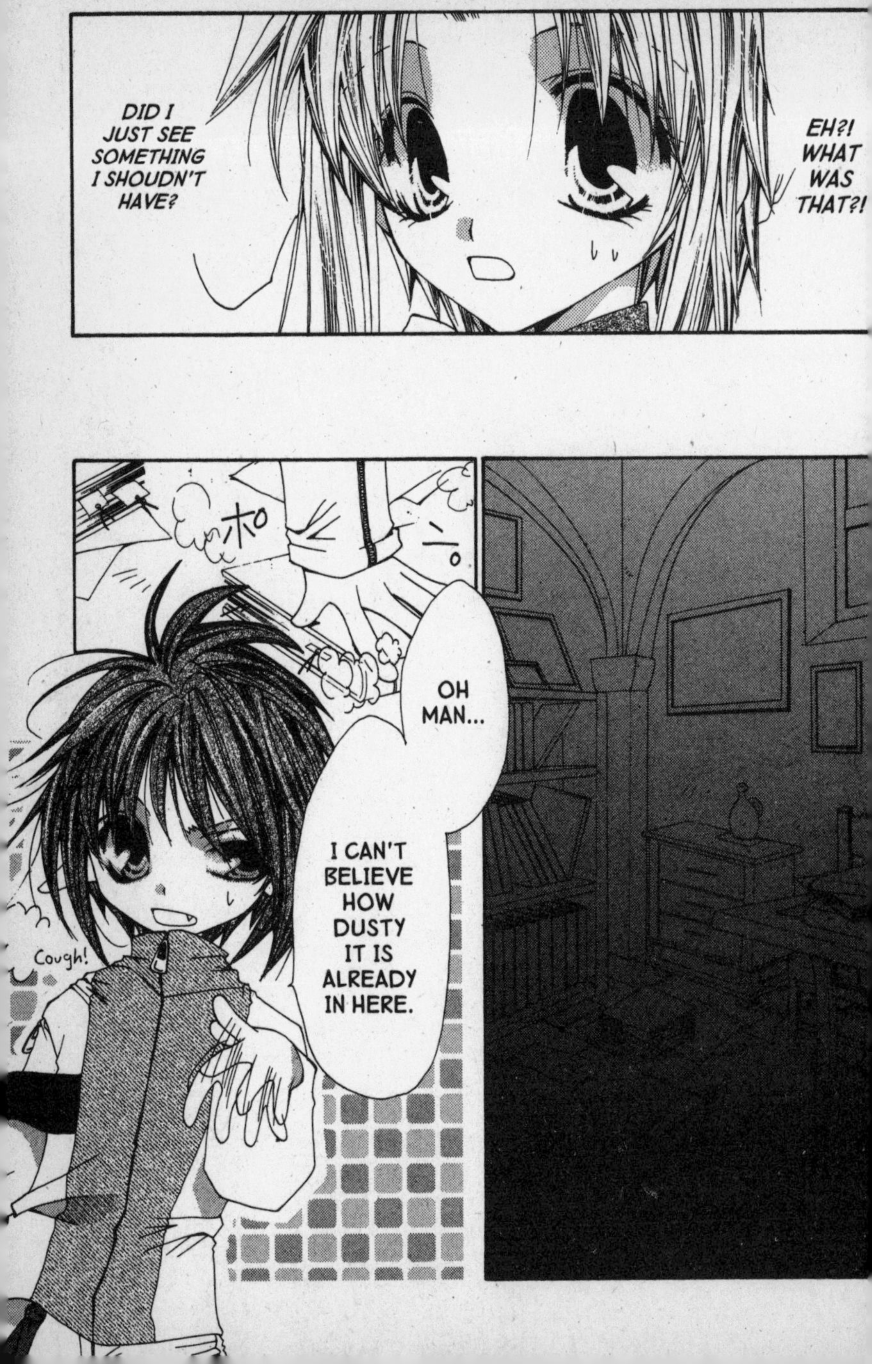
EH?! WHAT WAS THAT?!
DID I JUST SEE SOMETHING I SHOUDN'T HAVE?
OH MAN...
I CAN'T BELIEVE HOW DUSTY IT IS ALREADY IN HERE.
Cough!

OKAY!

LET'S DO THIS!

FERN?

WHAT?!

MEL!

HOW DID YOU--?!

I-I...

GAH! I'M BUSTED.

SHOULD I...

...HAVE NOT COME HERE?

...ool! You ...uld have ...en more ...areful!

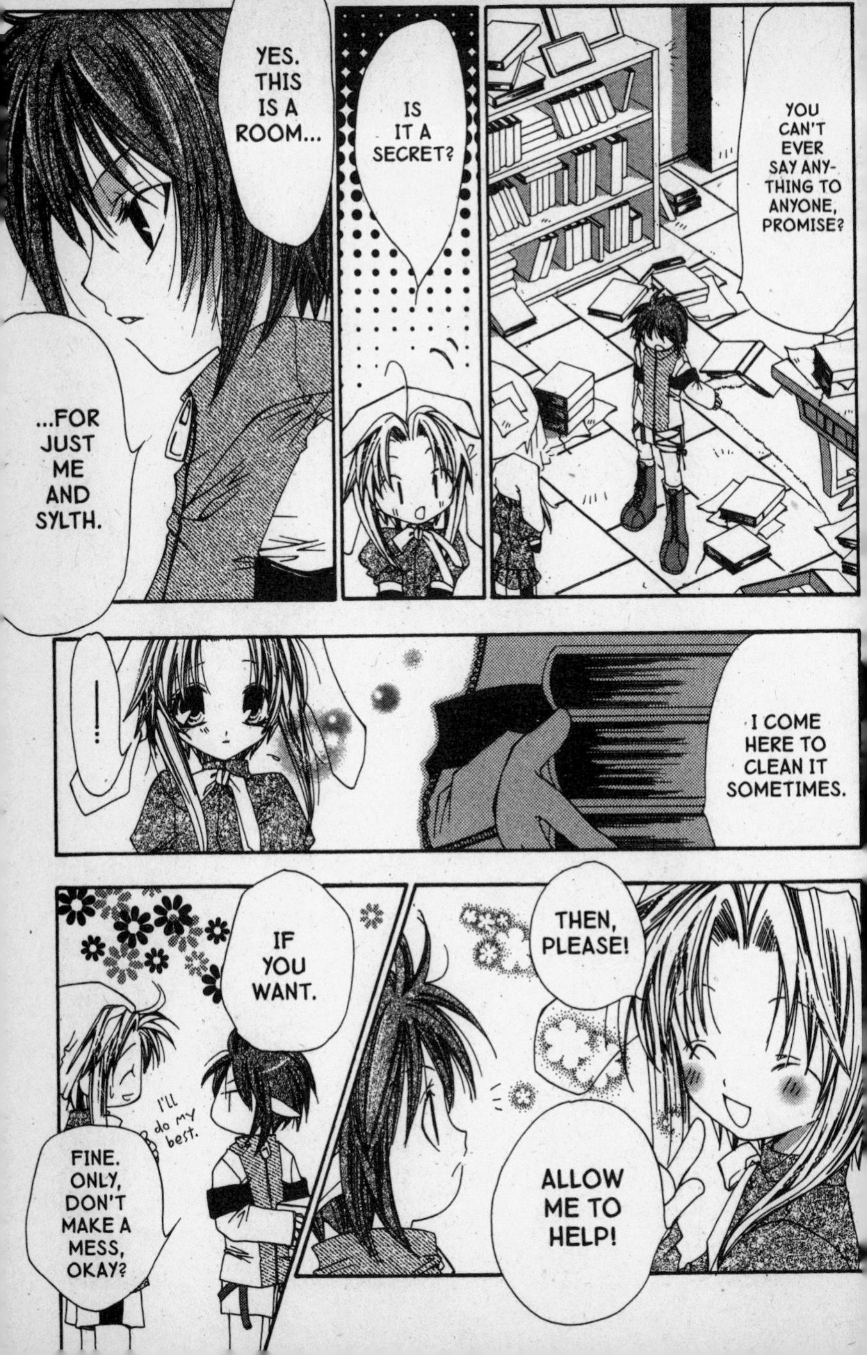
YOU CAN'T EVER SAY ANY-THING TO ANYONE, PROMISE?
IS IT A SECRET?
YES. THIS IS A ROOM...
...FOR JUST ME AND SYLTH.
I COME HERE TO CLEAN IT SOMETIMES.
...!
THEN, PLEASE!
ALLOW ME TO HELP!
IF YOU WANT.
I'll do my best.
FINE. ONLY, DON'T MAKE A MESS, OKAY?

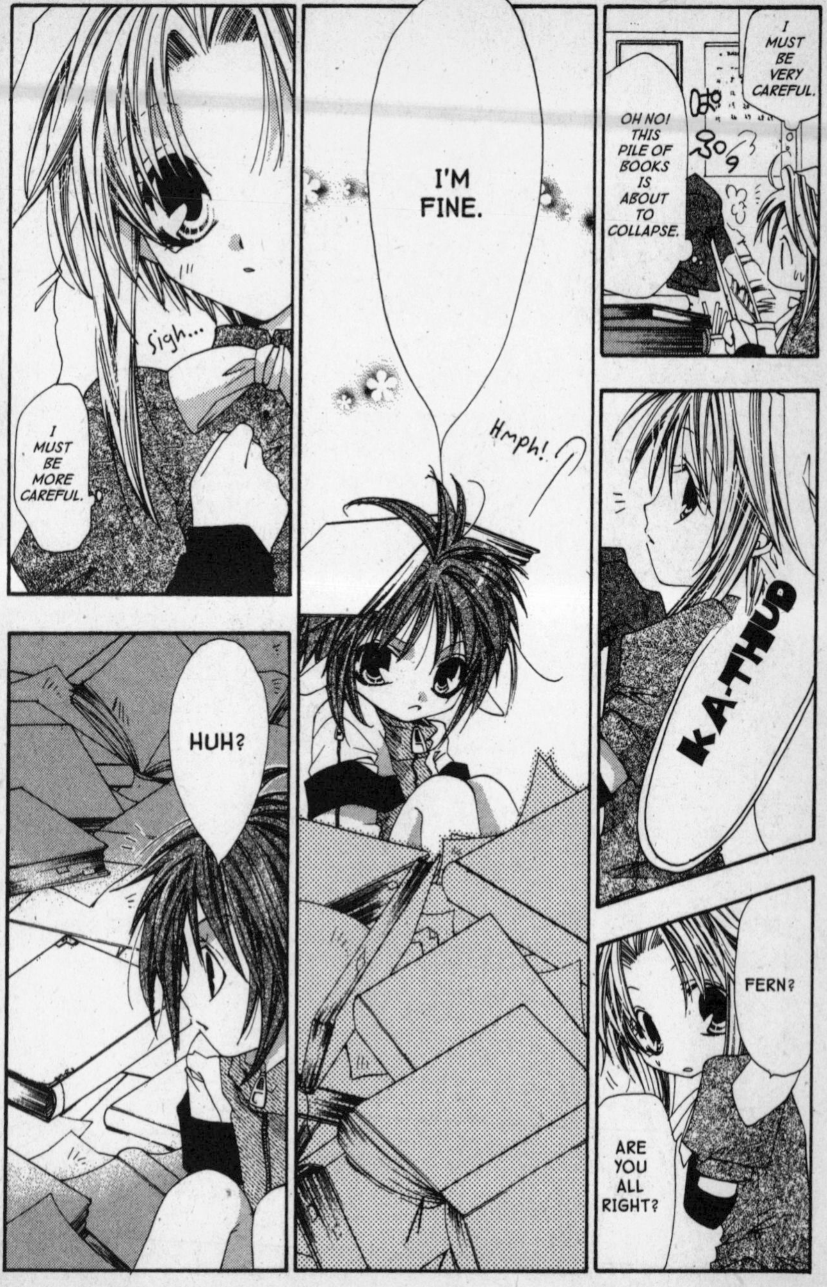

I MUST BE VERY CAREFUL.
OH NO! THIS PILE OF BOOKS IS ABOUT TO COLLAPSE.
KA-THUD
FERN?
ARE YOU ALL RIGHT?
I'M FINE.
Hmph!
Sigh...
I MUST BE MORE CAREFUL.
HUH?

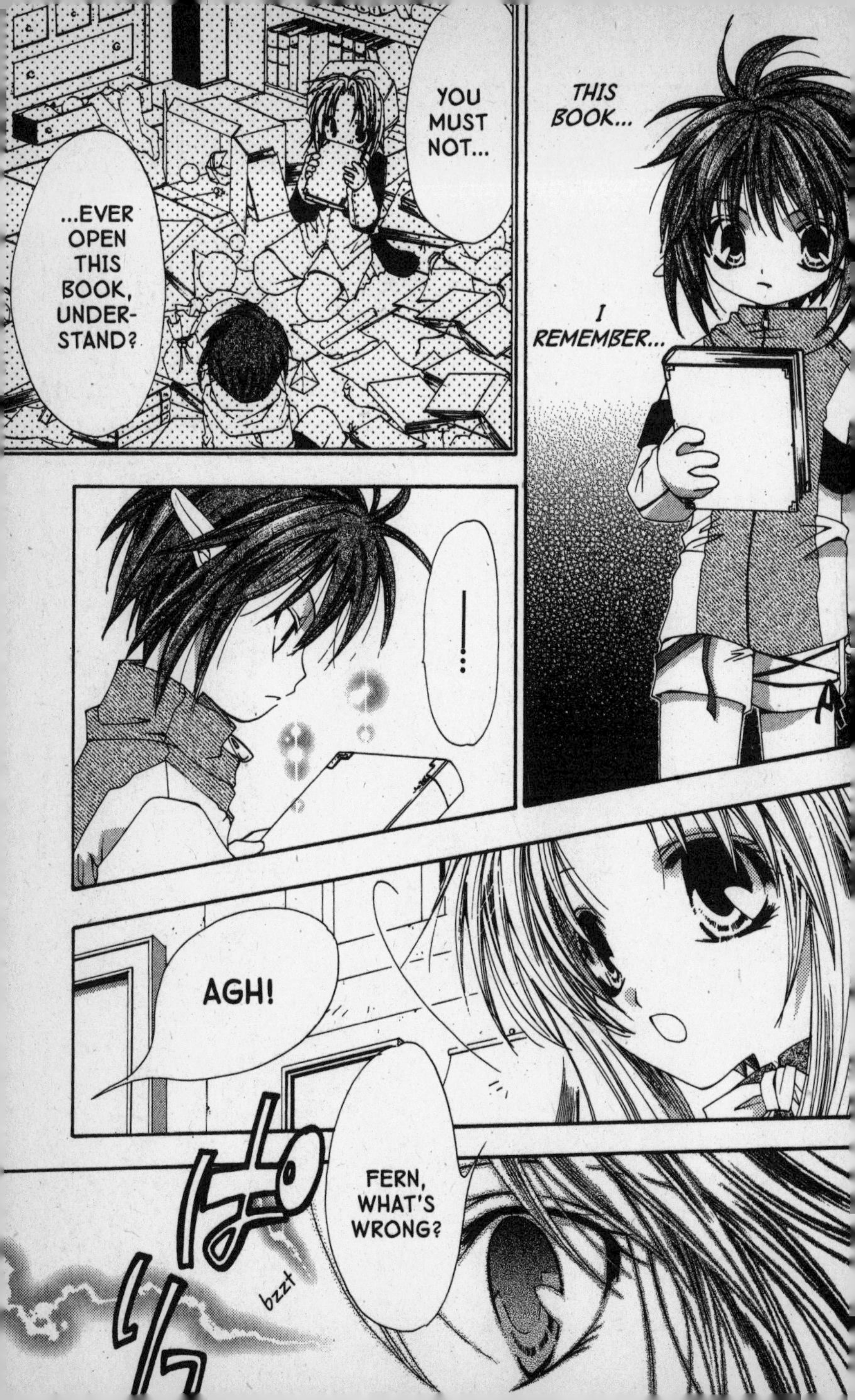
THIS BOOK...
I REMEMBER...
YOU MUST NOT...
...EVER OPEN THIS BOOK, UNDERSTAND?
!...
AGH!
FERN, WHAT'S WRONG?
bzzt

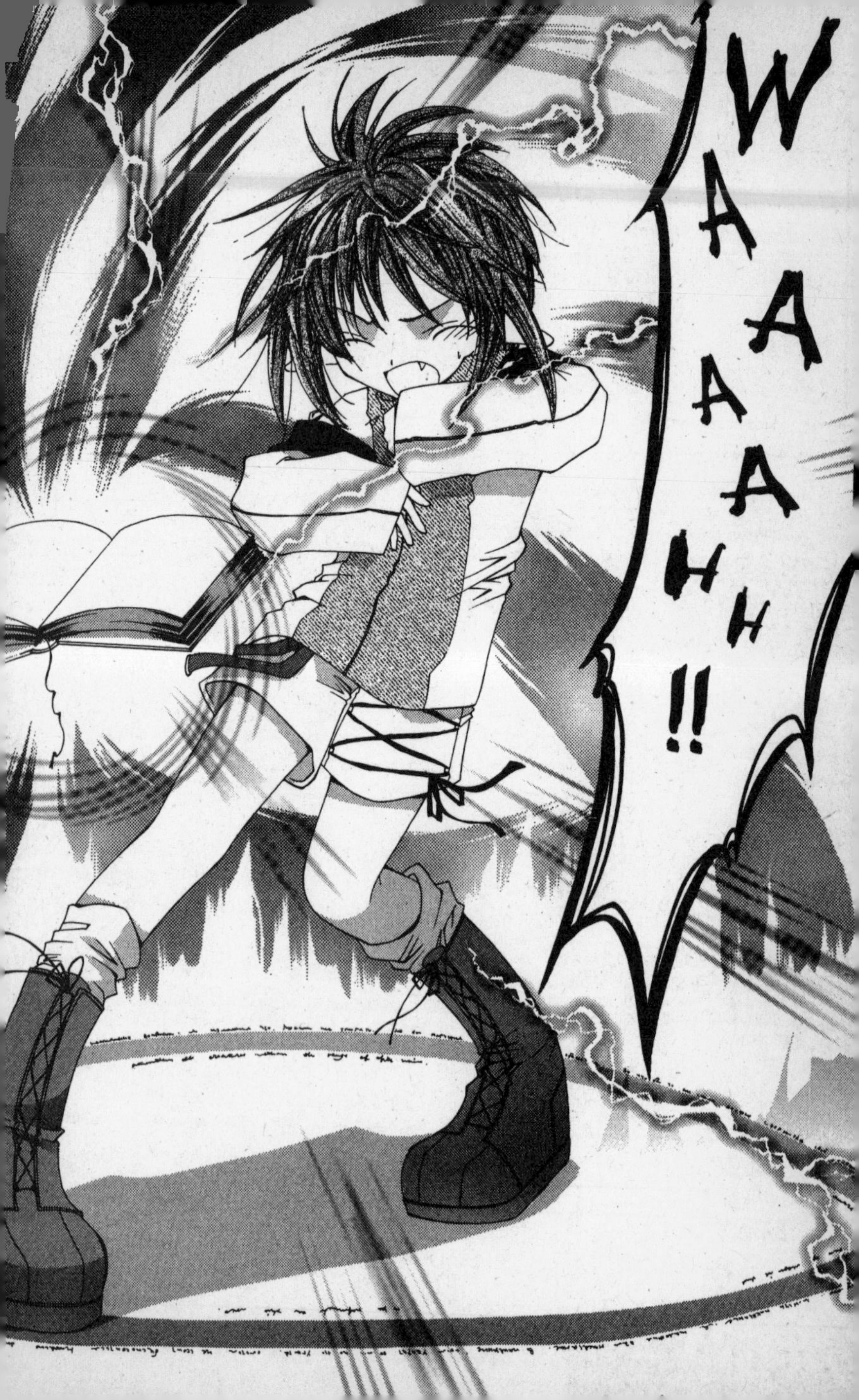
WAAAAAHH!!

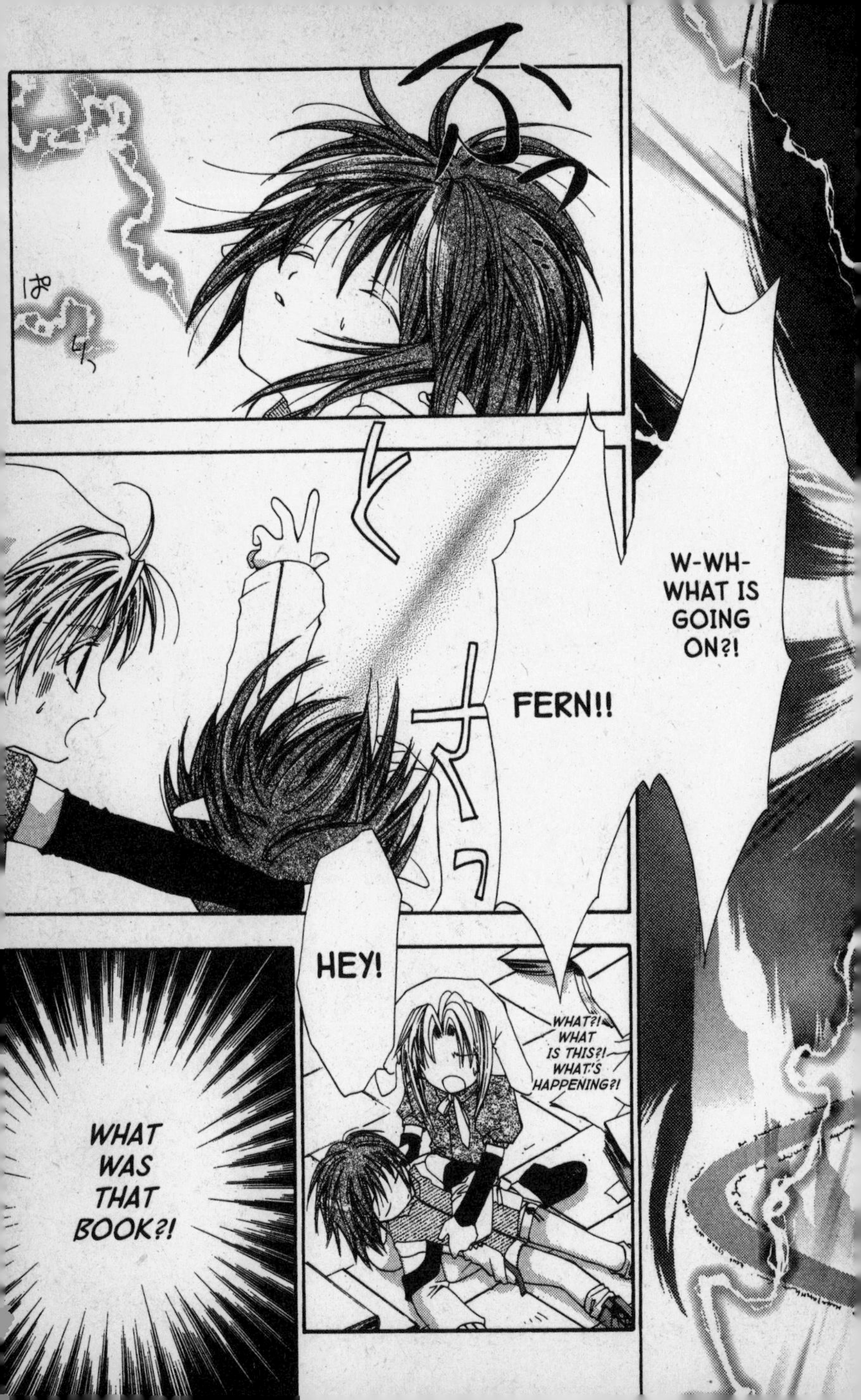
W-WH- WHAT IS GOING ON?!
FERN!!
HEY!
WHAT?! WHAT IS THIS?! WHAT'S HAPPENING?!
WHAT WAS THAT BOOK?!

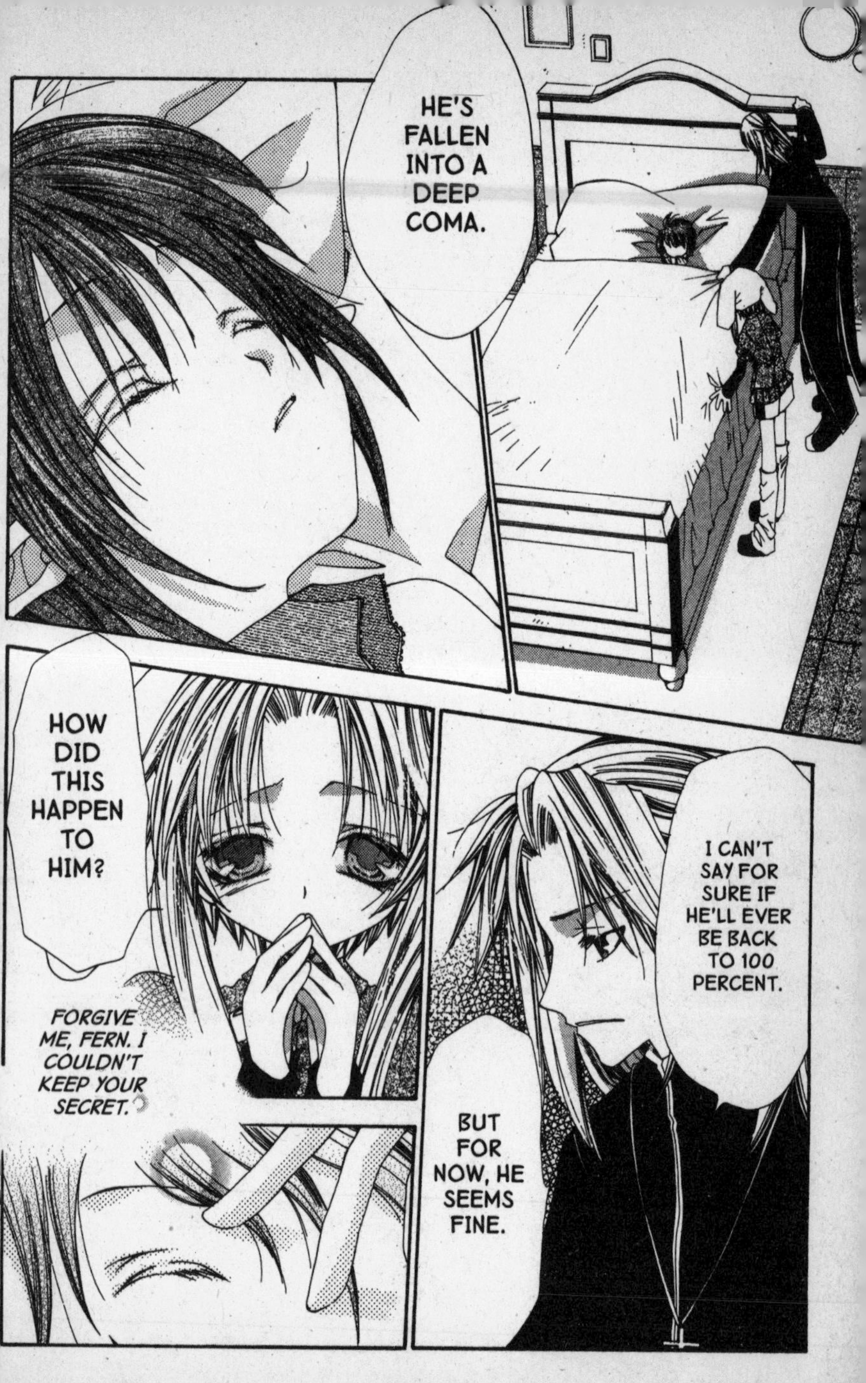
HE'S FALLEN INTO A DEEP COMA.
I CAN'T SAY FOR SURE IF HE'LL EVER BE BACK TO 100 PERCENT.
BUT FOR NOW, HE SEEMS FINE.
HOW DID THIS HAPPEN TO HIM?
FORGIVE ME, FERN. I COULDN'T KEEP YOUR SECRET.

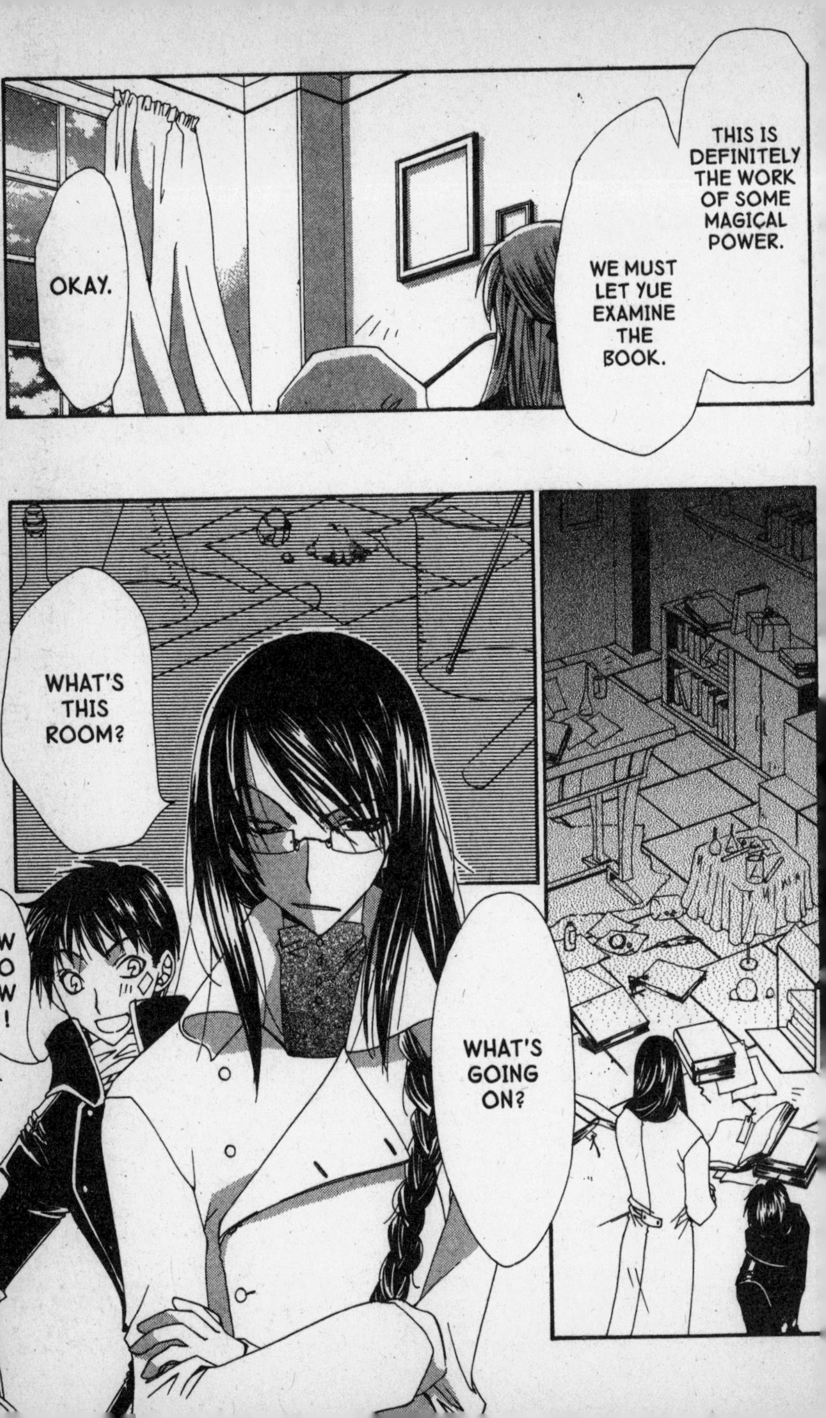
THIS IS DEFINITELY THE WORK OF SOME MAGICAL POWER.
WE MUST LET YUE EXAMINE THE BOOK.
OKAY.
WHAT'S THIS ROOM?
WHAT'S GOING ON?
WOW!

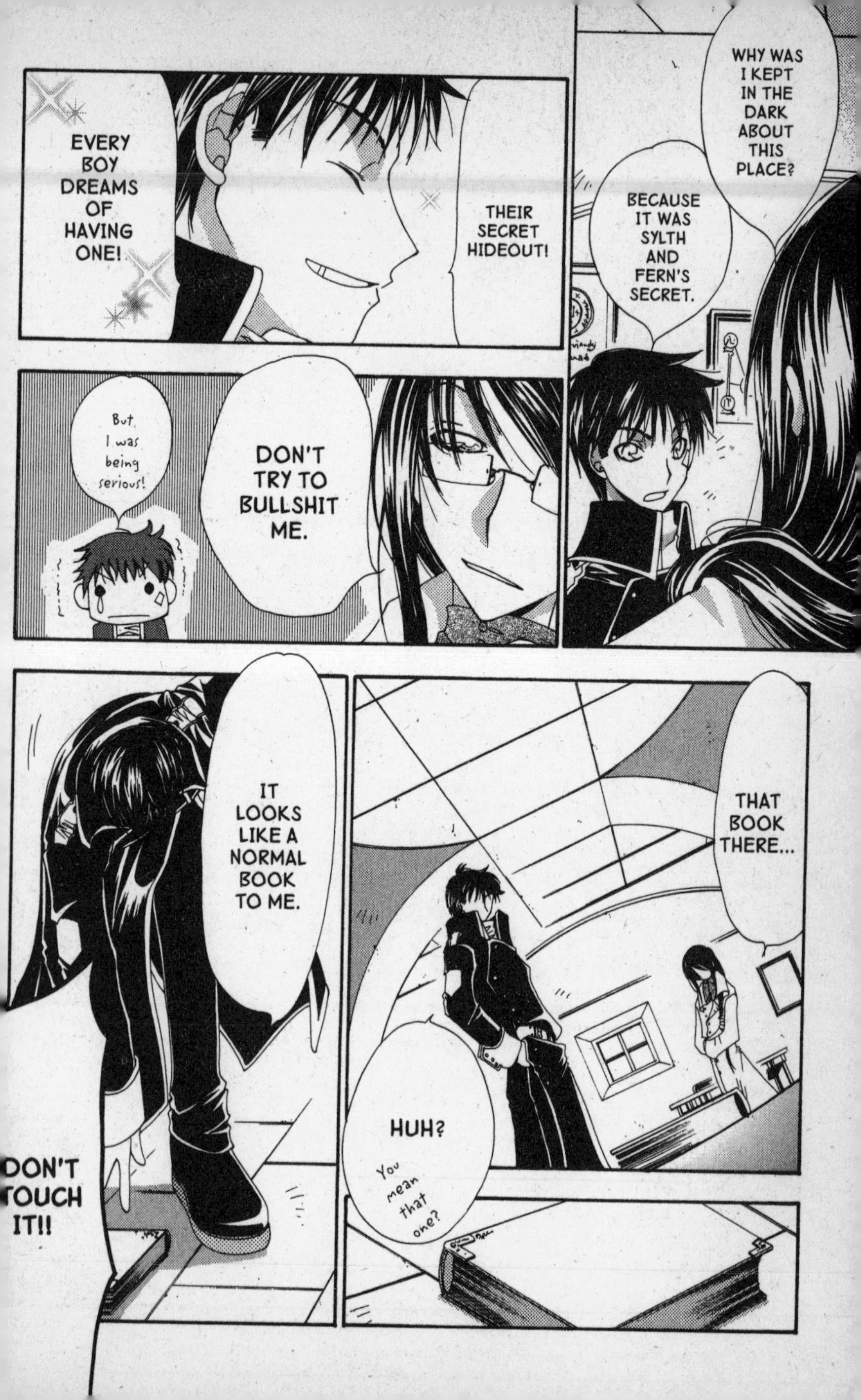
WHY WAS I KEPT IN THE DARK ABOUT THIS PLACE?
BECAUSE IT WAS SYLTH AND FERN'S SECRET.
THEIR SECRET HIDEOUT!
EVERY BOY DREAMS OF HAVING ONE!
DON'T TRY TO BULLSHIT ME.
But I was being serious!
THAT BOOK THERE...
HUH?
You mean that one?
IT LOOKS LIKE A NORMAL BOOK TO ME.
DON'T TOUCH IT!!

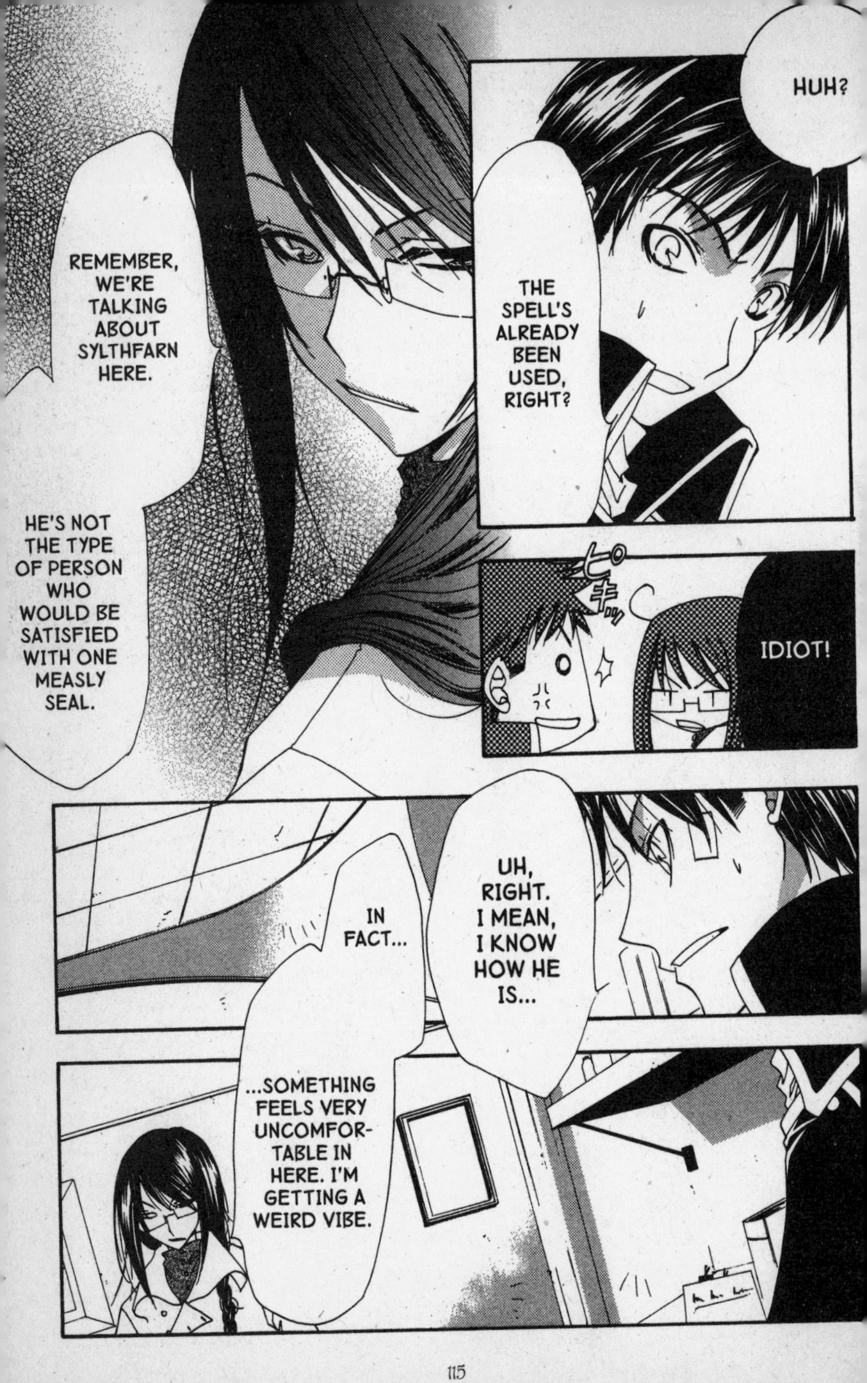
HUH?
THE SPELL'S ALREADY BEEN USED, RIGHT?
ピキッ
IDIOT!
REMEMBER, WE'RE TALKING ABOUT SYLTHFARN HERE.
HE'S NOT THE TYPE OF PERSON WHO WOULD BE SATISFIED WITH ONE MEASLY SEAL.
UH, RIGHT. I MEAN, I KNOW HOW HE IS...
IN FACT...
...SOMETHING FEELS VERY UNCOMFORTABLE IN HERE. I'M GETTING A WEIRD VIBE.

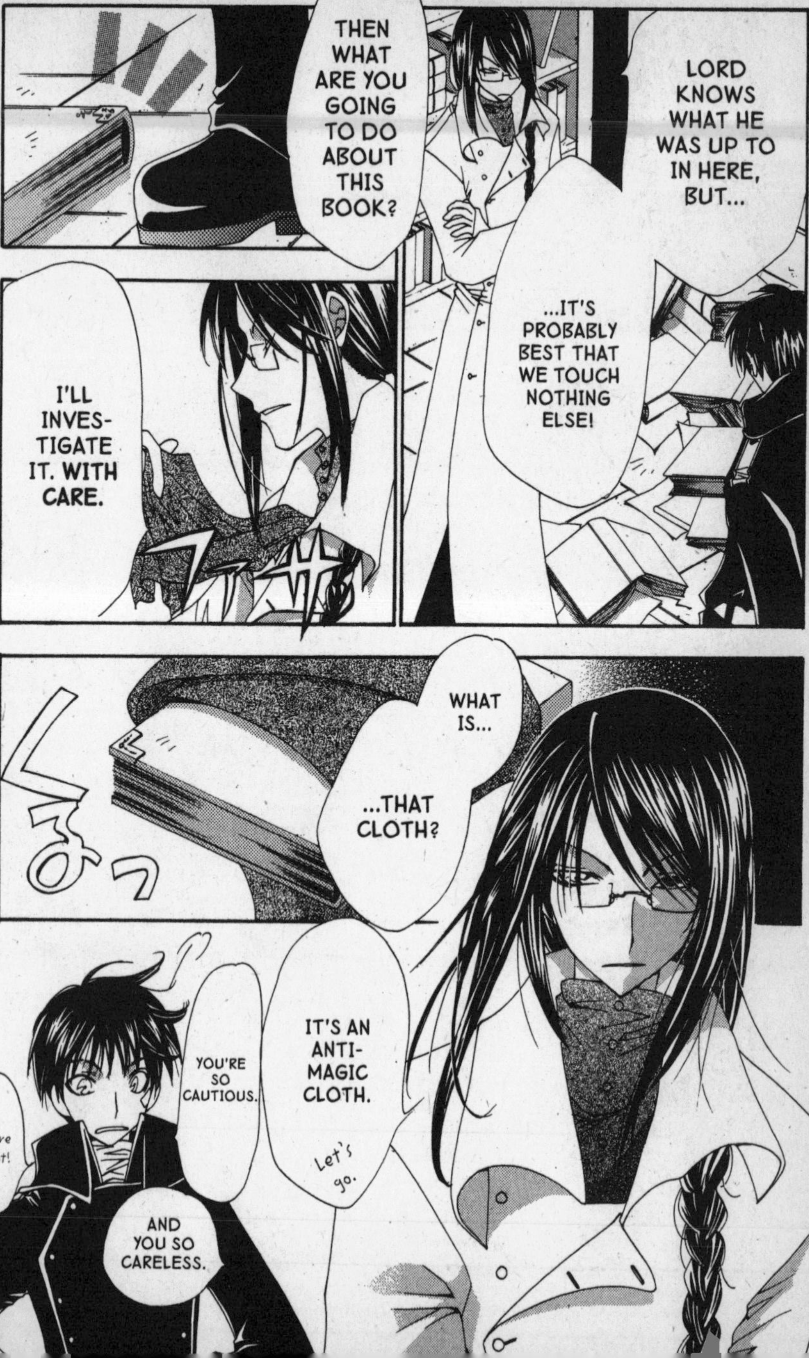
LORD KNOWS WHAT HE WAS UP TO IN HERE, BUT...
...IT'S PROBABLY BEST THAT WE TOUCH NOTHING ELSE!
THEN WHAT ARE YOU GOING TO DO ABOUT THIS BOOK?
I'LL INVESTIGATE IT. WITH CARE.
WHAT IS...
...THAT CLOTH?
くるっ
IT'S AN ANTI-MAGIC CLOTH.
Let's go.
YOU'RE SO CAUTIOUS.
AND YOU SO CARELESS.
You're right!

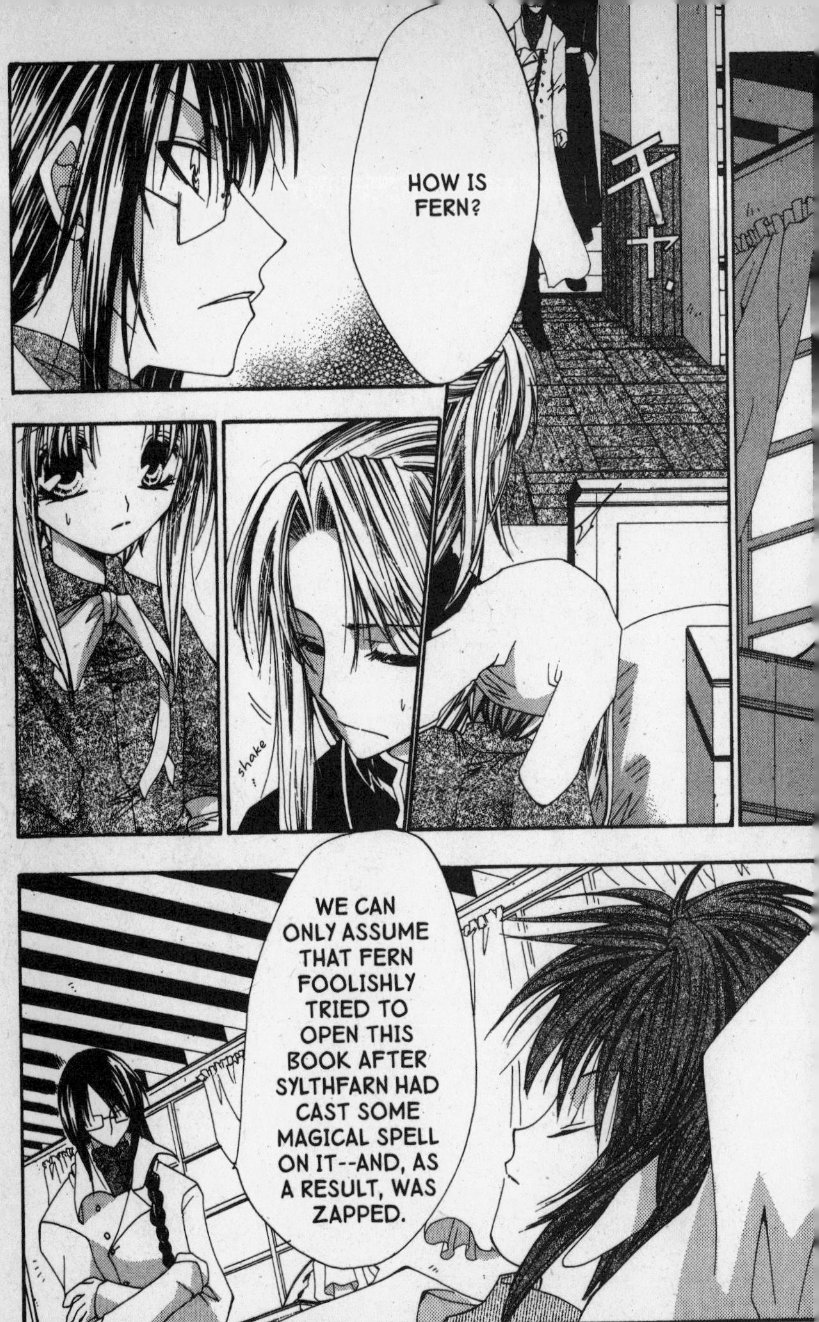
HOW IS FERN?
shake
WE CAN ONLY ASSUME THAT FERN FOOLISHLY TRIED TO OPEN THIS BOOK AFTER SYLTHFARN HAD CAST SOME MAGICAL SPELL ON IT--AND, AS A RESULT, WAS ZAPPED.

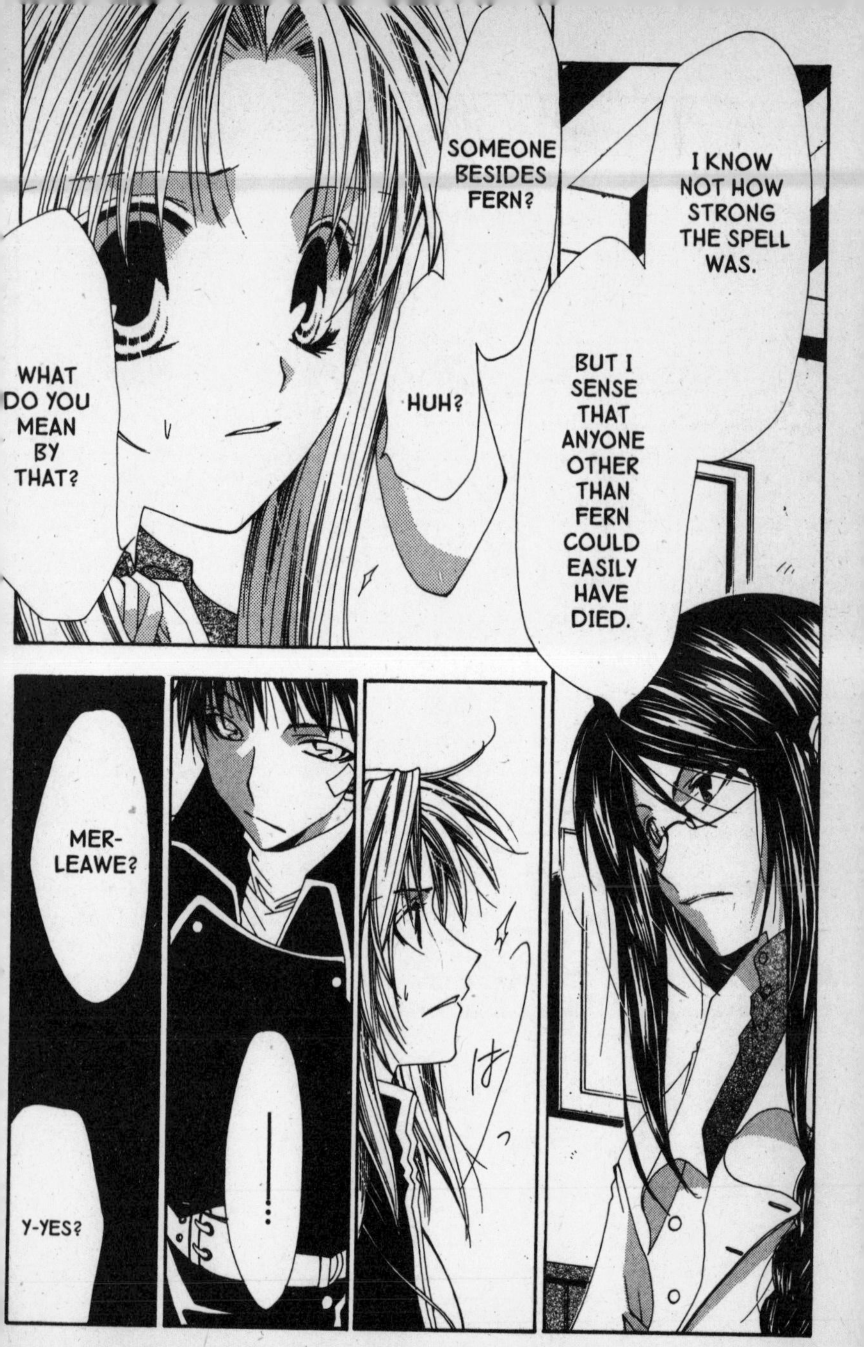
I KNOW NOT HOW STRONG THE SPELL WAS.
BUT I SENSE THAT ANYONE OTHER THAN FERN COULD EASILY HAVE DIED.
SOMEONE BESIDES FERN?
HUH?
WHAT DO YOU MEAN BY THAT?
は
—...
MER-LEAWE?
Y-YES?

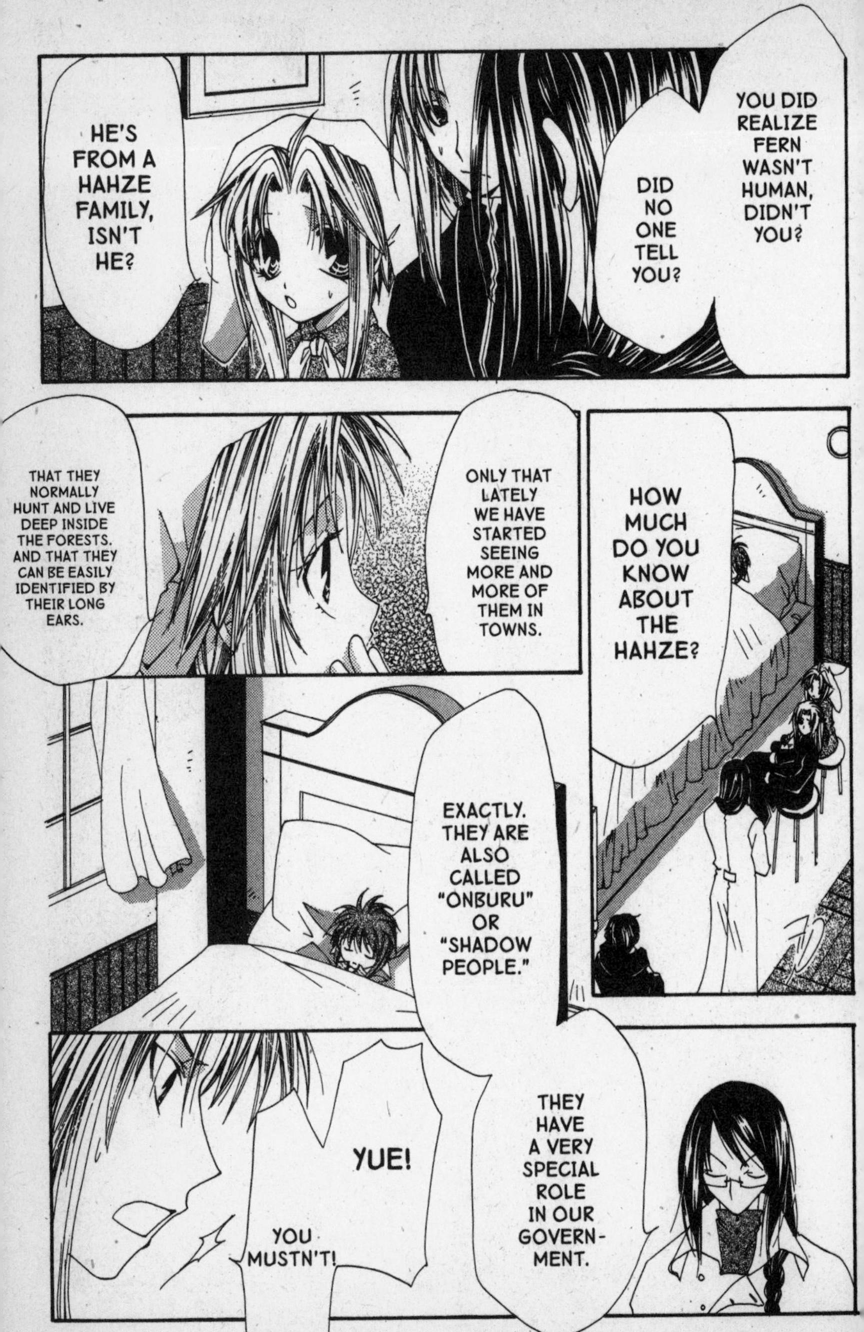
YOU DID REALIZE FERN WASN'T HUMAN, DIDN'T YOU?
DID NO ONE TELL YOU?
HE'S FROM A HAHZE FAMILY, ISN'T HE?
HOW MUCH DO YOU KNOW ABOUT THE HAHZE?
ONLY THAT LATELY WE HAVE STARTED SEEING MORE AND MORE OF THEM IN TOWNS.
THAT THEY NORMALLY HUNT AND LIVE DEEP INSIDE THE FORESTS. AND THAT THEY CAN BE EASILY IDENTIFIED BY THEIR LONG EARS.
EXACTLY. THEY ARE ALSO CALLED "ONBURU" OR "SHADOW PEOPLE."
THEY HAVE A VERY SPECIAL ROLE IN OUR GOVERN-MENT.
YUE!
YOU MUSTN'T!

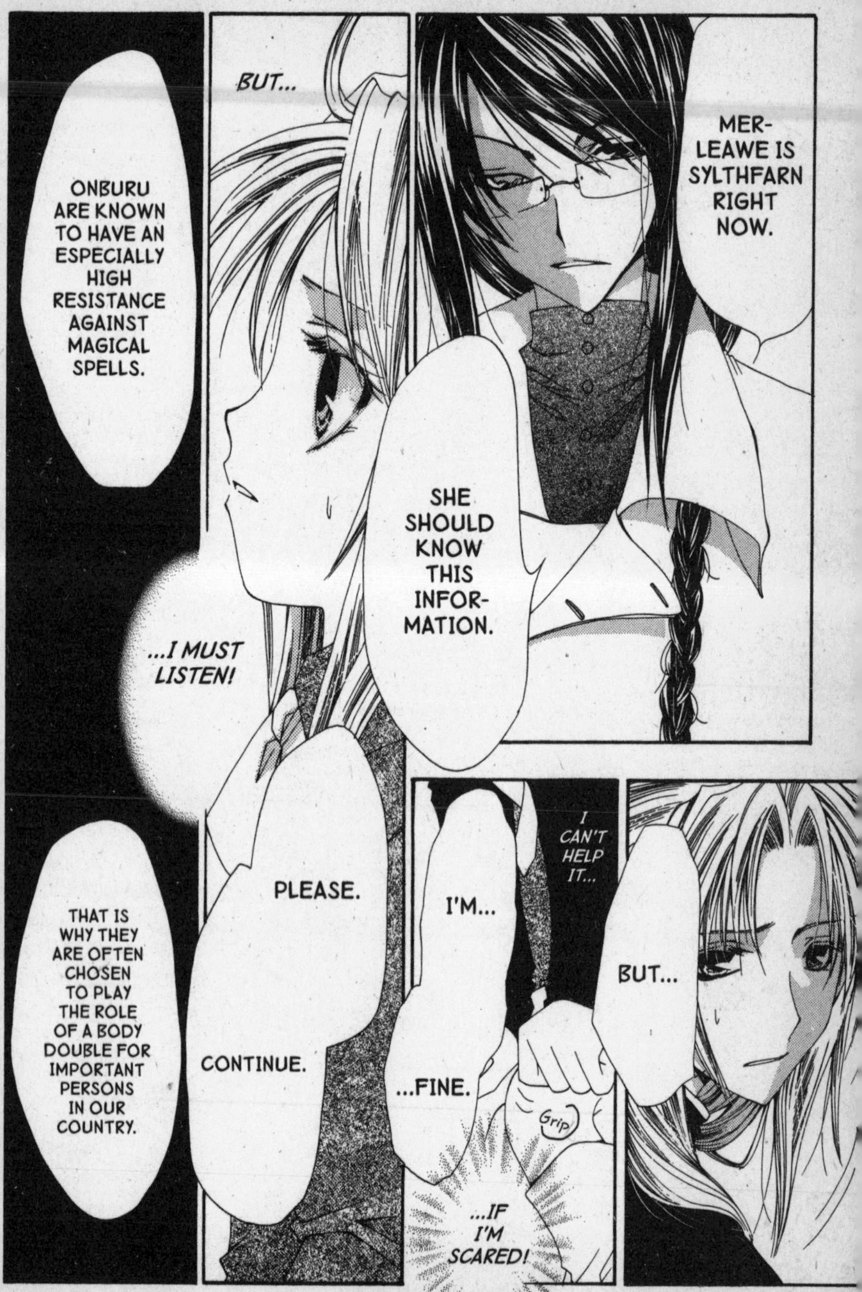
MER-LEAWE IS SYLTHFARN RIGHT NOW.
SHE SHOULD KNOW THIS INFOR-MATION.
BUT...
I CAN'T HELP IT...
I'M... ...FINE.
Grip
...IF I'M SCARED!
BUT...
...I MUST LISTEN!
PLEASE. CONTINUE.
ONBURU ARE KNOWN TO HAVE AN ESPECIALLY HIGH RESISTANCE AGAINST MAGICAL SPELLS.
THAT IS WHY THEY ARE OFTEN CHOSEN TO PLAY THE ROLE OF A BODY DOUBLE FOR IMPORTANT PERSONS IN OUR COUNTRY.

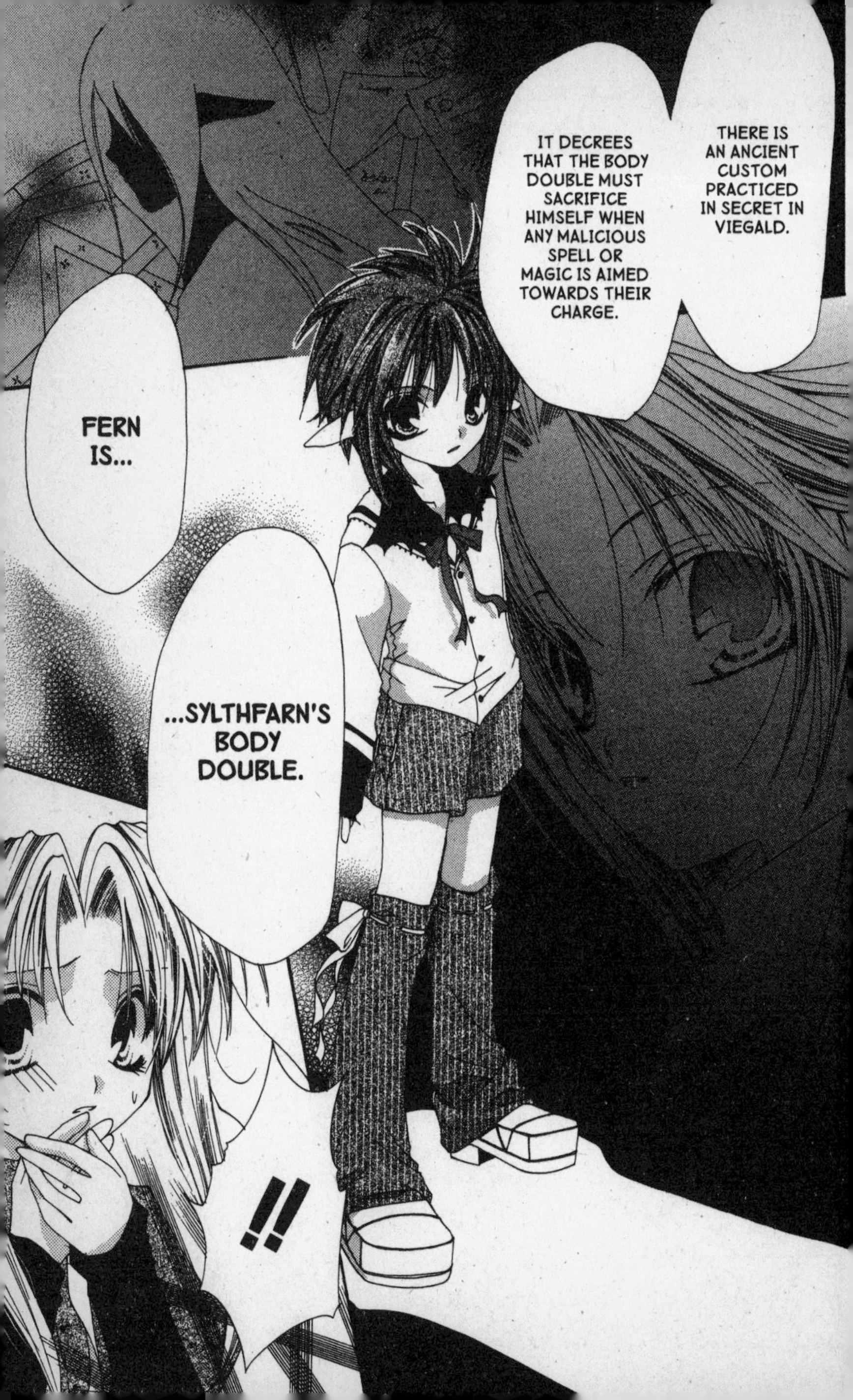
THERE IS AN ANCIENT CUSTOM PRACTICED IN SECRET IN VIEGALD.
IT DECREES THAT THE BODY DOUBLE MUST SACRIFICE HIMSELF WHEN ANY MALICIOUS SPELL OR MAGIC IS AIMED TOWARDS THEIR CHARGE.
FERN IS...
...SYLTHFARN'S BODY DOUBLE.
!!

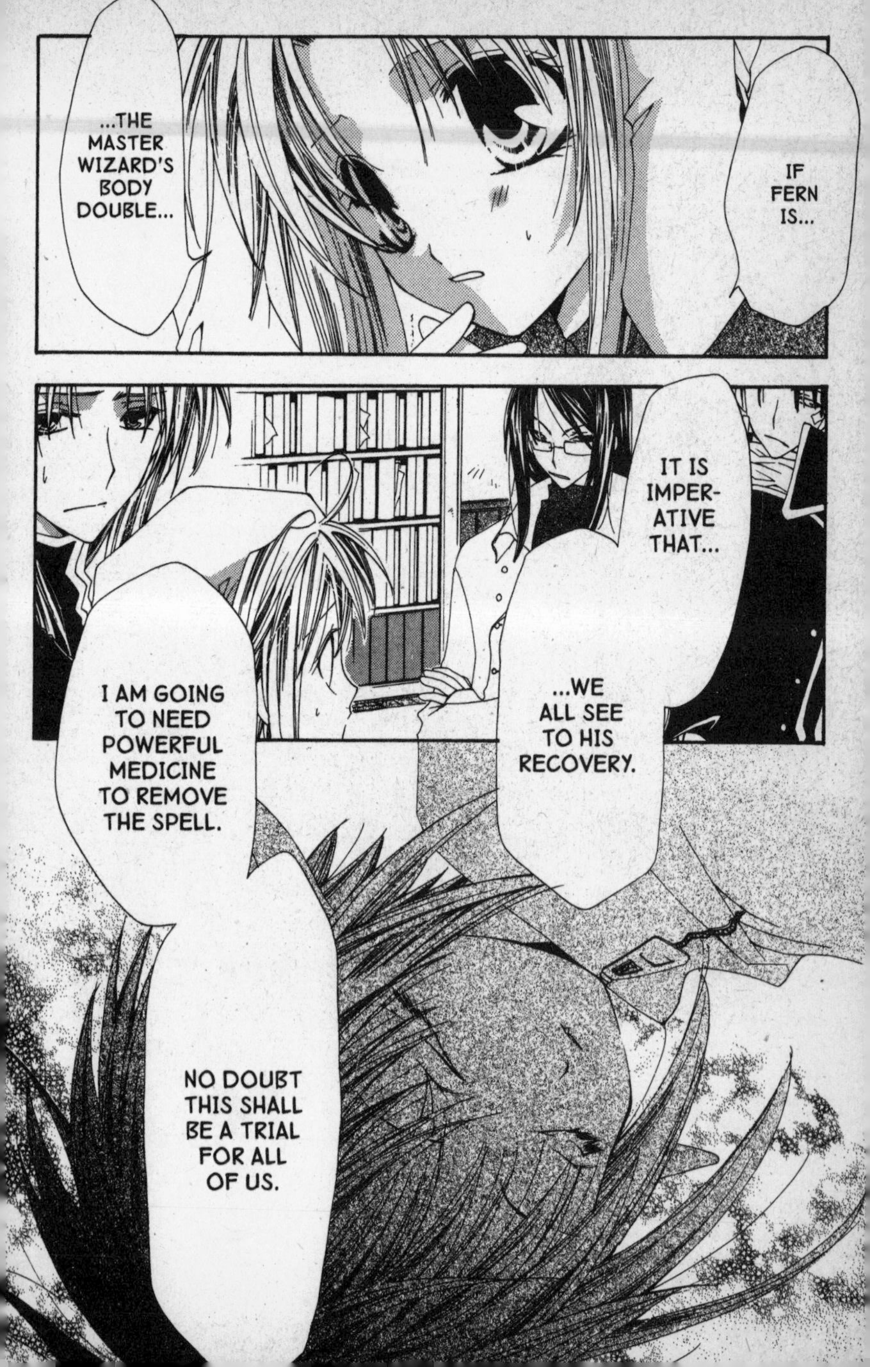
IF FERN IS...
...THE MASTER WIZARD'S BODY DOUBLE...
IT IS IMPERATIVE THAT...
...WE ALL SEE TO HIS RECOVERY.
I AM GOING TO NEED POWERFUL MEDICINE TO REMOVE THE SPELL.
NO DOUBT THIS SHALL BE A TRIAL FOR ALL OF US.

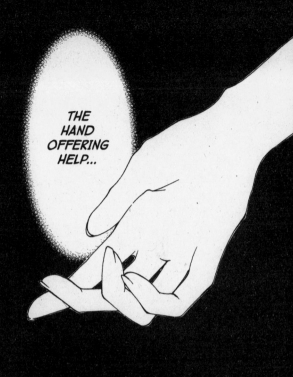

THE
HAND
OFFERING
HELP...

...AS
IF SOME
SPECIAL
LIGHT.

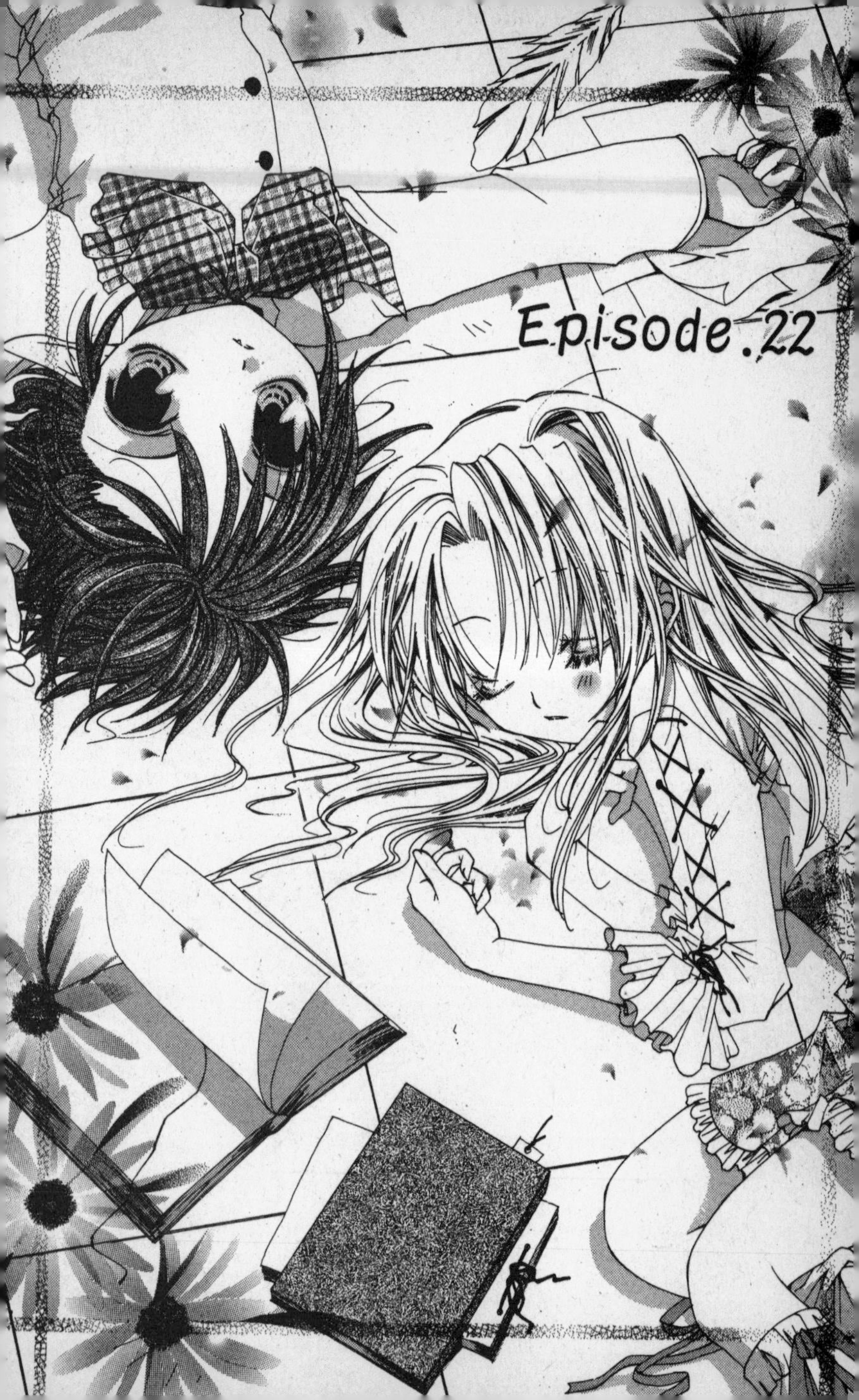
Episode.22

HERE ARE THE MAIN PROBLEMS.

FIRST, IT'S NOT AT ALL CLEAR HOW TO BREAK THE SPELL. ALSO, ONE OF THE MINERALS NEEDED FOR THE REQUIRED MEDICINE IS RARE IN VIEGALD.

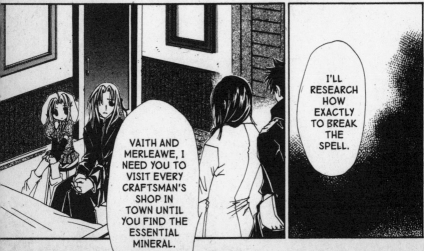

I'LL RESEARCH HOW EXACTLY TO BREAK THE SPELL.

VAITH AND MERLEAWE, I NEED YOU TO VISIT EVERY CRAFTSMAN'S SHOP IN TOWN UNTIL YOU FIND THE ESSENTIAL MINERAL.

125

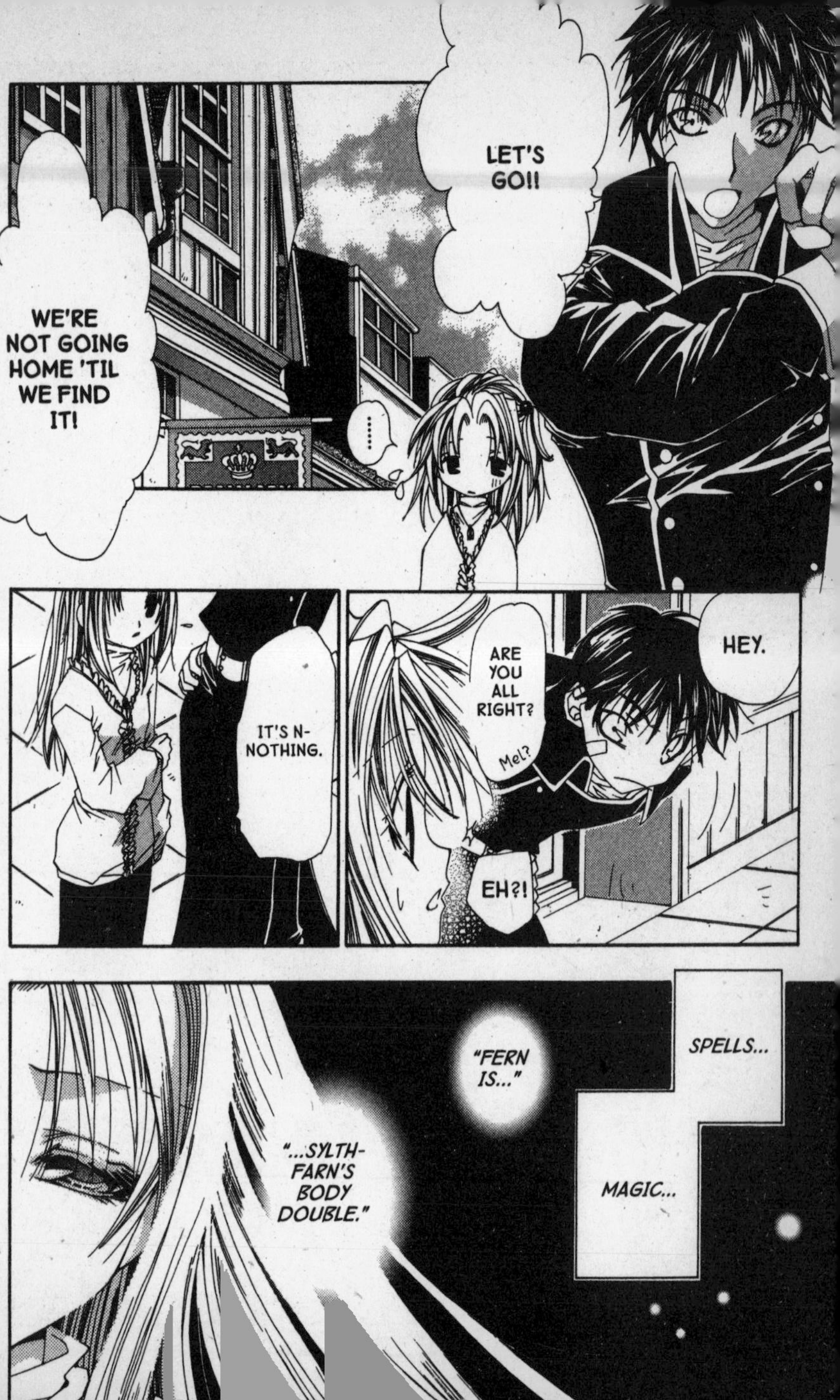
LET'S GO!!
WE'RE NOT GOING HOME 'TIL WE FIND IT!
......
HEY.
ARE YOU ALL RIGHT?
Mel?
EH?!
IT'S N-NOTHING.
SPELLS...
MAGIC...
"FERN IS..."
"...SYLTH-FARN'S BODY DOUBLE."

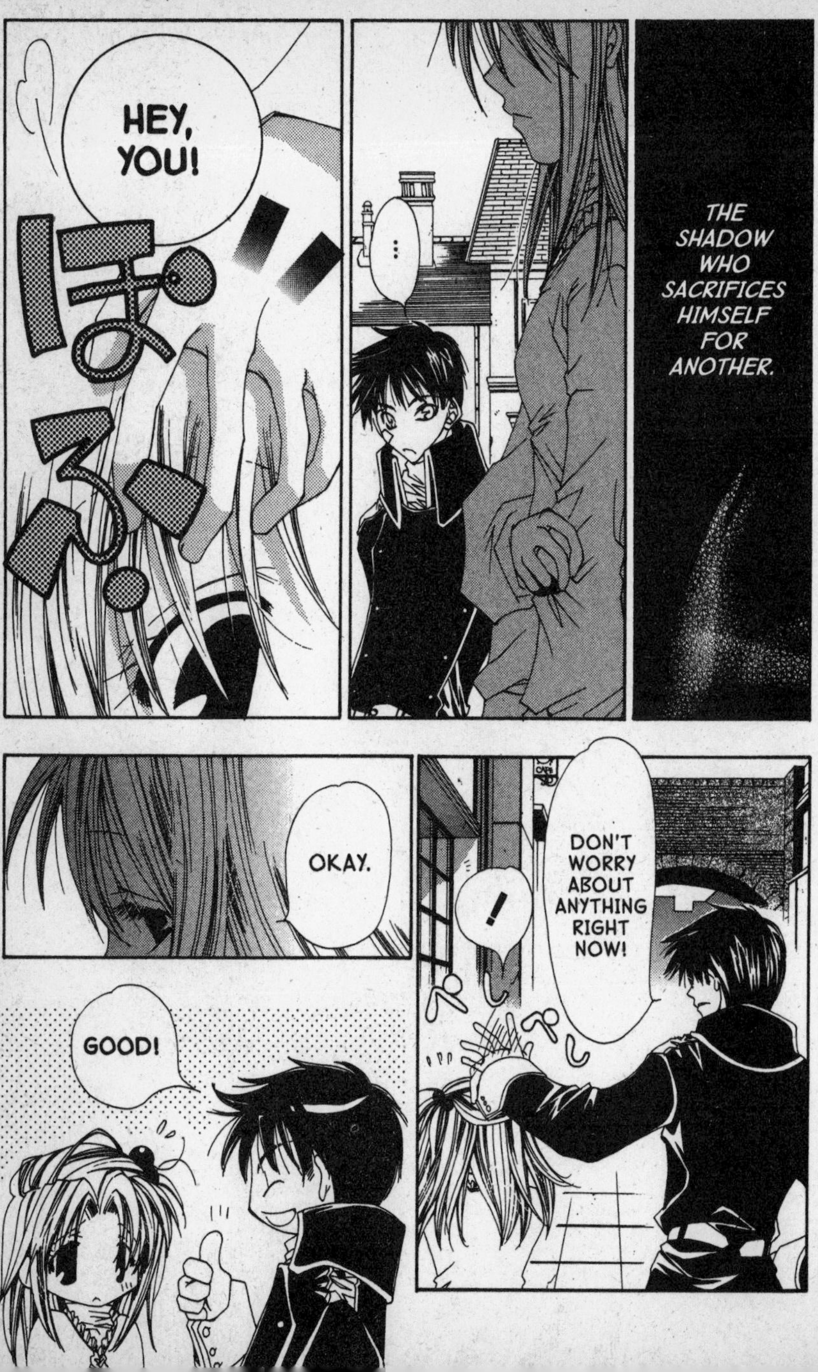
THE SHADOW WHO SACRIFICES HIMSELF FOR ANOTHER.
...
HEY, YOU!
ぽふっ
DON'T WORRY ABOUT ANYTHING RIGHT NOW!
!
OKAY.
GOOD!

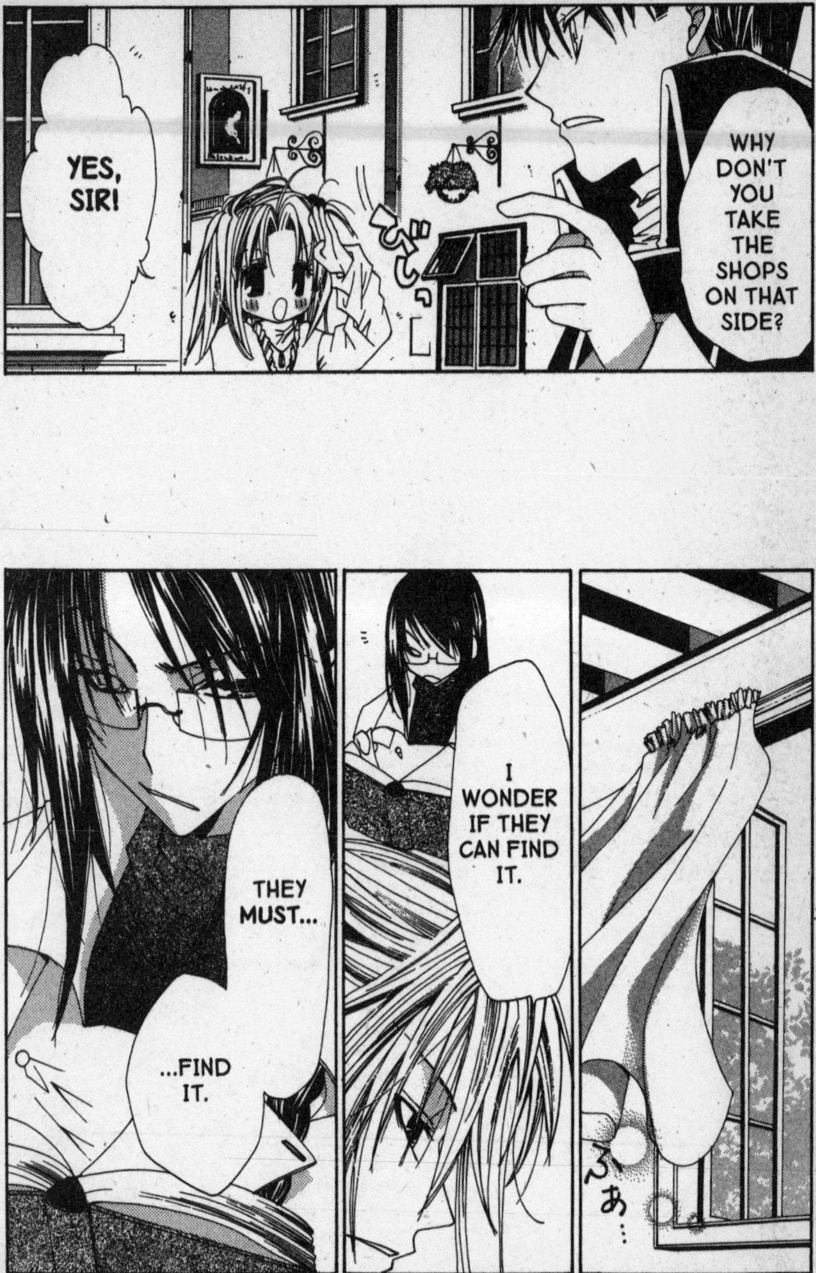
WHY DON'T YOU TAKE THE SHOPS ON THAT SIDE?
YES, SIR!
I WONDER IF THEY CAN FIND IT.
THEY MUST...
...FIND IT.

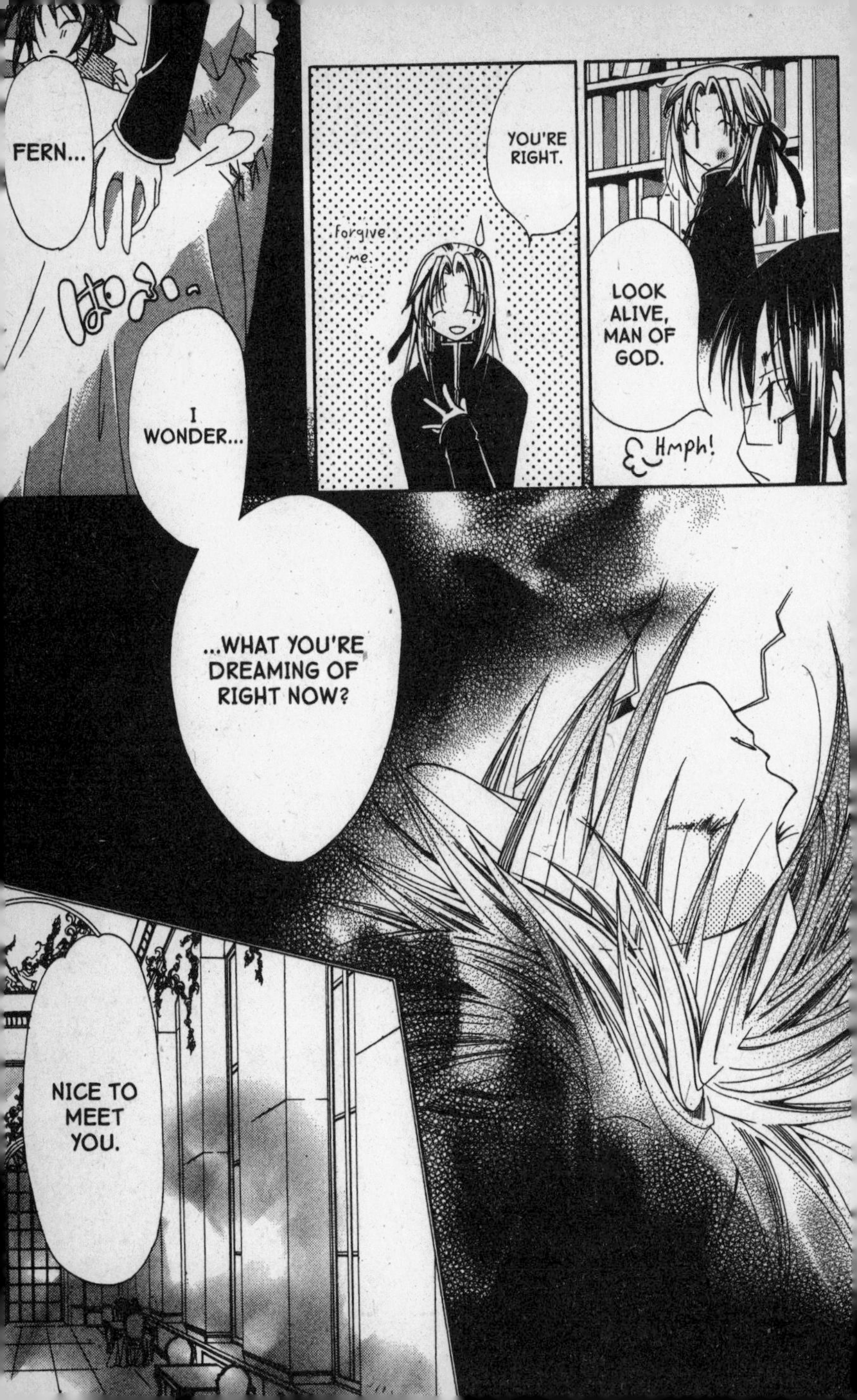
LOOK ALIVE, MAN OF GOD.
Hmph!
YOU'RE RIGHT.
forgive me.
FERN...
はふ...
I WONDER...
...WHAT YOU'RE DREAMING OF RIGHT NOW?
NICE TO MEET YOU.

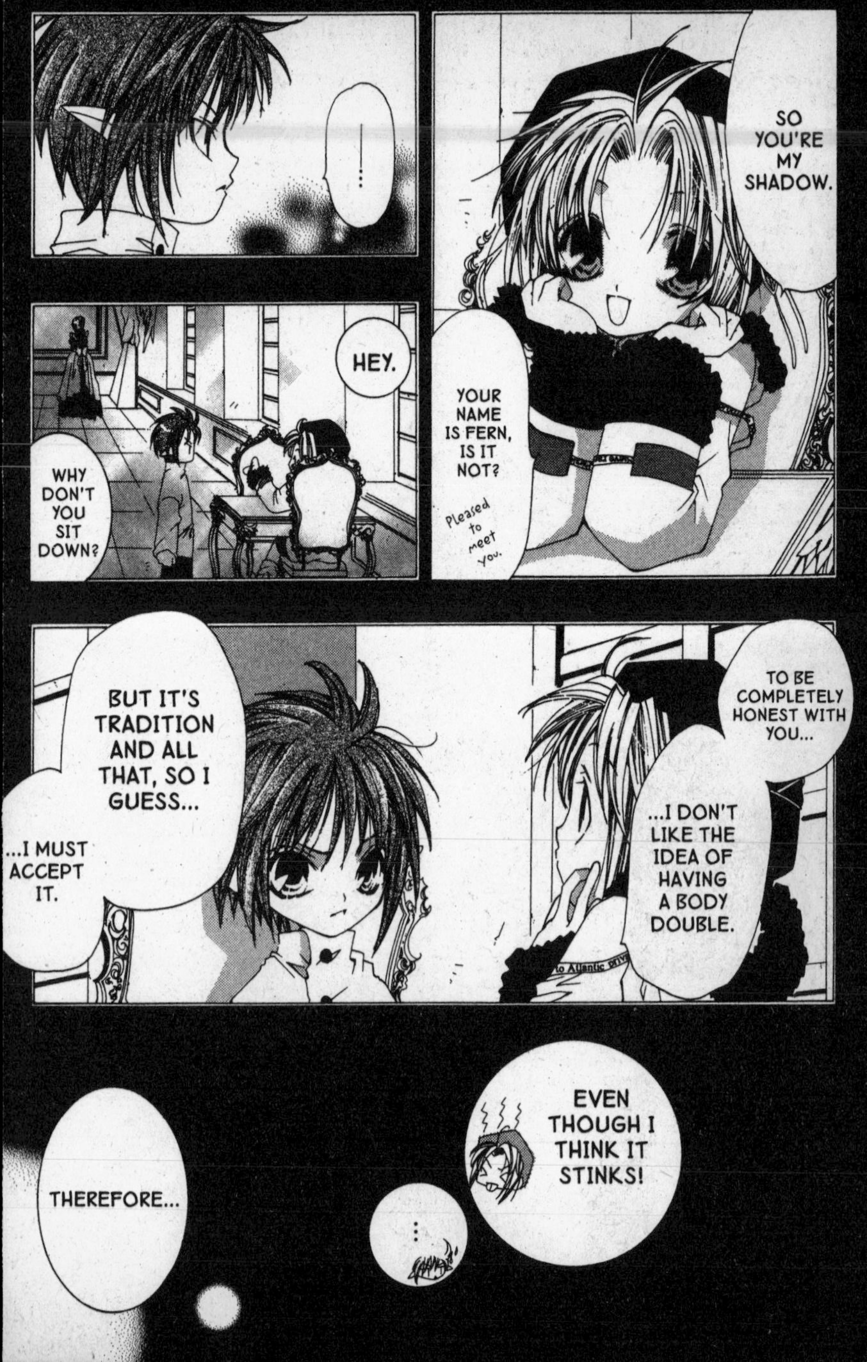
SO YOU'RE MY SHADOW.
YOUR NAME IS FERN, IS IT NOT?
Pleased to meet you.
...
HEY.
WHY DON'T YOU SIT DOWN?
TO BE COMPLETELY HONEST WITH YOU...
...I DON'T LIKE THE IDEA OF HAVING A BODY DOUBLE.
BUT IT'S TRADITION AND ALL THAT, SO I GUESS...
...I MUST ACCEPT IT.
EVEN THOUGH I THINK IT STINKS!
...
THEREFORE...

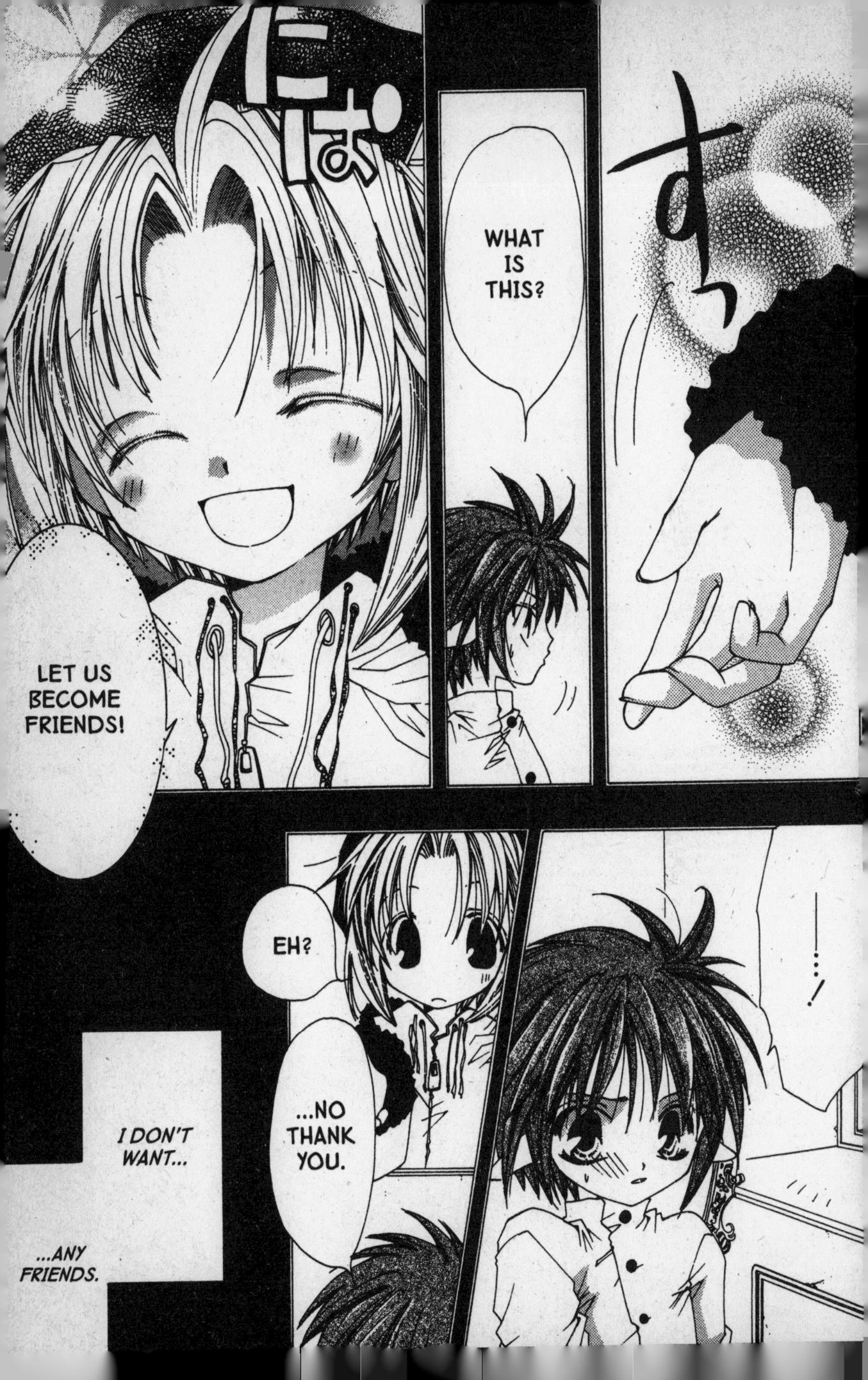
すっ
WHAT IS THIS?
にぱ
LET US BECOME FRIENDS!
...!
EH?
...NO THANK YOU.
I DON'T WANT...
...ANY FRIENDS.

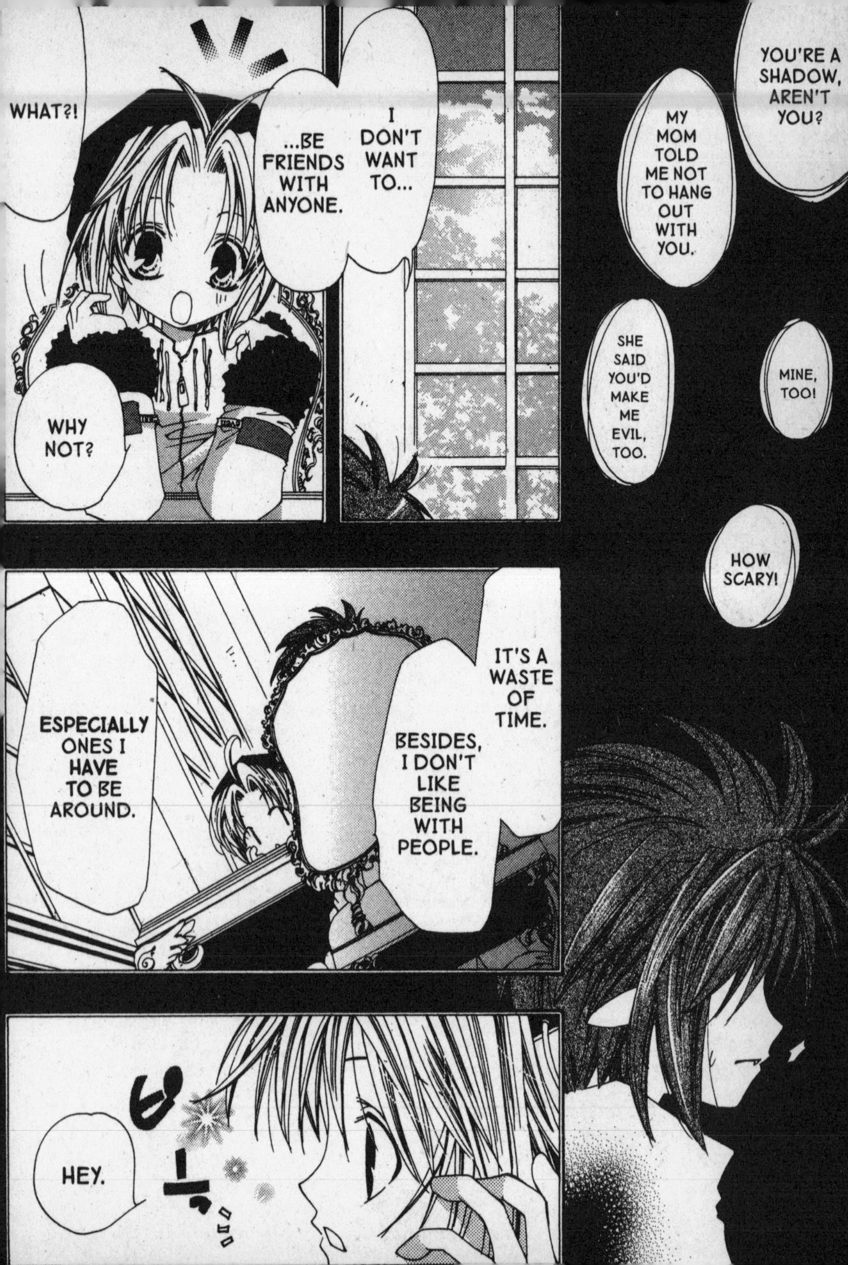
YOU'RE A SHADOW, AREN'T YOU?
MY MOM TOLD ME NOT TO HANG OUT WITH YOU.
MINE, TOO!
SHE SAID YOU'D MAKE ME EVIL, TOO.
HOW SCARY!
I DON'T WANT TO...
...BE FRIENDS WITH ANYONE.
WHAT?!
WHY NOT?
IT'S A WASTE OF TIME.
BESIDES, I DON'T LIKE BEING WITH PEOPLE.
ESPECIALLY ONES I HAVE TO BE AROUND.
HEY.

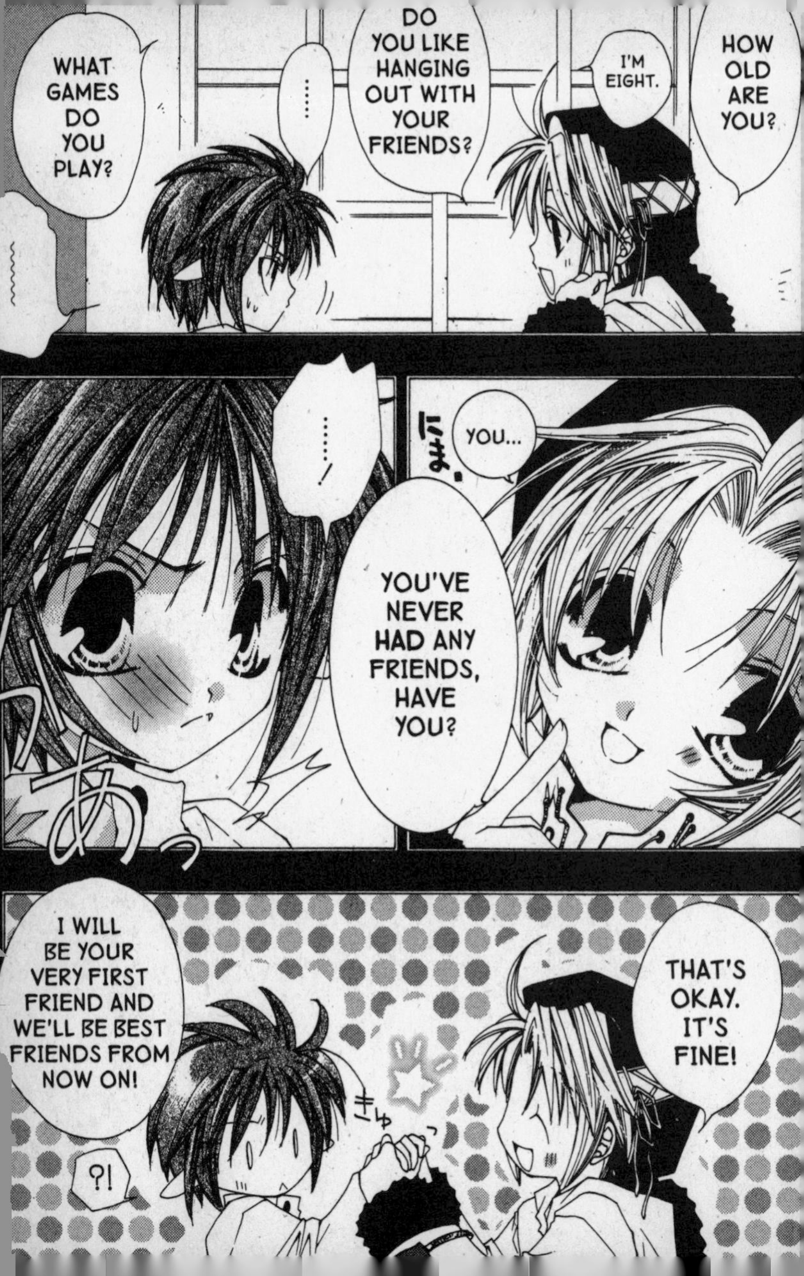
HOW OLD ARE YOU?
I'M EIGHT.
DO YOU LIKE HANGING OUT WITH YOUR FRIENDS?
......
WHAT GAMES DO YOU PLAY?
にま
YOU...
YOU'VE NEVER HAD ANY FRIENDS, HAVE YOU?
......!
あっ
THAT'S OKAY. IT'S FINE!
I WILL BE YOUR VERY FIRST FRIEND AND WE'LL BE BEST FRIENDS FROM NOW ON!
きゅっ
?!

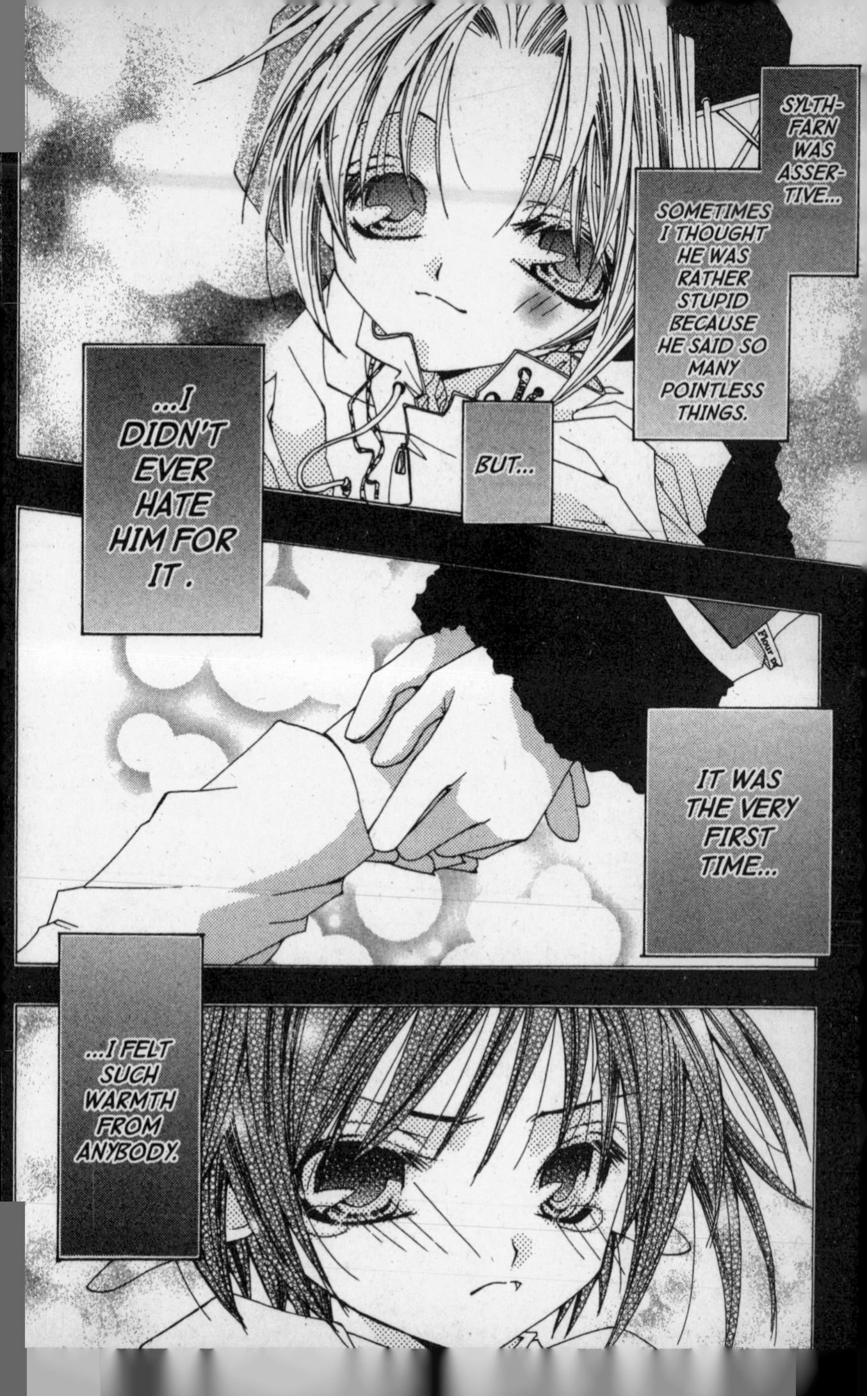
SYLTH-FARN WAS ASSERTIVE...
SOMETIMES I THOUGHT HE WAS RATHER STUPID BECAUSE HE SAID SO MANY POINTLESS THINGS.
BUT...
...I DIDN'T EVER HATE HIM FOR IT.
IT WAS THE VERY FIRST TIME...
...I FELT SUCH WARMTH FROM ANYBODY.

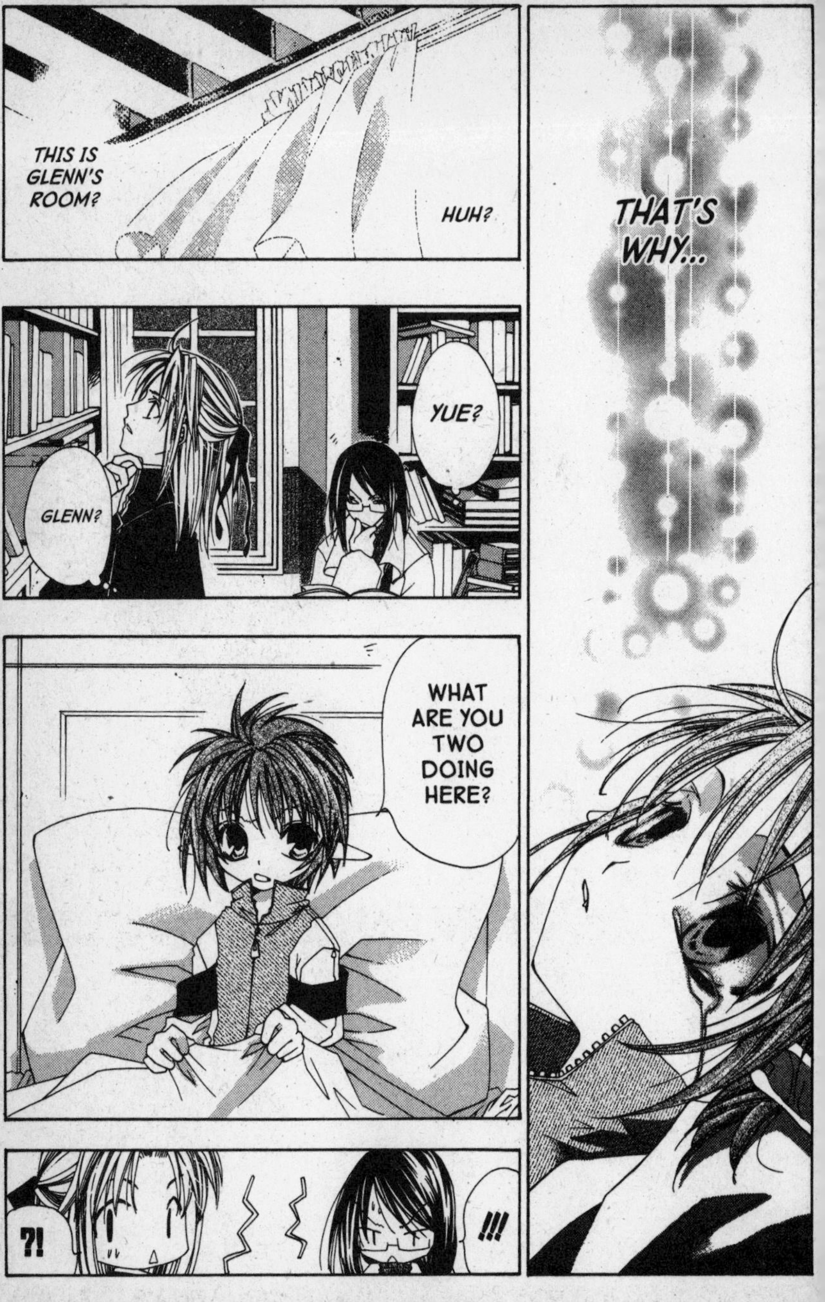
THAT'S WHY...
HUH?
THIS IS GLENN'S ROOM?
YUE?
GLENN?
WHAT ARE YOU TWO DOING HERE?
!!!
?!

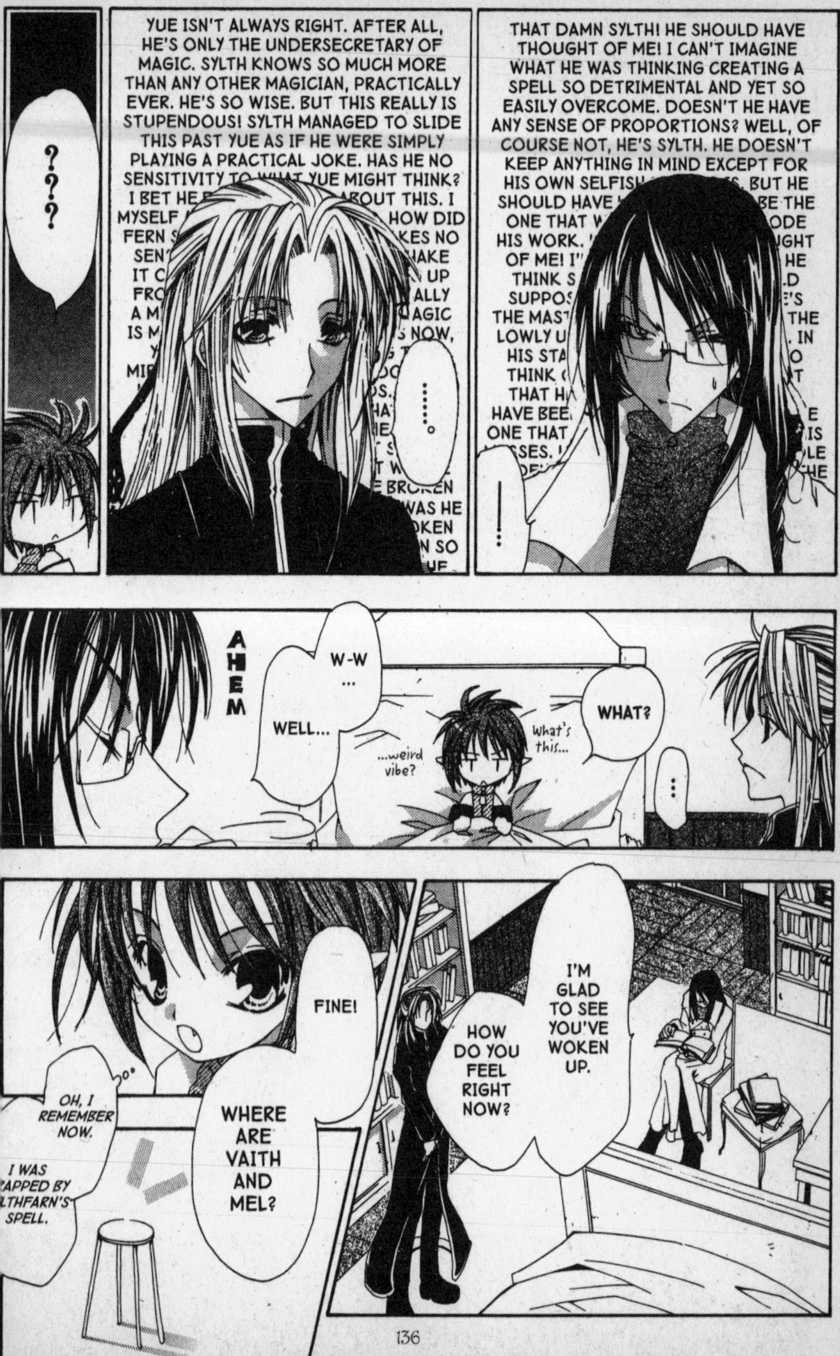
THAT DAMN SYLTH! HE SHOULD HAVE THOUGHT OF ME! I CAN'T IMAGINE WHAT HE WAS THINKING CREATING A SPELL SO DETRIMENTAL AND YET SO EASILY OVERCOME. DOESN'T HE HAVE ANY SENSE OF PROPORTIONS? WELL, OF COURSE NOT, HE'S SYLTH. HE DOESN'T KEEP ANYTHING IN MIND EXCEPT FOR HIS OWN SELFISH
!......
YUE ISN'T ALWAYS RIGHT. AFTER ALL, HE'S ONLY THE UNDERSECRETARY OF MAGIC. SYLTH KNOWS SO MUCH MORE THAN ANY OTHER MAGICIAN, PRACTICALLY EVER. HE'S SO WISE. BUT THIS REALLY IS STUPENDOUS! SYLTH MANAGED TO SLIDE THIS PAST YUE AS IF HE WERE SIMPLY PLAYING A PRACTICAL JOKE. HAS HE NO SENSITIVITY TO WHAT YUE MIGHT THINK?
......。
???
...
WHAT?
What's this...
...weird vibe?
W-W ... WELL...
AHEM
I'M GLAD TO SEE YOU'VE WOKEN UP.
HOW DO YOU FEEL RIGHT NOW?
FINE!
WHERE ARE VAITH AND MEL?
OH, I REMEMBER NOW.
I WAS ZAPPED BY LTHFARN'S SPELL.

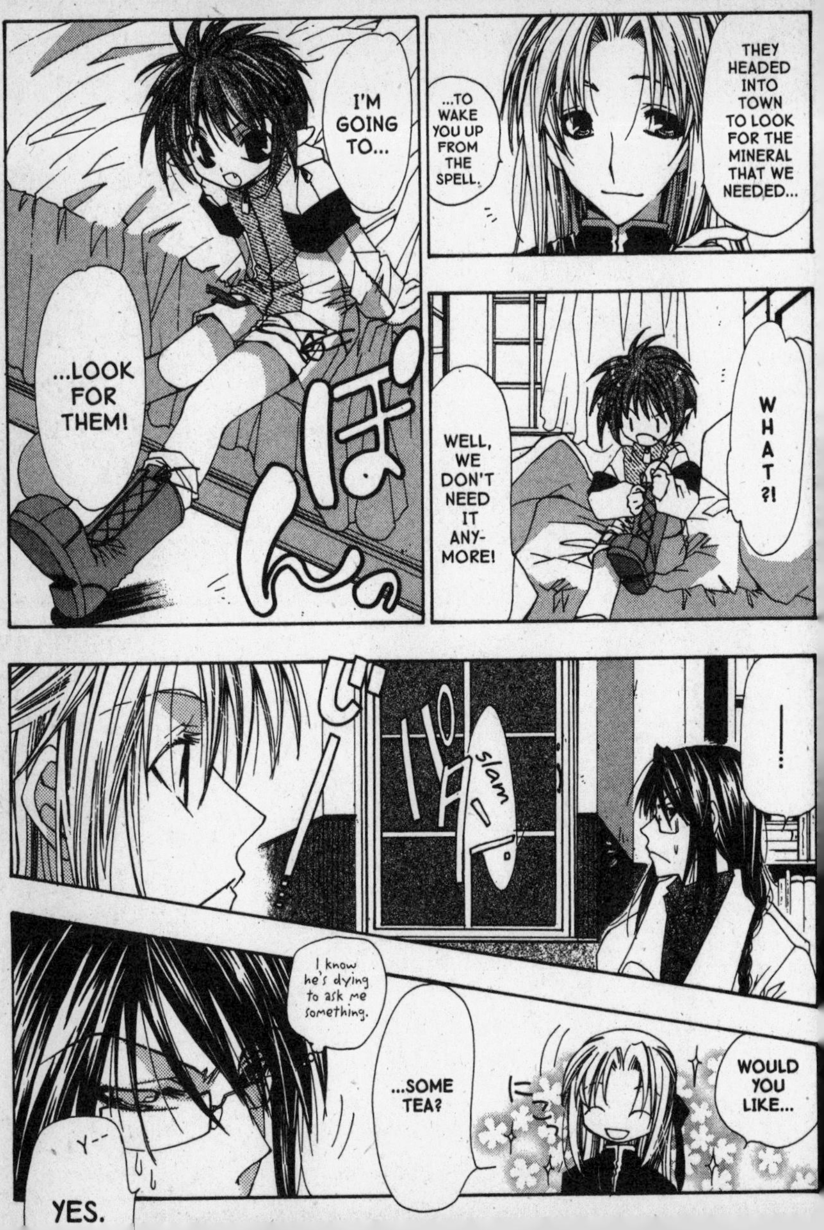
THEY HEADED INTO TOWN TO LOOK FOR THE MINERAL THAT WE NEEDED...
...TO WAKE YOU UP FROM THE SPELL.
WHAT?!
WELL, WE DON'T NEED IT ANYMORE!
I'M GOING TO...
...LOOK FOR THEM!
...!
slam
WOULD YOU LIKE...
...SOME TEA?
I know he's dying to ask me something.
Y--
YES.

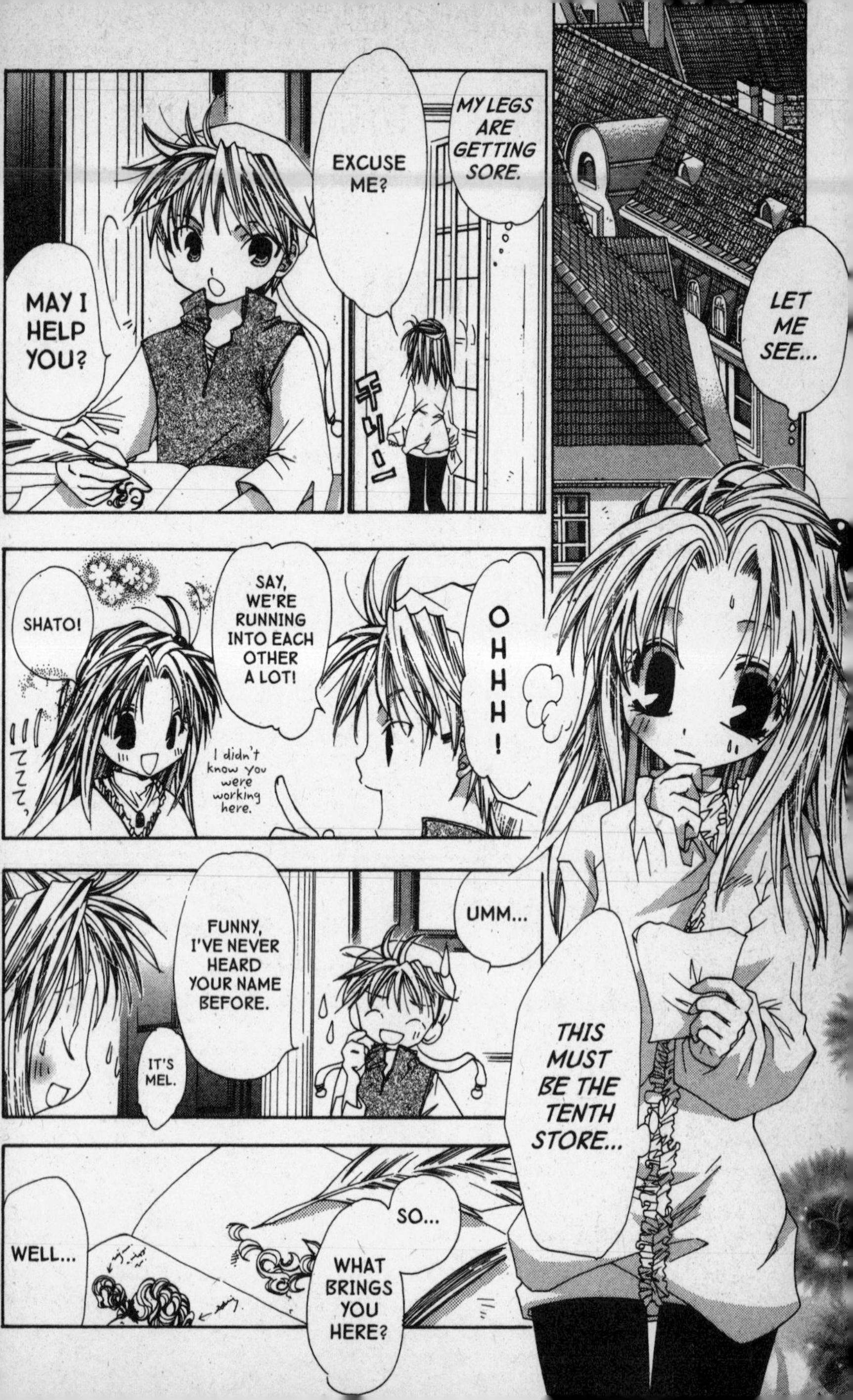
LET ME SEE...
THIS MUST BE THE TENTH STORE...
MY LEGS ARE GETTING SORE.
EXCUSE ME?
MAY I HELP YOU?
OHHH!
SAY, WE'RE RUNNING INTO EACH OTHER A LOT!
SHATO!
I didn't know you were working here.
UMM...
FUNNY, I'VE NEVER HEARD YOUR NAME BEFORE.
IT'S MEL.
SO... WHAT BRINGS YOU HERE?
WELL...

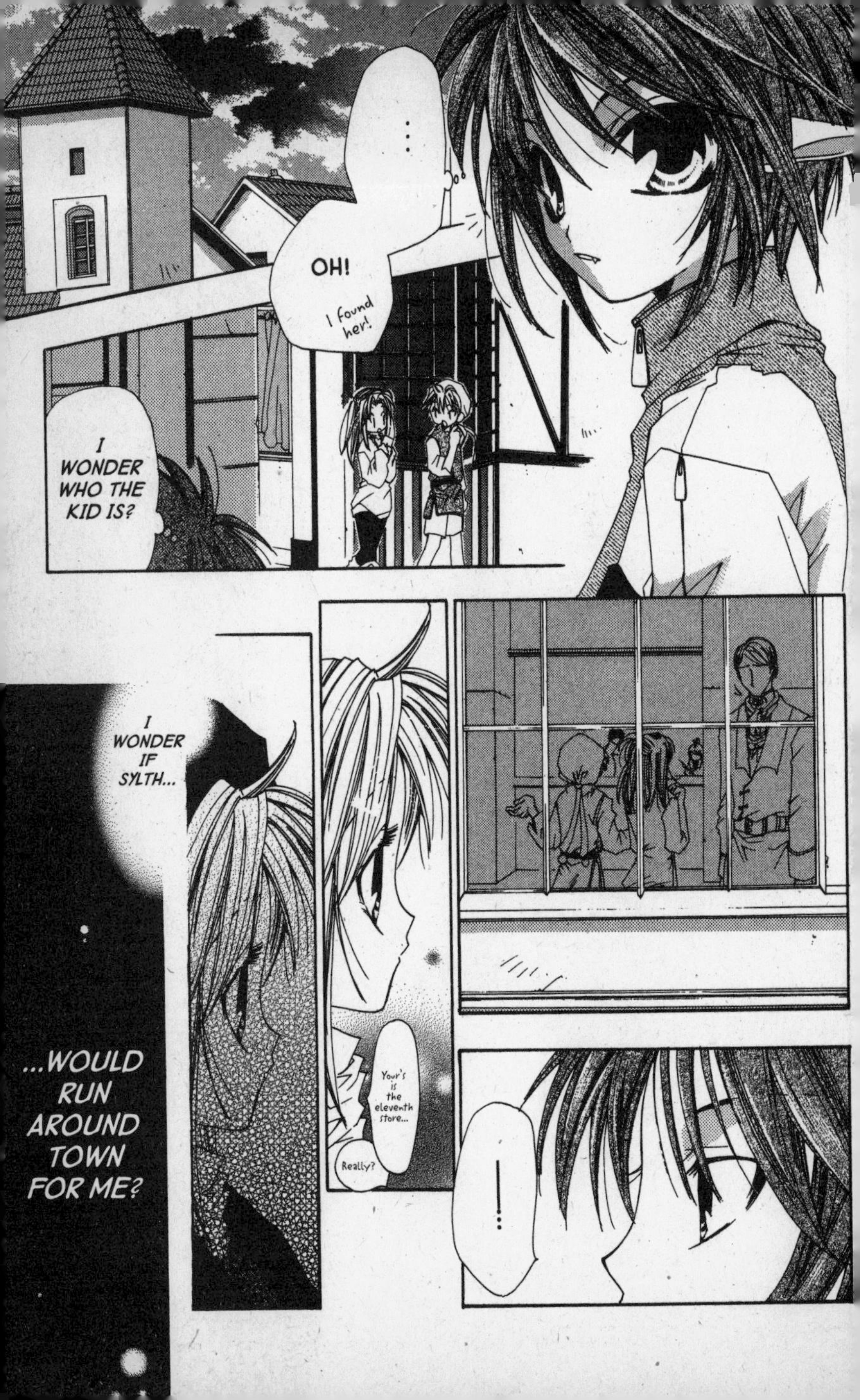
...
OH!
I found her!
I WONDER WHO THE KID IS?
...!
Your's is the eleventh store...
Really?
I WONDER IF SYLTH...
...WOULD RUN AROUND TOWN FOR ME?

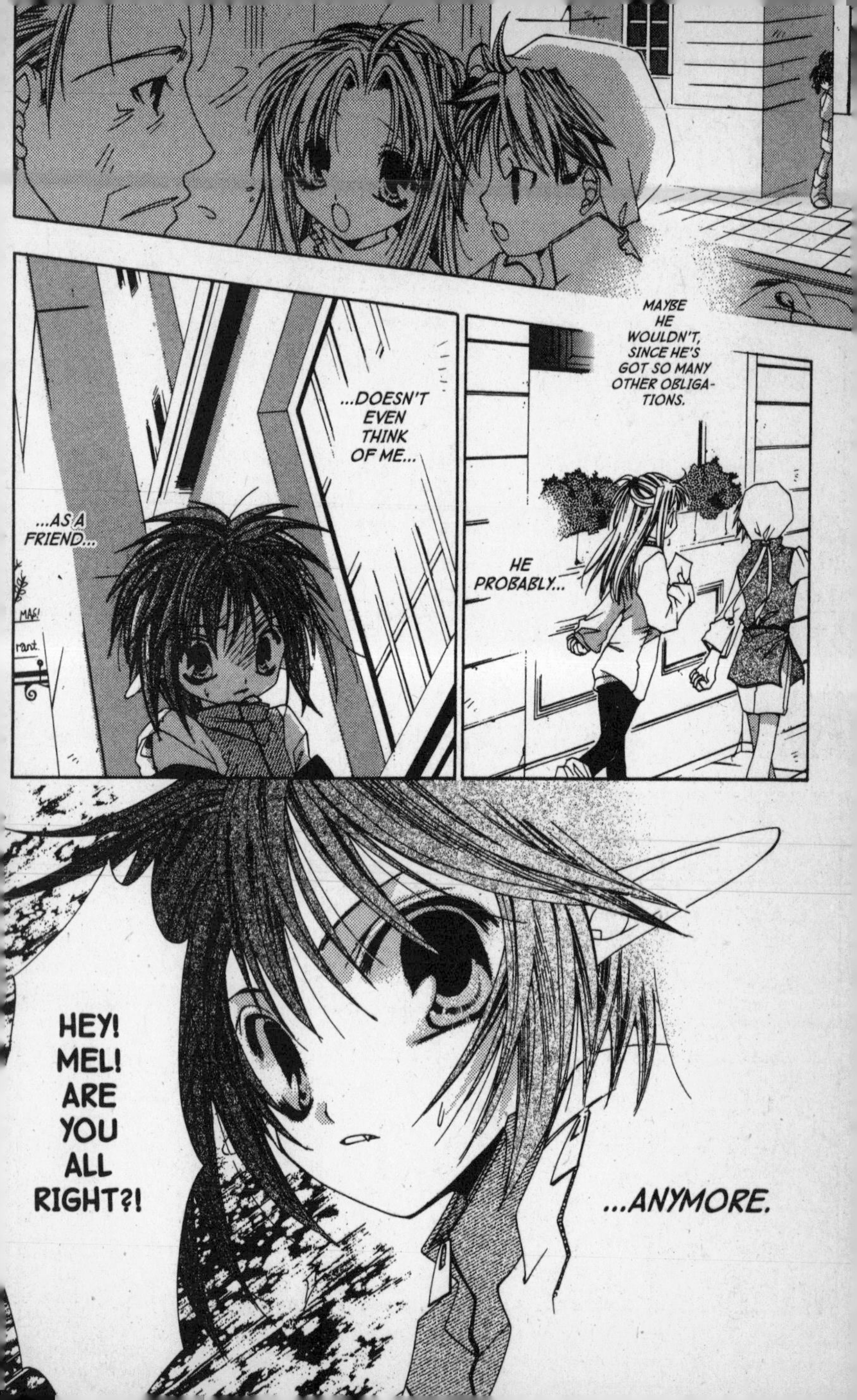
MAYBE HE WOULDN'T, SINCE HE'S GOT SO MANY OTHER OBLIGATIONS.
HE PROBABLY...
...DOESN'T EVEN THINK OF ME...
...AS A FRIEND...
...ANYMORE.
HEY! MEL! ARE YOU ALL RIGHT?!

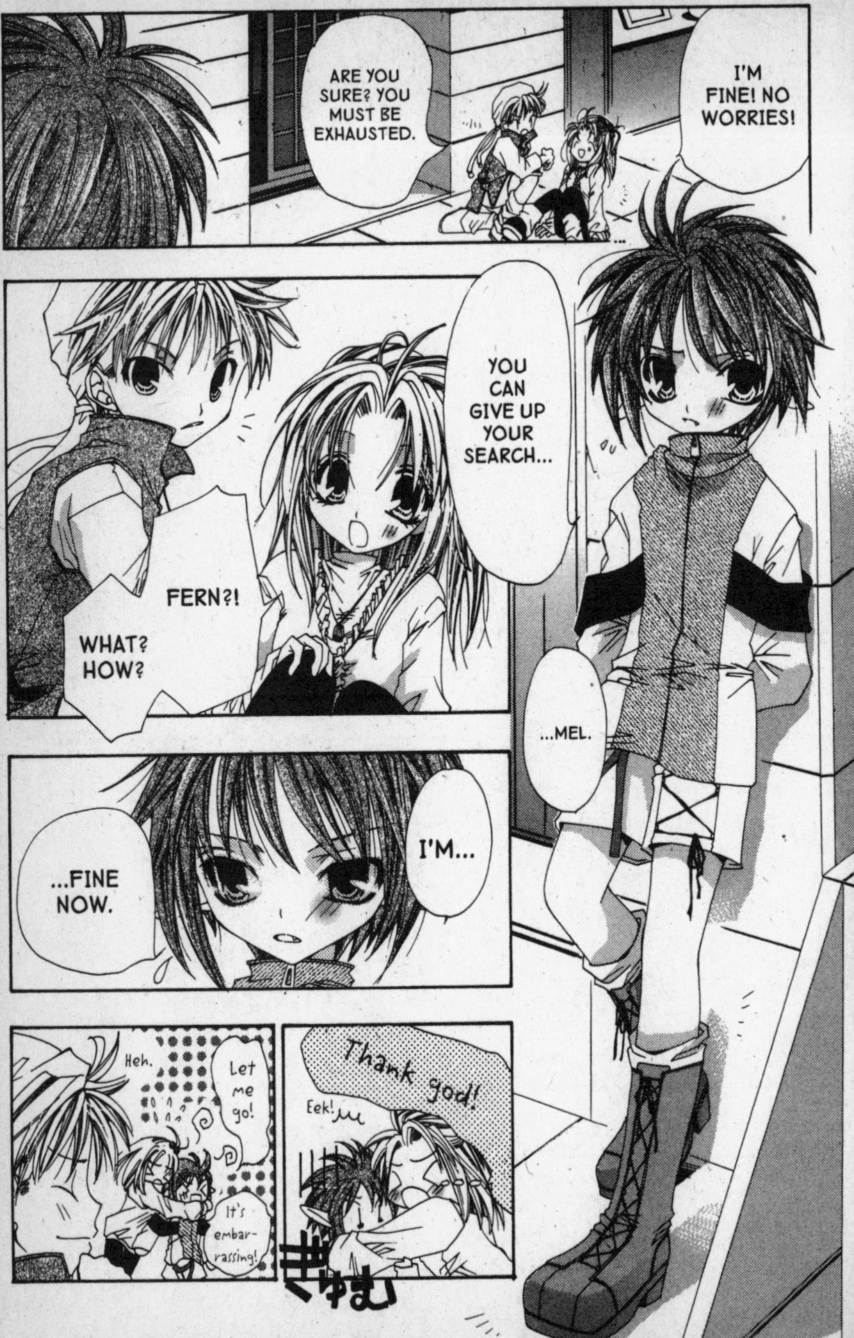
I'M FINE! NO WORRIES!
ARE YOU SURE? YOU MUST BE EXHAUSTED.
YOU CAN GIVE UP YOUR SEARCH...
...MEL.
FERN?!
WHAT? HOW?
I'M...
...FINE NOW.
Thank god!
Eek!
Let me go!
Heh.
It's embar-rassing!

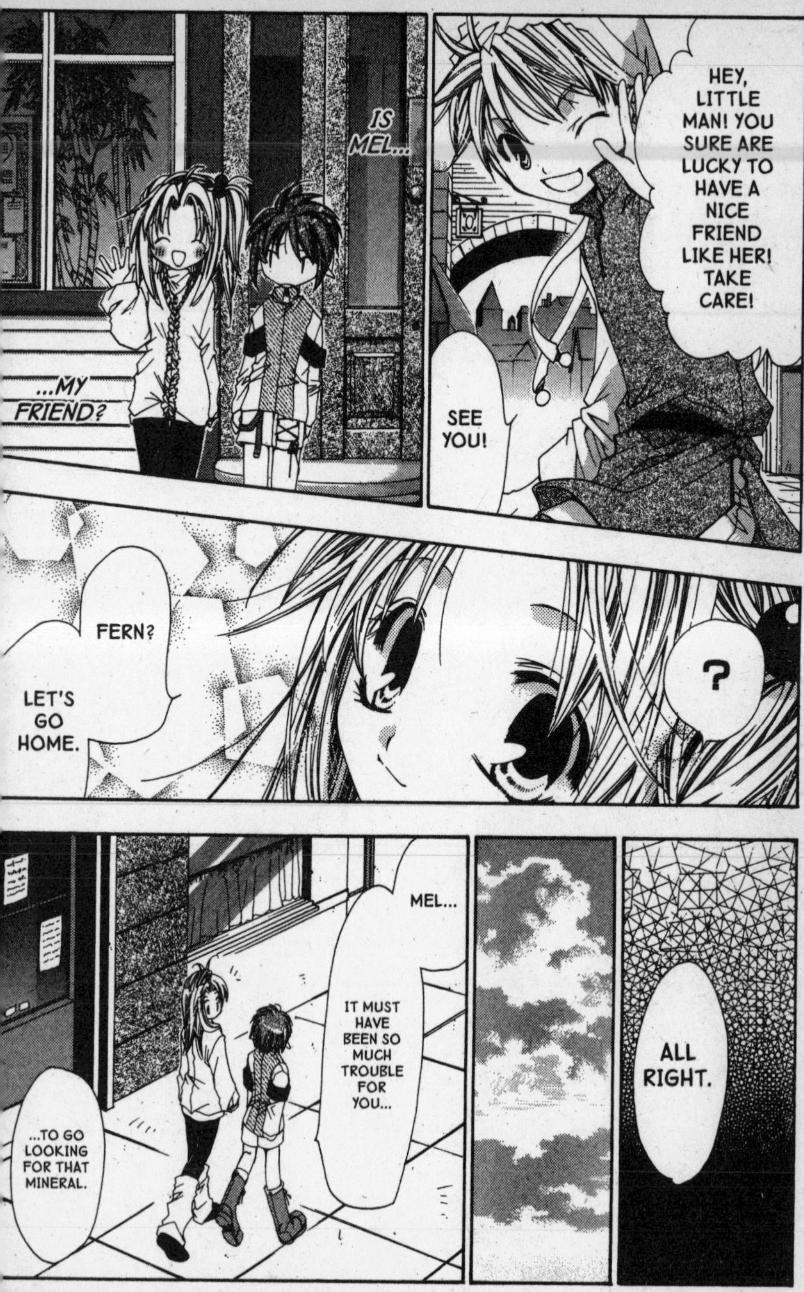
HEY, LITTLE MAN! YOU SURE ARE LUCKY TO HAVE A NICE FRIEND LIKE HER! TAKE CARE!
SEE YOU!
IS MEL...
...MY FRIEND?
?
FERN?
LET'S GO HOME.
ALL RIGHT.
MEL...
IT MUST HAVE BEEN SO MUCH TROUBLE FOR YOU...
...TO GO LOOKING FOR THAT MINERAL.

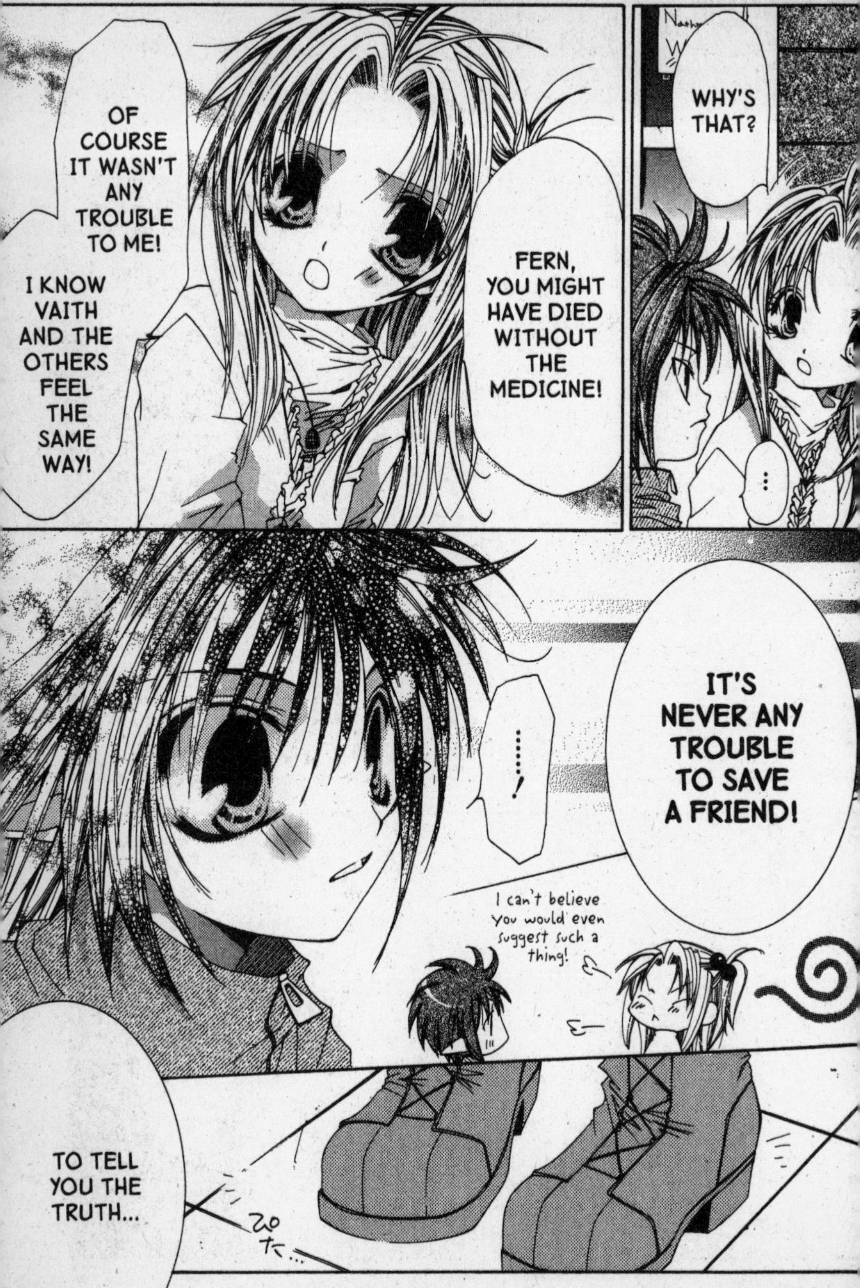
WHY'S THAT?
...
FERN, YOU MIGHT HAVE DIED WITHOUT THE MEDICINE!
OF COURSE IT WASN'T ANY TROUBLE TO ME!
I KNOW VAITH AND THE OTHERS FEEL THE SAME WAY!
IT'S NEVER ANY TROUBLE TO SAVE A FRIEND!
......!
I can't believe you would even suggest such a thing!
TO TELL YOU THE TRUTH...

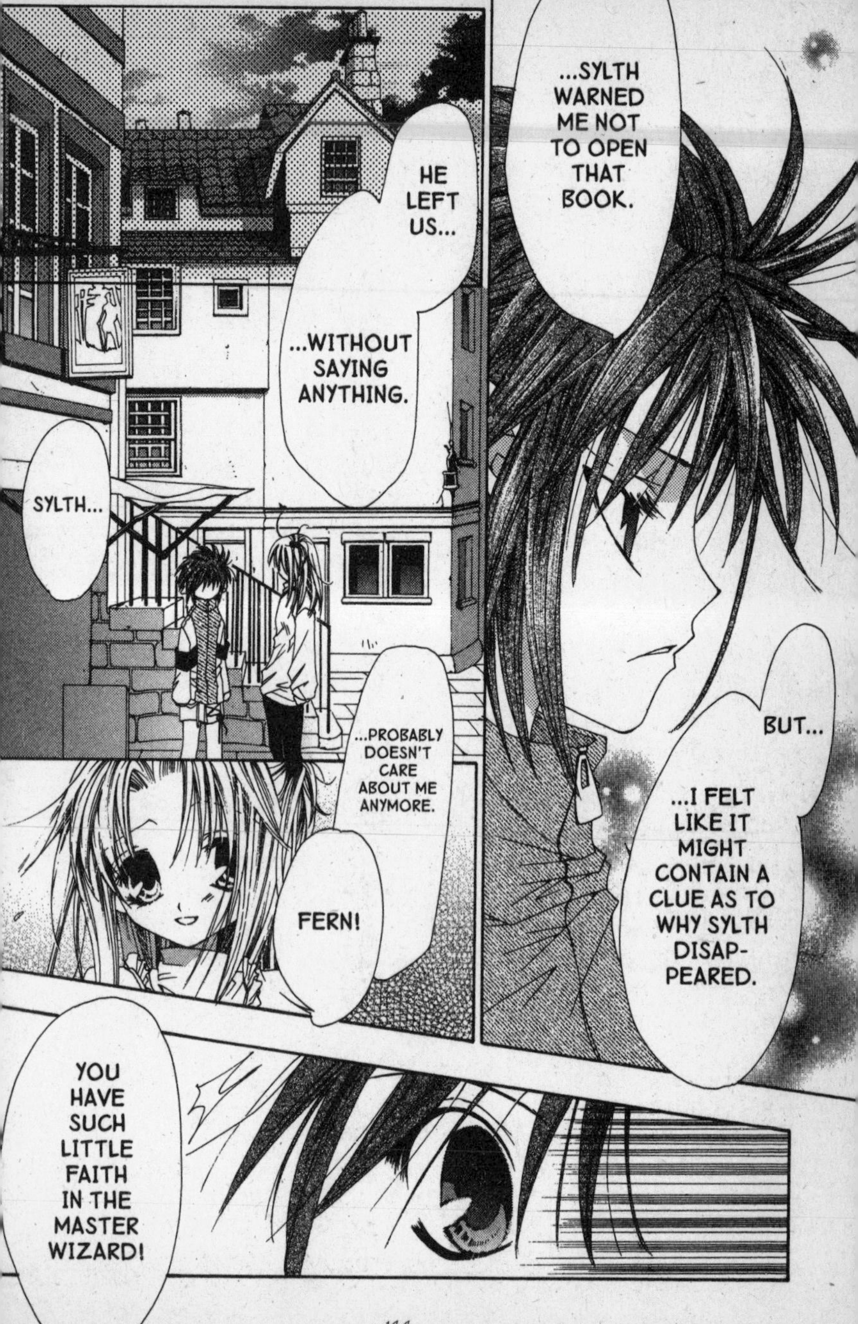
...SYLTH WARNED ME NOT TO OPEN THAT BOOK.
BUT...
...I FELT LIKE IT MIGHT CONTAIN A CLUE AS TO WHY SYLTH DISAP-PEARED.
HE LEFT US...
...WITHOUT SAYING ANYTHING.
SYLTH...
...PROBABLY DOESN'T CARE ABOUT ME ANYMORE.
FERN!
YOU HAVE SUCH LITTLE FAITH IN THE MASTER WIZARD!

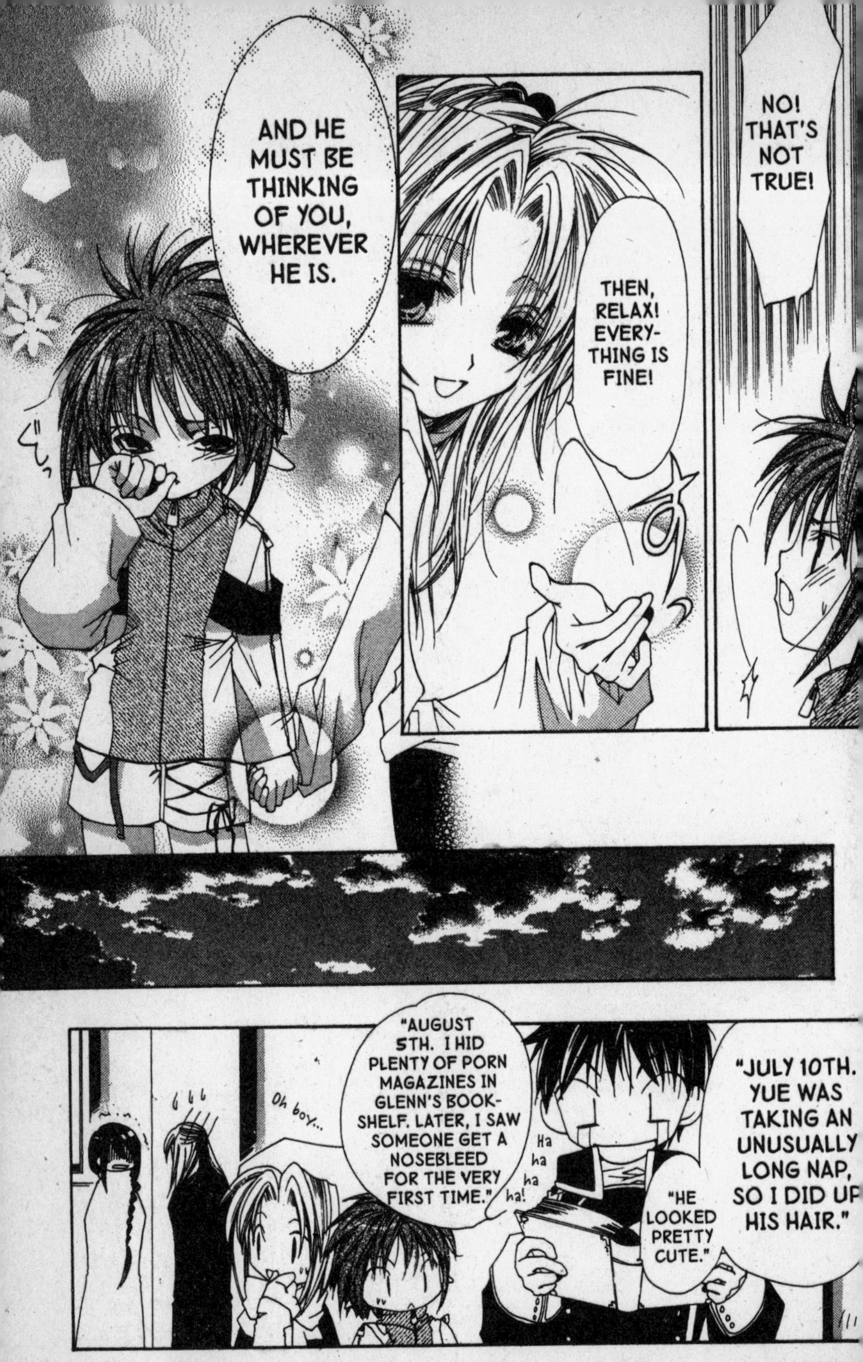
NO! THAT'S NOT TRUE!
THEN, RELAX! EVERYTHING IS FINE!
AND HE MUST BE THINKING OF YOU, WHEREVER HE IS.
"JULY 10TH. YUE WAS TAKING AN UNUSUALLY LONG NAP, SO I DID UP HIS HAIR."
"HE LOOKED PRETTY CUTE."
Ha ha ha ha!
"AUGUST 5TH. I HID PLENTY OF PORN MAGAZINES IN GLENN'S BOOK-SHELF. LATER, I SAW SOMEONE GET A NOSEBLEED FOR THE VERY FIRST TIME."
Oh boy...

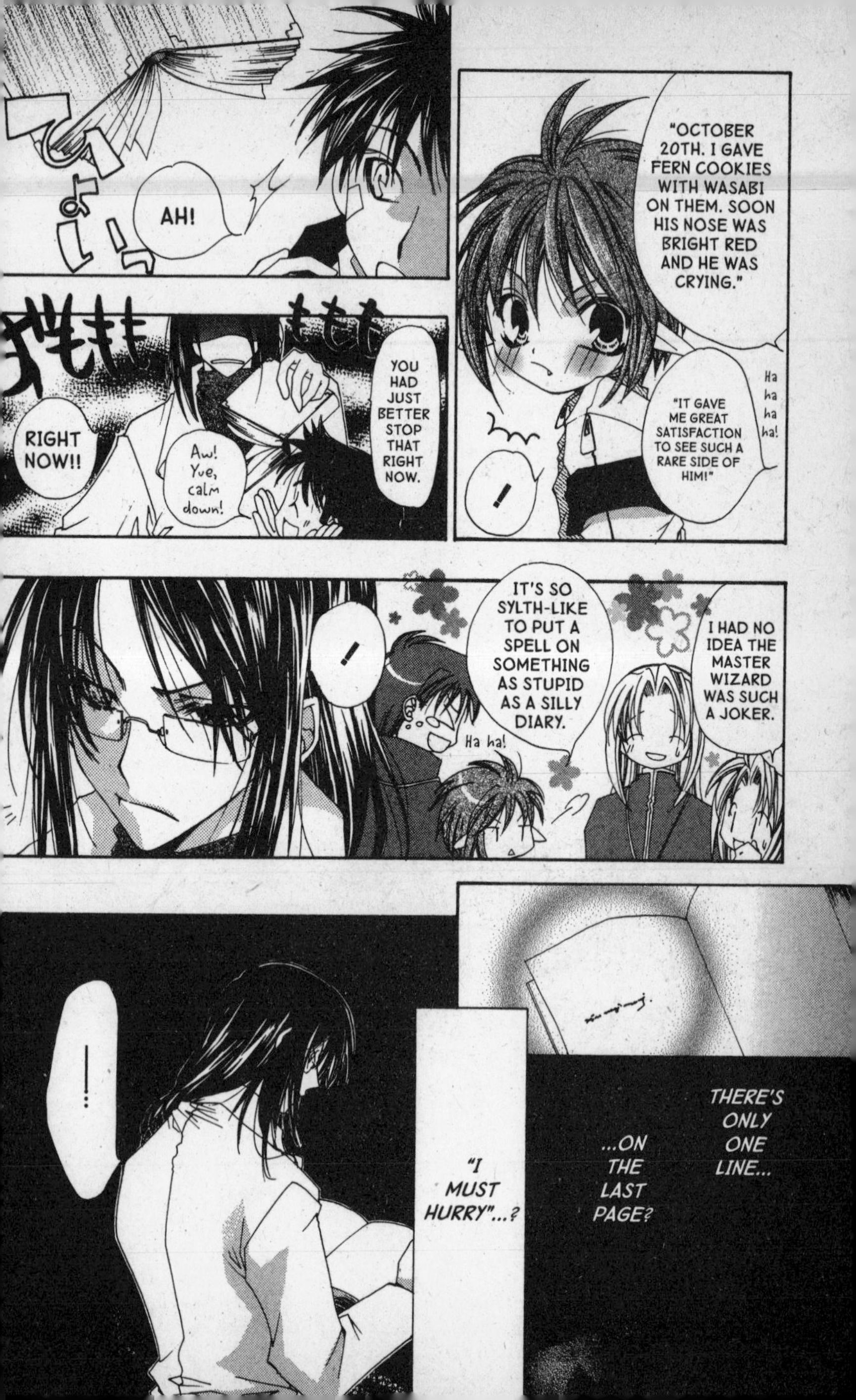

"OCTOBER 20TH. I GAVE FERN COOKIES WITH WASABI ON THEM. SOON HIS NOSE WAS BRIGHT RED AND HE WAS CRYING."
Ha ha ha ha!
"IT GAVE ME GREAT SATISFACTION TO SEE SUCH A RARE SIDE OF HIM!"
!
AH!
YOU HAD JUST BETTER STOP THAT RIGHT NOW.
Aw! Yue, calm down!
RIGHT NOW!!
I HAD NO IDEA THE MASTER WIZARD WAS SUCH A JOKER.
IT'S SO SYLTH-LIKE TO PUT A SPELL ON SOMETHING AS STUPID AS A SILLY DIARY.
Ha ha!
!
THERE'S ONLY ONE LINE...
...ON THE LAST PAGE?
"I MUST HURRY"...?
...!

Episode.23

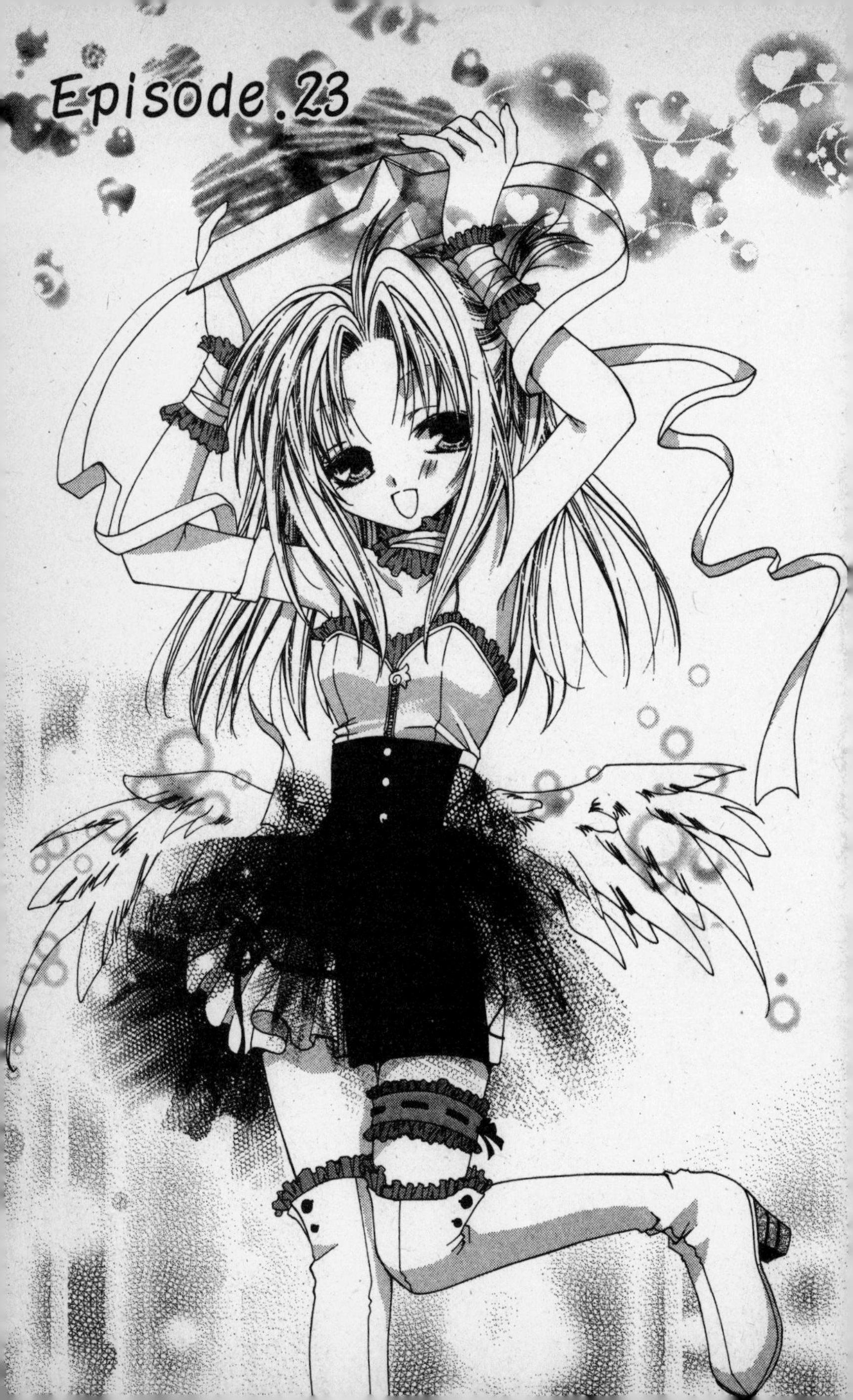

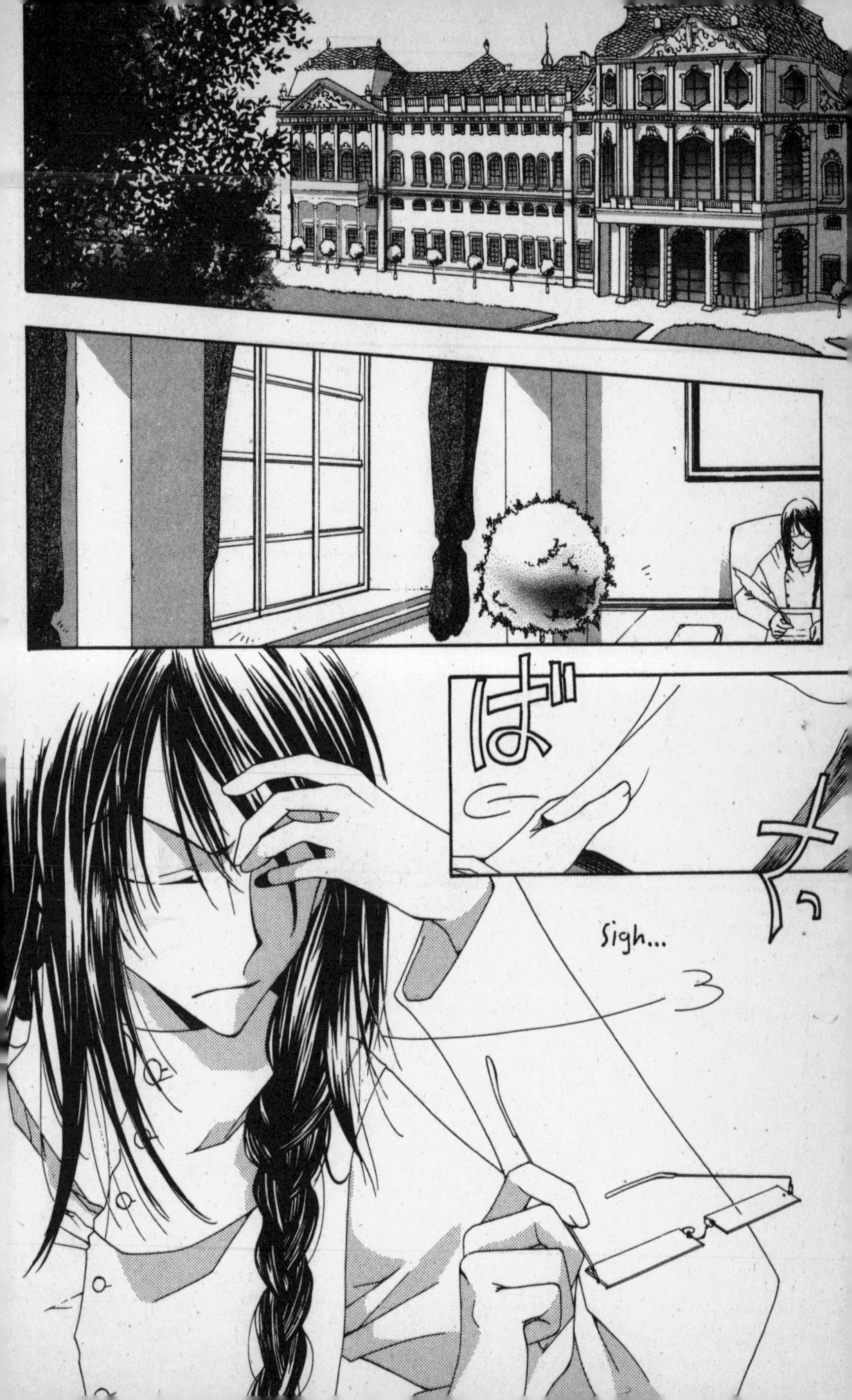
ばさっ
Sigh...

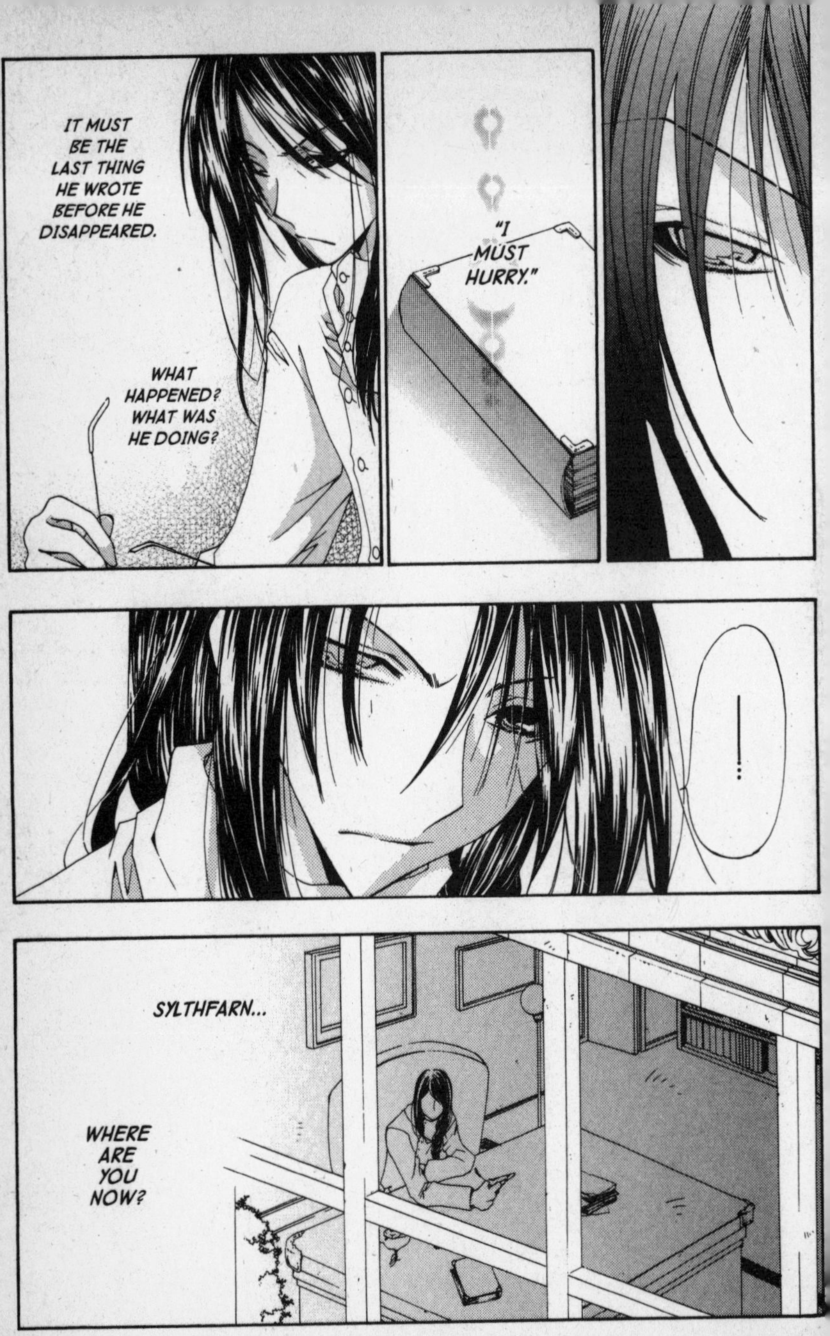
"I MUST HURRY."
IT MUST BE THE LAST THING HE WROTE BEFORE HE DISAPPEARED.
WHAT HAPPENED? WHAT WAS HE DOING?
SYLTHFARN...
WHERE ARE YOU NOW?

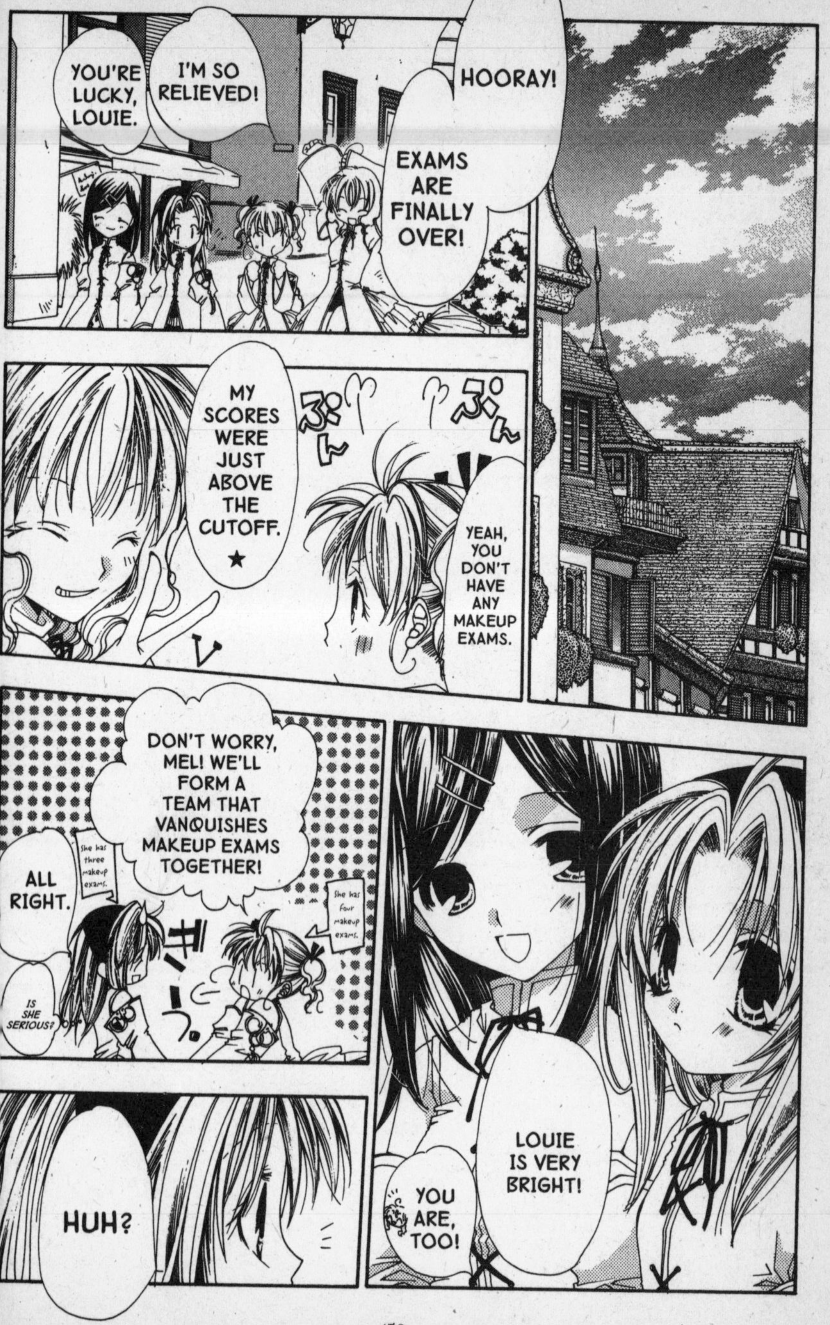

HOORAY!
EXAMS ARE FINALLY OVER!
I'M SO RELIEVED!
YOU'RE LUCKY, LOUIE.
ぷん ぷん
MY SCORES WERE JUST ABOVE THE CUTOFF. ★
YEAH, YOU DON'T HAVE ANY MAKEUP EXAMS.
LOUIE IS VERY BRIGHT!
YOU ARE, TOO!
DON'T WORRY, MEL! WE'LL FORM A TEAM THAT VANQUISHES MAKEUP EXAMS TOGETHER!
She has four makeup exams.
She has three makeup exams.
ALL RIGHT.
IS SHE SERIOUS?
HUH?

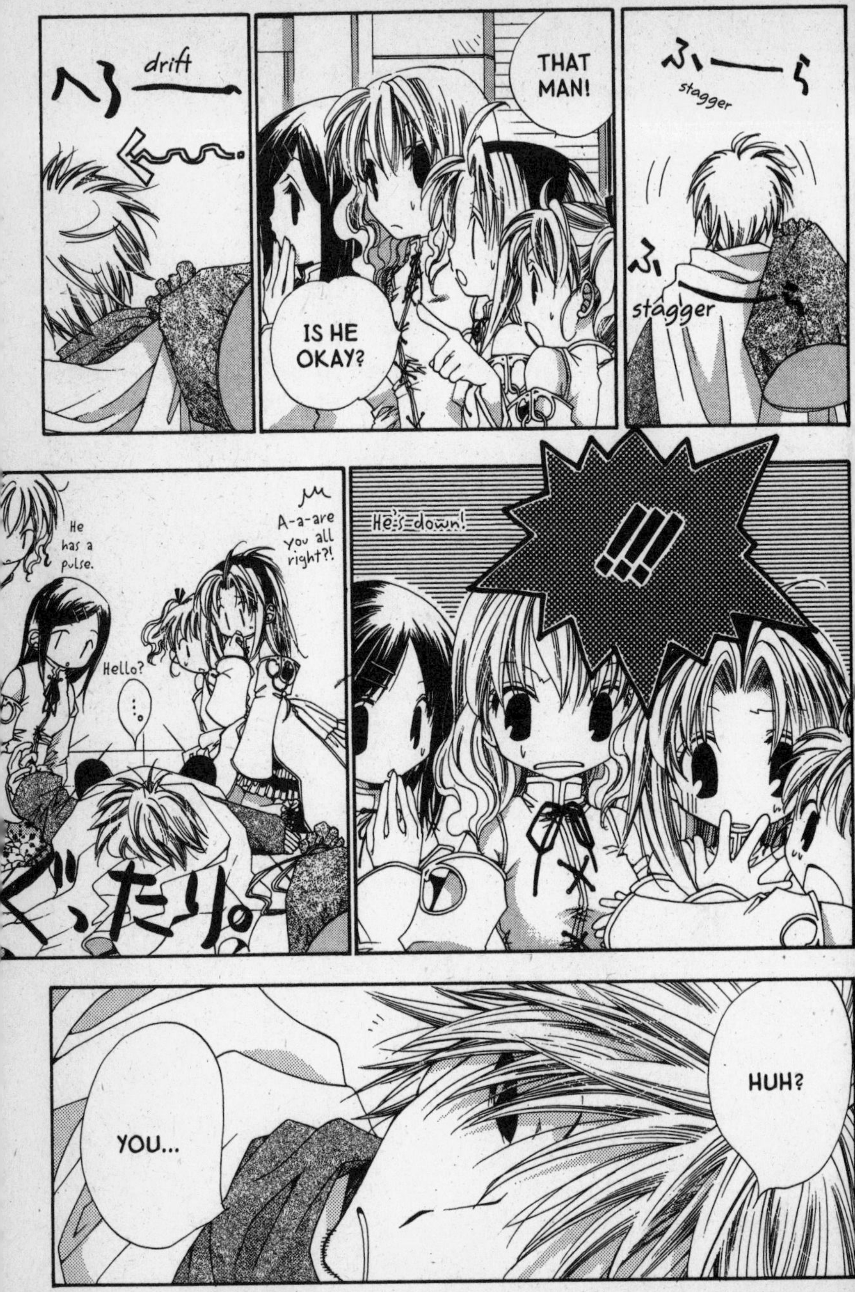
ふーら
stagger
ふー
stagger
THAT MAN!
IS HE OKAY?
へろー
drift
He's down!
!!!!
A-a-are you all right?!
He has a pulse.
Hello?
...
ぐったり。
HUH?
YOU...

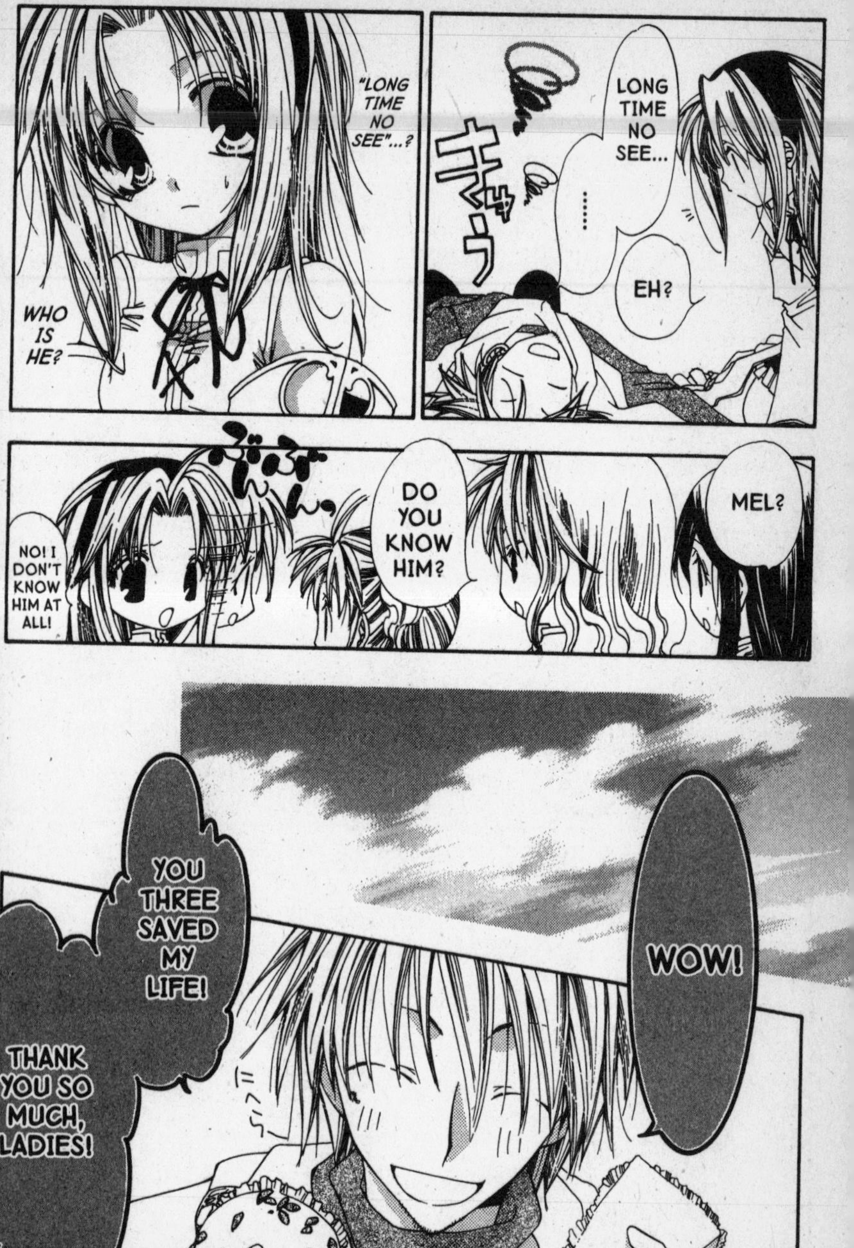
LONG TIME NO SEE...
......
EH?
"LONG TIME NO SEE"...?
WHO IS HE?
MEL?
DO YOU KNOW HIM?
NO! I DON'T KNOW HIM AT ALL!
WOW!
YOU THREE SAVED MY LIFE!
THANK YOU SO MUCH, LADIES!

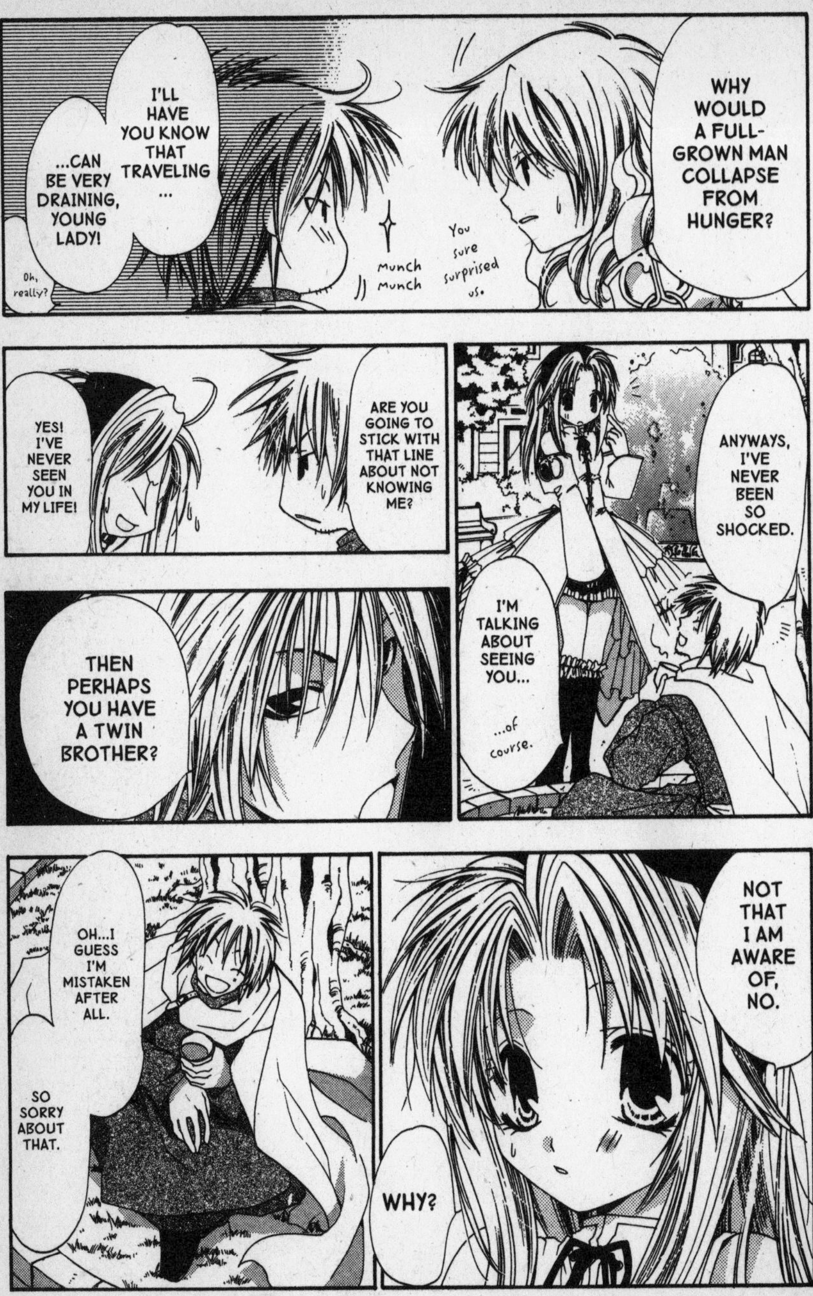
WHY WOULD A FULL-GROWN MAN COLLAPSE FROM HUNGER?
You sure surprised us.
Munch Munch
I'LL HAVE YOU KNOW THAT TRAVELING...
...CAN BE VERY DRAINING, YOUNG LADY!
Oh, really?
ANYWAYS, I'VE NEVER BEEN SO SHOCKED.
I'M TALKING ABOUT SEEING YOU...
...of course.
ARE YOU GOING TO STICK WITH THAT LINE ABOUT NOT KNOWING ME?
YES! I'VE NEVER SEEN YOU IN MY LIFE!
THEN PERHAPS YOU HAVE A TWIN BROTHER?
NOT THAT I AM AWARE OF, NO.
WHY?
OH...I GUESS I'M MISTAKEN AFTER ALL.
SO SORRY ABOUT THAT.

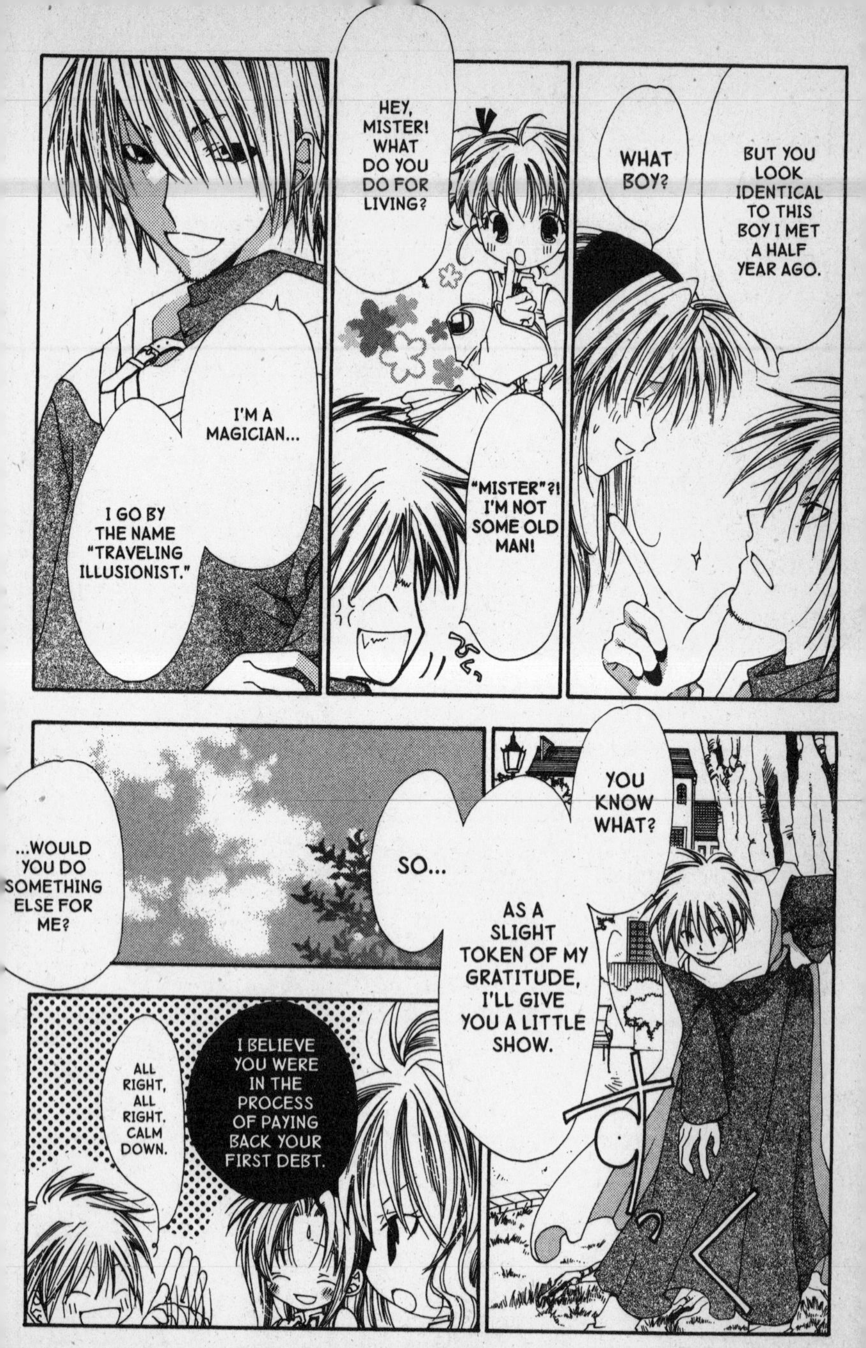
BUT YOU LOOK IDENTICAL TO THIS BOY I MET A HALF YEAR AGO.
WHAT BOY?
HEY, MISTER! WHAT DO YOU DO FOR LIVING?
"MISTER"?! I'M NOT SOME OLD MAN!
I'M A MAGICIAN...
I GO BY THE NAME "TRAVELING ILLUSIONIST."
YOU KNOW WHAT?
SO...
AS A SLIGHT TOKEN OF MY GRATITUDE, I'LL GIVE YOU A LITTLE SHOW.
...WOULD YOU DO SOMETHING ELSE FOR ME?
I BELIEVE YOU WERE IN THE PROCESS OF PAYING BACK YOUR FIRST DEBT.
ALL RIGHT, ALL RIGHT. CALM DOWN.

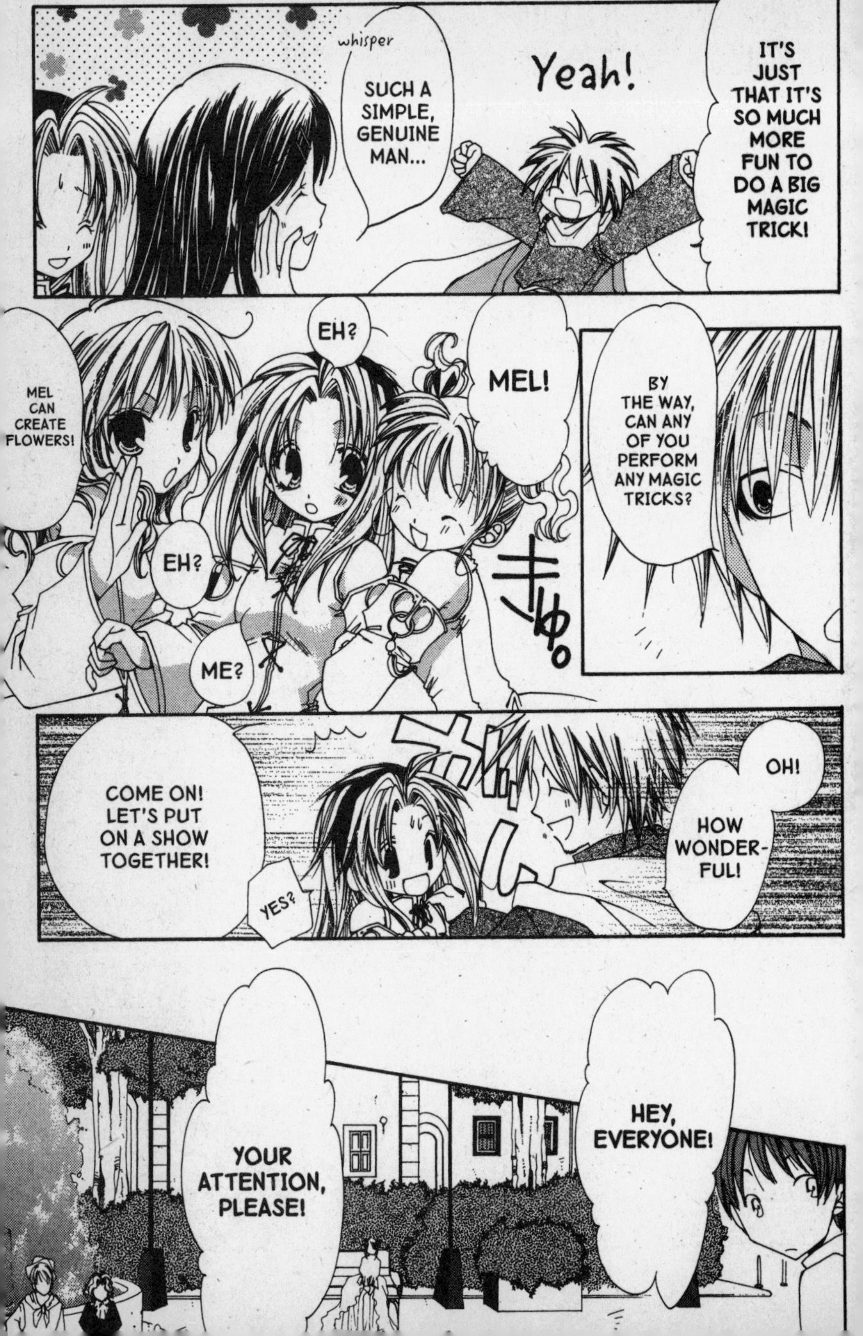
IT'S JUST THAT IT'S SO MUCH MORE FUN TO DO A BIG MAGIC TRICK!
Yeah!
whisper
SUCH A SIMPLE, GENUINE MAN...
BY THE WAY, CAN ANY OF YOU PERFORM ANY MAGIC TRICKS?
MEL!
きゅ
EH?
MEL CAN CREATE FLOWERS!
EH?
ME?
OH!
HOW WONDER-FUL!
COME ON! LET'S PUT ON A SHOW TOGETHER!
YES?
HEY, EVERYONE!
YOUR ATTENTION, PLEASE!

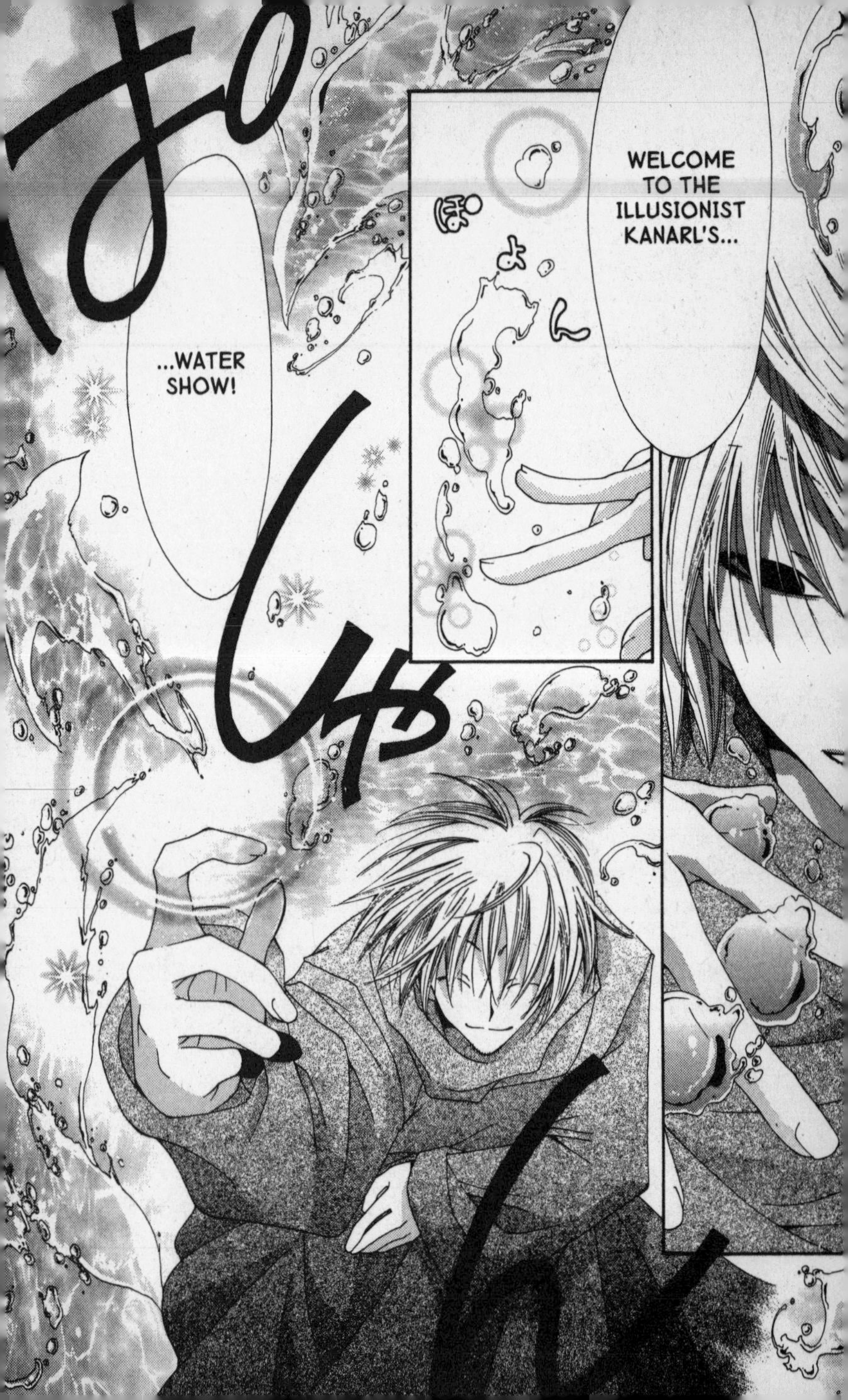
WELCOME TO THE ILLUSIONIST KANARL'S...
ぽよん
...WATER SHOW!

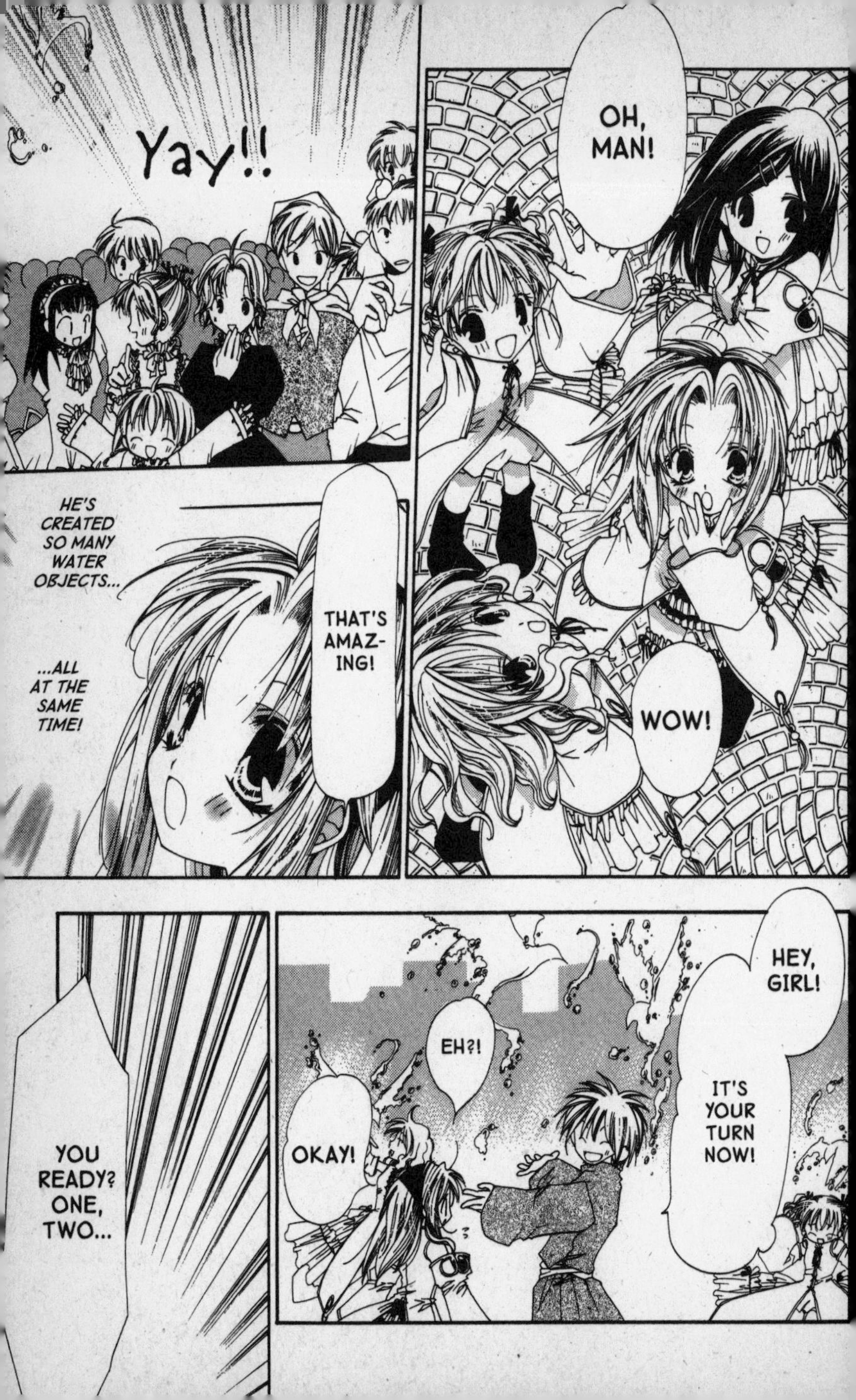
OH, MAN!
WOW!
Yay!!
THAT'S AMAZ-ING!
HE'S CREATED SO MANY WATER OBJECTS...
...ALL AT THE SAME TIME!
HEY, GIRL!
IT'S YOUR TURN NOW!
EH?!
OKAY!
YOU READY? ONE, TWO...

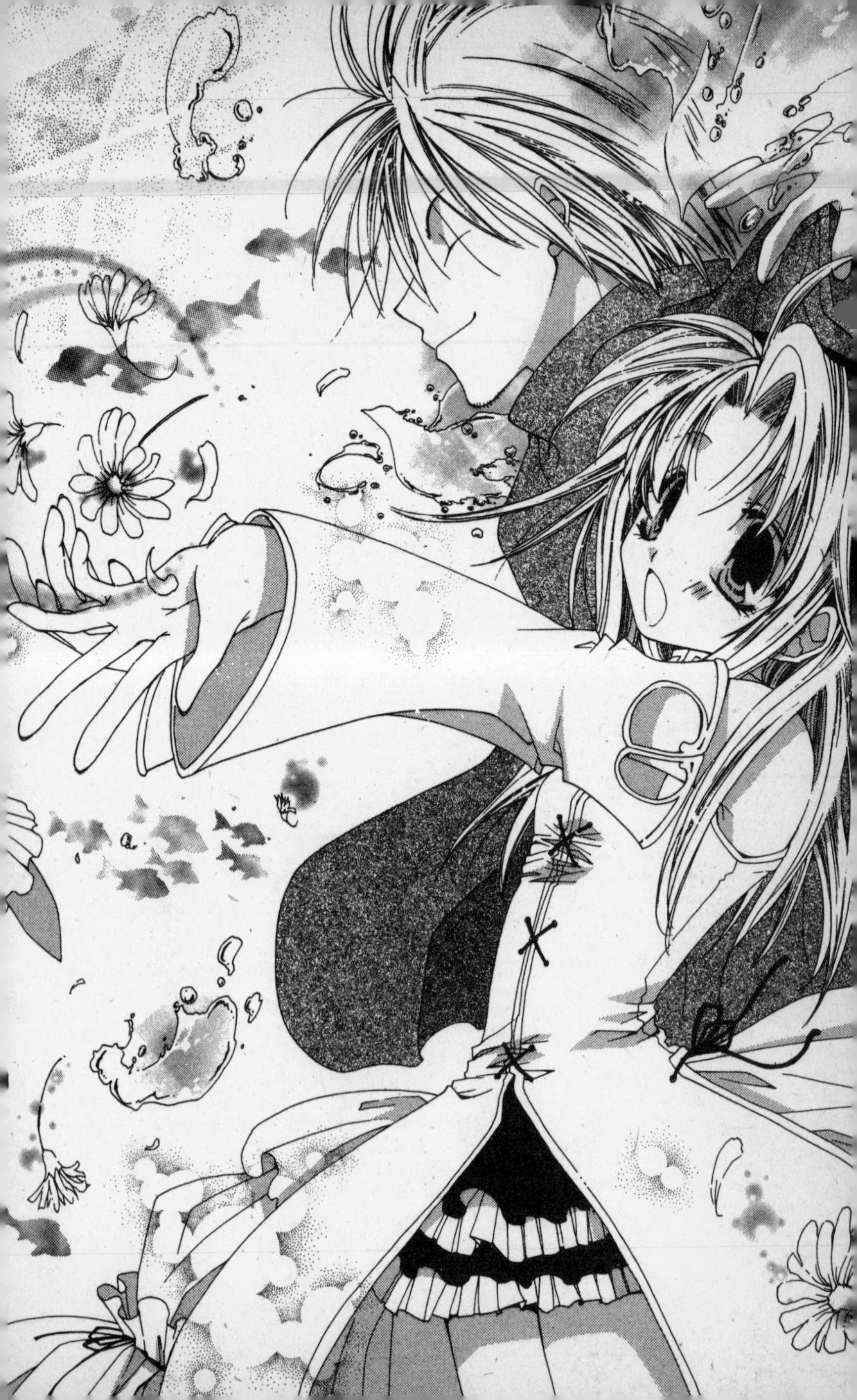

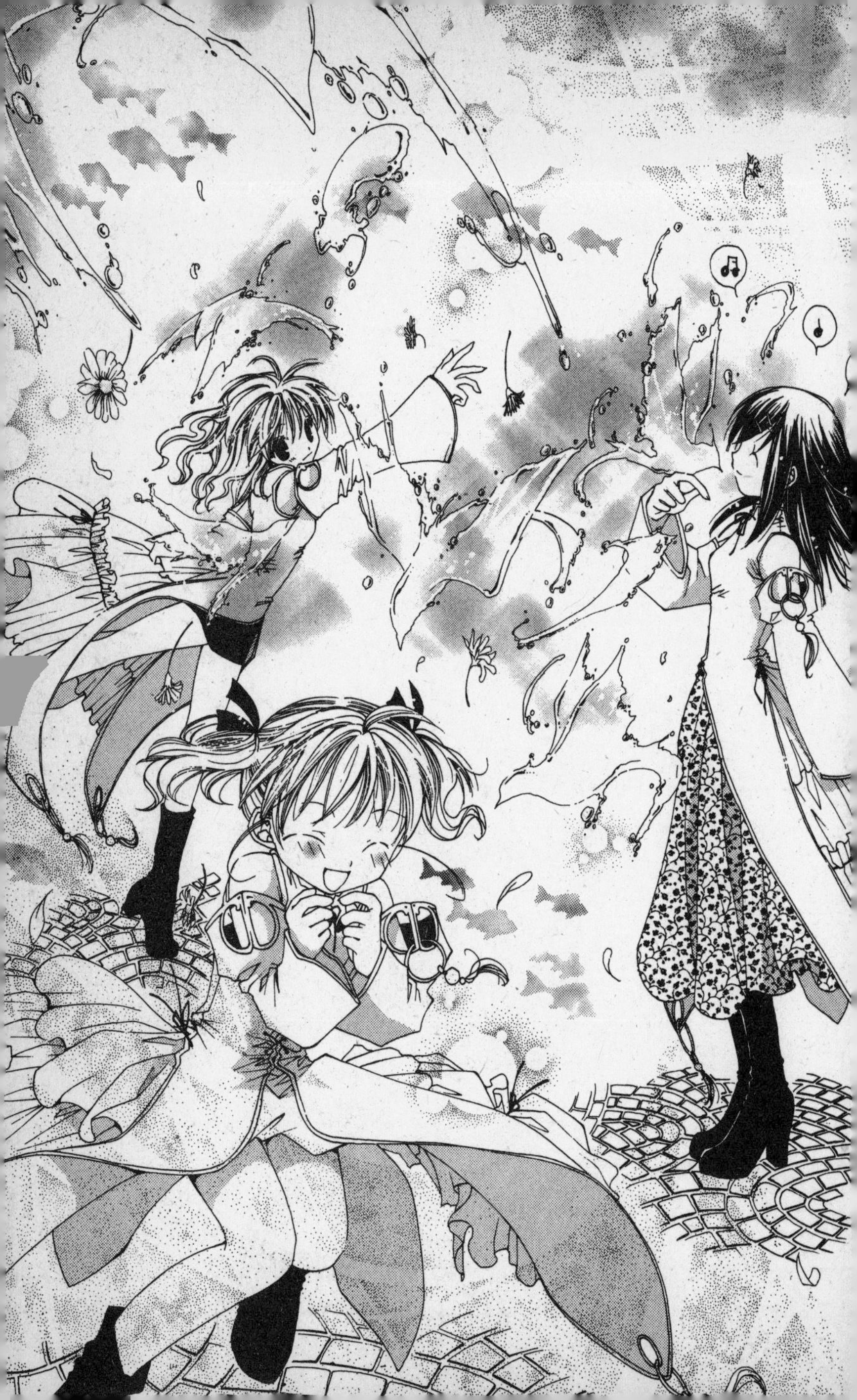

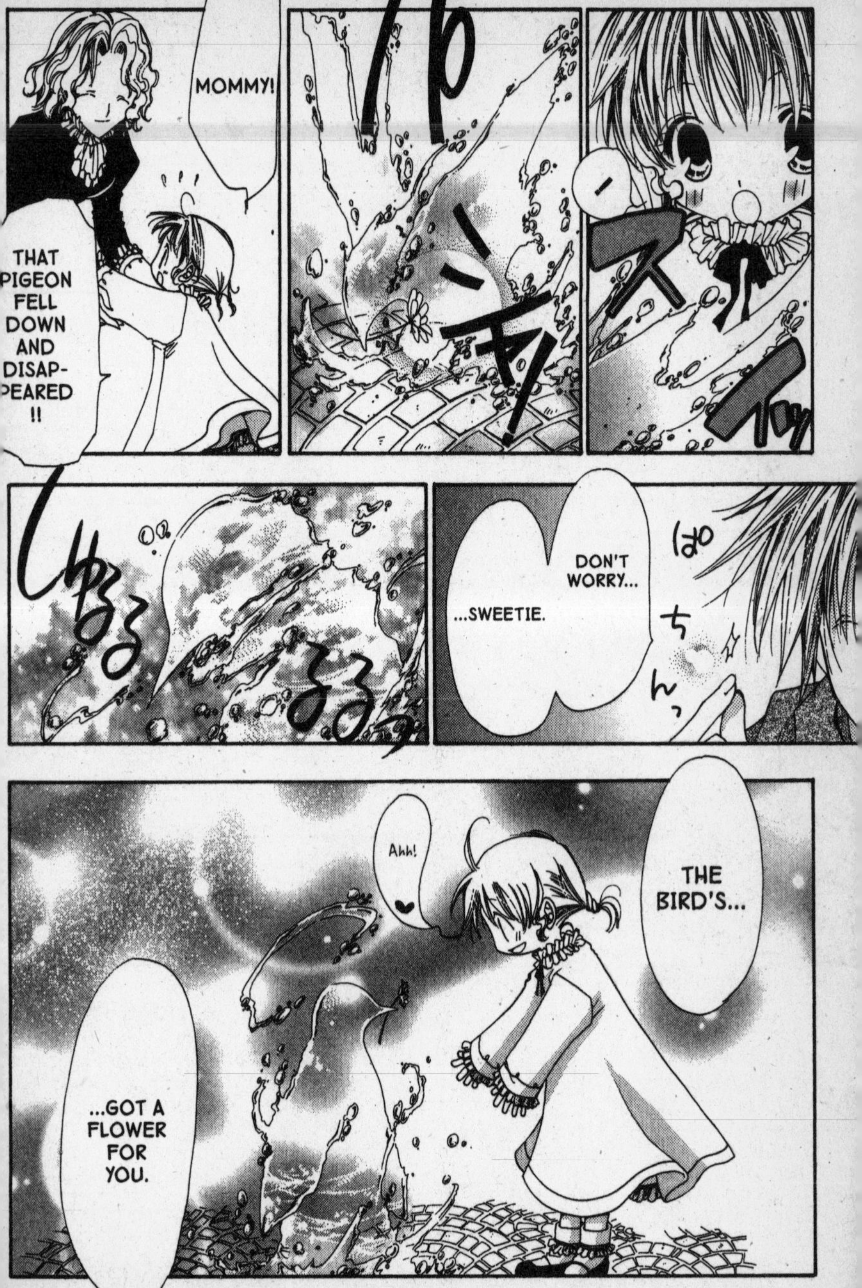
MOMMY!
THAT PIGEON FELL DOWN AND DISAP-PEARED!!
ぱちんっ
DON'T WORRY...
...SWEETIE.
THE BIRD'S...
Ahh!
...GOT A FLOWER FOR YOU.

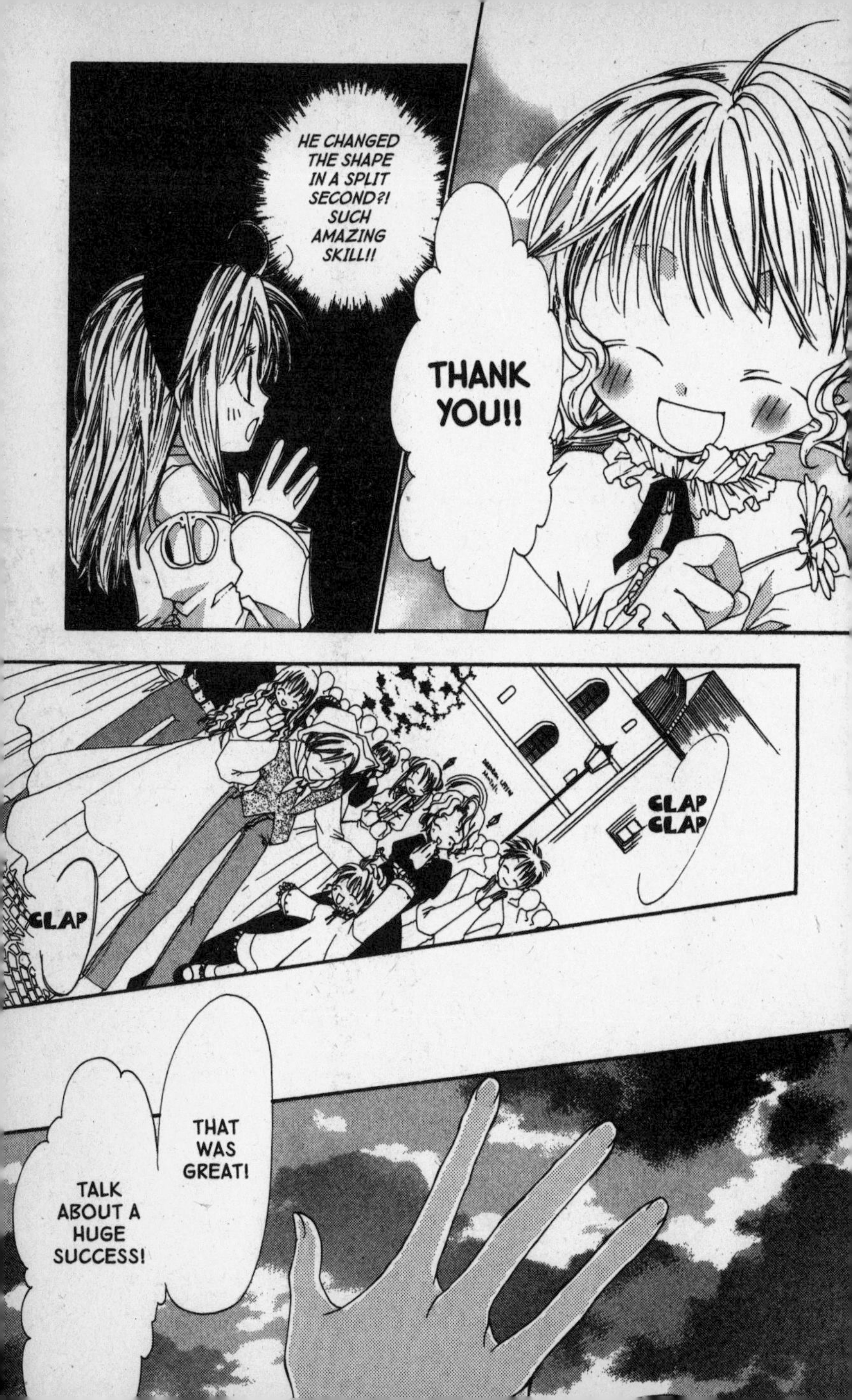
THANK YOU!!
HE CHANGED THE SHAPE IN A SPLIT SECOND?! SUCH AMAZING SKILL!!
CLAP CLAP
CLAP
THAT WAS GREAT!
TALK ABOUT A HUGE SUCCESS!

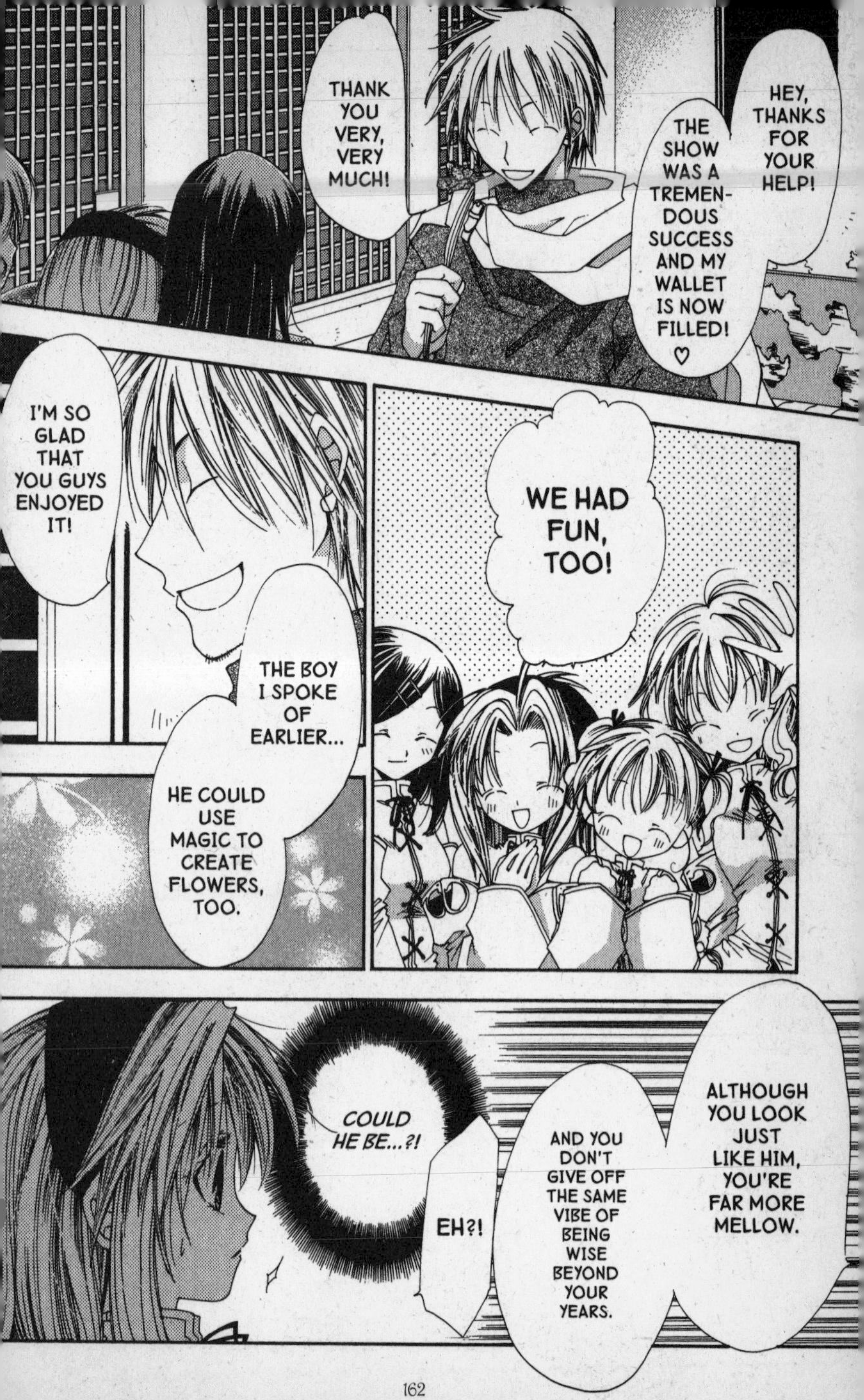
HEY, THANKS FOR YOUR HELP!
THE SHOW WAS A TREMENDOUS SUCCESS AND MY WALLET IS NOW FILLED! ♡
THANK YOU VERY, VERY MUCH!
WE HAD FUN, TOO!
I'M SO GLAD THAT YOU GUYS ENJOYED IT!
THE BOY I SPOKE OF EARLIER...
HE COULD USE MAGIC TO CREATE FLOWERS, TOO.
ALTHOUGH YOU LOOK JUST LIKE HIM, YOU'RE FAR MORE MELLOW.
AND YOU DON'T GIVE OFF THE SAME VIBE OF BEING WISE BEYOND YOUR YEARS.
EH?!
COULD HE BE...?!

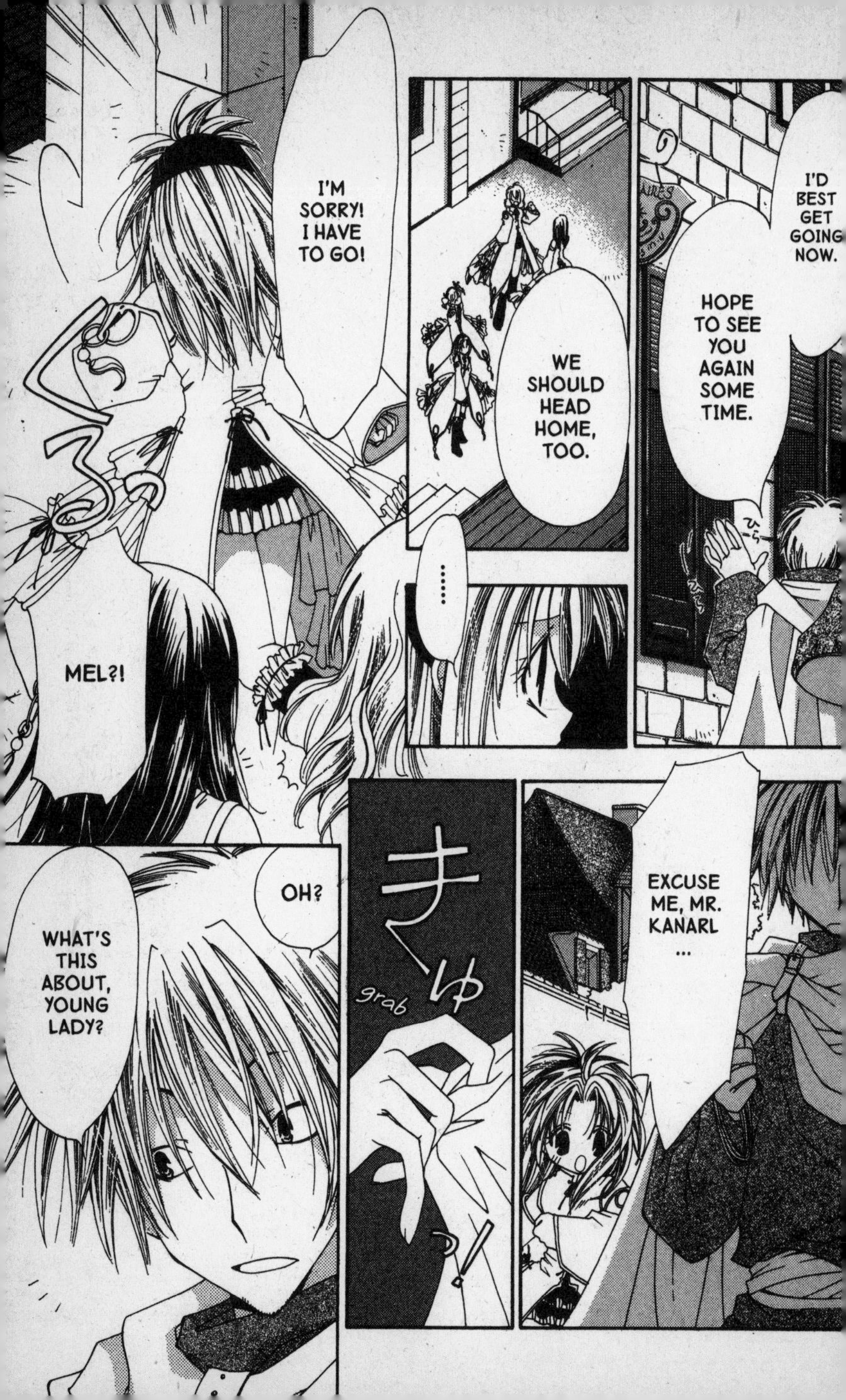
I'D BEST GET GOING NOW.
HOPE TO SEE YOU AGAIN SOME TIME.
WE SHOULD HEAD HOME, TOO.
......
I'M SORRY! I HAVE TO GO!
MEL?!
EXCUSE ME, MR. KANARL ...
grab
OH?
WHAT'S THIS ABOUT, YOUNG LADY?

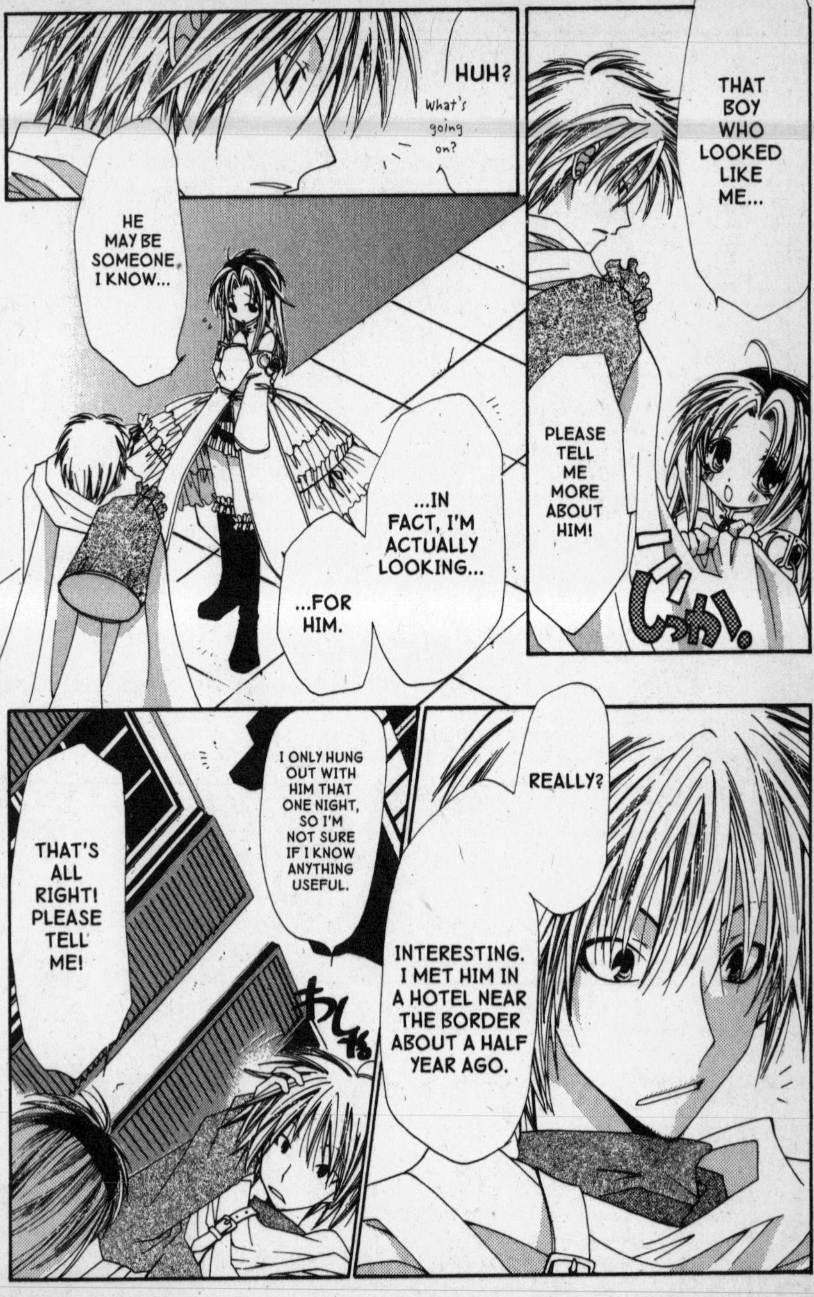
THAT BOY WHO LOOKED LIKE ME...
PLEASE TELL ME MORE ABOUT HIM!
HUH?
what's going on?
HE MAY BE SOMEONE I KNOW...
...IN FACT, I'M ACTUALLY LOOKING...
...FOR HIM.
REALLY?
INTERESTING. I MET HIM IN A HOTEL NEAR THE BORDER ABOUT A HALF YEAR AGO.
I ONLY HUNG OUT WITH HIM THAT ONE NIGHT, SO I'M NOT SURE IF I KNOW ANYTHING USEFUL.
THAT'S ALL RIGHT! PLEASE TELL ME!

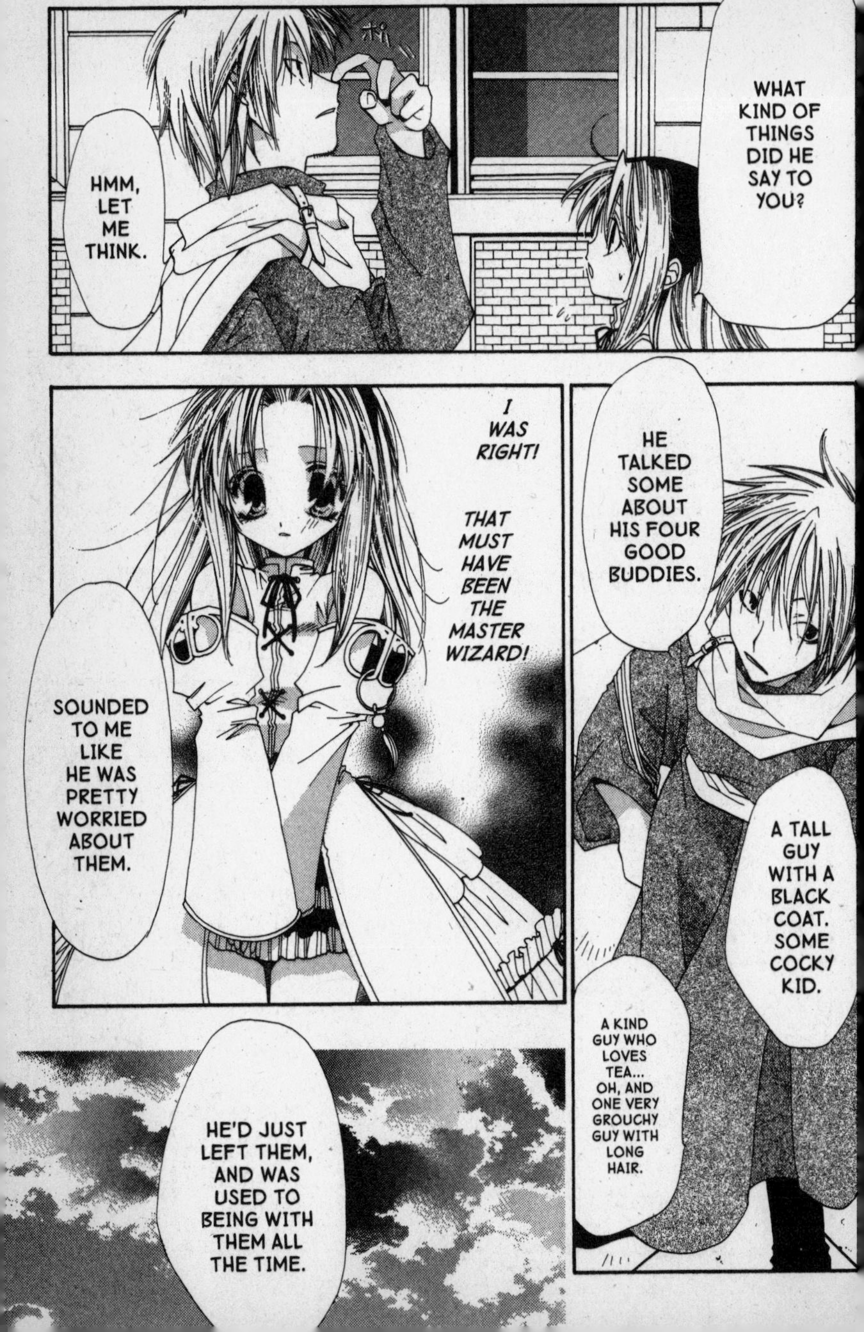
WHAT KIND OF THINGS DID HE SAY TO YOU?
HMM, LET ME THINK.
HE TALKED SOME ABOUT HIS FOUR GOOD BUDDIES.
A TALL GUY WITH A BLACK COAT. SOME COCKY KID.
A KIND GUY WHO LOVES TEA... OH, AND ONE VERY GROUCHY GUY WITH LONG HAIR.
I WAS RIGHT!
THAT MUST HAVE BEEN THE MASTER WIZARD!
SOUNDED TO ME LIKE HE WAS PRETTY WORRIED ABOUT THEM.
HE'D JUST LEFT THEM, AND WAS USED TO BEING WITH THEM ALL THE TIME.

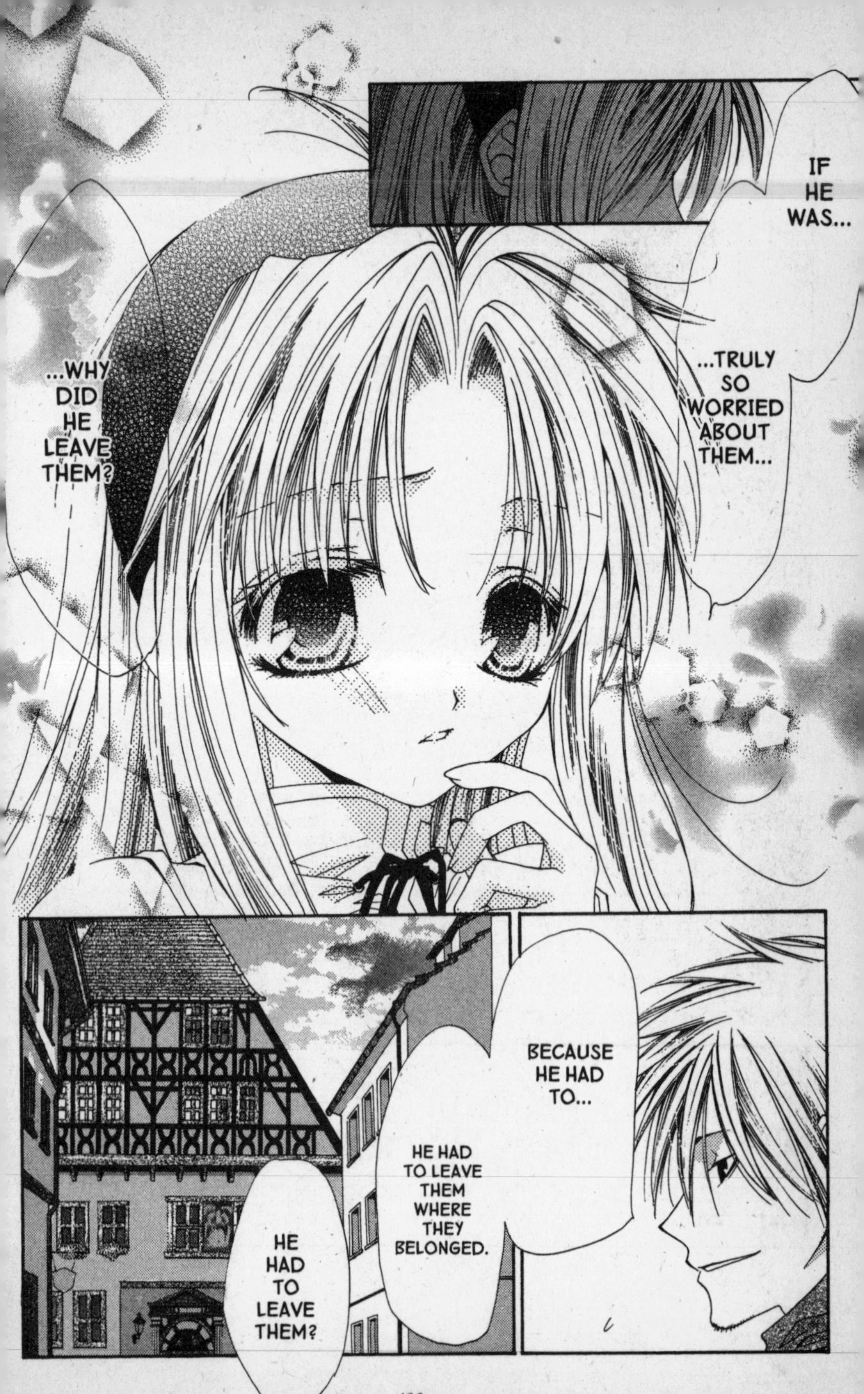
IF HE WAS...
...TRULY SO WORRIED ABOUT THEM...
...WHY DID HE LEAVE THEM?
BECAUSE HE HAD TO...
HE HAD TO LEAVE THEM WHERE THEY BELONGED.
HE HAD TO LEAVE THEM?

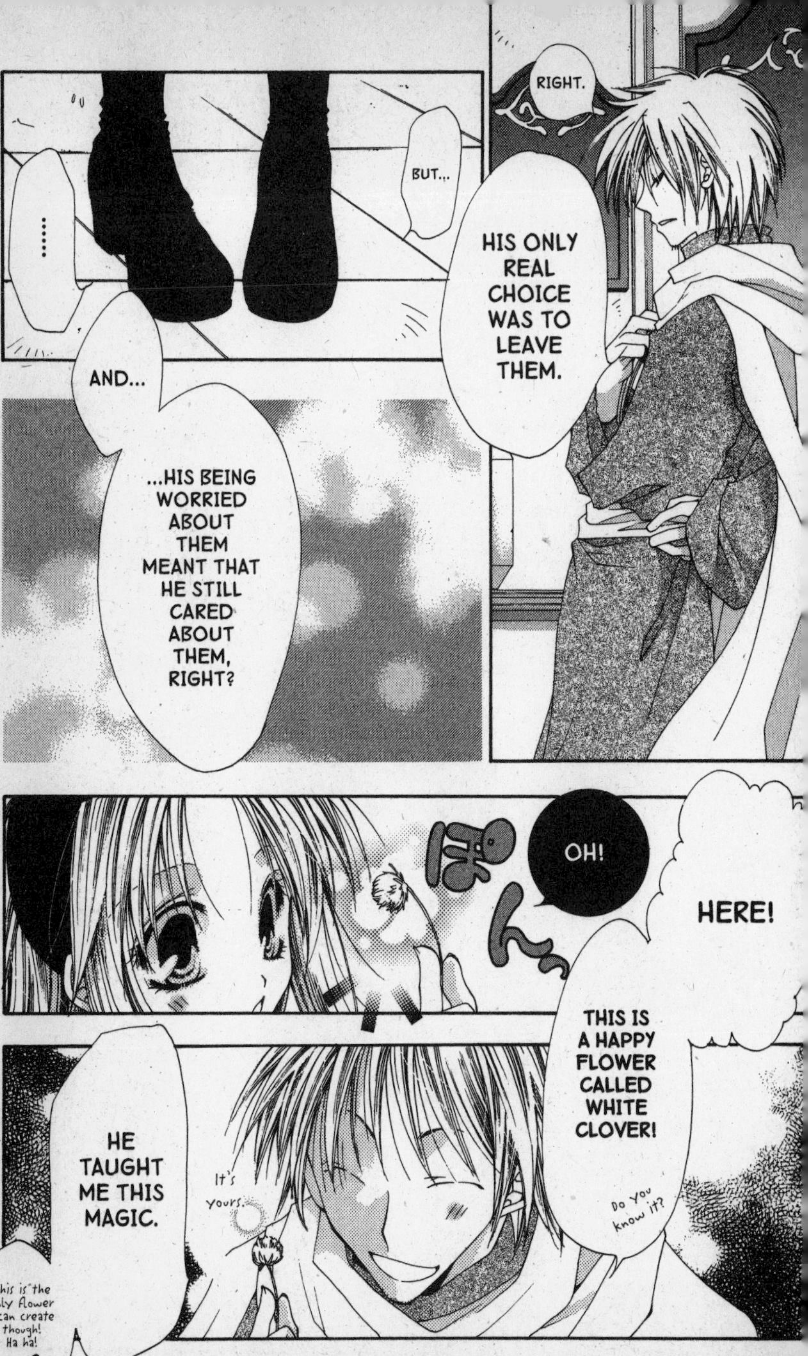
RIGHT.
HIS ONLY REAL CHOICE WAS TO LEAVE THEM.
BUT...
......
AND...
...HIS BEING WORRIED ABOUT THEM MEANT THAT HE STILL CARED ABOUT THEM, RIGHT?
HERE!
OH!
ぽん
THIS IS A HAPPY FLOWER CALLED WHITE CLOVER!
Do you know it?
It's yours.
HE TAUGHT ME THIS MAGIC.
This is the only flower I can create though! Ha ha!

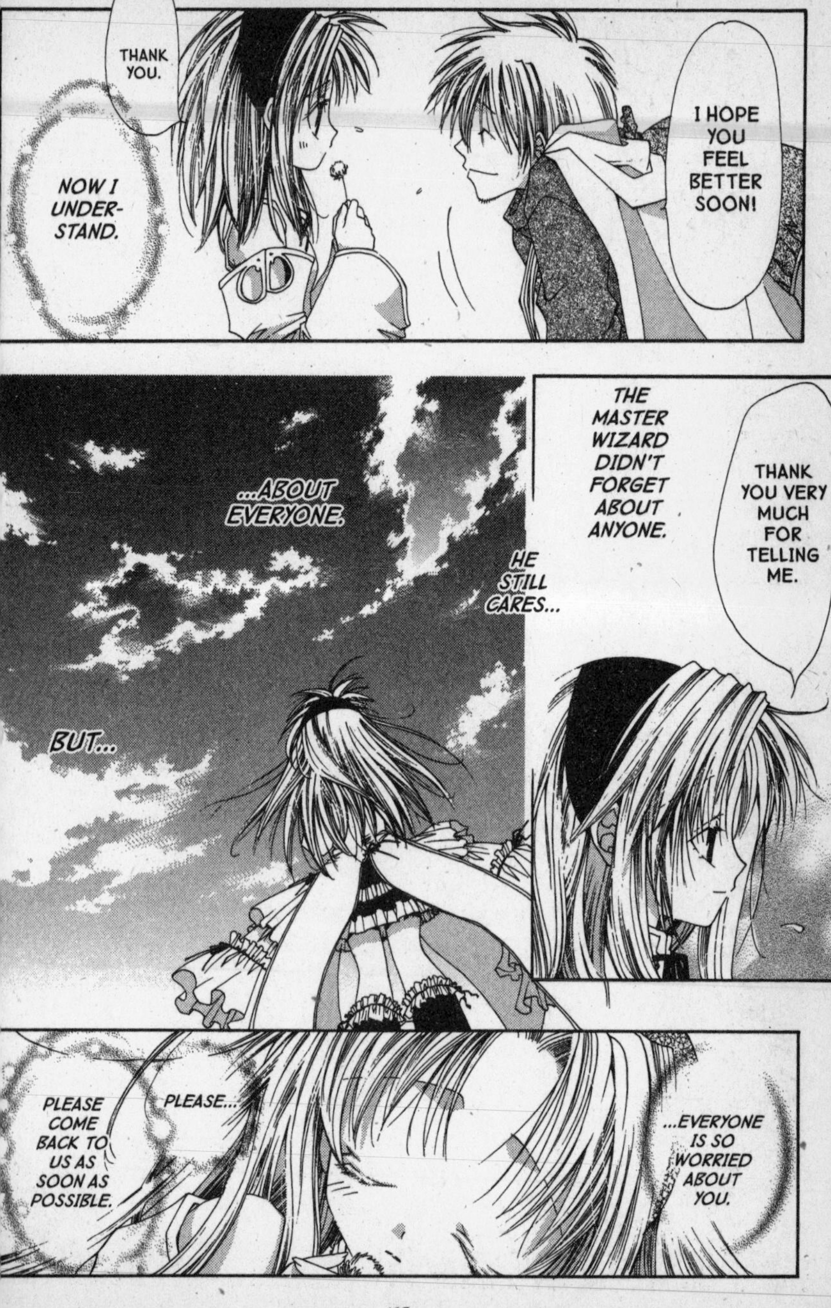
I HOPE YOU FEEL BETTER SOON!
THANK YOU.
NOW I UNDER-STAND.
THANK YOU VERY MUCH FOR TELLING ME.
THE MASTER WIZARD DIDN'T FORGET ABOUT ANYONE.
HE STILL CARES...
...ABOUT EVERYONE.
BUT...
...EVERYONE IS SO WORRIED ABOUT YOU.
PLEASE...
PLEASE COME BACK TO US AS SOON AS POSSIBLE.

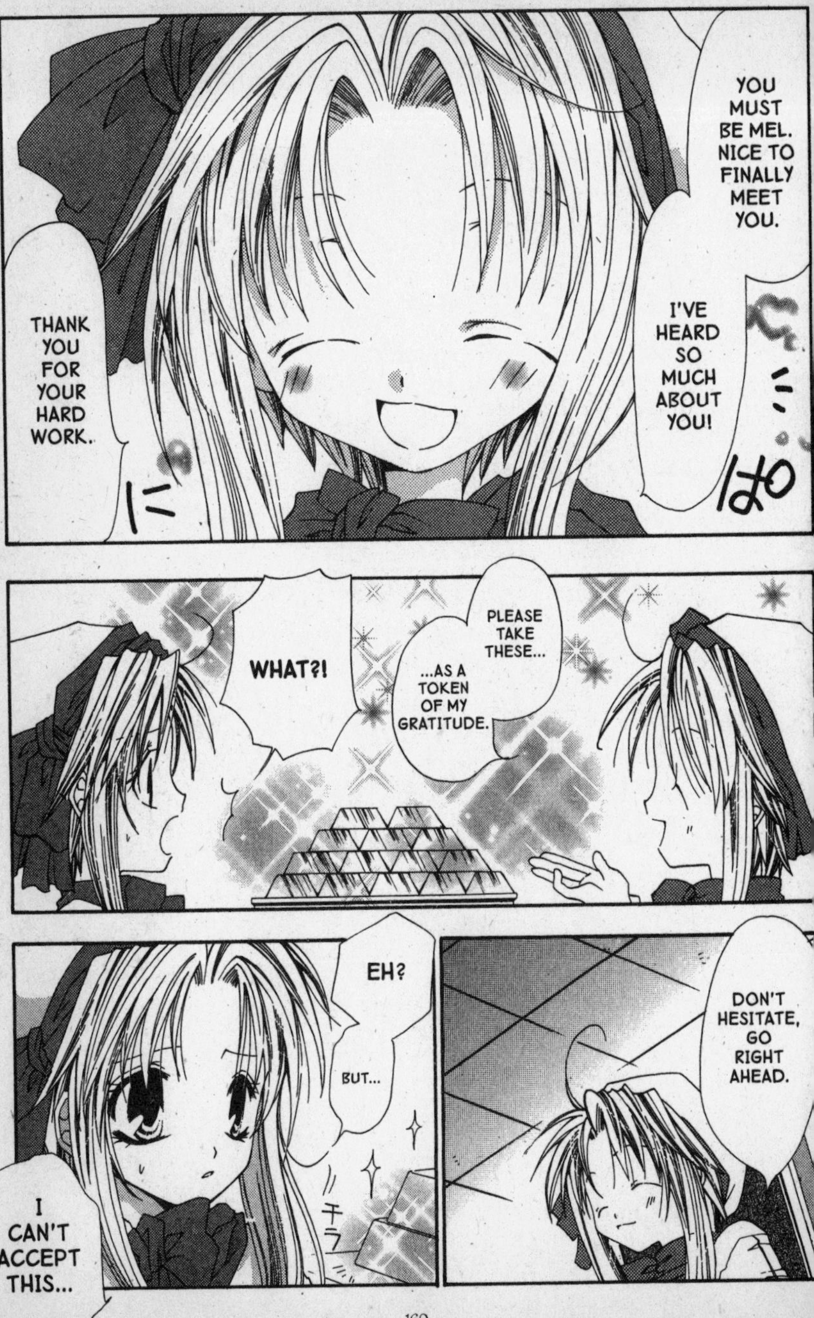
YOU MUST BE MEL. NICE TO FINALLY MEET YOU.
I'VE HEARD SO MUCH ABOUT YOU!
ぱ
THANK YOU FOR YOUR HARD WORK.
に
PLEASE TAKE THESE...
...AS A TOKEN OF MY GRATITUDE.
WHAT?!
DON'T HESITATE, GO RIGHT AHEAD.
EH?
BUT...
キラ
I CAN'T ACCEPT THIS...

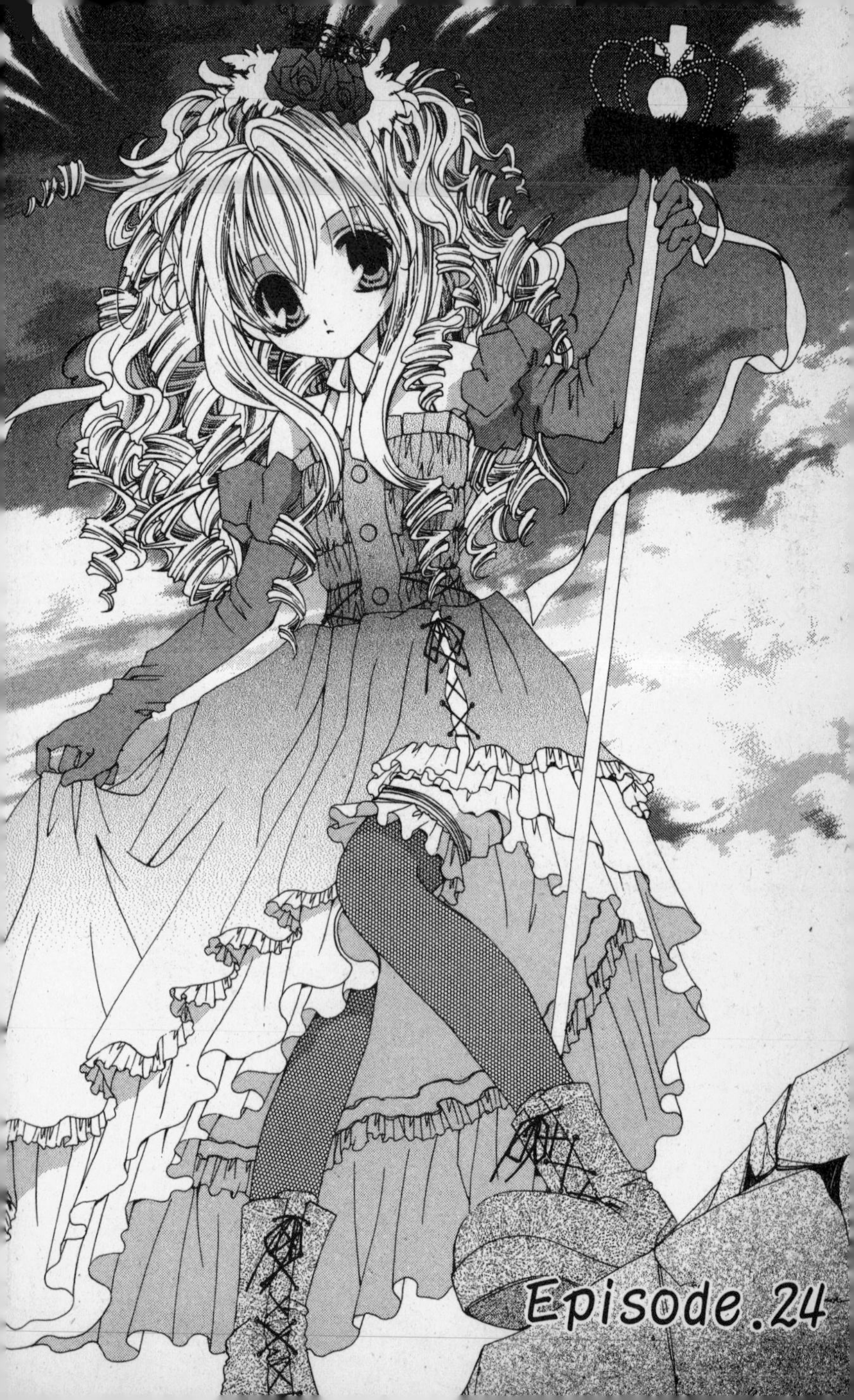
Episode.24

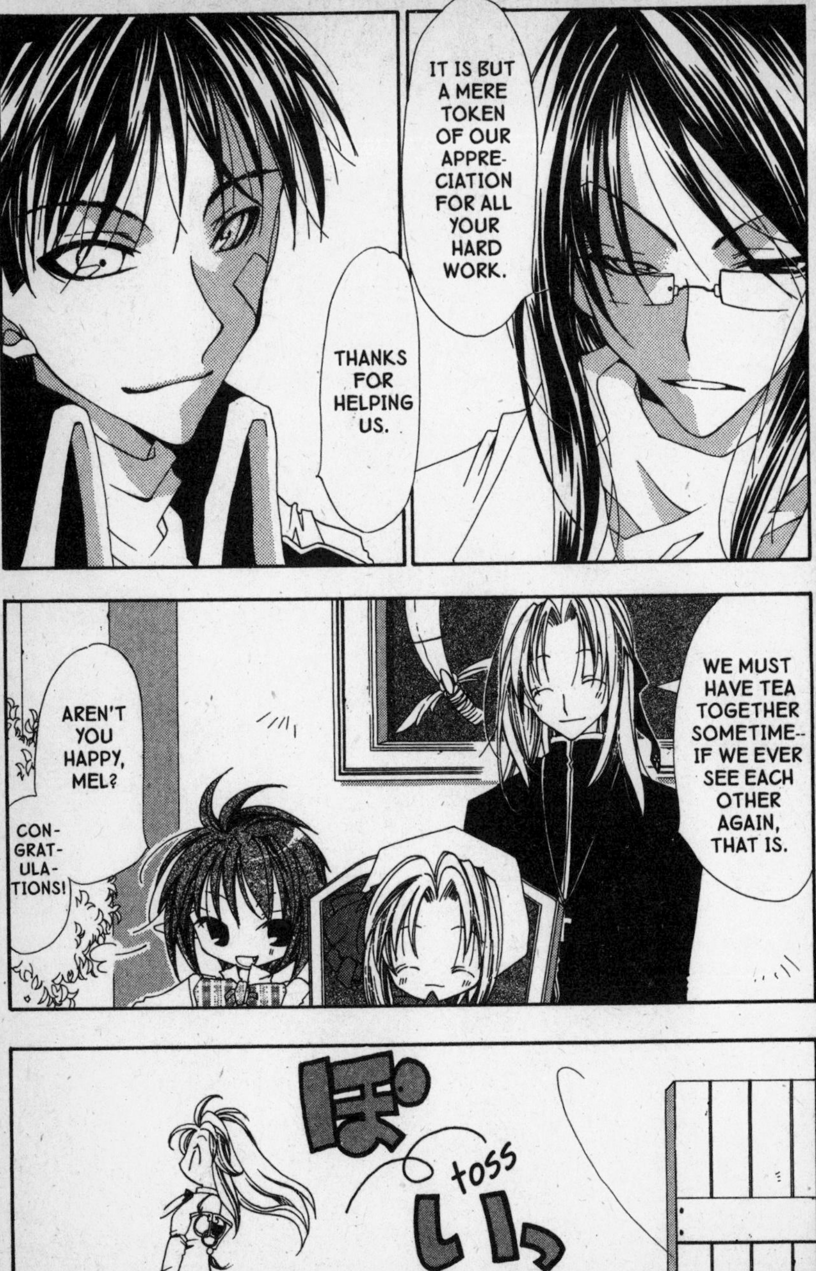
IT IS BUT A MERE TOKEN OF OUR APPRE-CIATION FOR ALL YOUR HARD WORK.
THANKS FOR HELPING US.
WE MUST HAVE TEA TOGETHER SOMETIME-- IF WE EVER SEE EACH OTHER AGAIN, THAT IS.
AREN'T YOU HAPPY, MEL?
CON-GRAT-ULA-TIONS!
ぽいっ
toss

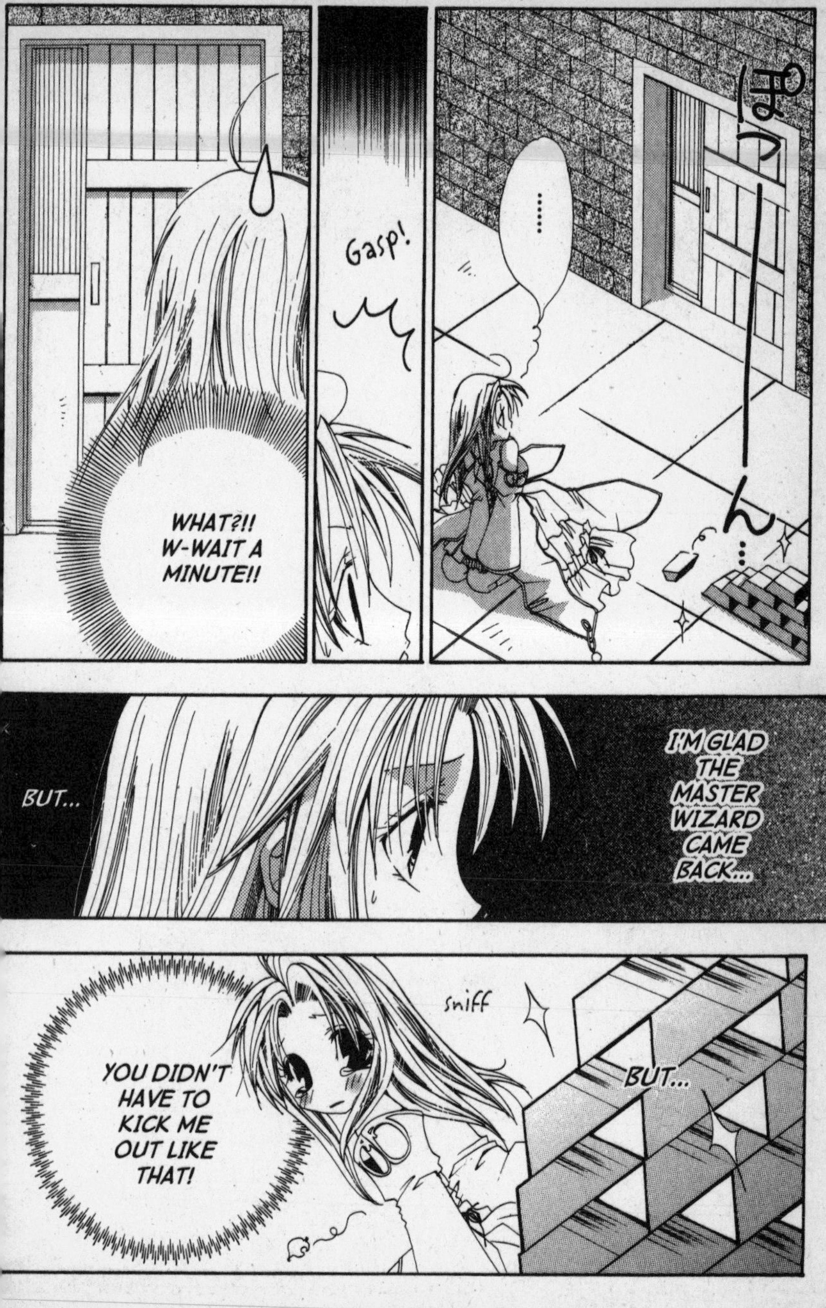
ぽつーん…
……
Gasp!
WHAT?!! W-WAIT A MINUTE!!
I'M GLAD THE MASTER WIZARD CAME BACK...
BUT...
sniff
BUT...
YOU DIDN'T HAVE TO KICK ME OUT LIKE THAT!

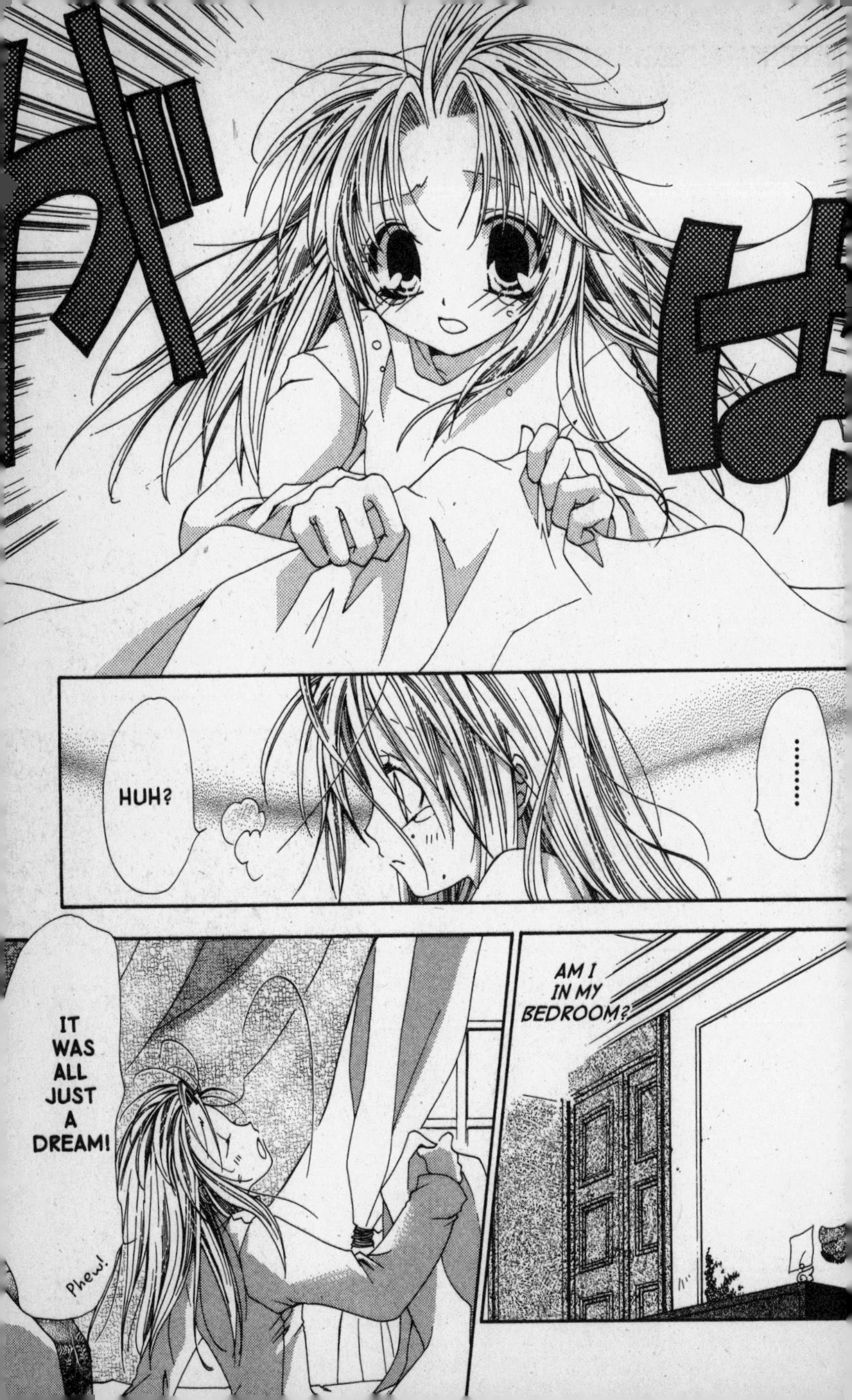

......
HUH?
AM I IN MY BEDROOM?
IT WAS ALL JUST A DREAM!
Phew!

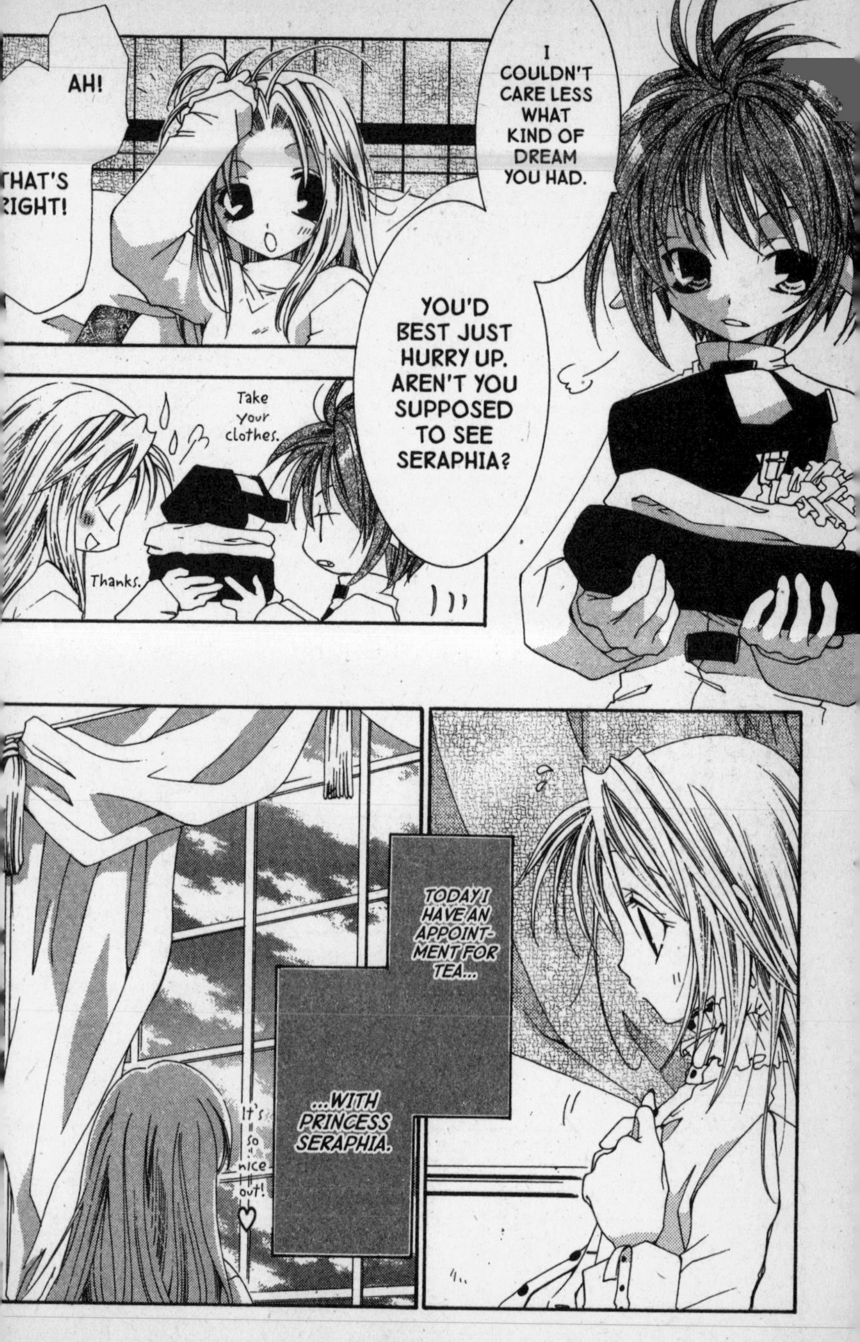
I COULDN'T CARE LESS WHAT KIND OF DREAM YOU HAD.
YOU'D BEST JUST HURRY UP. AREN'T YOU SUPPOSED TO SEE SERAPHIA?
AH!
THAT'S RIGHT!
Take your clothes.
Thanks.
TODAY I HAVE AN APPOINT-MENT FOR TEA...
...WITH PRINCESS SERAPHIA.
It's so nice out!

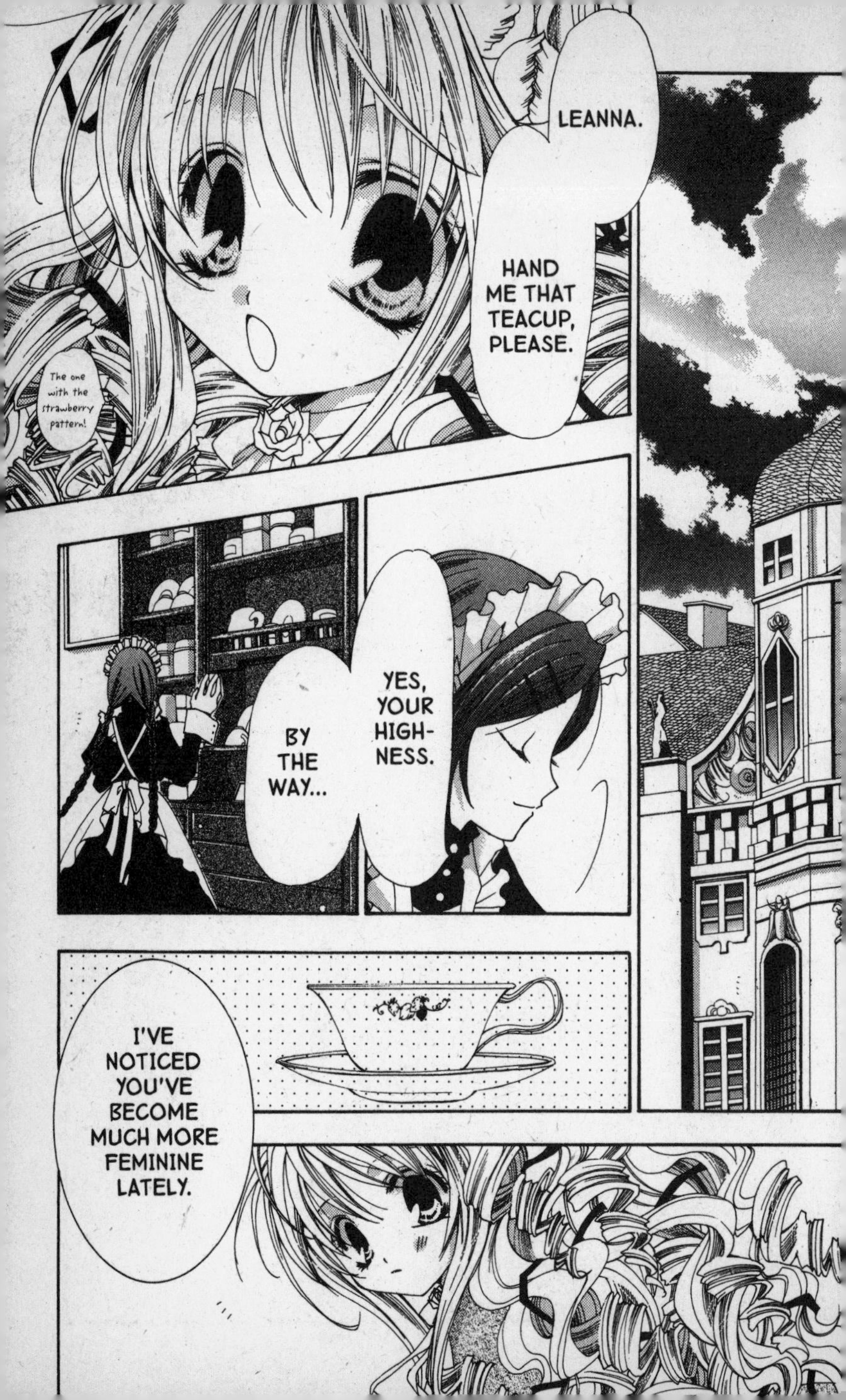
LEANNA.
HAND ME THAT TEACUP, PLEASE.
The one with the strawberry pattern!
YES, YOUR HIGHNESS.
BY THE WAY...
I'VE NOTICED YOU'VE BECOME MUCH MORE FEMININE LATELY.

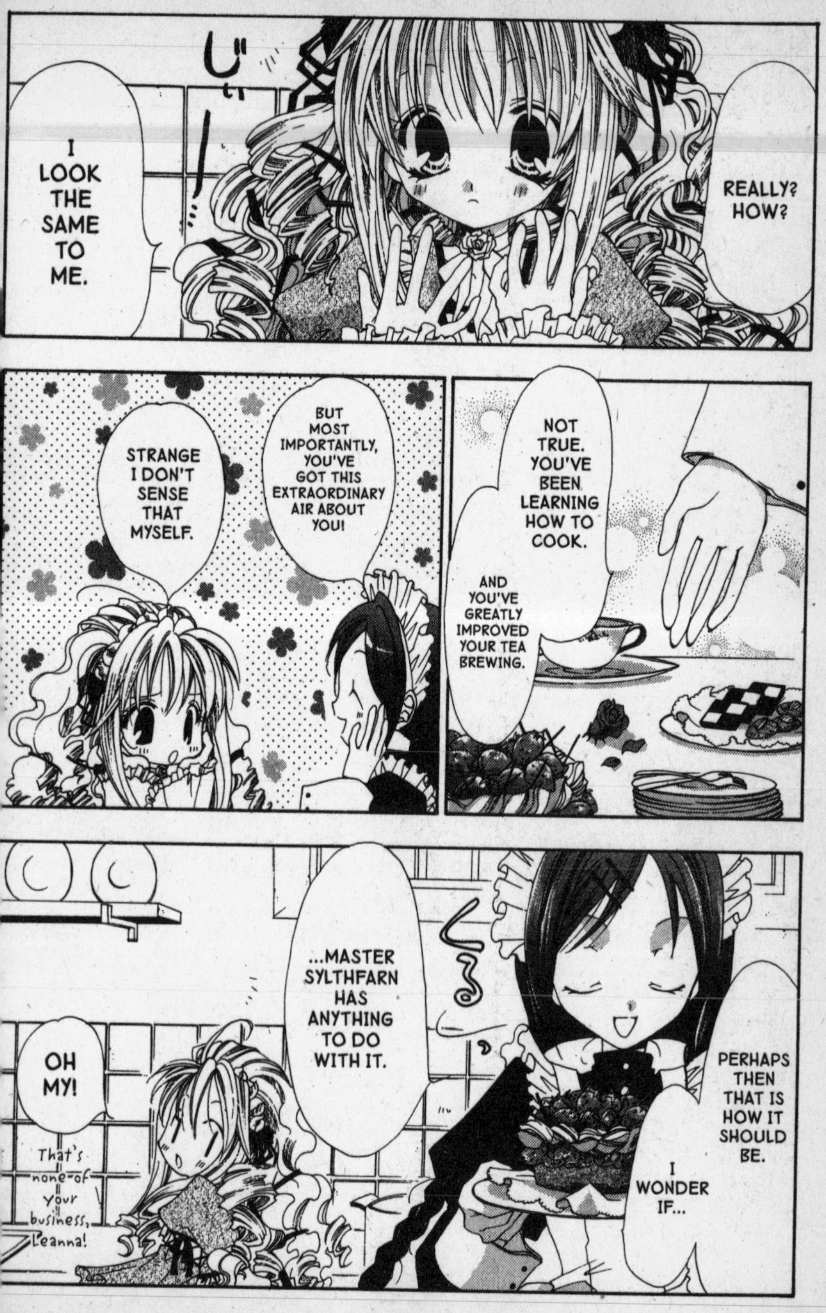
REALLY? HOW?
I LOOK THE SAME TO ME.
NOT TRUE. YOU'VE BEEN LEARNING HOW TO COOK.
AND YOU'VE GREATLY IMPROVED YOUR TEA BREWING.
BUT MOST IMPORTANTLY, YOU'VE GOT THIS EXTRAORDINARY AIR ABOUT YOU!
STRANGE I DON'T SENSE THAT MYSELF.
PERHAPS THEN THAT IS HOW IT SHOULD BE.
I WONDER IF...
...MASTER SYLTHFARN HAS ANYTHING TO DO WITH IT.
OH MY!
That's none of your business, Leanna!

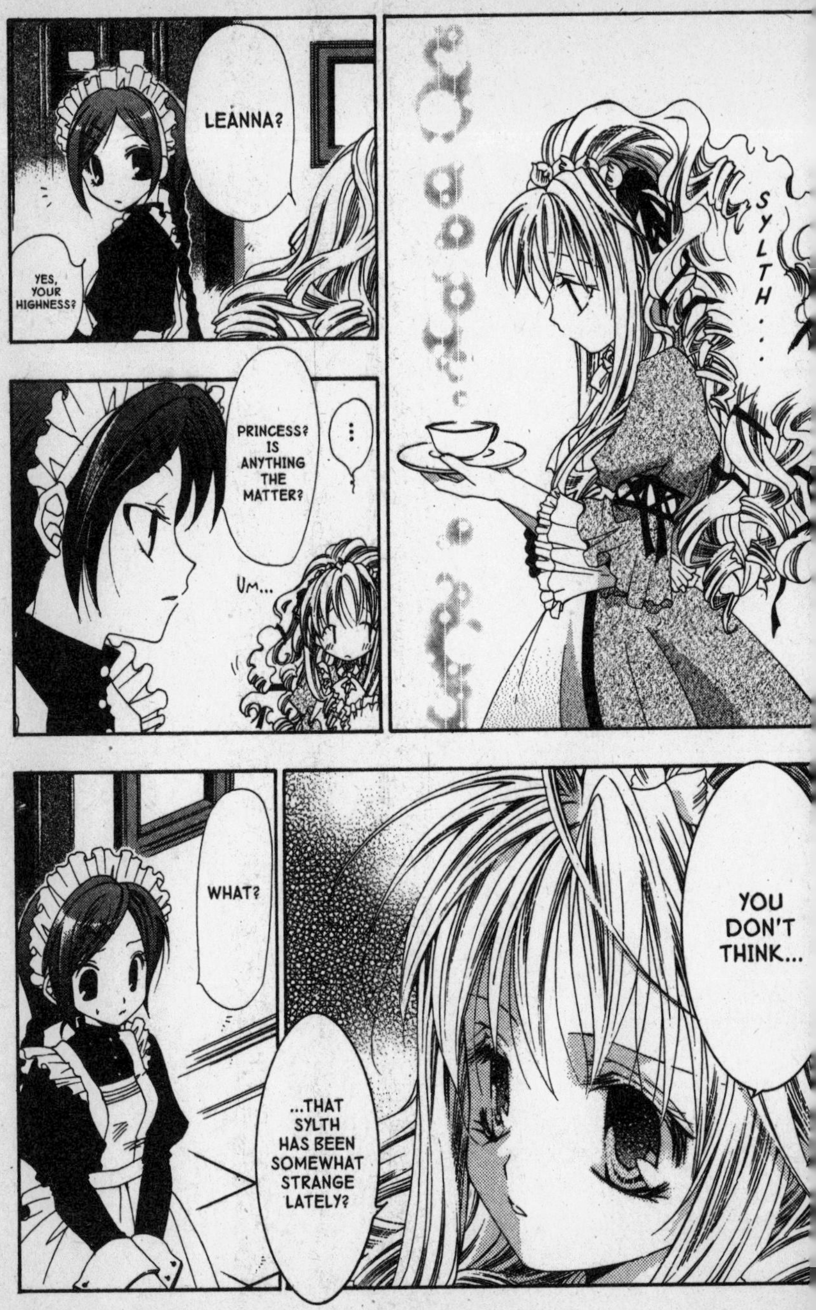
SYLTH...
LEANNA?
YES, YOUR HIGHNESS?
PRINCESS? IS ANYTHING THE MATTER?
...
UM...
YOU DON'T THINK...
...THAT SYLTH HAS BEEN SOMEWHAT STRANGE LATELY?
WHAT?

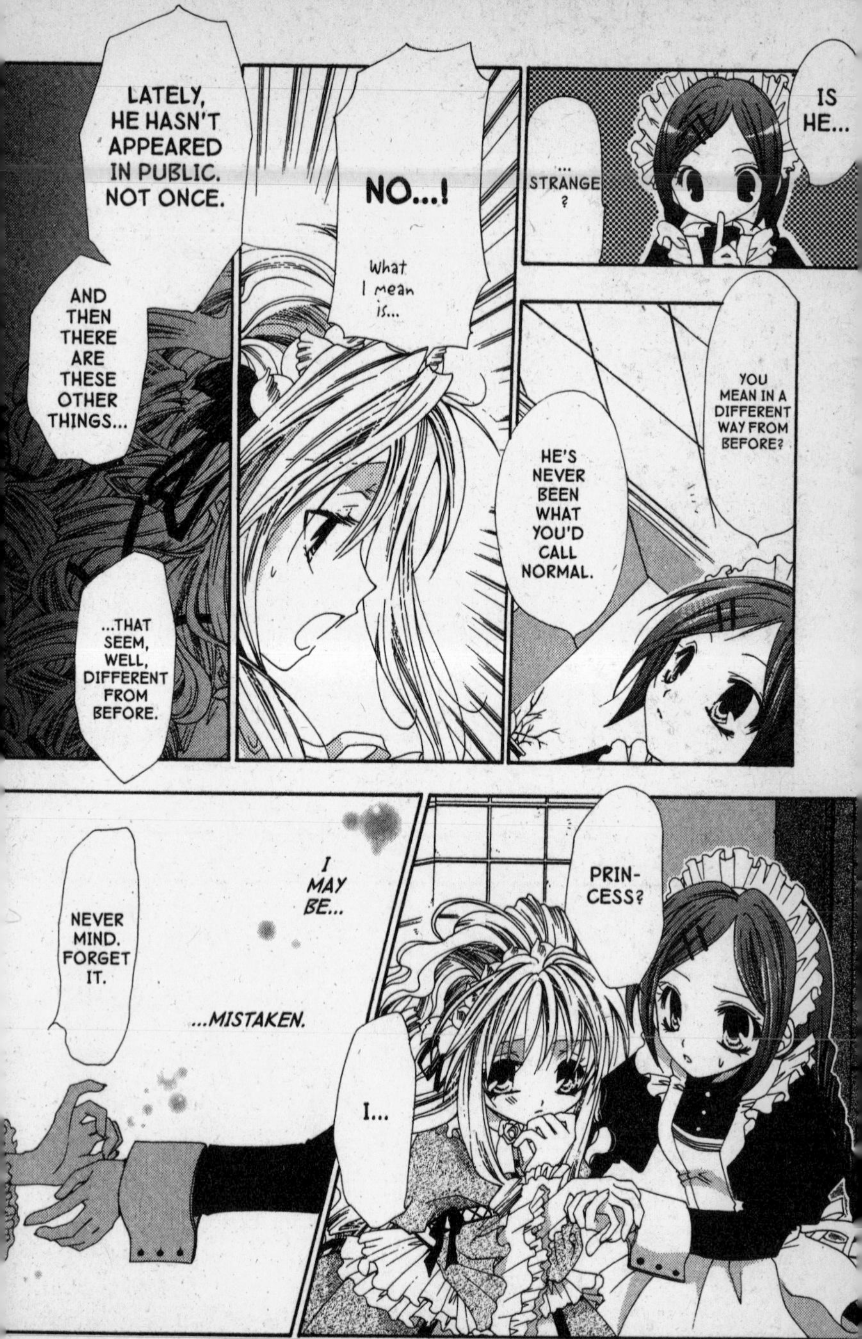
IS HE...
...STRANGE?
YOU MEAN IN A DIFFERENT WAY FROM BEFORE?
HE'S NEVER BEEN WHAT YOU'D CALL NORMAL.
NO...!
What I mean is...
LATELY, HE HASN'T APPEARED IN PUBLIC. NOT ONCE.
AND THEN THERE ARE THESE OTHER THINGS...
...THAT SEEM, WELL, DIFFERENT FROM BEFORE.
PRIN-CESS?
I...
I MAY BE...
...MISTAKEN.
NEVER MIND. FORGET IT.

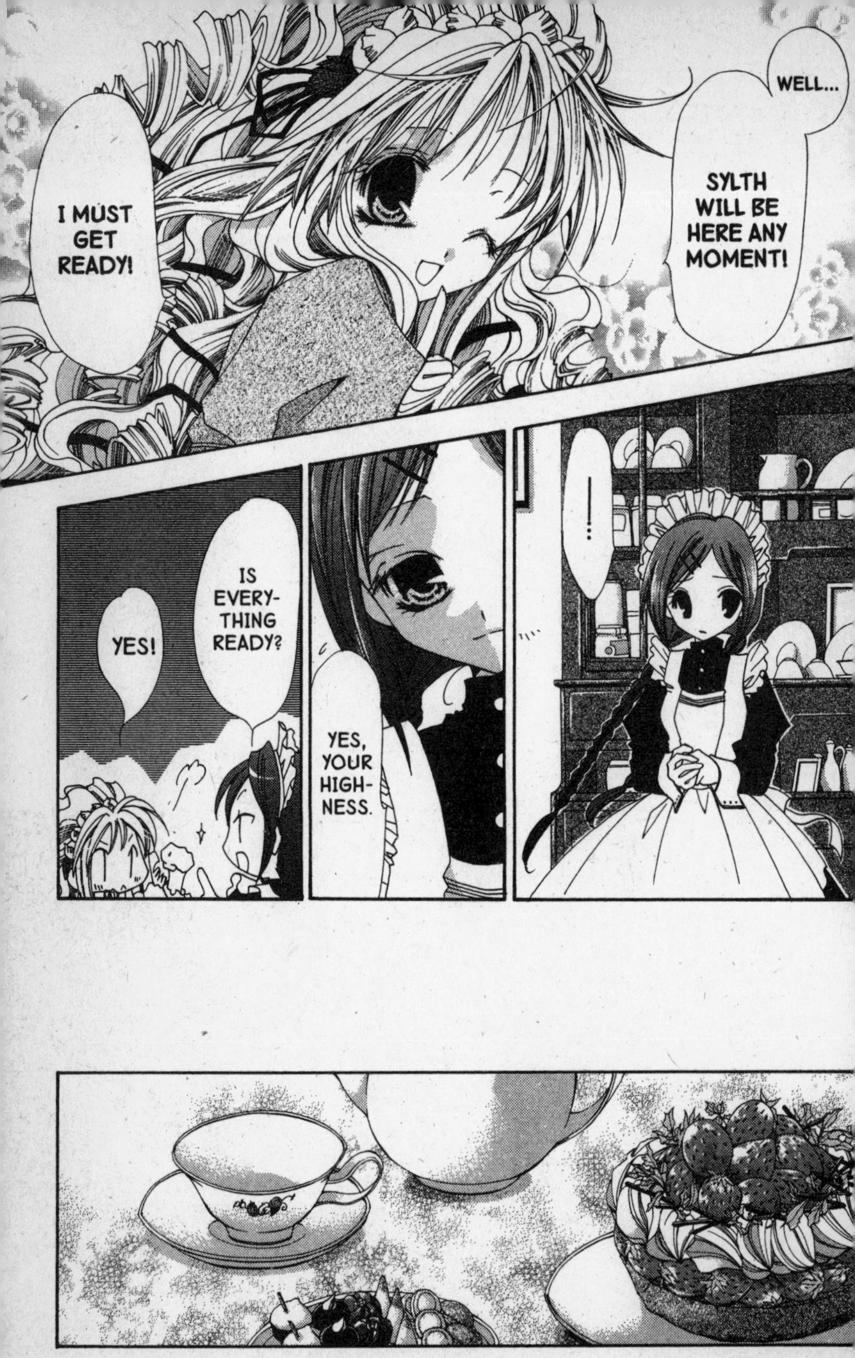
WELL...
SYLTH WILL BE HERE ANY MOMENT!
I MUST GET READY!
!
YES, YOUR HIGH-NESS.
IS EVERY-THING READY?
YES!

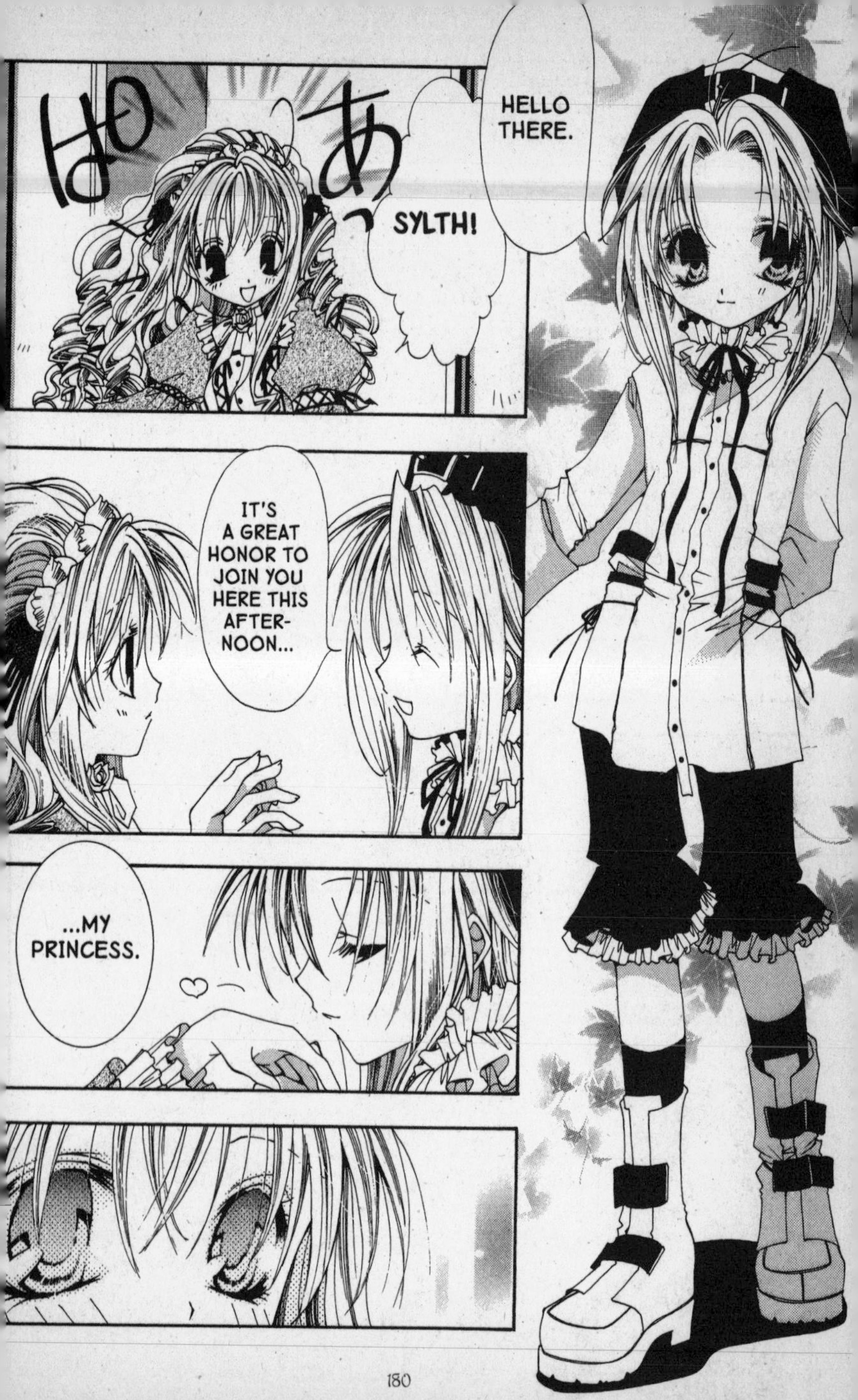
HELLO THERE.
はあっ
SYLTH!
IT'S A GREAT HONOR TO JOIN YOU HERE THIS AFTER-NOON...
...MY PRINCESS.

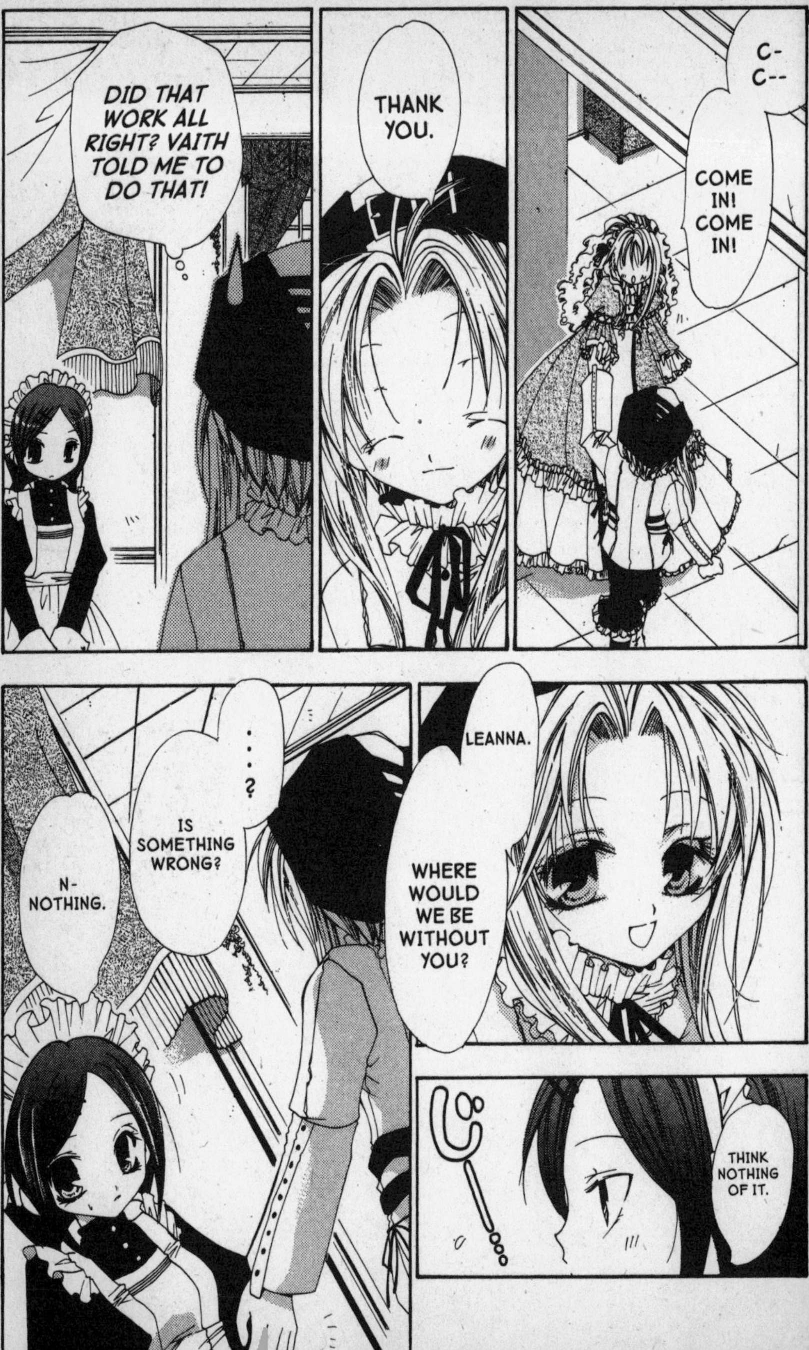
C-
C--
COME IN! COME IN!
THANK YOU.
DID THAT WORK ALL RIGHT? VAITH TOLD ME TO DO THAT!
LEANNA.
WHERE WOULD WE BE WITHOUT YOU?
THINK NOTHING OF IT.
...?
IS SOMETHING WRONG?
N-NOTHING.

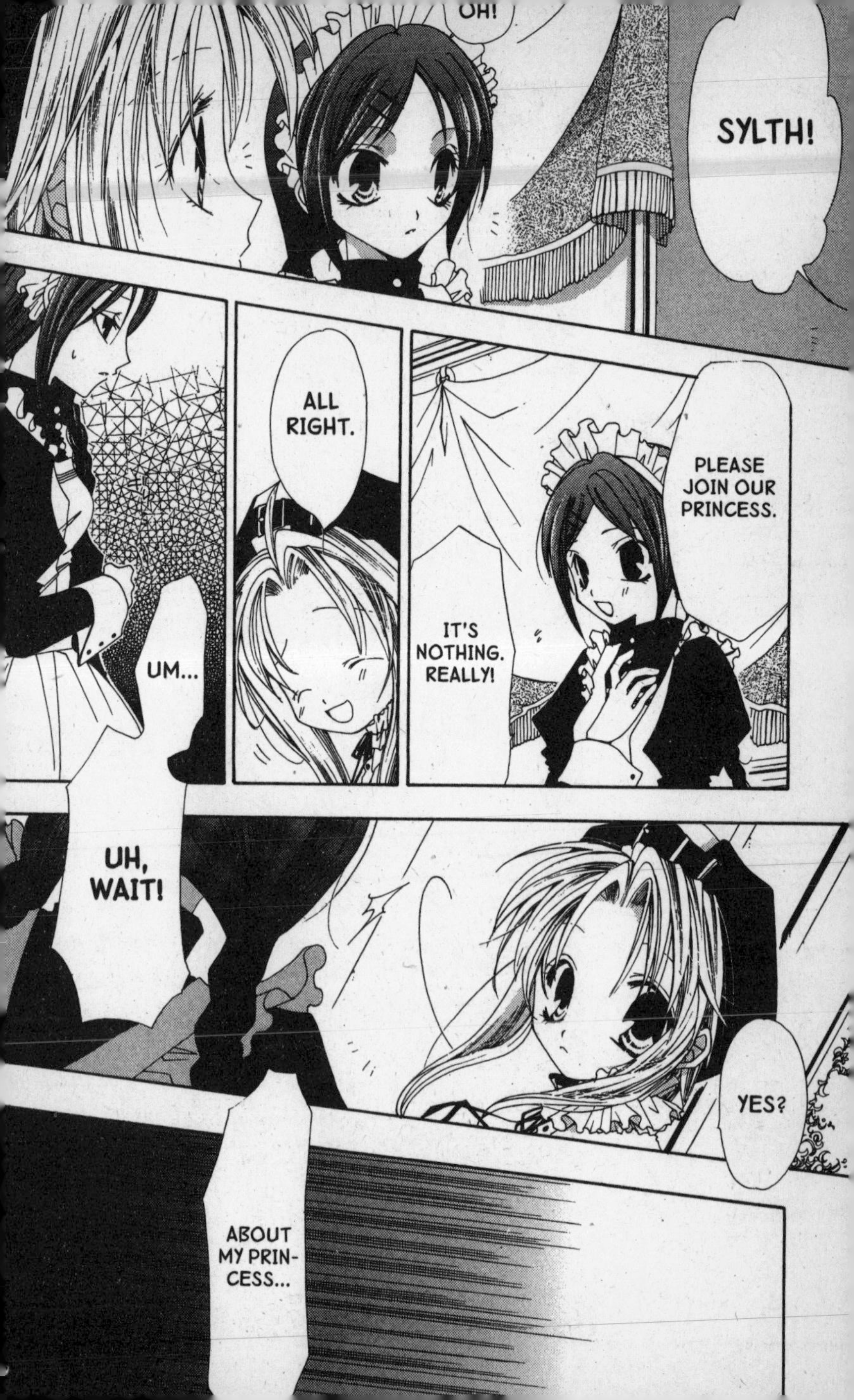
SYLTH!
OH!
PLEASE JOIN OUR PRINCESS.
IT'S NOTHING. REALLY!
ALL RIGHT.
UM...
YES?
UH, WAIT!
ABOUT MY PRIN-CESS...

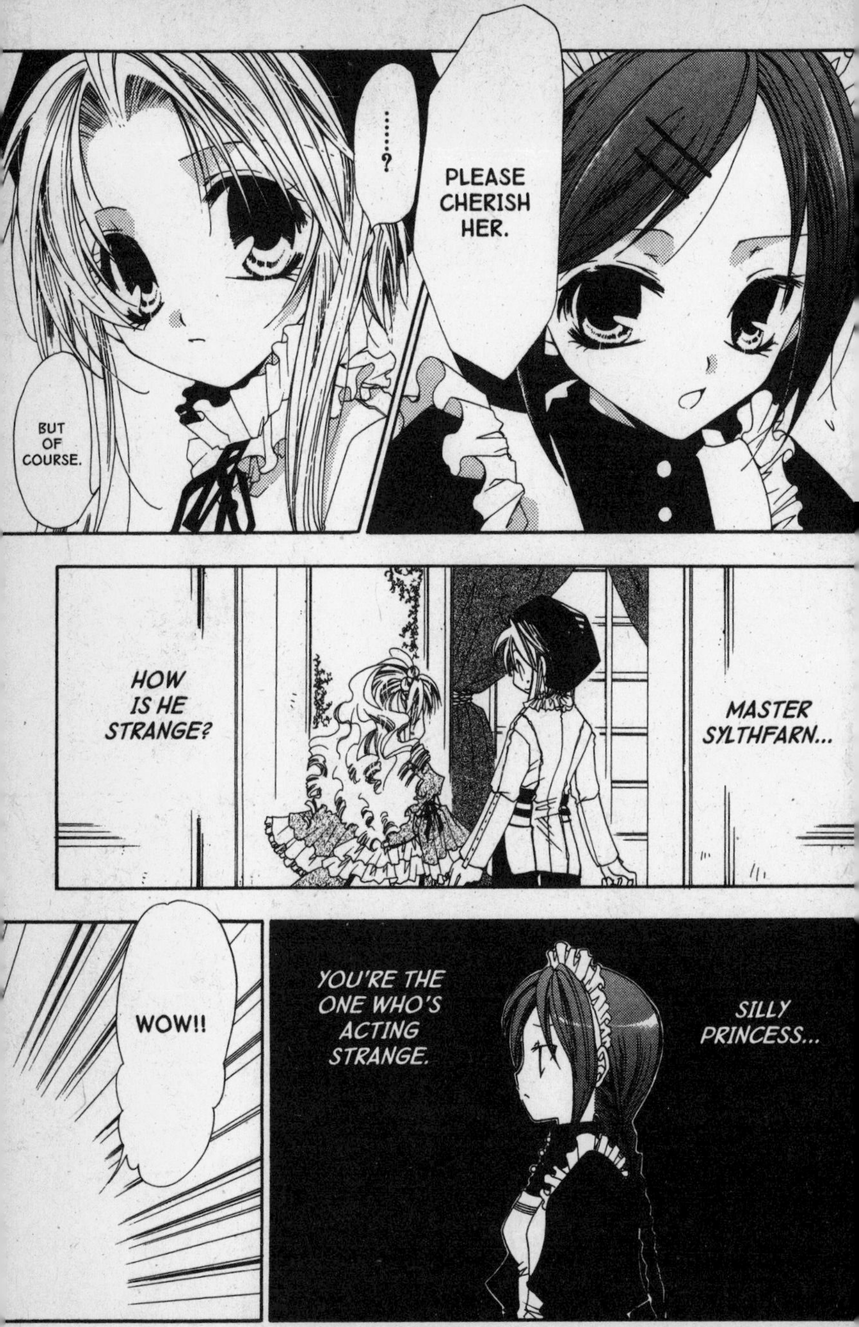
PLEASE CHERISH HER.
......?
BUT OF COURSE.
MASTER SYLTHFARN...
HOW IS HE STRANGE?
SILLY PRINCESS...
YOU'RE THE ONE WHO'S ACTING STRANGE.
WOW!!

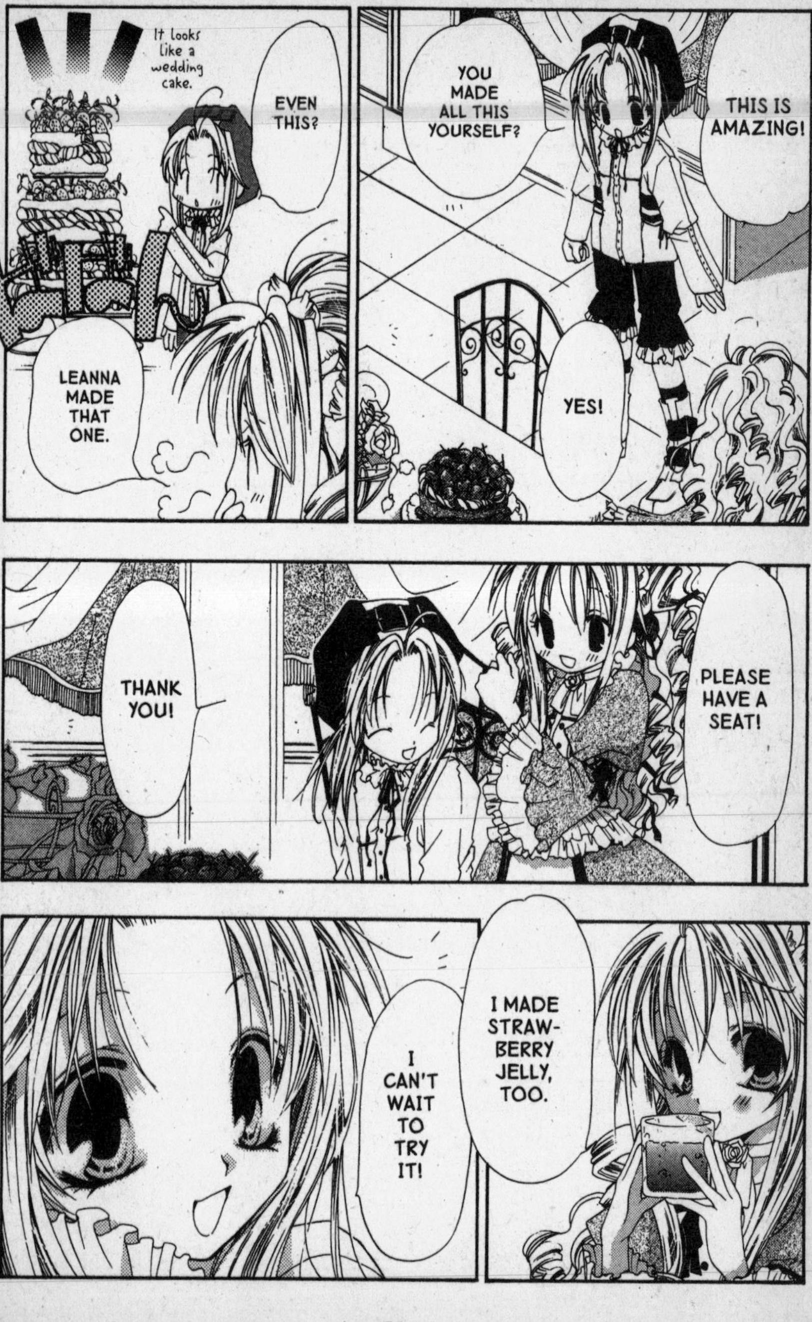
THIS IS AMAZING!
YOU MADE ALL THIS YOURSELF?
YES!
EVEN THIS?
It looks like a wedding cake.
LEANNA MADE THAT ONE.
PLEASE HAVE A SEAT!
THANK YOU!
I MADE STRAW-BERRY JELLY, TOO.
I CAN'T WAIT TO TRY IT!

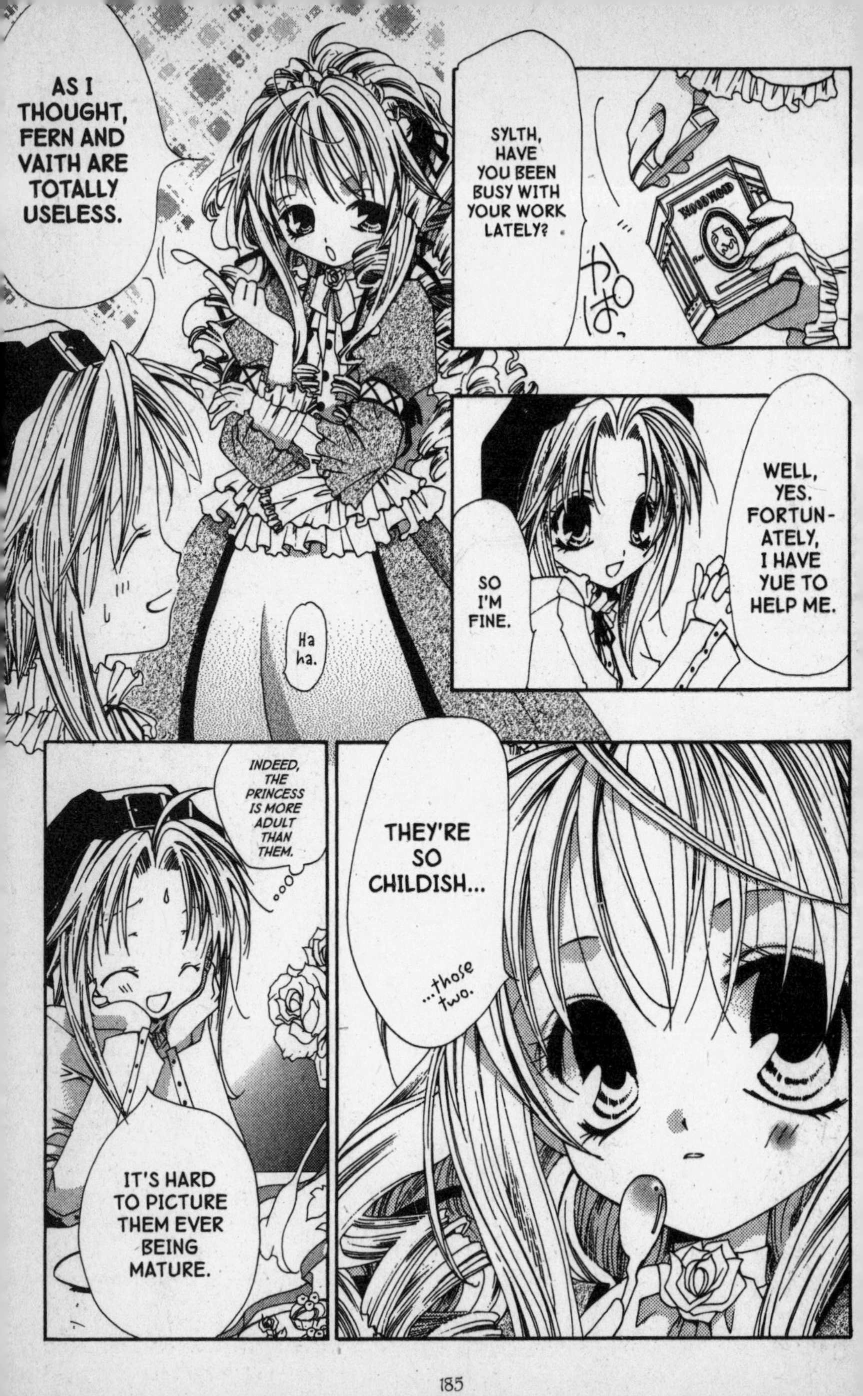
SYLTH, HAVE YOU BEEN BUSY WITH YOUR WORK LATELY?
WELL, YES. FORTUN-ATELY, I HAVE YUE TO HELP ME.
SO I'M FINE.
AS I THOUGHT, FERN AND VAITH ARE TOTALLY USELESS.
Ha ha.
THEY'RE SO CHILDISH...
...those two.
INDEED, THE PRINCESS IS MORE ADULT THAN THEM.
IT'S HARD TO PICTURE THEM EVER BEING MATURE.

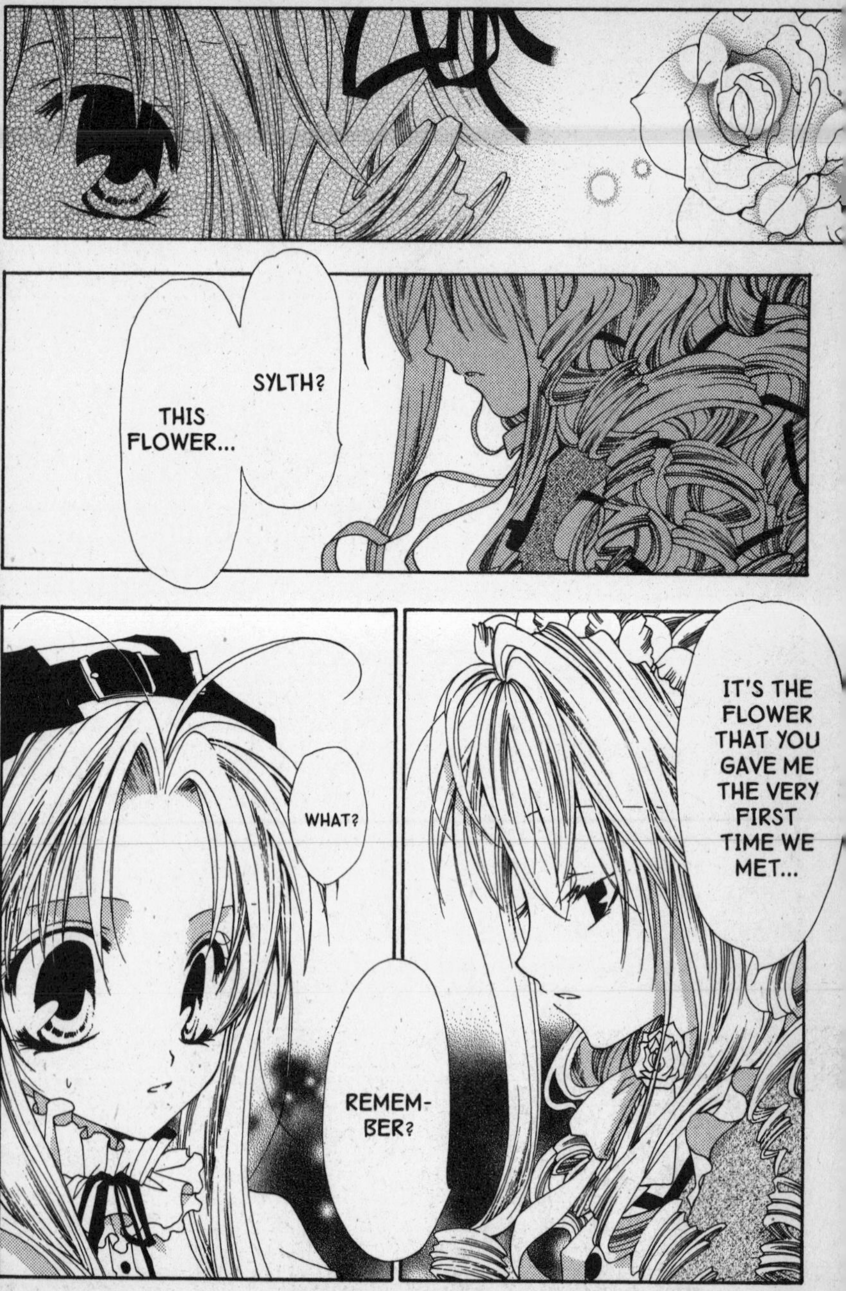
SYLTH?
THIS FLOWER...
IT'S THE FLOWER THAT YOU GAVE ME THE VERY FIRST TIME WE MET...
REMEMBER?
WHAT?

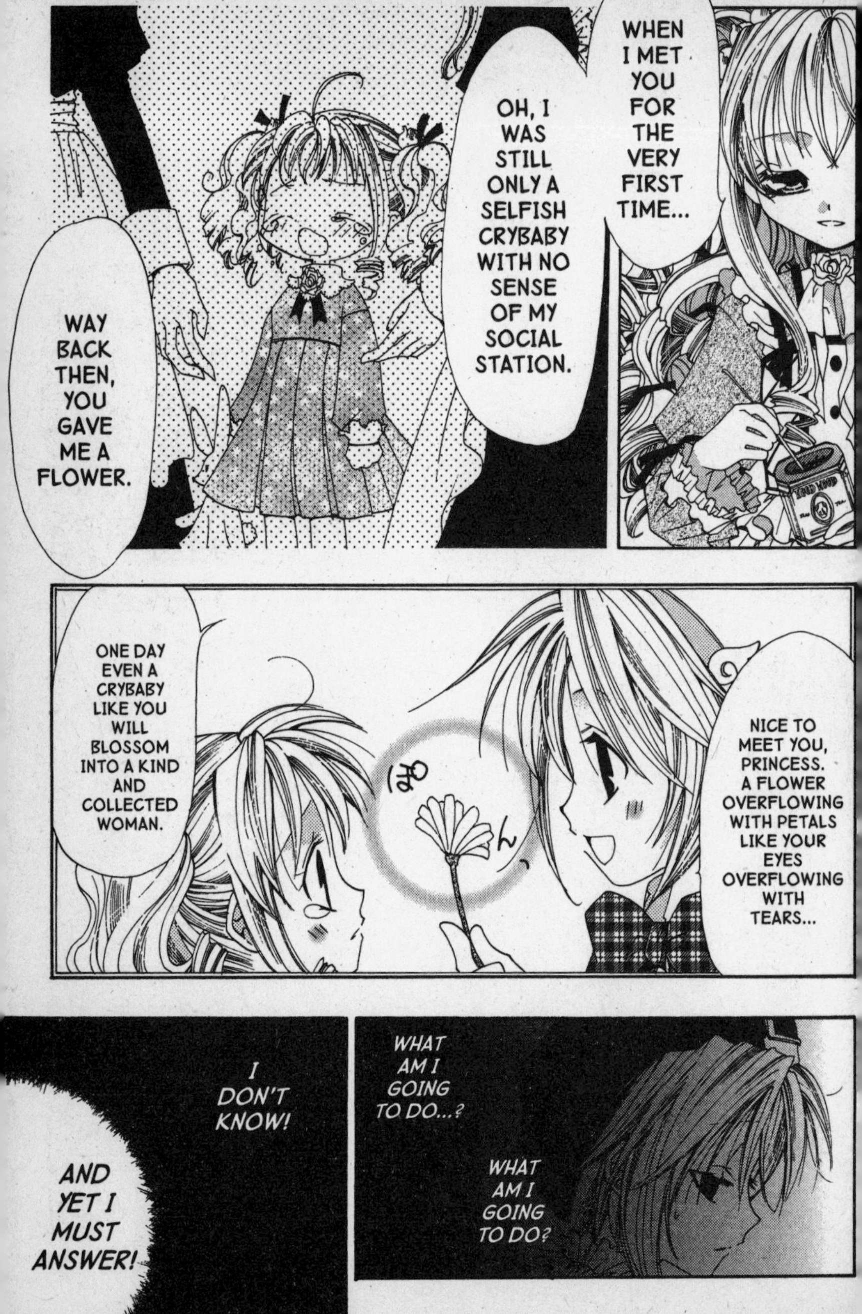
WHEN I MET YOU FOR THE VERY FIRST TIME...
OH, I WAS STILL ONLY A SELFISH CRYBABY WITH NO SENSE OF MY SOCIAL STATION.
WAY BACK THEN, YOU GAVE ME A FLOWER.
NICE TO MEET YOU, PRINCESS. A FLOWER OVERFLOWING WITH PETALS LIKE YOUR EYES OVERFLOWING WITH TEARS...
ONE DAY EVEN A CRYBABY LIKE YOU WILL BLOSSOM INTO A KIND AND COLLECTED WOMAN.
WHAT AM I GOING TO DO...?
WHAT AM I GOING TO DO?
I DON'T KNOW!
AND YET I MUST ANSWER!

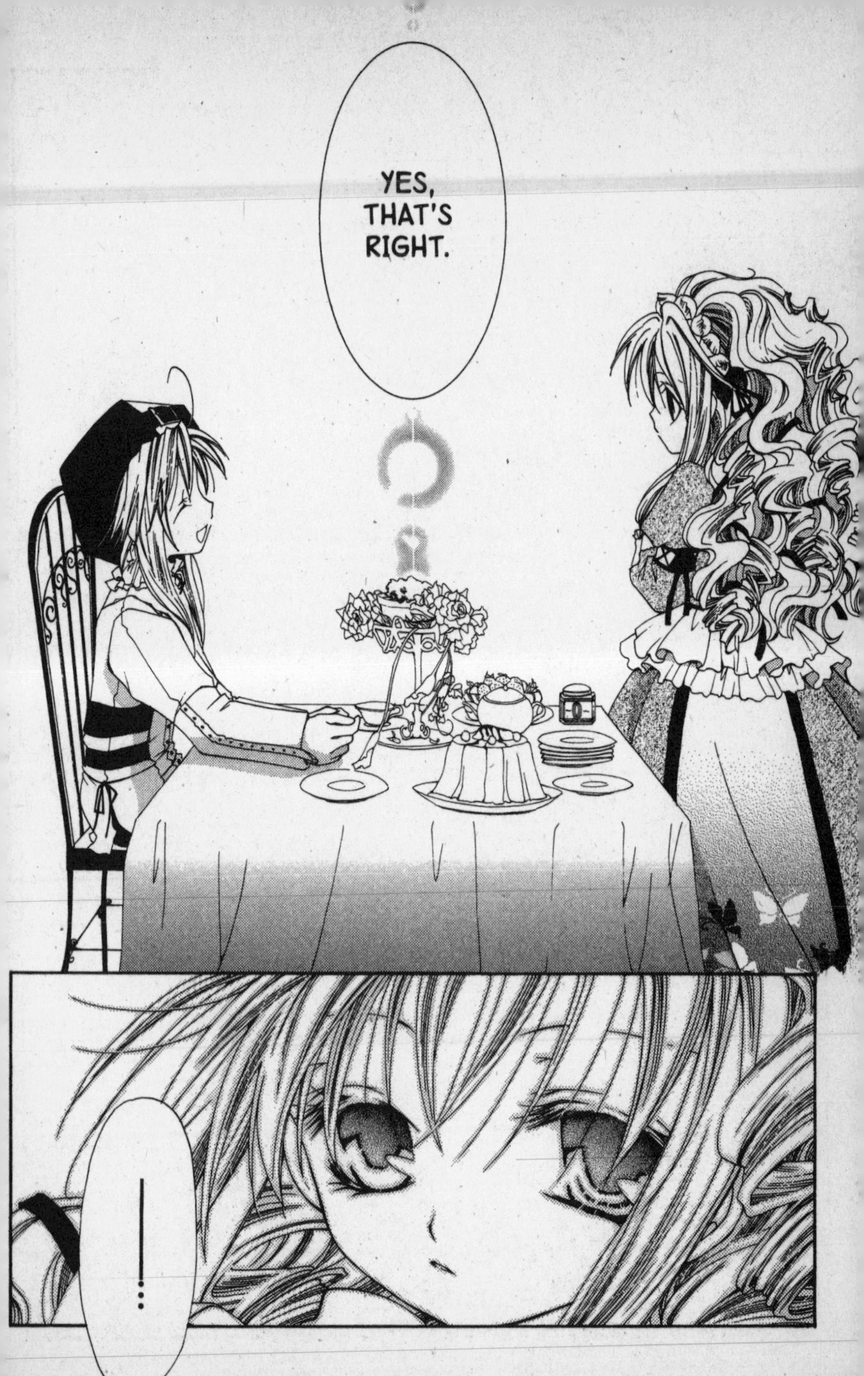
YES, THAT'S RIGHT.
—...

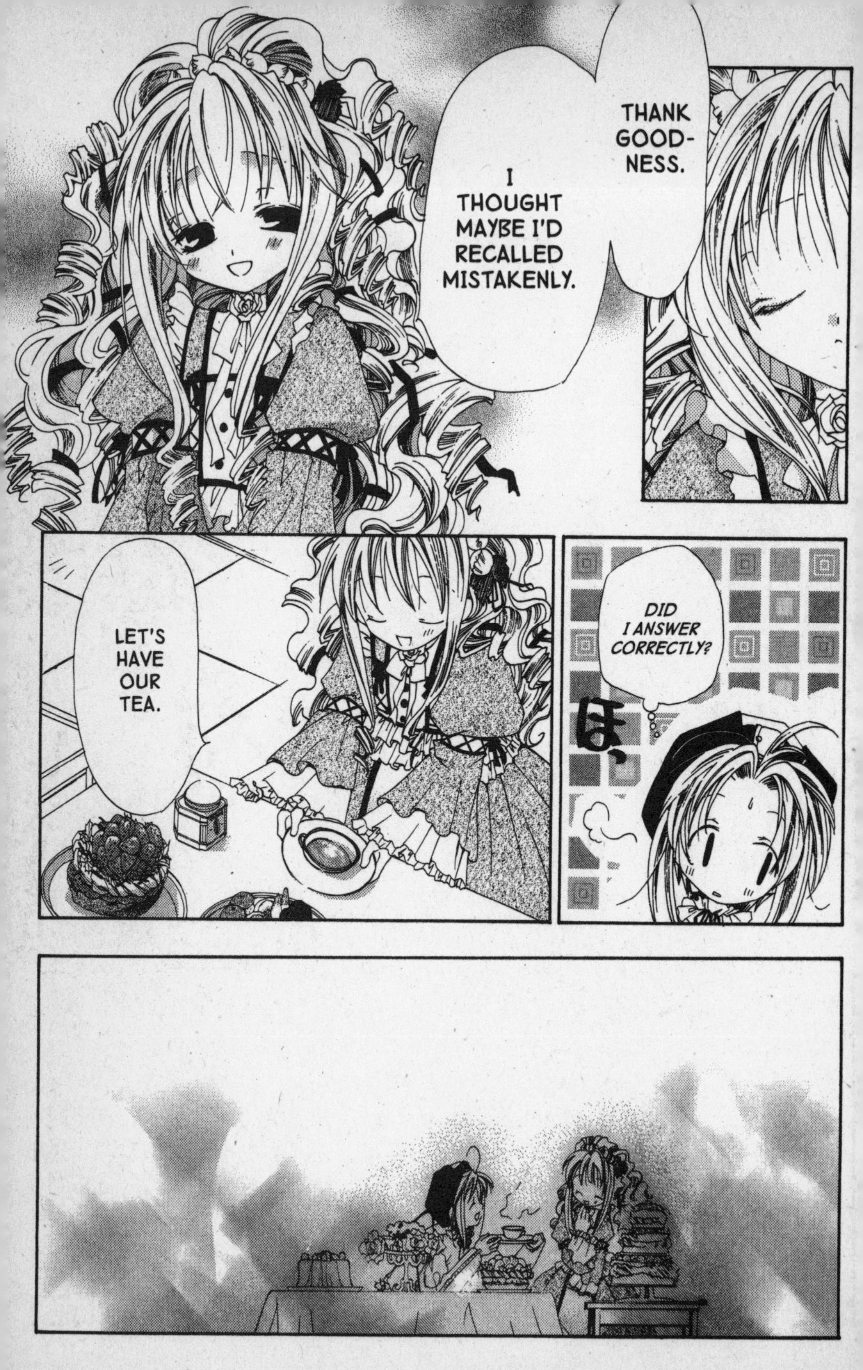
THANK GOODNESS.
I THOUGHT MAYBE I'D RECALLED MISTAKENLY.
DID I ANSWER CORRECTLY?
LET'S HAVE OUR TEA.

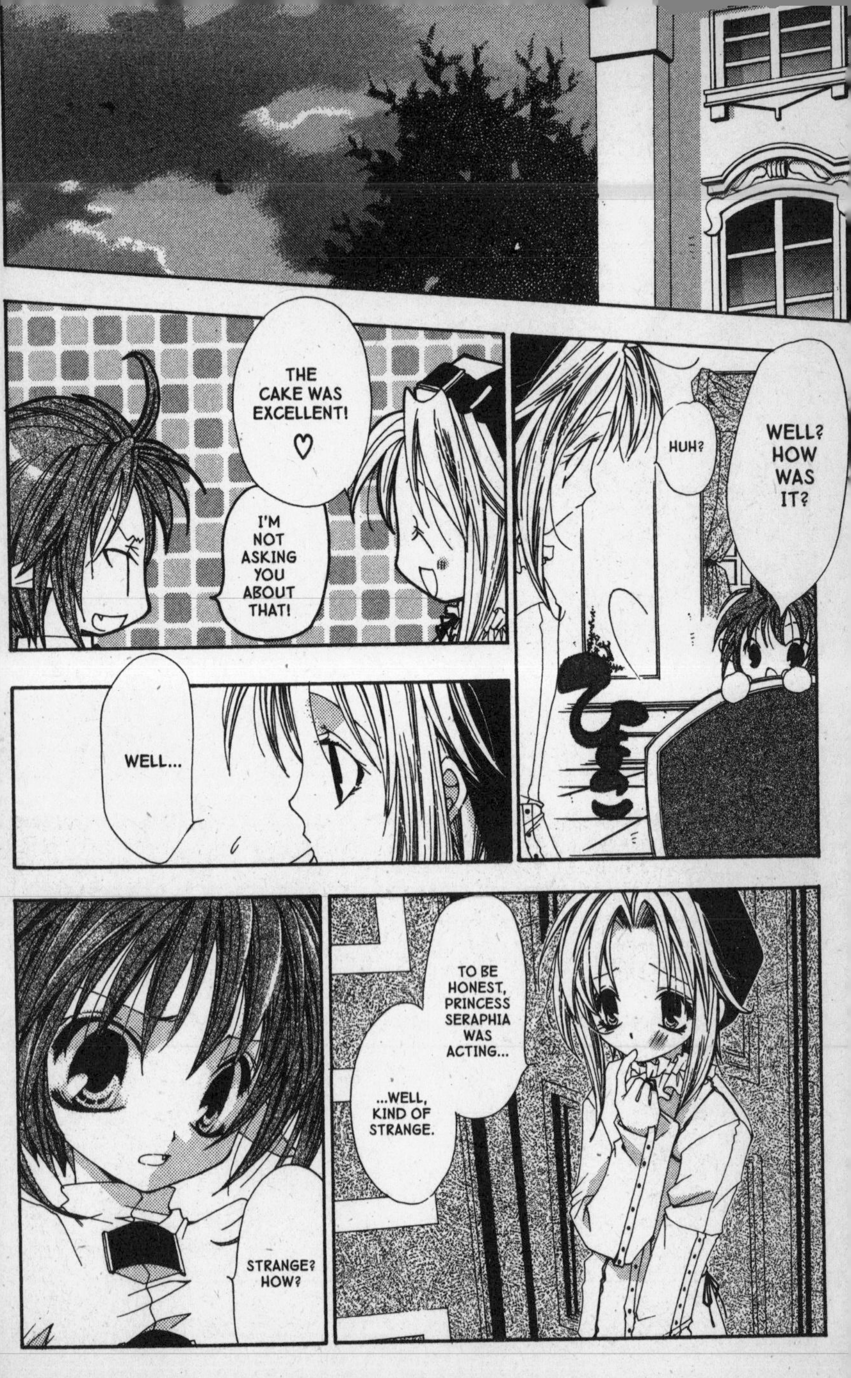
WELL? HOW WAS IT?
HUH?
THE CAKE WAS EXCELLENT! ♡
I'M NOT ASKING YOU ABOUT THAT!
WELL...
TO BE HONEST, PRINCESS SERAPHIA WAS ACTING...
...WELL, KIND OF STRANGE.
STRANGE? HOW?

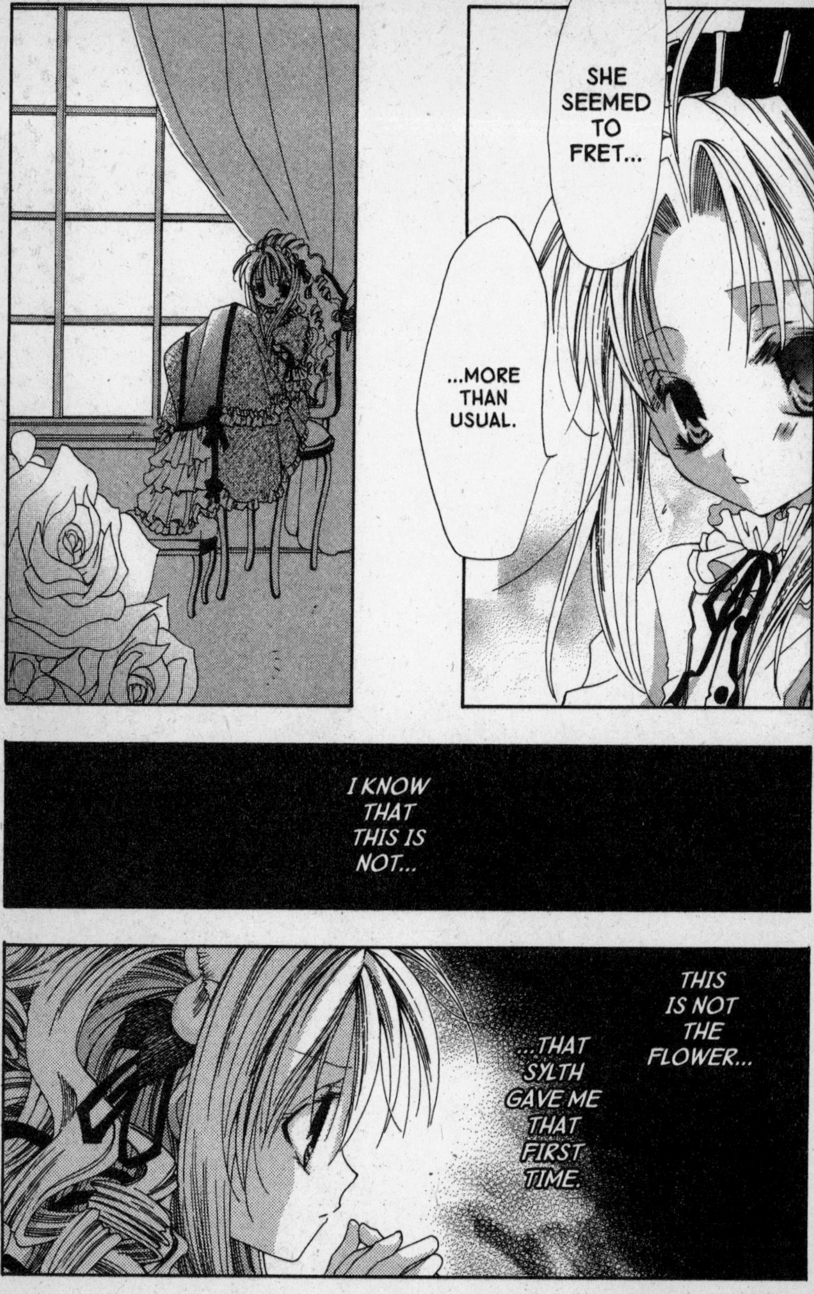
SHE SEEMED TO FRET...
...MORE THAN USUAL.
I KNOW THAT THIS IS NOT...
THIS IS NOT THE FLOWER...
...THAT SYLTH GAVE ME THAT FIRST TIME.

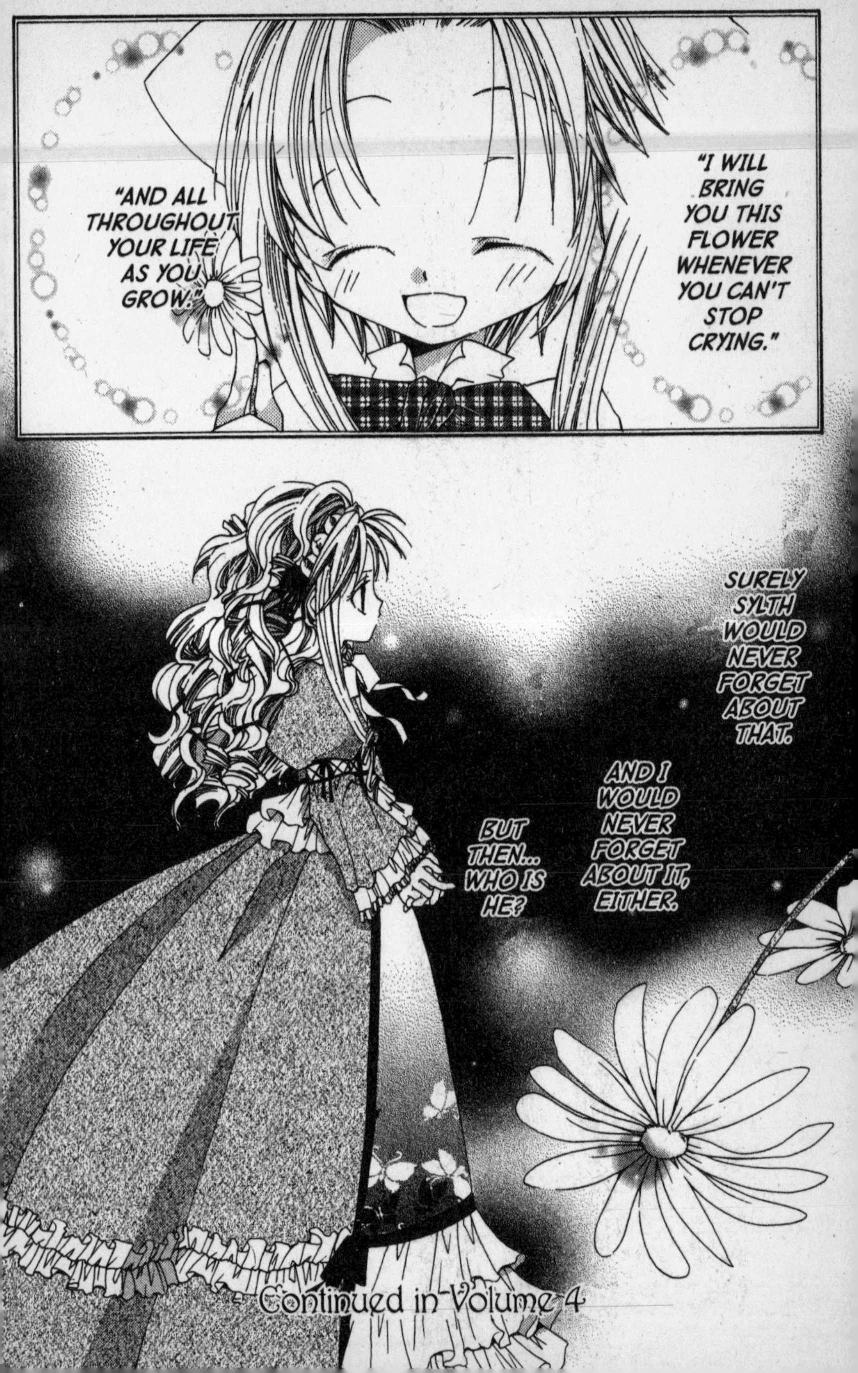
"I WILL BRING YOU THIS FLOWER WHENEVER YOU CAN'T STOP CRYING."
"AND ALL THROUGHOUT YOUR LIFE AS YOU GROW."
SURELY SYLTH WOULD NEVER FORGET ABOUT THAT.
AND I WOULD NEVER FORGET ABOUT IT, EITHER.
BUT THEN... WHO IS HE?

Continued in Volume 4

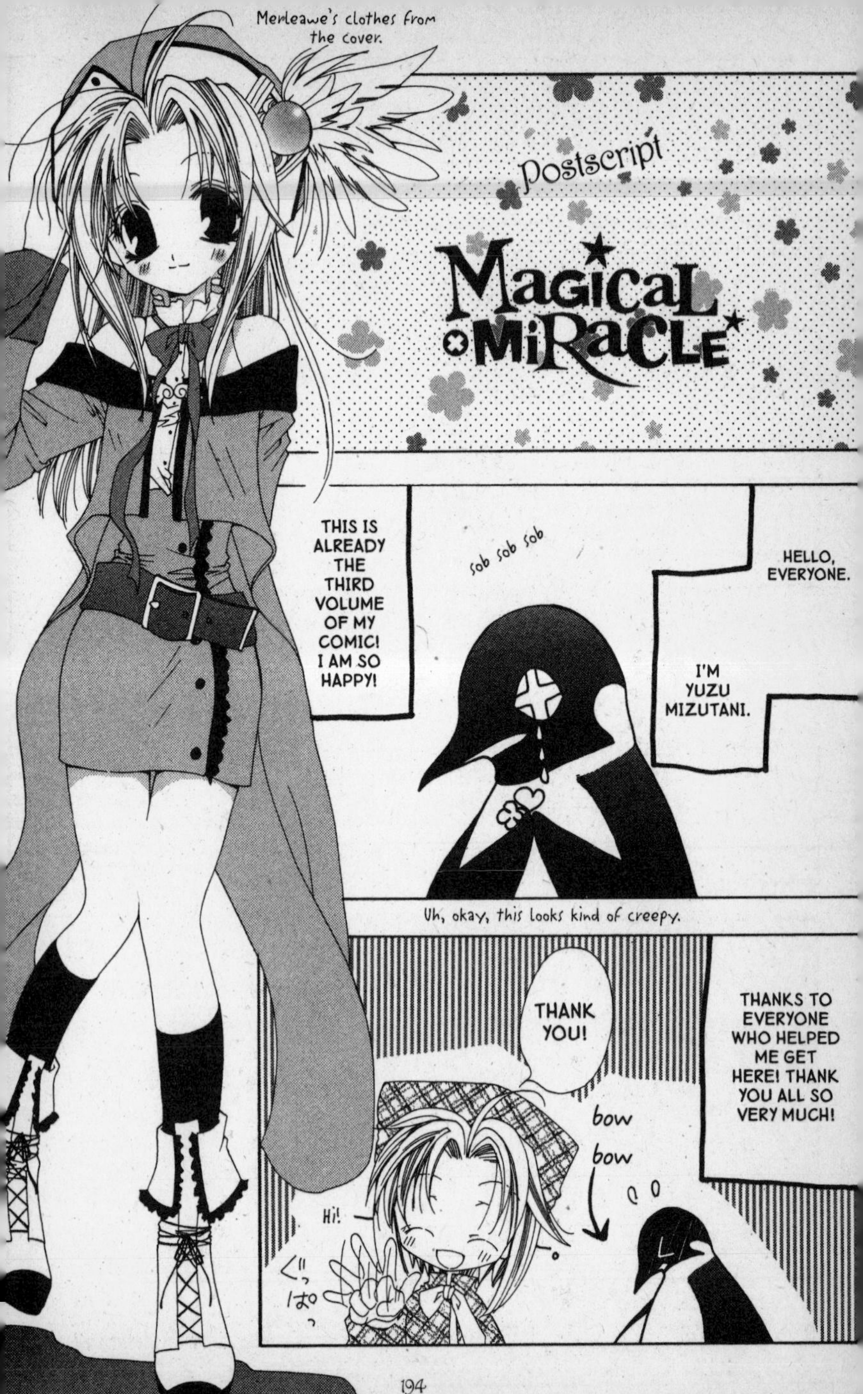

Postscript
Magical Miracle
HELLO, EVERYONE.
I'M YUZU MIZUTANI.
sob sob sob
THIS IS ALREADY THE THIRD VOLUME OF MY COMIC! I AM SO HAPPY!
Uh, okay, this looks kind of creepy.
THANKS TO EVERYONE WHO HELPED ME GET HERE! THANK YOU ALL SO VERY MUCH!
THANK YOU!
bow bow
Hi!
ぐっぱっ
Merleawe's clothes from the cover.

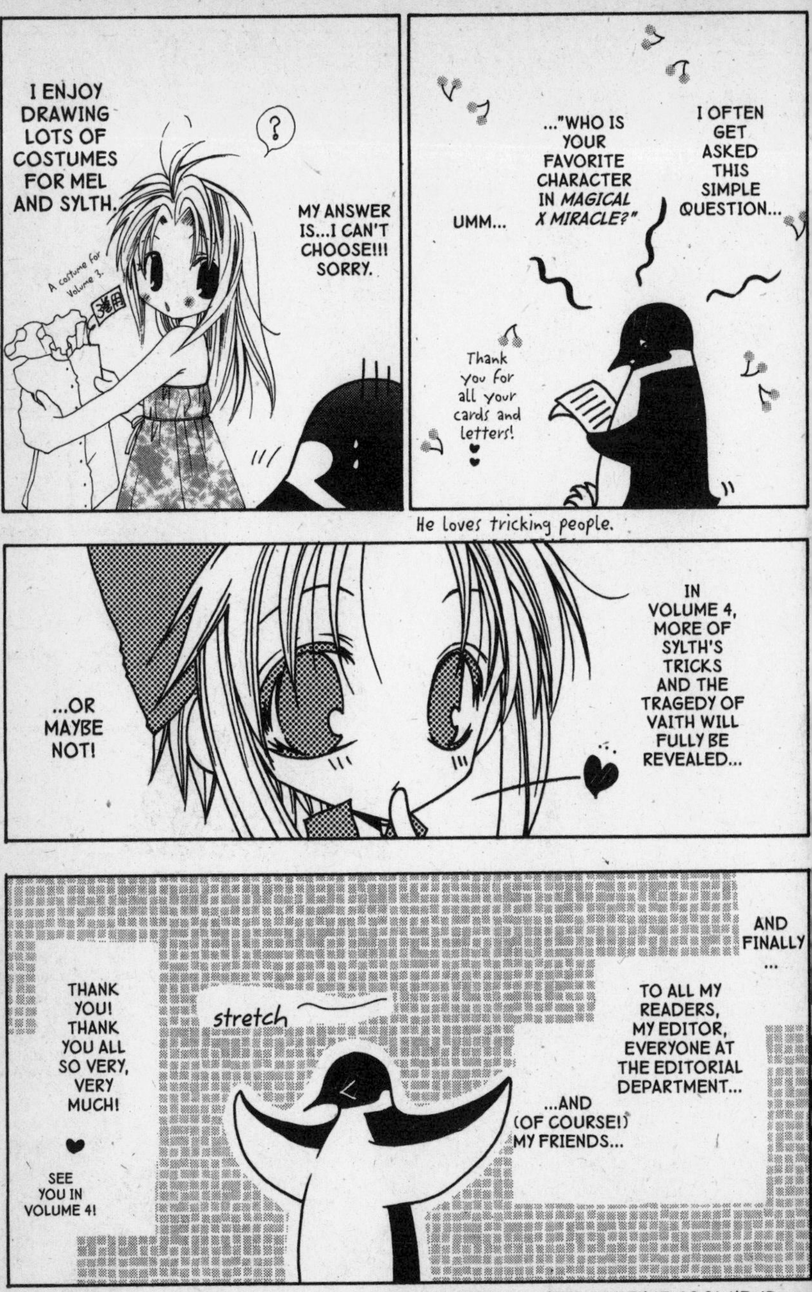
I OFTEN GET ASKED THIS SIMPLE QUESTION...
..."WHO IS YOUR FAVORITE CHARACTER IN *MAGICAL X MIRACLE?*"
UMM...
Thank you for all your cards and letters!
MY ANSWER IS...I CAN'T CHOOSE!!! SORRY.
I ENJOY DRAWING LOTS OF COSTUMES FOR MEL AND SYLTH.
A costume for Volume 3.
He loves tricking people.
IN VOLUME 4, MORE OF SYLTH'S TRICKS AND THE TRAGEDY OF VAITH WILL FULLY BE REVEALED...
...OR MAYBE NOT!
AND FINALLY...
TO ALL MY READERS, MY EDITOR, EVERYONE AT THE EDITORIAL DEPARTMENT...
...AND (OF COURSE!) MY FRIENDS...
stretch
THANK YOU! THANK YOU ALL SO VERY, VERY MUCH!
SEE YOU IN VOLUME 4!

MY WEBSITE → HTTP://MIZYUZ.COOL.NE.JP

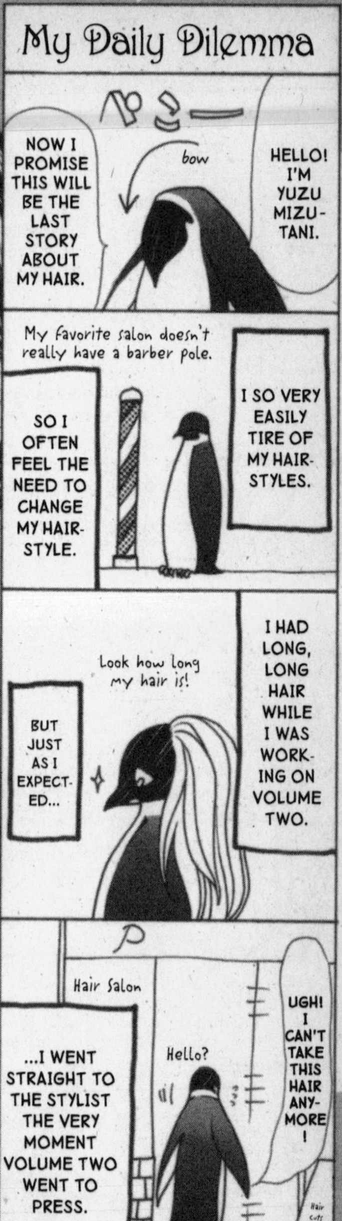
My Daily Dilemma
HELLO! I'M YUZU MIZUTANI.
bow
NOW I PROMISE THIS WILL BE THE LAST STORY ABOUT MY HAIR.
I SO VERY EASILY TIRE OF MY HAIR-STYLES.
My favorite salon doesn't really have a barber pole.
SO I OFTEN FEEL THE NEED TO CHANGE MY HAIR-STYLE.
I HAD LONG, LONG HAIR WHILE I WAS WORK-ING ON VOLUME TWO.
Look how long my hair is!
BUT JUST AS I EXPECT-ED...
UGH! I CAN'T TAKE THIS HAIR ANY-MORE!
Hair Salon
Hello?
...I WENT STRAIGHT TO THE STYLIST THE VERY MOMENT VOLUME TWO WENT TO PRESS.
Hair Cuts Perms Open at 11:00 a.m.

Since I had promised to grow my hair out, I knew I had to wait at least until volume two was published.

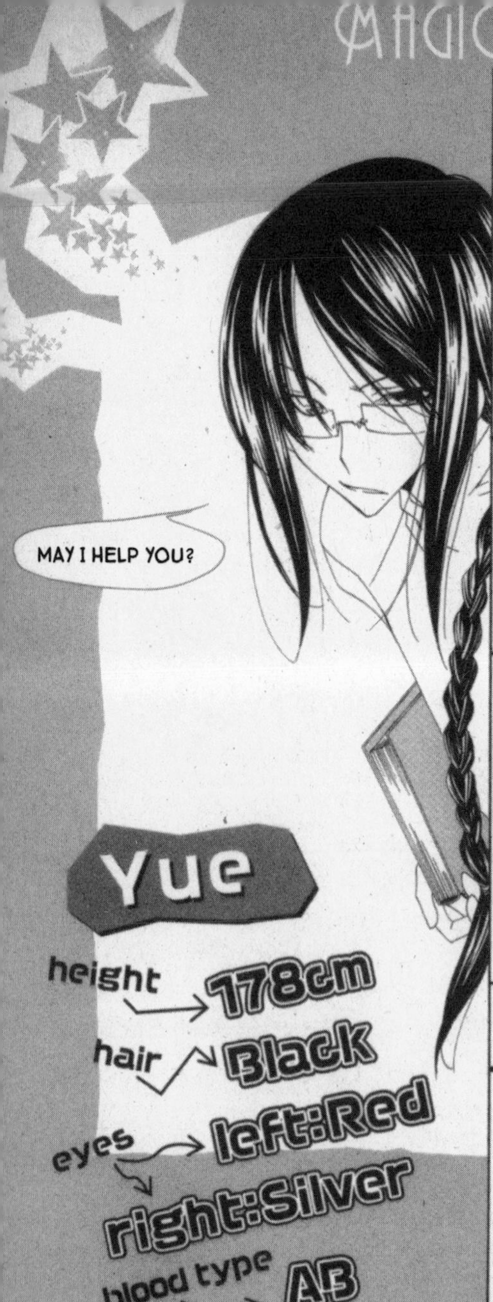
MAY I HELP YOU?
Yue
height 178cm
hair Black
eyes left:Red right:Silver
blood type AB

YUZU MIZUTANI

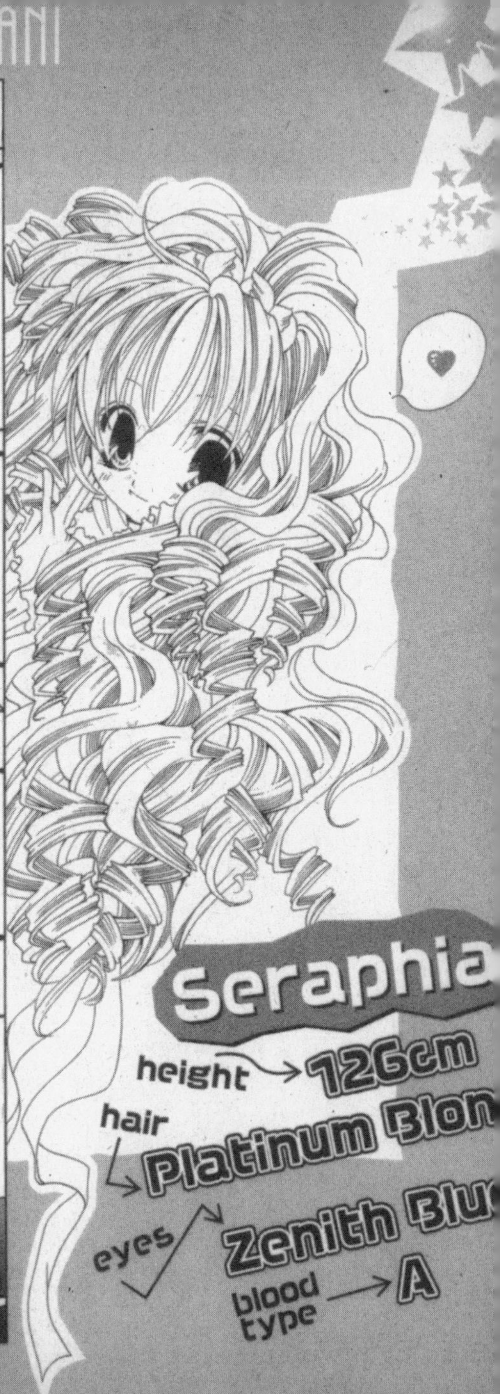

Seraphia
height
126cm
hair
Platinum Blon
eyes
Zenith Blu
blood type
A

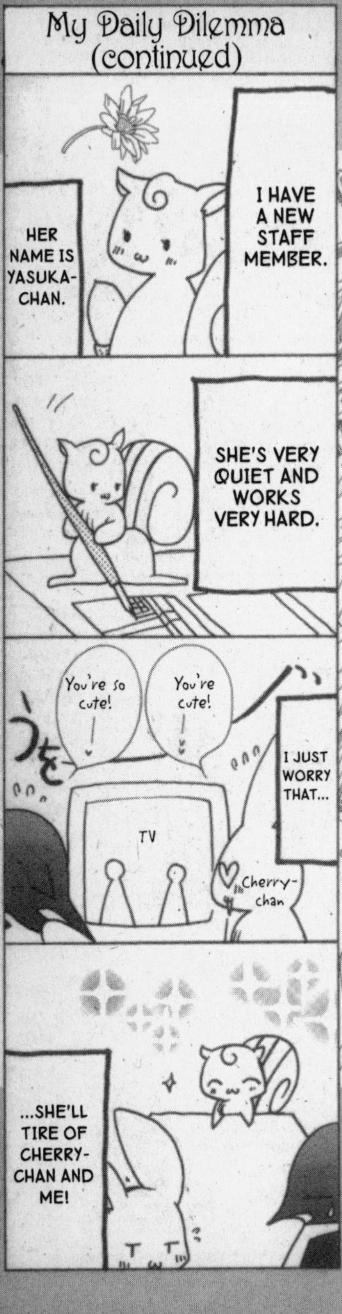

My Daily Dilemma (continued)
I HAVE A NEW STAFF MEMBER.
HER NAME IS YASUKA-CHAN.
SHE'S VERY QUIET AND WORKS VERY HARD.
I JUST WORRY THAT...
You're cute!
You're so cute!
Cherry-chan
TV
...SHE'LL TIRE OF CHERRY-CHAN AND ME!

Cherry-chan and I have such totally different taste (laugh).

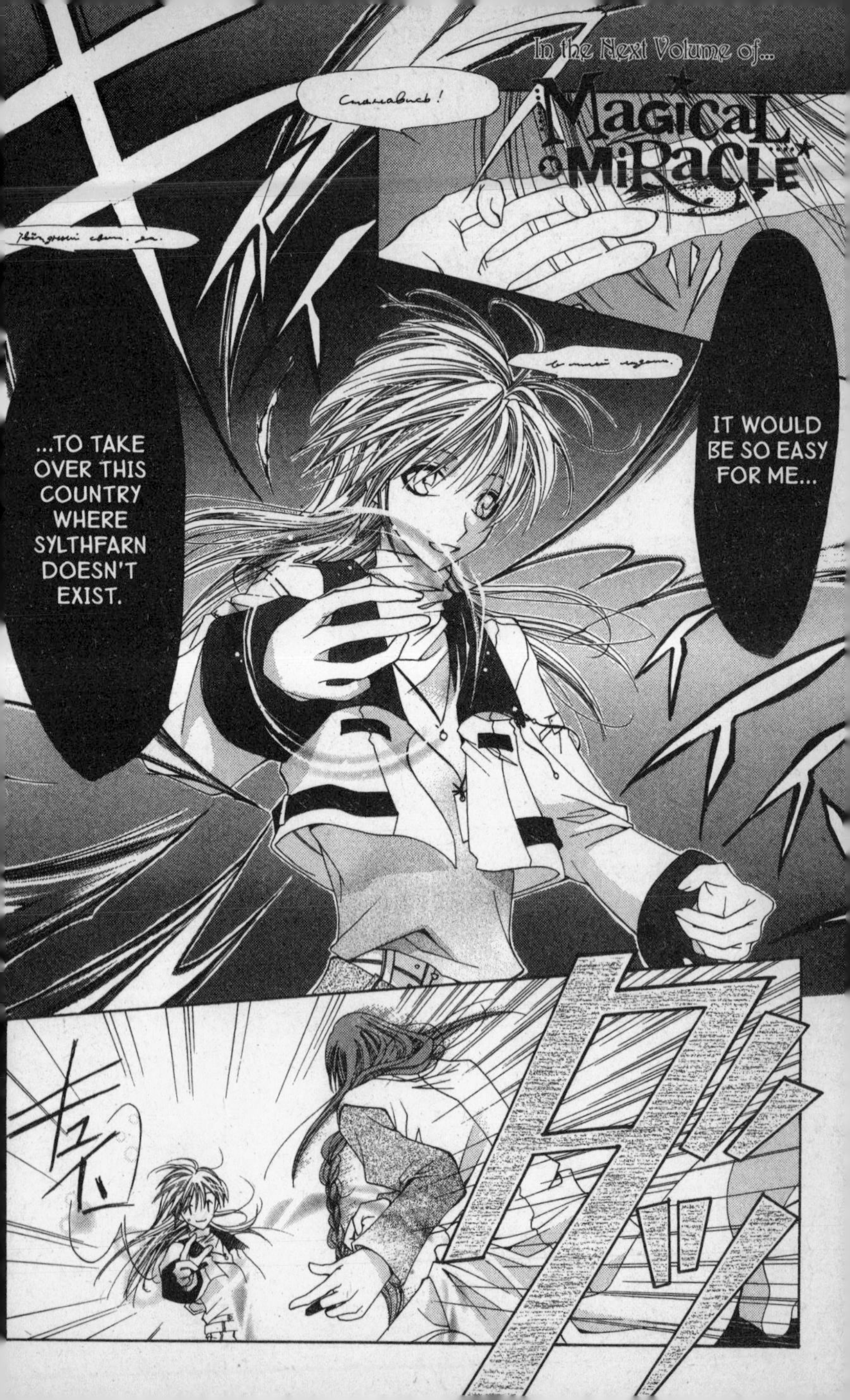
In the Next Volume of...
Magical Miracle
IT WOULD BE SO EASY FOR ME...
...TO TAKE OVER THIS COUNTRY WHERE SYLTHFARN DOESN'T EXIST.

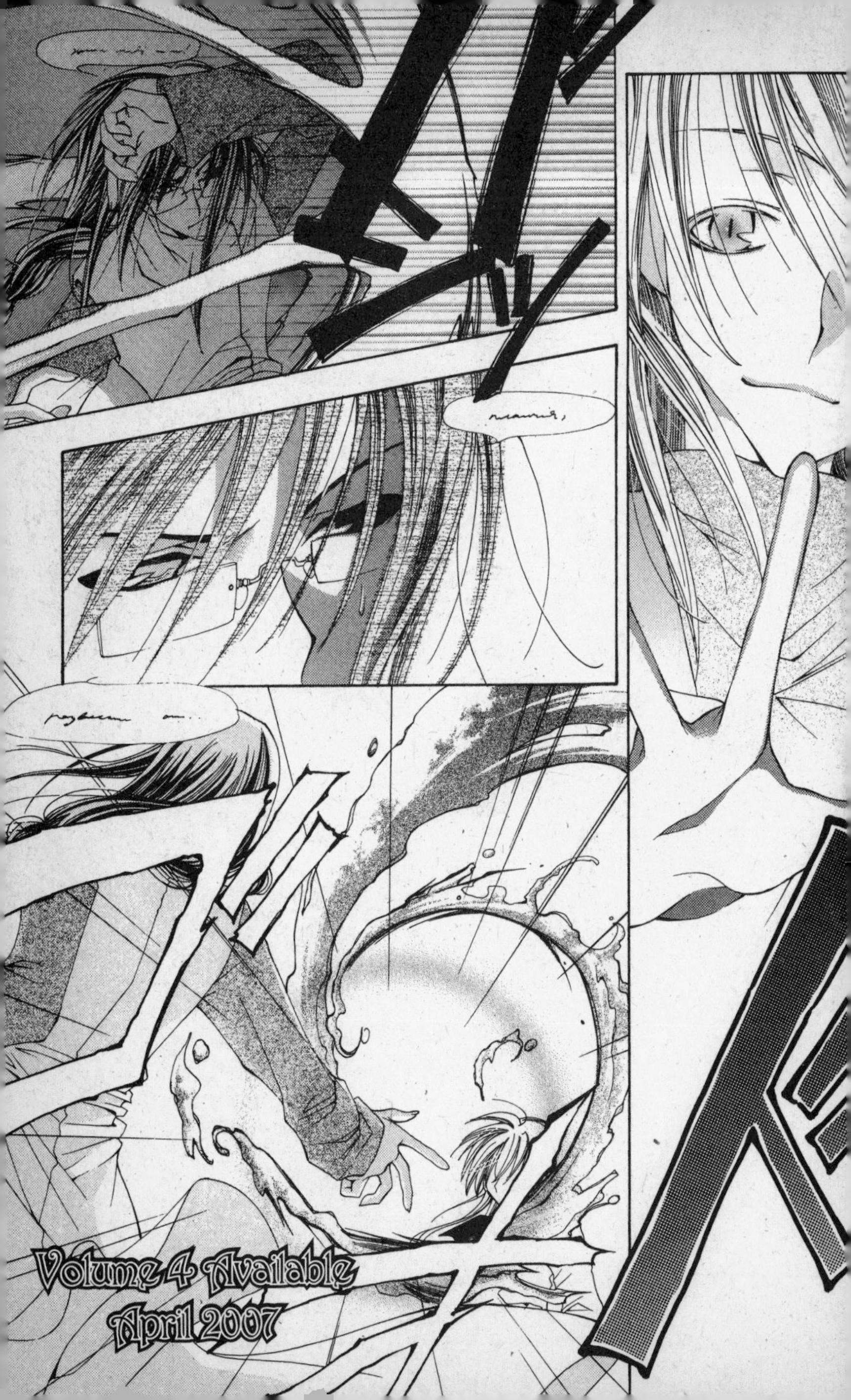
Volume 4 Available
April 2007

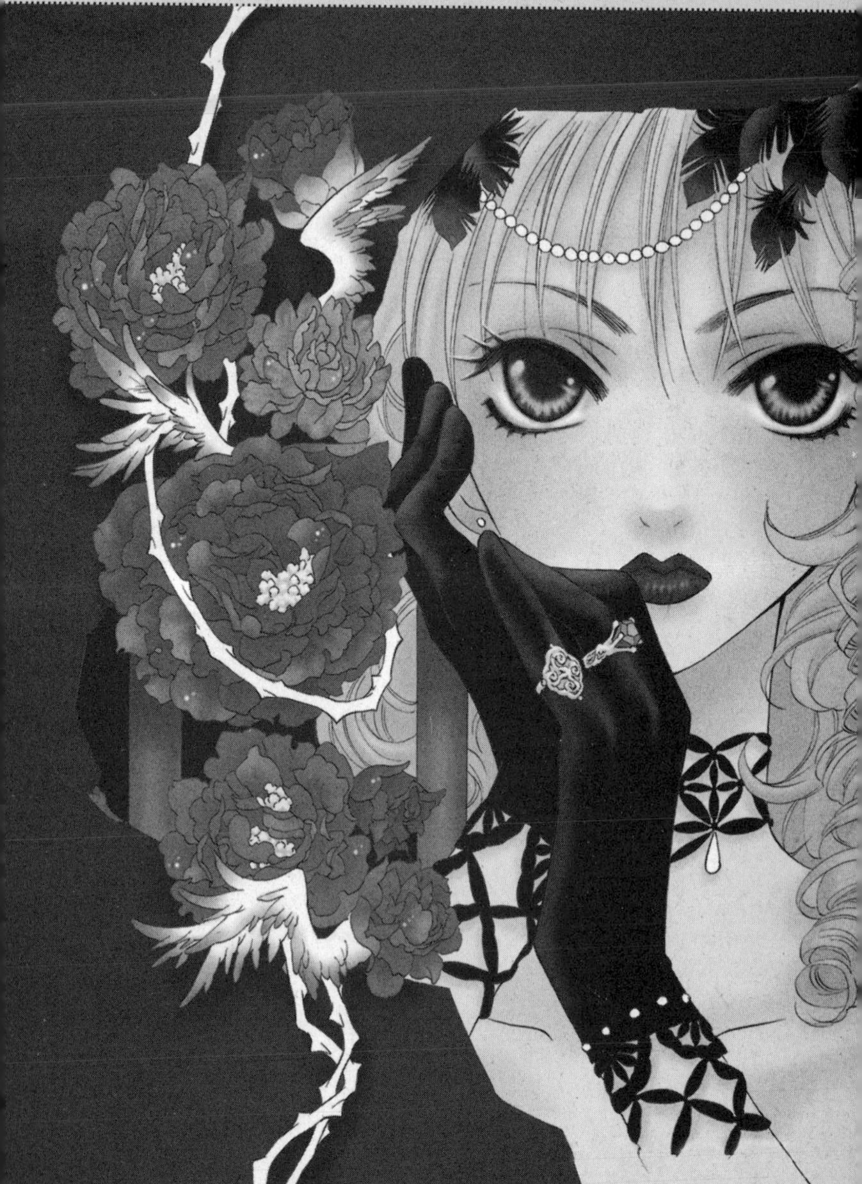

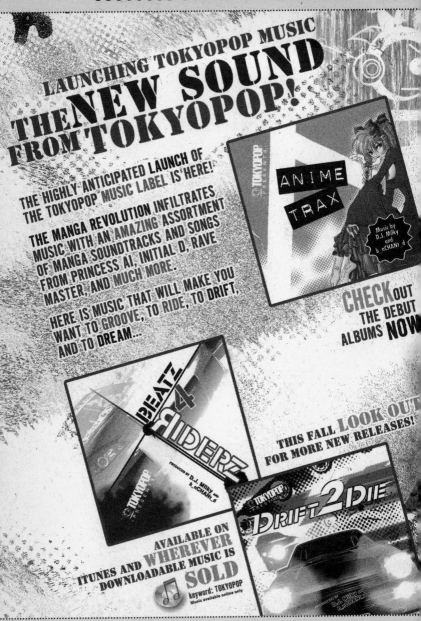

STOP!

This is the back of the book.
You wouldn't want to spoil a great ending!

This book is printed "manga-style," in the authentic Japanese right-to-left format. Since none of the artwork has been flipped or altered, readers get to experience the story just as the creator intended. You've been asking for it, so TOKYOPOP® delivered: authentic, hot-off-the-press, and far more fun!

DIRECTIONS

If this is your first time reading manga-style, here's a quick guide to help you understand how it works.

It's easy... just start in the top right panel and follow the numbers. Have fun, and look for more 100% authentic manga from TOKYOPOP®!